Unbreak My Heart

Dar Tomlinson

Genesis Press, Inc.

Indigo Love Stories

An imprint of Genesis Press, Inc.
Publishing Company

Genesis Press, Inc.
P.O. Box 101
Columbus, MS 39703

All characters in this book have no existence outside the imagination of the author and have no relation whatsoever to anyone bearing the same name or names. They are not even distantly inspired by any individual known or unknown to the author and all incidents are pure invention.

ISBN-13: 978-1-58571-315-8
ISBN-10: 1-58571-315-5
Manufactured in the United States of America

First Edition 2003
Second Edition 2008

Visit us at www.genesis-press.com or call at 1-888-Indigo-1

To Zac

Maker of beautiful memories

I wish I could have protected you more

one

Wilted, wrinkled, and pissed off at the desert heat, Cameron pinned the hotel desk clerk with a disbelieving stare. On her first day of a year's penance in this hellhole, she couldn't even check into her room.

"How can it not be ready?" She cast a glance at her watch. Two o'clock. "I'm Camellia Cameron Vickers. I've been expected for weeks."

Minus expression or haste, the clerk pecked a computer keyboard and stared at the screen until a phone rang. She cleared her throat to answer "Chastain Hotels, Salt River Inn, Scottsdale. How may I direct your call?" Cameron rolled her eyes at the five-star-hotel demeanor, then again when the girl turned to a companion lazing against the counter, announcing with a soft smile and tone, "It's your mama."

She returned to pecking keys, leaving Cameron to survey the worn lobby. A turquoise and coral color scheme. Cracked tile flooring. Fake R.C. Gorman paintings, cheaply framed. Faded draperies, hanging limp as chewed rags. So far, her mission was proving to be on target; the small hotel craved renovation. Miraculously, she had been given the chance. And if she succeeded, an opportunity to salvage herself, as well.

Eyes as dark as her own, but round, not almond shaped, gazed up from the screen. "Sorry. Housekeeping needs time to dean. You know?" The eyes held more patience than apology. "Check out time is noon. Check in is three o'clock."

An unreasonable policy. One Cameron, as manager, would seek to remedy. "All right, I'll wait." What choice did she have? "Which way is the restaurant?"

Anna, according to her nametag, pointed across the deserted lobby. Her dark head, sporting a long, thick braid dangling over one shoulder, nodded in that direction. As Cameron bent for her hand luggage, Anna proclaimed quietly, "But it's closed. Lunch ends at two. Dinner starts at five-thirty."

Her scalp pinching, the hellacious flight she had just completed reeled through Cameron's mind: crammed into a window seat, an irate infant next to her, a *snack* lunch she hadn't been able to get down. In defeat, she murmured, "Where can I get something to drink?"

This time the nod designated a long, tile-fronted counter lined with tall stools. A large window behind the back counter framed the pool area. "The bar is open."

Cameron's stomach fluttered, then clenched. The sensation moved through her chest, passed her throat and formed a mist in her brain. The girl's voice brought her back. Almost.

"If you're hungry, the bar serves fry bread nibbles." She grinned. "Maybe."

Fry bread? "What do you mean, maybe?"

Anna shrugged one solid shoulder. "It depends."

"On what?"

Dark eyes pivoted in the direction of the bar, then lowered. "On the bartender. He runs the bar. I can't promise anything."

Cameron shouldered the strap of her briefcase and clutched her purse to her ribs. Grasping the handle of the Pet Taxi at her feet, she made her way to the bar.

Framed by harsh window light that obstructed a view of his features, the bartender leaned against the back counter, arms folded across his chest, watching her approach. A nearby radio played haunting flute music, the kind she had heard playing in the airport gift shop. She chose a stool opposite the end where he stood, hooked her purse strap over a pine back-spindle, unloaded her burdens on the floor, and hoisted herself onto the cane seat. The man—she could now see that he was tall, lean and dark, and his hair, caught in a silver clip at his nape, was as long as her ponytail, but thicker, blacker—made no move. No acknowledgement.

Weariness seeped across her shoulders. She felt peevish, cross.

Drawn to the liquor display behind him, her eyes took inventory while her hands melded in a tight clasp. Her throat tightened as dreaded, senseless guilt flooded in. She looked away, then back, soundlessly reading bottle labels. Her mind filled with the irony of her reason for being in Arizona, her reason for not wanting to be. How could they be one and the same?

I can't fail. So much is riding on…this.

Too much time passed before her host stubbed out the small cigar he'd been smoking. He shoved away from his leaning post and ambled toward her, stopping midway, eyes seeking hers. He looked as if he recognized her, but that wasn't possible.

"What would you like?" His voice was deep. Quiet, void of inflection.

"Could you give me some water…for my cat?" Since landing, she'd had no time to replenish the shallow water container, a fact that stirred more guilt spasms.

The man's dark gaze shifted to the lobby desk, reminding her she had already erred by breaking the no-pets rule. Finally, he murmured, "No problem."

He filled a clean ashtray with water and handed it to her. She got off the stool, opened the carrier's webbed steel door, and placed the water inside. Stroking the silky pelt of a groggy Mikela, she crooned assurances that might well have been for herself. Then she climbed back onto the stool, taking pains to adjust her short skirt, and found the man waiting, his full mouth almost smiling.

"What kind of cat?" He quirked a heavy brow.

"Siamese."

He smiled then, a kind of concession, murmuring, "Sky blue eyes."

"Yes." She tried not to look at the rows of bottles behind him, every color, hue, shape and size. She tried not to consider the havoc just one bottle was capable of leveling. Stalling, wrestling fatigue and hunger, she ventured, "The desk clerk said you might have...fry bread?"

"Squaw bread." His mouth formed a rigid line.

"Excuse me?" No reply. "Nibbles...I think she said. I haven't eaten."

The black-as-pitch eyes glistened, softened. Again, she had the sense of one-sided familiarity. "It's all gone."

His voice was uncommonly quiet, but resonant. She could hear him easily, but couldn't lose the feeling she might not if she didn't listen carefully. "Umm...." She took inventory again, then eyed the condiments in a metal container on the counter. Olives, black and green. Plump cherries. Lemon slices that brought saliva rushing between her tongue and teeth. Robust stalks of trimmed celery. Her voice came from far away. "I'll have a Bloody Mary. Lots of celery, please." Her throat cinched, face warming, as if she'd been caught stealing. "Just barely wave the vodka over the glass," she managed.

He moved closer. She caught a whiff of cigar smoke. "A virgin, maybe?"

She leaned forward, drawn by his quiet delivery, his meaning unclear for a moment. And then it was.

Her eyes fastened on the silver belt buckle at his slender waist, wondering if this stranger were part of a conspiracy. Sudden sweat drenched her forehead. Loosening the top button of her shirt, she lifted her ponytail off the back of her damp neck, shaking her head.

"No, but just go *very* light on the vodka." Swiveling in the chair, she searched her bag for a cigarette. She lit it, blew smoke toward the ceiling, then fanned the residue with her palm. Additional guilt stung like bees attacking a honey thief. So much for her plan to celebrate this turn in her life by quitting smoking today.

The bartender slid an ashtray into range, then made no further movement, drawing her gaze. He had high cheekbones topping a straight, strong nose and granite chin.

"Beer is better in the heat," he said. "It cools you off."

Twelve ounces of beer instead of a mere trace of vodka? Her stomach roiled as she reminded herself it was irrelevant, and fought not to snap her reply. "No beer, thank you." She managed a smile. She would have a sip of the Bloody Mary—no more than two—then ask for water.

With languid grace he filled a highball glass with celery stalks and placed them before her, along with a salt shaker. *Nibbles*. When he turned away finally, she observed narrow hips, legs, long and slender in tight jeans, a wave of back muscles beneath a T-shirt, a rough rawhide string restraining his hair. The name Lukas had been hand-tooled into his rich leather belt. His skin, darker than her own, boasted the patina of weathered bronze.

Indian. Native American, her mind corrected. Navajo? Hopi? Zuni? Exotic local color. Native to his surroundings. How would that hallowed distinction feel? Taste? How would the assurance of belonging rest on you mind when you closed your eyes each night?

A tall, frosted Bloody Mary glass dressed with another bushy stalk o celery appeared on the bar. Lukas sauntered back to his resting place at the opposite end and re-fired his cigar, staring out the window at the fair-haired children playing Marco Polo in the azure pool. The flute music ended, replaced by a low drumbeat, chanting, and then more flutes. She tasted he drink, stirred the red liquid with celery tasted again, then concluded he had not heard her clearly. Mr. and Mrs. T's mix, most likely. Definitely *virgin*.

In her raveled mind, an emotion close to relief wrestled with irritation and curiosity. While smoking her cigarette, she made circles on the scarred bar top with the glass, her napkin shredding in the wet residue. Then, mired in crucial thought, she sipped the benign drink and devoured celery, as children's raucous laughter competed with flute music on the edge of her awareness.

I didn't sign my employee agreement in blood. One would hardly expect to have to do that when working within their family dynasty, although she'd always been an exception to the rule where family favoritism played a role. But she didn't have to stay here where loneliness and a job she felt less than confident in placed her thousands of miles from the one thing she cared about. She could go back to Vancouver, petition her uncle for a different assignment. In Canada. Where was it written that proving herself, making up for the past, earned a higher grade if it was accomplished under duress? She could strive for absolution in familiar surroundings.

Surroundings that included Jarrid.

But if she left Scottsdale without trying, her giving up would go down on her résumé as failure. She had been allotted a third chance. Two others had been wasted on mourning a dismal childhood and settling for a marriage that had neither soothed nor healed her wounds.

Hayden Chastain had made it clear there wouldn't be another chance—not with Chastain Hotels. Neither would she stand a chance with Jarrid if she failed.

Gradually, her confusion merged with relief and determination. Once more she had conquered her urge to flee, to quit. She would see this through. But her life and future with Jarrid depended on her own strength, not her uncle's mercy. She finished the drink, stubbed out the cigarette and laid five dollars on the bar.

Somehow she would find the resolve to stand on her own feet.

శ

Lukas watched the woman slip down from the stool, cross the lobby and disappear down a corridor. So this was Cameron Vickers. Her industry reputation preceded her. Even though the Salt Water Inn staff was unable to prioritize enough to have a room ready for her, they had waited weeks for her to appear and begin a touted miracle of restoring the little inn. Aesthetically and profitably.

From what her uncle had told him, Lukas had prepared himself for a brash blonde with women's breasts and men's balls. Definitely not this tremulous, exotic creature with black-as-a-raven's curly hair, hot-coffee eyes, and skin the golden color of the desert at sunrise.

Never mind her sultry mouth, the image of which traveled from his intellect to his groin.

His mind lingered on her travel-poster image that would look contrived on another woman. Picture-perfect breasts beneath a fine white shirt. A short, flowered skirt wrapping her hips like a sarong. Strappy little sandals that clicked on the old tile floor as she'd walked away, listing to one side with the weight of the cat and its cage, head held high, shoulders back, dark hair swaying.

Her exotic image fit the Scottsdale scene like a three-fingered glove.

Anna slipped onto the stool Cameron Vickers had occupied, pulling him back. He reached for the empty glass, noting all the celery was gone, too.

"That's Cameron Vickers." Anna rolled her eyes in the direction her new boss had gone. To Lukas' nod, she prompted, "What you think, brother?"

He blotted the bar with a dry towel. "Life is full of surprises. *Enit?*"

two

With reluctance, Cameron unlocked a carved wooden door and stepped into the dimness of her assigned room. She lowered her hand luggage and Mikela's kennel to the floor and opened the drapes. Underlining the deafening quiet, the air hung hot and oppressive, stale as old beer and dead cigar butts. She had requested a non-smoking room, but this one smelled as though it had been transferred to non-smoking status the moment Anna handed her the key.

Studying the shoddy interior, she sensed a kind of broken promise in the faded verve of fabrics and carpet, the concave impression in the double-size mattress. Her reflection in a dresser mirror made her glance away, unready to meet her own eyes and acknowledge proof of solitude.

The instant Cameron unlatched the gate, Mikela scampered to the kennel's back corner and knotted up. "It's all right, baby," Cameron crooned, unlocking and sliding open a glass door. It opened onto a small arid patio enclosed by a masonry wall laden with greenery and voluptuous, unfamiliar blooms. "You venture out when you're ready."

In answer, the Siamese clawed the carpeted floor of her hiding place.

The rest of the luggage had been delivered to the room while she had nursed her misgivings at the bar. After lowering the thermostat, small compensation for the open door, she hoisted her two cases onto the bed, unzipped the smaller one and rifled through until she located a pill bottle. In the cramped bathroom, she shook two capsules into her hand, then stopped short. Her head pounded like the drums that had thudded from the radio in the bar. She clenched her eyes, then opened them, staring at the bottle. Although the warning glared in her memory she read the label again, and then read it once more, pushing back disturbing images.

May cause drowsiness. Do not take with alcohol.

Resting her brow against the cool mirror, fingertips pressed to her temples, she reminded herself she had drunk no alcohol. Thanks to the bartender. As for drowsiness, she would welcome it. She tilted her head, placed the pills on the back of her tongue, swallowed them down with tepid tap water. Then, wearing only a robe, she curled fetal-like in the indention on the bed, where her mind whirled like a run-away movie reel, eventually settling into memory.

Discipline forced her to pick and choose bits of recall carefully, in order to filter out bad times, embrace good. Her mind skimmed over Vancouver summers, convent schools less austere than others, the one Christmas where she and her mother had been included in family ritual. An Easter egg hunt with cousins—that memory tainted suddenly by ghostly echoes of a scolding voice when she'd torn her too-small, lacy dress on a grape briar.

Cameron turned over in the mattress well, drew her knees closer to her chest and tucked the robe around her feet. In her mind, she deliberately traveled the road backward from Scottsdale to Vancouver.

"If you want a college education, you'll major in something useful to the family business." Her Uncle Hayden's edict still echoed in her head. He had actually been saying, "something to earn your keep." Something other than the art classes she still longed for.

"Commercial art, then." Cameron had petitioned deaf ears. Eventually acquiescing, she had enrolled in business, selected a second major, hotel management, graduated with honors, and worked her way up in Chastain Hotel management hierarchy.

Mikela leapt onto the bed, startling Cameron back to the present. As the cat thrummed deep in her throat, her fine-boned head butted Cameron shoulder with surprising strength. Mind racing, stomach twisting, Cameron turned onto her back to accommodate the feline's favorite position and await the promised drowsiness. Her headache had ebbed, and Mikela's soft warmth, stretching from Cameron's thighs to her breasts, should have been a comfort Instead, Cameron bolted up, and Mikela scampered out the door to the patio.

Gripping her face in her hands, she moaned, sickened at her lack of power over memory. She reached for her bag on the night table, rummaged and found a cigarette. Her hand halted halfway to her desert-dry mouth as her gaze sought out and settled on the smoke alarm above the door, barely visible in the darkening room. Catching her disheveled reflection in the dresser mirror, she moaned again, crumpled the cigarette and reached for the phone, dialing by rote. His voice. That's all she needed to get her through the night. A continuous, unanswered ring echoed in her ear until she broke the connection.

The hot, close room became another unfamiliar prison.

౿

As if he'd been nudged by *chindi*, or the white man's ghosts, Lukas looked up from slicing limes and peered into the mirror behind the back bar counter. An unwelcome sensation whispered on the skin between his shoulder blades, tickling the hairs at his nape.

Cameron Vickers crossed the lobby in shoes as tall as Pinnacle Peak, little more than phantom-thin straps across her toes and buckled around her ankles. As her reflection in the mirror drew closer, her hair bounced loose and curly, wet, maybe. Behind each ear she had pinned a clump of bougainvillea that was already wilting. That, and the way her short, black dress wrapped and tied at her waist, forming an eyenabbing V where some kind of pendant on a thin chain dangled into her cleavage, put him in mind of a displaced, mourning Polynesian princess.

As gracefully as a woman could manage, she climbed onto a barstool and quickly lit a cigarette, holding the smoke in. Then, eyes closed, she tilted back her head to slowly release it, surrendering to pleasure.

Closer than he had been earlier that afternoon, he turned to remove an ashtray that held a crushed, unfiltered cigarette butt, slipping a clean one into her reach. With a towel, he took a needless swipe at the tile bar top while observing beads of sweat lurking between her dark brows and lining her upper lip. The pendant proved to be a round locket. Old, he would wager. Beat up. Its shoddiness mocked her earrings and bracelet, the matching ring on her left hand. Familiar with jewelry making, he judged the stones to be authentic black pearl.

"What can I get you?"

She studied him, looking surprised. "Oh…" A glance at her watch. "You're still here?"

He figured that didn't require an answer.

As before, her gaze inventoried the liquor cache on the back counter. Most people knew what they wanted before they came through the front door. So did she, and he saw that it bothered the hell out of her. That led him to suspect validity in the tip-off he had been given, the one he had sworn to ignore until he could judge for himself.

He waited, taking inventory. She had high cheek-bones. Fat and glossy lashes lined almond eyes. Perfect teeth gleamed within a lipstick frame the color of ripe strawberries, leaving him to speculate on how she would taste.

Making her into the Cameron Vickers he had expected was hard as hell.

"Excuse me." He ambled to the other end of the bar, took an order, filled it. By the time he ambled back, her mind was made up.

"Vodka Collins." Her tone bouncing between triumph and defeat, she took a deep breath that elevated her shoulders. Her throat pulsed. He caught the scent of bougainvillea and too-sweet perfume.

"Beer's good and cold," he suggested.

Her eyes narrowed. "An Absolut Vodka Collins." She looked like a deer testing the wind with its nose in the air, ready to take flight. Or do battle. Bu she had good taste in vodka.

"You want more celery with that?"

"No," she fired, but then added, "thank you, but I'm on my way to dinner."

Turning away, he watched in the mirror as he concocted her drink. Their eyes met. Hers jerked away as if she had sinned. She turned her eyes to the lobby, smoking her cigarette. He set the drink before her with a napkin bearing a Salt River Inn logo, then returned to slicing limes, watching. She extinguished the cigarette and sipped, tongue catching an errant drop on he lip. Lukas' gut clenched. She sipped again, frowned and took a full drink, her dusky throat moving as she swallowed. Raising the drink, she sniffed as if vodka had a scent, then set the glass down with a soft slap.

"Excuse me." She employed a low, cultured, don't-mess-with-me tone.

His gaze met hers in the mirror.

"May I speak with you?"

He lowered the paring knife, dried his hands on a towel and approached her. "*Enit?*" He quirked a brow.

"Do you know who I am?"

Her name, yeah. But regardless of how he had been tipped off, he was a hell of a long way from knowing who she was, her values, her wants an needs. He kept quiet.

"I'm Cameron Vickers. I represent Chastain Hotels. As of tomorrow, I'll be assuming management of the Salt River Inn."

He nodded. No news there.

"And you're…Lukas." Her attention shifted to his belt buckle, then bolted back to his face. "Isn't that right?"

He nodded again, folding his arms over his chest. The silver bracelet on his wrist jangled, drawing her eyes there, then to the other wrist, where he wore no watch. Just more bracelets, and on his finger, the silver and lapis ring his father had made. Her eyes lifted to the cross at his chest, the silver stud in his ear. Between her perfect brows, a shallow, judgmental furrow deepened.

"There's no vodka in this drink." Did he hear anger or condescension in her voice? Her color heightened, turning those soft cheekbones to rusty pith.

"There's some." Thumbing the underside of his ring, he kept his ton neutral, as if she were. complaining about the hotter-than-Hades weather.

"But not what you'll charge me for." She squared her shoulders and hiked her chin. "And most likely, not what the other patrons at this bar will pay for. Am I right?"

"About you, or about the others?"

Fire sprang up in her dark eyes. "I see you have an automatic dispenser gun back there." She nodded to the back counter. "Why aren't you using it?"

"I used it on the *others*."

One brow rose in artful skepticism. "And why not me?"

Aware that the customer two stools down had witnessed her accusations of *knocking down on the till*, Lukas kept his reply to a murmur. "As pricey as it is, we don't have a big call for Absolut. It's not hooked up to a gun. I free pour it."

"Well, you chose the wrong customer to short-change."

He didn't make a practice of arguing with women, but her claim didn't warrant ignoring. "This afternoon you told me to just wave the bottle over the glass."

"Which you neglected to do."

She had him there. He took away her soiled ashtray without replacing it.

She met his waiting gaze. "If you intend to continue working here, I'll expect you to give Salt River patrons what they order, and that includes me." She searched the little bag she carried, pulled out three one-dollar bills and slapped them on the bar, mad as a wet wasp. "This should cover the Collins mix. Make sure it gets into the register."

He might have found the way she stalked away in her out-of-place, exotic fury humorous, if her indictment had not felt like a gash in his honor.

☙

Cameron asked for a table in a far corner of the dining room. From there she could observe the level of patronage and quality of service, as well as take the stigma, imagined or real, off her solitude. The wait staff proved to be Anglo. The busboys and kitchen help, revealed by a scarred and kicked swinging door, were Native American. Dark skin and hair, black, brooding eyes, languid, graceful movements. Like Anna at the desk. Like the bellman and the maids she had noted in the halls pushing turndown carts.

She mulled that over, cocking her head to see across the lobby and into the bar. Native American, like the bartender, Lukas, who, unlike the commonly square and stocky build of the others, was tall, lean, and muscular. He had dark, almost sad I-can-see-through-you eyes and a smile capable of rendering a woman mute, should he ever choose to use it. He tended to his work with fixed and elegant rhythm. His male beauty and masculinity could insure female patrons lining the bar to look, even if not to touch. She felt a hesitant stirring. How much of her anger toward him, her resentment of his making decisions for her, hinged on false accusations leveled on her in the past? It wouldn't matter, she knew. He would be Salt River Inn history the moment she found someone to replace him.

❦

She woke near dawn, drenched, tangled in the bed linens. Darkness formed a shroud around her, except for the eerie green light cloaking the bed.

Her mind hurled possibilities. A closet? Dormitory? Cell?

A hospital room? No monitors beeped, no carts jangled, no nurses laughed.

Somewhere traffic filed by, tires strumming concrete, music playing too loudly. Amber light edged between the floor and the heavy drapes. A green clock face proclaimed four a.m. Her mind identified yet another hotel room.

Beside her, warmth stirred, hummed, then curled into a ball of protest.

Mikela. They were in the cursed Salt River Inn. *Damn the past*.

Ghostly faces roiled behind her closed eyes. Phillip. Jarrid. And Hayden, who held her fate. She rose from the bed and went onto the patio to await dawn.

☙

When Cameron appeared in the coffee shop the next morning, the hostess greeted her solicitously by name, assurance that word of her Scottsdale arrival had spread. She did a quick check of the girl's nametag for future reference. Yolanda. Blonde, barely past puberty. Skirt too short, shoes too tall, too much makeup for early morning.

Cameron returned the girl's brilliant smile. "Good morning. I'd like a quiet table, please, and I'm meeting a Mr. Dancer, an architect. When he arrives—"

"Yes, ma'am. He's here." She indicated a back table, a four-top littered with papers and a briefcase, where a man sat alone with his back to the door. He wore a cowboy hat. A thick, black braid hung halfway down the back of a faded denim jacket.

Native American—Indian, as she had overheard them referring to themselves. She began to feel like a minority, something she'd not expected in her new environment.

"He's waiting for you," Yolanda half whispered.

Cameron checked the business card in her hand again. *I. L. W. Dancer*. Architect and *Contractor*. She stared at the back of the man at the table. "That's Mr. Dancer?"

"Wind Dancer. Yes, ma'am." An affirmative nod, a conspiratorial smile.

Yolanda seized a menu and led the way, pencil-thin heels clicking on worn tiles, derriere swaying like a charmed cobra. As they drew nearer the table, the man rose and turned. Shock streaked up Cameron's spine. Her breath snagged. She halted, barely aware of Yolanda placing the menu on the table and swishing away.

"Good morning." The bartender, Lukas, offered a handshake.

three

Eternity passed before Cameron regained enough composure to accept the gesture. Her hand disappeared inside his, silky smooth on top, callused in the palm. For such a large and powerful hand, the gesture was surprisingly gentle. An elaborate turquoise ring chilled her fingers.

"You're J. L. W. Dancer," she said dumbly.

He released her hand. "Jay Lukas Wind Dancer, my legal Navajo name,' he said. "We meet again." His chiseled features revealed no clue as to how he felt about that. His voice, also devoid of intonation, held the same riveting quietness as before.

Her cheeks singed as every word of the reprimand she had issued the night before, the threats, echoed in her head.

"I don't understand." Before she could swallow her confusion, the confession had escaped, along with her command of the situation. "There must be some mistake."

"We'll see." A velvet gaze penetrated hers, but divulged no feeling.

"You're not a bartender?"

"Not by profession."

He pulled out a chair and waited until she slipped into it in front of a place setting. As he placed his beaver-brown hat, crown side down, or an empty chair, she caught a glimpse of the brand inside. Stetson. He resumed his seat, slouching back, cocking a well-shined, silver-trimmed, snake skin boot over one knee. Levi's, well-washed, but newer than those he had worn yesterday, tightly encased long legs with strong-looking thighs. Beneath the denim jacket, a white T-shirt strained across his broad chest, revealing the clear impression of a Christian cross beneath.

Breaking the silence, he announced, "I moonlight. Have jigger, will travel."

She waited for a smile. Apparently last night's harsh accusations had eliminated that possibility. *Not by profession*, he had said. Just as she wasn't a bitch, by profession. "You're an architect. The one Hayden Chastain hired for this project?"

"Architect and contractor. I specialize in politically correct renovations."

Was he being glib, or trying to amuse her? His stoic nature prevented her from knowing. "Have you been in business long?" She hedged around the real questions. Was he successful? Could he handle this project?

Had Uncle Hayden lost his mind?

"Long enough."

At that moment, a waiter appeared with a platter of flat, saucer-size pastries. They steamed, gleamed, and smelled like grease. He placed a pitcher of honey next to the platter, filled her coffee cup, and topped off the cup next to Lukas' plate. With slender, deft fingers, Lukas raised his cup in a kind of toast. When she failed to lift her cup, he lowered his, eyes expressionless, jaws hard as sun-baked brick.

"What is this?" She indicated the pastries.

"Squaw bread." He shrugged. "Fry bread, if you are gender conscious. You wanted it yesterday."

Just as she had wanted him to only wave the vodka bottle over the glass of Bloody Mary mix. Did he recall every word she had uttered in his presence? Was he the kind of man to hold a grudge? Thus far, his demeanor gave no clue. "You have quite a memory," she ventured.

"Not always a good thing."

She felt he had looked into her being. In diversion, she asked the question she could no longer resist. "Why are you tending bar?"

He hesitated, then his precise black brows hiked. A smile gleamed, rain diamonds splattering on clean bronze glass. "I have a mission."

With his fork, he speared a piece of fry bread and deftly moved it to her plate. As she watched, he served himself, slit the pocket of bread, drizzled honey inside, rolled the creation into a cylinder, and ripped off a hearty bite with strong, straight teeth. His jaw muscles flexed, chewing. His throat moved, swallowing. Then the tip of his tongue raked between full lips briefly enough to have been imagined.

"Fry bread is better hot." He employed the dinner-size paper napkin before draping it half folded across one thigh, his movements unhurried and supple. "So is coffee."

"I'm not very hungry." A cigarette would do her nicely, but she was quitting. *Today.* She stirred cream into the coffee and took a sip, trying not to show her amazement when he stoically split the bread he had served her, applied honey, rolled a second cylinder and placed it seam side down on the plate.

Obligated, she took a bite. Her taste buds rallied. She took another bite, realizing what all the fuss was about. "It's…wonderful."

"Now you know." His tone held a triumphant edge.

He pushed his plate away, moved the bread platter, and reached into the stack of papers she now realized were architectural renderings. Hastily finishing the bread in her hand, she blotted her mouth and followed his lead in pushing her plate aside. He uncapped a cardboard tube and spread the rolled-up contents between them. Cameron ducked her head to study the drawing. Her hair fell forward; she held it back one-handed.

"This is how I see it." His breath, scented with coffee and yeast, stirred her hair, tickled her ear.

She recognized the present building's elevation, with no obvious changes. Pueblo Indian architecture, authentic, she suspected. Apparently this architect lacked imagination or was proposing restoration, as opposed to renovation. Had Hayden seen these drawings? Approved them? If so, he'd failed to mention it.

Taking her time, she lifted pages one by one, studied electrical and plumbing specs that could have been drawn in a foreign language, all the while conscious of the architect's nearness. Conscious that he awaited her comments, she flipped back to the first page depicting the proposed structure, beautifully drawn and signed by Jay Lukas Wind Dancer in the corner.

"This is nice. Interesting."

"But?"

She raised her eyes to his, finding them placid. "Not what I have in mind."

"Which is?" He tapped the end of a mechanical pencil on the table. A silver and pearl ring on his left hand and a lapis-bezeled watch caught the filtered sunlight.

"I want a replica of a South Seas hotel. Complete with thatch roof and a sand beach around the swimming pool—which I want enlarged, by the way."

"Why?" He took a small cigar from the intricately tooled leather briefcase and rolled it, still wrapped, between his thumb and forefinger.

"The present pool is too small for the customer increase we'll have," she said.

"*Enit.*"

She had no idea of the word's meaning, but his tone seemed affirmative.

He unwrapped the cigar and resumed fingering it, drawing her eyes to the enervated, rhythmic motion. "But why South Seas?"

She had misunderstood his original question. "I have a reason."

He ran the cigar beneath his nose, then damped his teeth around it viselike, his jaw line pulsing when he spoke. "Which is?"

Which is, for thirty-two years I've borne the brunt of my mother's folly. Converting this Inn into a Samoan clone is the only way to change that. But exposing her reasons to this stranger, this man who already considered her deranged, wasn't an option. "It will draw tourists. Travel agents can sell space based on its uniqueness to the area."

So long did he study her that she ached to check her lipstick. Instead, she flicked her tongue over her lips, hoping to catch any fry bread residue that might be clinging there. Her mouth, however, wasn't his focus. He stare into her eyes so deeply she felt he entered her soul. She tore her gaze from his and took a drink of lukewarm coffee.

At last he said, "A South Seas hotel wouldn't draw tourists."

"We'll run a market survey. Immediately. I don't want to delay reconstruction a moment longer than necessary."

A brow quirked, then straightened, leaving his classic face devoid of expression, eyes veiled. "Why is that?" He spoke around the unlit cigar.

Because there's another place I ache to be.

"The inn has to have more occupancy to show a profit. I'm responsible for that, but it won't happen until we can have state of the art accommodation and offer something our competition doesn't."

He plucked the cigar from his mouth. "Tourists come to Arizona to see Indians and anything they think spells Indian."

"I didn't, Mr. Wind Dancer." And if his narrow, set-in-his-ways thinking was an example of *Indian* culture, she wanted no part of it. "I came to get a job done. If we can't agree—"

Her head jerked up as he shoved back his chair and stood. She watched him slowly roll and stuff the architectural rendering back into the tube with care, then gather together what must be the contract Hayden had told her to sign. After storing the cache of papers inside the briefcase, he retrieved and donned his hat. A narrow silver hatband gleamed in the soft lighting.

"Let's take a walk," he said.

"What?"

Catching her upper arm, he drew her gently but firmly from the chair before she could protest. He handed her the oversized shoulder bag that served as purse and briefcase.

"In this heat?" She had almost lost her breath when she opened the slide for Mikela at dawn. "Walk where?"

"Around Old Town Scottsdale." He shrugged out of his jacket, wrapped and tied it around his waist. Beneath the sleeves of his T-shirt, corded arms and biceps appeared smooth and hard as river rock. Wordlessly, he eyed the linen blazer she wore with a skirt and pumps, inviting her to follow suit.

"I…can't take a walk. I have a meeting."

"A meeting with me," he reminded. "One I would like to finish."

To establish peace, she would humor him. Then he would gratefully comply with her design dictates for the privilege and prestige of revamping the old hotel.

Shedding her jacket, she folded and draped it over the shoulder bag, pulled her hair off her neck into a ponytail and secured it with a band she kept tucked away in the bottomless bag.

His gaze settled on her bare shoulders and arms in the floral silk tank top, segued to her breasts and lingered before their eyes met. "That works."

He stepped aside for her to precede him. Then his hand at the small of her back guided her with purpose out of the hotel and into the God-awful September heat.

On the street, he wordlessly lit his cigar as he headed her in the direction of the narrow Salt River Canal a block away. Bulldozers labored at clearing the land, a prelude to the Scottsdale Waterfront Project. The future shopping and entertainment mecca fronting the canal would blend into the historical section of Scottsdale, which included the Salt River Inn. Hayden Chastain had learned of the planned development three years earlier when it was no more than a whispered rumor, then managed to buy the inn for a pittance of its worth. Cameron would ready it to take advantage of the windfall, reopening the hotel and eventually instating new management. The barren, sandy soil the dozers worked reminded her of the miles she had to go before returning to Vancouver.

"This is a tremendous project," she interjected into Lukas' silence, blotting her brow with the back of her hand. "Chastain Properties is fortunate to be part of it."

"Enit." Nothing more, but he stopped, taking the heavy bag from her shoulder and placing it on his own, his somber expression rejecting her protest. A man of lesser stature would have looked peculiar. But not J. L. W. Dancer. His presence struck her as stately, confident, commanding. A man used to and expecting to have his way.

Following his lead, she strolled with him onto Fifth Avenue, winding past galleries and antique shops. Some of the buildings were antiquated, some only camouflaged to look old, all constructed of adobe and tile and weathered wood. Her body pulsed with the Latin music blaring from the Tortilla Factory on West Main. From a tobacco shop, two doors beyond, seeped lonely sounding strains of flutes.

On Craftsman Court, a wide, straight boulevard of interior design shops and upscale furniture stores, they ambled past Dos Gringos, a small adobe café. Even at midmorning, people in lightweight clothing crowded the patio and stood two-deep at the open-air bar, sipping beer and frosty drinks, eating chips, smoking, talking, laughing. *Networking.* A graying woman tending bar waved to Lukas. He waved back, awarding his soul-stirring smile and a native greeting.

Walking in silence, other than his occasionally pointing out a landmark, had unnerved Cameron at first, before she settled into his reassuring presence and an awareness of his gentle, persuasive strategy. With silence that spoke volumes, he pointed out proof of his theory: the hotel she proposed would clash like cymbals with Scottsdale culture. But to Cameron, swimming up-stream in a cultural river was a familiar way of life.

Covertly, she studied his strong profile beneath the brim of the Stetson. Aware of his dark, virile attractiveness, she grew overly conscious of the surreptitious stares he drew from women of varied age and color. He smelled of cigar smoke and aftershave going stale in the blistering heat. His thin, sweat-dampened shirt stuck to his shoulder blades. It dipped at the shallow indention in his lower back, just above the stenciled belt bearing his name. The belt reminded her that, by not identifying himself last night during her tirade, he had tricked her, repaying her for her distrust and embarrassing accusations, whether or not they'd been warranted.

Lukas Wind Dancer was proving complex and cagey. Working with him on the renovation could be a challenge she lacked the time and energy to accept.

She could not risk slowing down production.

Having come full circle around Old Town, they reentered the inn and the welcome cool of the lobby. With her big bag and the briefcase he'd retrieved from the coffee shop resting on the floor between them, they stood perspiring, Cameron catching her breath. Anna eyed them curiously from behind the desk. Yolanda watched guardedly from the hostess stand.

"Thank you for the tour. I enjoyed it."

"Is that right?"

He observed the damp tank top clinging to her body, then looked into her sweat-drenched face. Surprising her, he reached to tuck a straggle of wet hair behind her ear, his movement slow, decisive, his touch warm as Indian summer. She stepped back before he could do the same with the damp hair hugging her other cheek.

"I'll be honest," she rushed. "Your point is well taken, but I haven't changed my mind."

Dark-as-thunder-cloud eyes locked into hers. "Neither have I."

"That's a moot point. The decision is mine. If you're unable to come up with a design I approve…" When his exquisite mouth formed a taut line, she let the alternative lie.

He tugged the hat low on his forehead. Framed by the brim, his eyes seemed even darker, more luminous. "To renovate the way you want would be a mistake."

Would be. Not will be. *Stubborn.* "I'll take my chances."

"Scottsdale has strict building codes. Too much variance would never get past the city planning commission." He slid his hands, palms out, into the rear pockets of his starched jeans. He tilted his chin a bit, emphasizing a damp, muscled chest. "Red tape could delay the project. You wouldn't want that."

She'd thought him too amiable to issue a threat. Still…"Most likely Properties will be able to influence building codes."

He took the tube containing his drawings from the brief case, extended it. "Hold onto these. In case you come to your senses."

Before she could level a rejoinder, he smiled so engagingly he might have rehearsed before a mirror. She offered her hand, as he'd done earlier. He took it, his handshake gentle and brief.

"Thank you," she said with finality.

"For what?" A brow lifted, touching the low-set hat brim.

"For the time you put in. The drawings are impressive, but—"

"Not what you're looking for." His smile lost some of its guileless quality. Lifting his briefcase, he rummaged through, withdrawing another cigar, which he unwrapped and held in his hand like a slender sucker. "I wish you good luck." His tone, not the formality of his words, suggested she would need good fortune.

After giving him a head start, she ventured outside and stood stealing two puffs from a seductive cigarette, watching him saunter away, get into an aged Chevrolet Suburban, and pull into mid-day traffic.

Now she'd be faced with replacing both the bartender *and* the architect.

❦

When Lukas turned into the driveway of his Tempe townhouse, the rusting Toyota belonging to Chuey Run Amok occupied guest parking. The front wheels of the battered auto rested a few inches too many beyond the end of the concrete, crushing the groundcover maintenance had planted yesterday. Even in his junior year at ASU, Lukas' nephew had not outgrown his family nickname: Chuey Run Amok. While working part time at Wind Dancer Construction, and as Lukas' houseboy in exchange for his college tuition, he had managed to break or destroy more than he took care of. But he possessed an uplifting spirit and was trustworthy as the gospel.

Chuey looked up from polishing silver as Lukas entered the kitchen. An alcohol-free O'Doul's beer sat on the counter next to the polish. "Hey, Uncle Bro." He wrinkled his nose as Lukas came within sniffing distance: "You been in a tribal sweat box?"

"More or less." Lukas veered out of range, opened the refrigerator, and took out a liter of bottled water. "Any calls?"

"Enit, man." Chuey recited a list of names, mostly women. "They're still on the machine. One of them is pissed. She called you a—"

Lukas raised a hand. "Don't spoil the surprise."

Chuey sat aside a meat fork, picked up and promptly dropped a ladle. It whanged and thudded on the shiny plank floor. He grinned when he dropped the sponge while stooping to retrieve the ladle. "That Salt River thing go okay?"

The way his nephew watched from beneath hooded brows alerted Lukas that he had failed to hide his frustration. "Could be better."

"Yeah, how?" He rinsed the ladle in hot water.

"Cameron Vickers is short on appreciation of ethnic architecture."

"You're probably long enough to convince her." Chuey grinned, gray-bronze eyes flashing, teeth gleaming in his pale umber half-breed face. "Sexual pun intended." At the tender age of nineteen, he was too good looking, as Lukas' sister had been, too ready to play.

"So far she's immune."

Chuey copped a swig of O'Doul's. "You aren't dropping the ball, are you Luk? The *Diné* are counting on you. Your butt will be steak tartar at the next tribal council."

"Do I look like a quitter?"

Chuey eyed him as if considering. "Just a little pre-pussy whipped maybe?"

Lukas seized the dishtowel and popped Chuey's arm with the tip, raising an immediate red welt. The boy danced around, exaggerating the wound.

"That's what I need, brother," Lukas chastised. "A vote of confidence."

"She's just a female," he needled back. *"Gringo,* at that. A pale face."

"Gringa," Lukas corrected. "But the Navajo term is Anglo, Mr. Run Amok."

And Cameron Vickers was neither *gringa* nor Anglo.

❦

He thought about that in the shower. *Gringa?* Anglo? Half maybe. For sure, some uncommon ethnic mingling had taken place. But the term pale face in no way applied. Except maybe in her non-meditative reasoning. She was quick to jump the gun, quick to form an opinion that might not stand up under fire. Too damn quick. *Scary.*

He hated like hell to see her make a mistake. Apparently, she had a lot riding on this venture. Hayden Chastain, who surely had the final word, had seen the drawings and made no mention of wanting to see anything different. He seemed savvy concerning Scottsdale and the Waterfront Project. Legally, Chastain Properties could be made to stand by their prior agreement, one he and Cameron Vickers had been scheduled to sign today. But that working environment wouldn't bring honor to the *Diné*, Lukas' people.

His warning that the planning commission would give her months of hassle, then reject her idea, had been only a half bluff. Cameron was hell-bent to get back to Canada, and he had a feeling it was more personal than professional. No big surprise. A beautiful woman like her had to be involved from her long, slender neck down to her trim ankles.

Hard as he tried to avoid it, her image from the day and night before—when she'd left off power dressing—rammed itself into his mind behind the closed eyes he tilted up to the water spray. Flowery perfume, erotic clothing draping her breasts and hips, shoes so skimpy she looked to be barefoot. Her nails and toenails painted blistery-hot pink. His groin winced. If she had dressed for effect, she had succeeded. Or maybe her clothing seemed alien because she had been cast into expatriate status. He remembered what that felt like. He could empathize. Still, there was something methodical about the way she decked herself out.

He lathered his loosened hair, scrubbed and squeezed, then stuck his head beneath the stream, reflection finished, until she insinuated her way back in. How would she look in buckskin, fringe swaying when she walked that walk? Or in the vivid velvet skirts his mother and aunties—and Kai Blackwater—favored?

Who the hell cared? She wasn't Navajo. Neither was she Apache. And Jay Lukas Wind Dancer wouldn't be making that mistake again. Still, he wondered what bedding her might entail, if it might douse some of her fire, wondered what might surface in the aftermath? No way. She was off limits.

As he re-braided his wet hair, his thoughts migrated to a past that truly dogged him, nipping at his heels and psyche like a neglected reservation puppy—an ache he sometimes thought was easing, those times when he was buried deeply enough in a woman for temporary memory loss. Over the last five years, since he had returned from the north to Arizona, deciding to remove himself from the sights of the white man's firing squad, bitterness had evolved to scar tissue. But thoughts like those about this displaced *asdzání*—a woman both spirited and vulnerable enough to rattle his reasoning—invited bad memory with an invitation hand-engraved in grief.

Consolation came with knowing he had learned his lesson.

four

The cold from the concrete steps Chuey sat on chilled the seat of his jeans, spread down his legs and into his Nikes. Autumn's breeze, dry but biting, swayed piñon branches, then sn eaked inside his shirt collar. He untied the arms of an ASU sweatshirt from around his waist and pulled the shirt over his head. Not enough. He hugged himself, fingers tucked into his armpits. Nippy. Around him wild grasses waved and the smell of sage filled the afternoon. A rusting three-wheeler, minus its seat and a wheel, lay up-ended beneath a pine tree. In the distance, half a dozen sets of kids' jeans and denim shirts draped a clothesline, whipping, sweeping the ground when the wind picked up.

Clothespins might be in order here. He'd try to remember to bring some.

He shifted his weight on the hard seat, leaning back, the pine logs that made up the hogan sturdy and rough against his shoulders.

Tzin-yah' dee klin'. Logs stacked up.

He toyed with the words and mind pictures of Navajos building the shelter long ago with their hands, no tools needed. According to legend, between battles with the Utes, they'd held up in hovels like this, licking their wounds and regrouping.

Hogan. Structures as traditional as the woman who lived here. Never mind the holes in the mud mortar and worms invading the logs at the back corner, low to the sticky red clay the shelter sat on. Probably a few *chindee* around, too, the way the little hut creaked in the wind. Not that he believed in that stuff. For real.

Chuey eyed the watch Lukas had given him for Christmas last year. He'd have to hump like a sumbitch to make that night class. If he missed it, he'd face the wrath of God, channeled through Lukas. Confronting disappointment in Lukas' eyes was worse than being lashed at the stake. Not that he'd been, but he'd rather be.

Where the hell was she, anyway? What was she going through? He closed his eyes, envisioning driving the two-hundred miles back to Tempe without answers. That's what phones were for. Except she didn't have one, didn't want one. There had been a time when he'd considered that cool. He now considered it backward. Selfish.

Drawn by the sound of an engine, he glimpsed a vehicle climbing the road that ran beneath the bluff supporting the hogan. Yep. The school bus. A yellow and black ritual as comforting as time. Part of every kid's life. Navajos, gringos—Anglos, Lukas had reminded him—and *breeds* like him. Mutual ground, school buses. A common denominator. In his primordial life, his years on the rez, he'd ridden this same rusting contraption now snaking up the road a million miles, give or take a few. Now he waited for it. Glad to see it.

Had anybody ever waited for him?

Brakes whined. The bus lumbered to a stop a quarter mile away. Chuey pushed up from the steps, strode in that direction, wishing to hell he'd worn boots. He hadn't planned on staying past morning, or getting far from the pavement of Kayenta. Things changed when your heart got caught in a vise too rusty to pry open. He had run amok a few years back. Big time. Someone had straightened him out. Now he didn't have the balls or heart to put a stop to payback.

The boy hopped down from the bus, spotted him and began to run, dark hair flying, backpack slapping his back. His dented Tarzan lunch box rattled, probably shattering the thermos inside. *Agile little shit*. The way he jumped the ruts in the lane without missing a step. But where the hell had the clay stains on his faded jeans come from? Shooting craps in the schoolyard? Little young for that. Maybe.

Chuey quickened his step and they came together, the boy's arms wrapping Chuey's thighs, coal eyes genial but questioning. "Where's Mama?"

"What? Disappointed to see me?" Not according to the strength of the hug.

He shrugged back, cheeks rosied by wind and humility. "I'm glad. But Mama usually comes." Chuey watched as he got the message. "When she's here."

"Congrats, Nash Bridges. You figured it out." He turned him by his bony little shoulders, heading toward the hogan. "She went to the doctor."

"Oh…yeah." The shoulders drooped, his step heavier. "I forgot."

Chuey's heart flipped. It was hell to count on somebody being there, hell when you weren't supposed to show your disappointment. Or fear. "She asked me to run you down to the trading post, case she's late getting back." Navajos, especially women, spent half their rez lives in clinic waiting rooms. And died anyway. "She thought you might like a burger." He roughed the coarse, springy hair, buzzed on top, long in the back. "You hungry, chief?"

"Yeah. Cool." His eyes clouded, joy short-lived. "But I got no money."

"I gotcha covered, little man." *This week's gas money, but hell…*

"Okay. Cool."

They stashed the school gear inside the hogan, climbed into Chuey's Toyota, bumped across the weedy yard and onto the road.

"How's school?"

Gad pushed in the radio knob, then abused the seek button, remembering to say, "Cool."

"You taking any language classes, I hope?"

The dark eyes leveled on him, measuring. "Huh?"

Chuey chuckled. The kid was too young for second grade, but he'd tested out of kindergarten and first with through-the-roof scores. His daddy—whoever—must be an awesome brain. His mama was no slouch either, but she leaned to the arts. Pots and baskets and rugs. A regular Spider Woman when it came to those rugs.

Chuey tapped the steering wheel, enjoying thirty seconds of Pearl Jam, before the radio changed to a classical station. But he got a rueful smile in return for his groan. The boy was more of a humanitarian than a rock music advocate, always bringing home sick or dying derelict animals, saving most, cratering when he lost one. Getting that attached didn't pay. One of these days, he had to try to explain that to the kid.

Ten minutes into the trip, halfway to the trading post, a pickup jostled toward them, a dust wake streaking out behind. The boy stopped fiddling with the radio, watching, anticipation and apprehension mixing in his gaze. "It's Mama," he whispered.

Chuey pulled to a stop in the narrow road and waited. The pickup, dented, one headlight dangling, but clean as an old bone, pulled alongside, front bumper even with his rear. The driver rolled down the window.

The boy crowded Chuey, his grin a little weak, his concern genuine, the burger tabled for now. He waved a grimy hand. "Hi, Mama."

She waved back, smiling, done in but hiding it.

"Hi," Chuey said. "We were just on our way. How'd it go?"

Kai shrugged, eyes somber. A loose fist went to her mouth to catch a cough, then pressed to her chest. "I got a lecture and new medicine. I'm caught up on the back issues of *People Magazine*, though." Her stern mouth fished for a smile, revealing not-quite perfect, but very white, teeth. "That's a relief."

Chuey shrugged. "Well, something good in everything." Homily he'd stolen from her a few years back.

"I'll take him back home." She nodded toward the boy, the new gray streaks in her raven hair snagging the soft light. "You have miles to go."

Feeling the boy tense beside him, he laid a hand on his knee. "I...dunno. about that. You got any burgers back there in that shack?" He read the answer in her eyes. "Park that thing and get in. We'll eat fast. I'll still make the class.

Or die trying.

They watched her guide the pickup to the road's edge, get out, cross the road and round the hood of the Toyota. Graceful. Her long legs glide beneath the burgundy velvet skirt, the full sleeves of her blouse ruffling in the breeze.

Chuey nudged the boy, who now straddled the center console. "Your mama's pretty, chief." He countered the boy's skeptical grin with, "A real Indian princess." Another nudge. "Don't you think?"

"She's cool." He scrambled to open the car door, then back onto the console.

When she was inside the car, filling the void of her absence, her musky, smoky smell settling on him, Chuey wrote off the night class. *Screw it.* Lukas could chew his ass if he felt like it. He'd be due. Justified.

Then again, Uncle Bro had a history of screwing up priorities, too.

five.

Cameron sensed the first hint of trouble while gazing into her makeup mirror a week after her meeting with Wind Dancer. On the television in the adjoining bedroom, a Scottsdale station droned. Sound bites such as "old hotel rests on former Navajo burial ground" and "Canadian conglomerate" nudged her awareness as she lined her lips. She stepped into the bedroom, gaping at the television while an attractive, dark-skinned, onyx-eyed female anchor shared the local news.

Sacred? Hallowed? Burial grounds? Impossible. Hayden Chastain's horde of lawyers would have discovered that while searching titles. Where had such nonsense come from? The story, no doubt concocted by the minor-league station, had to be outlandish speculation, entertainment for the excitement seeking *snowbirds* and the more romantic minded tourists. Rather than allow concern, she chose to consider the story good publicity for the inn, especially the future café and bar.

In the gift shop, *Scottsdale Tribune* headlines sowed the first seeds of bona fide anxiety:

DOES LOCAL HOTEL REST ON SACRED INDIAN LAND?

A small-town paper scavenging for news, Cameron concluded, until Hayden's midmorning call changed the enigma to a predicament.

"Cam?" His tone spelled dissatisfaction.

"Good morning, Uncle Hayden."

"What's this about Salt River sitting on a burial ground?"

In her office, hastily converted from a storage room, Cameron glanced at the newspaper lying on the visitor chair. Did Hayden subscribe to the *Scottsdale Tribune*? If so, his copy would be days behind hers. Unless, for some unfathomable, extravagant reason, he had overnight delivery.

"I'm as surprised as you," she said. "How did you hear?"

"The damned media." A phone buzzed in the background. "Hold on."

Her mind darted frantically, negating the Muzak meant to soothe hex ear. *Media*? A hazy picture of paparazzi chasing Princess Diana's Mercedes formed.

The phone clicked in her ear. "A Scottsdale journalist woke me up this morning, asking if I knew about the Indian involvement when I acquired the inn."

"Did you?" She reluctantly granted the story credence.

"Hell, no, and there's no truth to it. What's going on?"

"I'm sure it's local hype. Paper-selling strategy." She couldn't imagine the story—rumor—ever being plucked from the *Scottsdale Tribune* by national media.

"The journalist saw the story on a Scottsdale station, Cameron." The disclosure sounded accusatory, rather than informative. "So it's spread to television—or vice versa."

"You're sure there's nothing to the…claim?"

"Absolutely." He shoved a directive into her silence. "Let's get to the bottom of this. Do you hear?"

"I'll take care of it."

"Have you met with Lukas Dancer yet?"

An unwelcome but stirring image winged across her mind. "Jay Lukas Wind Dancer, you mean."

"The Navajo. Did the two of you connect?"

Connect? She wrestled more images. "We met. I suppose you know he tends bar at Salt River."

"A jack-of-all-trades fellow, wouldn't you say?" Irony coated the remark.

"Have you already okayed the drawings he showed me?"

"I'm leaving the okay up to you, as long as they're workable. You know the amenities required to operate a hotel."

Precisely. Her breath came easier. "Wind Dancer's drawings need adjustment. I'm on top of it."

"Fine. Get this *hallowed ground* fable cleared up before it escalates." An-other line buzzed. "And keep me informed." The phone went dead.

ॐ

From the bathroom doorway, while brushing her teeth before bed, Cameron watched the second act unfold.

A network-affiliated Phoenix station opened the ten o'clock news by featuring the "hotel on sacred ground" saga. While their wording veered only slightly from the small Scottsdale station's report, photography enhanced it. Pictures of the inn, its proximity to the Scottsdale Waterfront Project, worldwide Chastain Property holdings. The finale featured the opulent home office in Vancouver.

Lying in bed cuddling Mikela, she assured herself the spreading propaganda represented publicity that money could not buy. The story would run out of fuel and die, but the inn would lodge in locals' minds. When she staged the grand opening a year from now, they would remember, come for drinks and dinner, approve the ambience and return, their visiting relatives and friends in tow. Revenue for the inn. An enhanced personal résumé. Still, anxiety kept her sleepless.

Hayden's call woke her the following morning. "Cam? Are you sleeping?"

A definitely incriminating greeting, even though dawn remained a coming event. She glanced at the lighted clock dial. Why wasn't *he* sleeping?

"I'm awake, Uncle Hayden." She attempted to clear the huskiness from her throat.

"What have you done about squelching that sacred ground business?" he barked.

So, in Hayden's mind the report had evolved from fable to business.

Tucking the receiver between shoulder and chin, she massaged her temples, ran her fingers into tangled hair. Mikela stretched, pressing her paw pads against Cameron's bare thigh. "I called the station to assure them there's no truth in it."

"What else?"

What else? Her mind scrambled backward, all the while craving a cigarette and an end to the developing dilemma. "I suggested they immediately cease and desist reporting untruths."

"I just got a call from an *Arizona Republic* reporter." The widely circulated Phoenix paper.

Her heart thrummed like guitar strings, then raced. "Checking on the story you mean?"

"He didn't call to discuss hotel rates."

Verbally, she ignored the barb. "What did you tell—"

"Not to print the rumor unless they want trouble. The same thing you *say* you told the television station."

Not exactly. Based on her belief that the publicity would benefit rather than harm the inn, her response had leaned more toward a suggestion than a warning.

A sudden, crucial urge to turn on the television seized her. But even news anchors didn't get up this early. She located the remote control in the bed covers anyway, and began flipping soundlessly through the channels. Infomercials only.

"Uncle Hayden, have you considered this might be good publicity for the hotel?"

"Do you take me for an idiot?" His voice boomed.

"I assume you don't think it would work."

"And don't you be thinking that either. Don't give any interviews, no matter how much you would like to see yourself on TV."

Rolling her eyes at Mikela, she scratched the feline's soft tummy, needing to hear her reciprocal purr. "So how did your conversation with the *Republic* reporter end?"

"With me threatening to sue his ass if he prints a lie, and hanging up on him."

"Hmm…" The Chastains practiced guerrilla tactics. "You're sure there's nothing to the claim?"

Chilled silence. Then, "I'm warning you, Cam. Get this stopped or I'll send someone who can."

Someone chosen from the cache of golf-loving cousins that envied her Scottsdale assignment. "You have my word."

She replaced the phone and sank against the pillows. Even with her impressive work history, he wasn't above testing her, threatening to jerk the gilded ring from her hands.

Her mind hurled backward to her first assignment at a fishing lodge in the tundra then forward to the industry award she had won for managing a five-star hotel in Vancouver. There, hosting a thousand-dollar-a-plate political event, she had met Phillip. After sharing her troubling, threatening secret with him on their second date, she eloped with him two months later. Without costly wedding or media attention to which the family would object, Phillip Vickers, influential in business and politics, had joined the ranks of Chastains.

And then Phillip had cost her the only thing that mattered. Jarrid.

She must remember, Salt River and Hayden's blessing could change that.

Watching the news that morning and evening, reading the *Republic* cover to cover and finding nothing, led her to believe the storm had passed. Relieved, she began devising a list of possible replacements for Jay Lukas Wind Dancer.

❦

As Cameron entered the lobby from her room, bound for a late morning appointment, the list tucked into her bag, Lukas was opening the bar. She ducked inside the gift shop and watched from there.

He worked with his back to her, those same tranquil movements, the imposing stature and rawhide-bound braid familiar now. A twinge of annoying regret for her morning mission nagged. As if her thoughts had winged through space and tapped him on the shoulder, he stared into the back bar mirror, then turned. Even veiled by distance, his gaze penetrated. Too challenging to ignore.

She bought a pack of cheese crackers and strode to the empty bar. As she climbed onto a stool, they made mirrored eye contact. She asked for a Coke.

He turned, settling a hip against the low back counter, arms folded across his chest. "Diet or regular?" A soft, deep, I've-been-verbally-stoic-until-now timbre.

"Regular."

"Caffeine or caffeine free?" His eyes pierced like hot, blunt needles.

"Free, please."

"Would you like bourbon with that?"

"No." Her muscles tensed.

"Rum?" He cocked a raven brow.

A smile escaped, surprising her. She waggled the crackers. "Just Coke to wash down my breakfast."

"Ice?"

"I'm running late, Wind Dancer." When he failed to budge, she sighed, "Yes. Ice."

He turned away, poured the Coke and placed it before her. "I wanted to get it right, *enit*?" Cameron now knew the word ran a full spectrum, from perfect agreement to question, doubt or skepticism. He flashed a beautiful but constrained smile. "And of course I could pilfer more pocket change if you ordered alcohol."

So he *was* capable of holding a grudge. But capable of gripping it tightly enough to set the media on her tail? "Especially if it's mostly virgin," she quipped.

One eyebrow flickered. "Is that an oxymoron?"

The pulse in her throat rioted. Meeting his eyes, she attempted to keep her face deadpan. She took out her first cigarette of the day, then changed her mind and dropped it back, loose, into her bag.

"If I want a legitimate drink, I'll stop by Dos Gringos." She sipped, sparing a smile. "Just put this on my account. That way, no money will change hands." She offered a prankish smile.

He eyed her as if she spoke a foreign language, then returned to counting bills and placing them in the cash register. Apparently, he possessed a limited sense of humor. With his movements, the solid braid swayed between his shoulder blades, half mesmerizing her. The radio hummed on a talk show. Periodically the host touted *KTNN-AM 660* out of Window Rock as "the voice of the Navajo nation." High in a corner, a television offered local fare, volume mute.

Finishing the last cracker, she decided to breach the silence. In view of this morning's mission, she felt compelled to give Lukas a last chance to comply. "Do you have any revised drawings for me to look at?"

"No." He closed the register with a soft thud. "My pencil draws only what my ancestors honor. If you're waiting for me to change my mind..." He leveled a gaze as sharp and unyielding as a sniper sighting down a rifle barrel. "I won't."

Her sentiments exactly. *Arrogant bastard.*

She crumpled the cracker packet and left it on the bar, along with a tip. Shouldering her bag, she caught a curious glimpse of the hotel on the TV screen, then an elderly man in elaborate Indian headdress. Lukas watched the screen raptly, black eyes reverent, classic features serene.

Not the televised images but Lukas Wind Dancer lodged in her mind.

§

Lukas sat across a cluttered desk from Aaron Wallis. A runt with tarnished-chrome eyes and matching hair, he repeatedly fingered a clip-on bow tie. Lukas had not met the *Arizona Republic* journalist before, but followed his column and judged him friendly to thecause.

Evidently Wallis had seen or heard of the piece about the Salt River Inn on the local news. When he called, Lukas had agreed to see him.

Lying awake the night before, he had weighed Wallis' possible intent, pondering the best response, should his hunch turn out valid. True to his creed, he would tell the truth, take his chances. If his hunch was wrong and Wallis proved to be a red herring, he would bide his time, see what developed elsewhere.

Wallis rocked back in a ragged chair, run-down ankle boots propped on the desk, fingers tented, flexing like spider legs. "So you think the ground the inn sits on *could* be sacred?"

"Apenimon thinks it could. He's eighty-two. Not usually wrong." Lukas shrugged and played his trump card. "He is descended from a long line of Apache chiefs. He tells the tribal council he has some kind of mystical knowledge connection to his ancestors." And a passed-down warring spirit, according to Apache lore. A spirit that sometimes surfaced in Lukas' own character, albeit subtly. Thus far.

"And screwing the land up with…" Wallis glanced at notes scribbled earlier in the meeting. "…South Seas, you say?"

Lukas nodded.

The journalist grinned, continuing, "Screwing it up with South Seas architecture would be sacrilege."

"Apenimon thinks so." A far weightier opinion than his own. Crossing a boot over a knee, he formed a steeple with his own fingers, his eyes on Wallis. "He's dead set against disturbing it period, but he warns that if it is, it had damn sure better honor history. And…" Saying more could overplay his hand.

"And what?" Wallis swung his bandy legs down and sat forward.

Lukas took his time. "Only Indians should do the disturbing." Indians like his construction crew, eager as bridegrooms to tackle his designs.

Wallis' ragged brows hitched. "You say he's an Apache chief?"

"Descendent. Apenimon means 'worthy of trust'."

Wallis touched the bow tie. "And you're Navajo, you say?"

"And Apache."

"No shit?"

"It happens." Lukas forced a grin, letting mixed heritages run through his mind. When different tribes intermarried, the males followed Indian tradition of moving in with the female's tribe. Thus, Lukas had been raised Navajo. In Apenimon's case, when his wife died, he had moved in with Lukas' family. Lukas' father had been dead by then, but since that tragedy didn't bear upon this tale, he kept his sorrow concerning his father buried in his heart.

"Do you have any documentation to back up this land claim?"

"I'm not sure 'claim' is the right term. And the reservation is not famous for its library system." He smiled to temper any bitter edge in his tone. "I've learned to pay attention when Apenimon speaks."

Wallis' mouth tightened, puckering his chin. "I'm seriously considering playing around with it, seeing what I come up with. I'd hate to see the Waterfront Project screwed by the wrong architecture." His eyes quickened. "How about if I meet…" He checked his notes again, mouth attempting to form the name.

"Apenimon. I could ask how he feels about it." No sense in revealing the old man was a ham, loved to tell his stories, and relished attention.

Lukas stood. So did Wallis, offering his hand, tilting his head till their eyes met.

"Interesting tale. Kind of mystical…like you said. But damned interesting."

"No matter what you decide, I would be grateful if you left my name out of it."

"Conflict of interest, you mean."

Whatever. "Just focus on Apenimon. Any knowledge I have comes from him."

six

On her way to breakfast the next morning, Cameron discovered the staff, including housekeeping and kitchen help, hovering around the windows over-looking the inn's driveway and covered entrance. The group included Chuey Run Amok, frequently present at the inn, and Lukas, towering over the rest, easy to identify.

Cameron swerved in that direction, addressing the crowd as she approached. "What's going on here?" Across the lobby, the phones at registration buzzed like flies in a bottle.

Dozens of dark heads swiveled, leveling dusky, somber stares. Yolanda, distinctive as a lone star in a desert night sky, pointed out the window. Shouldering her way through, Cameron wedged between Anna and Lukas, catching a heady whiff of Lukas' cologne, a sense of his male warmth.

"Hi, Cameron." Anna spoke quietly, as though a baby slept.

"Why aren't you at the desk? Can't you hear the phones ringing?"

The girl nodded, braids bouncing. "I'm watching."

Exasperated, Cameron turned to the window. "Watching what?"

"History, maybe?" Anna's brows puckered.

Lukas grunted, a soft amen-like sanction. Standing so close to Cameron their arms brushed, he spread his feet, silently settling. She felt his tolerant smile, but denied herself the visceral pleasure of looking at him.

A large dented and rust-pocked van idled beneath the overhang fronting the lobby. Back and side doors yawned wide. From the side opening, a dark-skinned woman passed out cardboard placards attached to spindly tree branches still sprouting green leaves. The woman's hair hung to her waist and swayed with each unrushed movement. Children—Cameron counted ten, toddlers to preteens—grabbed placards and settled them on their shoulders. The boys wore fringed buckskin and breeches. The girls, along with three elderly women stationed in the background, looked groomed for church in starched blouses and long skirts. Moccasins clothed their feet. Grave expressions masked their faces.

Scalp tightening, throat warming, Cameron strained to read the message on the big cards, catching glimpses of words she managed to string together.

CHASTAIN PROPERTIES v. NATIVE AMERICA
Oh, my God!

A Channel 3 News truck turned onto Salt River property, parking a cautious distance from the van. In a rush, a familiar-faced female journalist and photographer bearing a shoulder camera joined the group around the van.

As though tethered to a speeding arrow, Cameron's head turned and tilted up. "Lukas, do something."

He gazed at the woman hopping down from the van now, one hand gathering her purple velvet skirt around trim legs, knees so dark-skinned she might have been kneeling in soot.

"Too late." His comment reeked of detached inevitability.

"Who's responsible for this?" Her stomach roiled into her throat.

"Probably her." No need for nodding or finger pointing.

"I can't believe *anyone* would stoop to this tactic."

"Freedom of speech." His voice held a reverent quality.

"Stooping to use women and children?" Her voice escalated half an octave.

"You think this should be man's work?" Finally he looked at her. His perfectly sculpted mouth tugged out an indulgent smile.

"Don't you, for God's sake? Those signs are heavy."

"Especially the message," someone behind her murmured. A chorus of stereotypical grunts migrated through the group, ending with Yolanda's.

"Modern technology," Lukas commented, barely audible.

"What the hell does that mean?"

"Microwave ovens."

"Look, Wind Dancer—"

"They freed our women for causes worthier than cooking," he said gravely, and then with more levity, "Cable television introduced them to the needy causes."

Beside her Anna giggled, then clamped it off with a palm.

Outside, three women in yellow and burgundy velvet, laden will squash-blossom necklaces, lined up the children according to height.

Cameron pressed her temples and ran her fingers through her hair. Believing the controversy over, she had lowered her guard and been ambushed. "Cut the propaganda, Wind Dancer. This is taking advantage of children." *And it's blackmail.*

"Making them grow up on the rez is taking advantage. They're happy to have a day in town, snowbird watching."

"They look miserable," she countered.

Another nod. "They have been coached to look that way."

"By whom?" She glared at him.

"Not by me, Yazhi." He held up his hands, palms extended toward her the corners of his luminous eyes crinkling.

Quiet fell until Anna stage-whispered, "He's giving you a Navajo name. Yazhi means little one."

Little one, like hell. Cameron's hands moved to her hips, her oversized bag banging between her thigh and Lukas'. His gaze shifted there, taking her back to the day he had shouldered her burden. That simpler time now seemed prehistoric. The scene before her reeked of conspiracy.

If Jay Lukas Wind Dancer, Navajo and Apache, architect, contractor, and part-time bartender wanted a fight, he had chosen the right battleground. She had nothing to lose, everything to gain. "I'll stop this."

Like oil from water, the group separated allowing her passage. Once outside, she sensed dozens of pairs of dark eyes behind her, waiting, judging as she approached the woman in command.

"Good morning. I'm Cameron Vickers. I manage the Salt River. And you are…?" She offered an ignored hand, then withdrew it. A silent response and a solemn, middle-distance gaze came as no surprise. Wordlessly, the woman passed out another placard. Somewhere across the parking lot, a car door slammed. Running footsteps. Excited voices. More media! "What's your name?" Even to her own ears, Cameron's tone echoed a hated sense of urgency.

Instead of an answer, anxious onyx eyes shifted to the lobby window before focusing on Cameron's chin. The journalist fiddled with a portable microphone, then held it close to the woman's head while the cameraman aimed a lens across her sturdy shoulder at Cameron's face.

A second cameraman, tall with inky braids and scarred boots, appeared.

"I'm Kai Blackwater," the woman announced. An almost too soft voice and perfect poise signified she had been waiting for their audience to settle waiting to hear the whir of the cameras.

Cameron paused for a beat, praying for both her own and her adversary's composure. "Please tell me why you're here."

"We're protesting." Covering a rattly cough with a loose fist, Kai Blackwater eyed the squirming children.

"Against what?" If only her professed ignorance were valid bliss.

Kai held up a sign for Cameron to read before passing it to a woman with pewter-colored hair and a wrinkled-raisin face. "By ignoring our heritage, CF Ltd. mocks the Navajo."

"How?" Cameron attempted to lower her voice, urging, "How do we—Chastain Properties—mock you?" The camera inched closer.

"This hotel must remain authentic Indian architecture rebuilt by Indians."

"Is Lukas Wind Dancer behind this?" She could no longer stifle the query. Aware of the microphone, she lowered her voice another octave, despite the wasted effort.

"I act alone." A placid dark face turned to stone; full lips grimaced. She touched the head of a child who clung to her thigh, hands tangled in purple velvet. "Will you have us arrested?" She coughed again, swallowed deeply, dark eyes moistening.

Whirring quietly, the second camera inched closer.

The need for preservation reared its head, resolute as thunder. Shunning the camera, Cameron sought eye contact with Kai Blackwater, who proved adept at avoidance. "Of course not." Her mind spun, grappled, settled. She dredged up a coaxing smile. "I want to invite you inside."

Kai shot a look at the window. Cameron followed the lead, noting Lukas' absence from the inside gathering.

"Why?" Kai's dusky gape refocused on Cameron's chin.

"Our chef makes excellent—" Her mind searched, coming up with, "Waffles. Perhaps the children would like some." Getting no reaction, she added, "Belgian waffles." *Try harder.* "With powdered sugar and berries."

"We had fry bread before we left the reservation." Kai's head hiked a fraction, hair swaying. "At dawn," she stressed, ignoring the child who stared up at her, eyes imploring, cued by the mention of food.

Though she saw no sign of weakness, Cameron urged, "Come inside. We'll talk. This misunderstanding can be worked out."

For the first time, the woman's eyes met hers. "Can *you* change hundreds of years of broken promises with more Anglo talk?"

Look at me, Kai Blackwater. Look at my skin. I see your pain and feel your hopelessness. Yet, I see your fire.

Cameras hummed. A microphone, then another, split the space between herself and Kai. Too many times Cameron had complied. Not this time. She would use this woman's spirit to stoke her own fire.

"You are free to march or free to come inside. It's your choice." She waited, heart thumping, palms moist.

Kai stepped to the head of the line of children, holding fast to the child at her side. Pursued by media, she led the protest onto the sidewalk fronting the inn.

Only then did Lukas appear, phantom-like, rounding the corner of the building. Within speaking range of Kai Blackwater, ear range of the others, he said, "Bring the children away from the street, *at'ééd*. People are cruel. Do not take that chance." His tone, the upward tilt of his chin, his outstretched hand, defied argument.

With noble spirit, eyes cast distantly, Kai honored his request.

៩

"Big trouble in River City," Chuey murmured, gauging Kai's and Lukas' expressions through the window as most of the staff drifted away.

"No joke." Reminding him she was still there and had overheard, the new blonde hostess, Yolanda, nudged his arm. "Lukas is pissed, I'd say."

He spared her a glance, a grin. Nice, saint-blue eyes. Which didn't match her dare-the-devil body or the low-cut, sleeveless blouse and mini skirt not quite covering her curves. "You know him that good, huh?" Enough to read his body language?

"Not at all, actually."

Damn right. Not Uncle Bro's type. Not anymore, anyway. Not after Suzanne Stanton turned him wrong side out and ass backwards. Stomped his heart.

"But I feel negative vibes from here," she said. "He's pissed off, for sure."

She hugged a stack of menus to breasts so round and firm he wondered if they were padded. Silicone, maybe. Or maybe the narrow Anglo waist gave them that look. That waist sure as hell paved the way to the nice wide hips topping her long, bare legs.

"The woman's not scared, though," she half whispered. "You notice that?"

Chuey laughed. "Kai Take-No-Prisoners Blackwater? Not on your life."

"My kind of woman."

"Enit, girl?" Her cynical smile made him wonder about the basis for the declaration, challenged him to find out. She was too young and fine for cynicism.

They watched silently for a moment as Lukas maintained a territorial stance, arms folded, observing the procession. Yolanda's perfume homed in on Chuey's senses, too sweet and heavy for early morning and the night he had passed. He shifted away, announcing, "Think I'll have some breakfast. Is that your department?" The thought of eggs gagged him, but oatmeal, maybe, and fry bread.

She smiled conspiratorially. "Once I've seated you, you're on your own. I couldn't cook water." She turned, hips swaying, and Chuey followed in her path, wondering if she'd been claiming her expertise lay outside of cooking.

Stopping later to align a chair at the table next to his, she watched him drizzle honey from a plastic container onto the last piece of fry bread. "She's still out there, her and those cute kids."

He had noticed, paying silent tribute to Kai's legendary staying power.

"That's what I call standing by your man." Yolanda sounded wistful.

He shoved the bread into his mouth, washed it down with strong, black coffee, and tipped his chair onto its back legs. "Whether he wants her to or not." He hadn't been able to hear the earlier exchange between Kai and Lukas but, from his sullen reaction when the van pulled in, and later, Chuey suspected his uncle wasn't a party to the protest. And he had damn sure looked frustrated when his new boss hailed a cab and departed in a huff.

Trouble in River City, all right. Just like Saturday morning cartoons.

"They keep the minions entertained," Yolanda murmured, turning so the window light showed off her profile. *Nice, like her eyes.* "Lukas and Ms. Vickers, I mean." She slurred Ms. into Mzzz. "They go from one sparring match to another, thinking they're being discreet." She grinned. "They've got the hots. They just don't know it yet. Or she doesn't, anyway."

A gnarly new wrinkle. "You think so?"

"For sure." She struck a pout. "But he'd never tell her. He hardly talk and when he does…he talks funny. Like formal. No one's fooled, though, about what he's after."

Though Lukas spoke flawless Anglo and had converted slang to an art form, his random habit of rejecting contractions sometimes made him sound like he was reading from highbrow literature. Their ancient grandfather talked like that, plus Lukas had cut his adolescent teeth on the Old Testament. No contractions in there. "They're up to suppressed hanky panky, huh? Well, it doesn't take much to entertain Indians."

With both hands, she lifted her yellow hair off her neck, held it high, breasts pressing against the thin blouse, then released it to spill on her shoulders. The hair might be bleached, might not. Only one sure way to know without asking.

She pouted a little. "I'm here, too, if you haven't noticed. I'm a minion, not an Indian."

He tossed his napkin onto the plate. "So what does that make me?"

"I'm deciding. Not a minion if you're related to the boss—Lukas, mean."

So she had bothered to find that out. "But Indian, by the same token."

"Not quite a real one, though." She sidled closer, jammed a thigh against his table. "I bet a pale face got in your mama's wood pile." Her smile dared. "Right?"

He shrugged, never having heard his mother's downfall expressed quite that way. Or expressed much at all, one way or the other. "That's what I hear. So does my mama's hanky-panky make me better or worse?" He knew the answer, had learned it the hard way at an early age. But he liked confirmation.

"My brothers would say worse." She frowned. "But they're assholes."

The back of his neck tingled a warning, not enough to keep him quiet. "And what do you say?" Might as well get this settled before he invested any feelings beyond lusty speculation. Plenty of other shiny goldfish in the stream.

She leaned forward. The blouse dipped, affording a faint view of cleavage as she ruffled his hair. "I'd say being part Indian gave you those funny gray-brown eyes. And great hair. Chocolate." Her tongue traced over bare lips. "My favorite."

"That's encouraging." He drained the coffee and stood. "Unless you're trifling with my affections." He gave her a hayseed grin, ready to retreat.

She stared at him, her creamy throat pulsing.

"Or maybe you get off on playing cowgirl and Indian."

"I thought you'd never guess." Flipping hair over one shoulder, she gave him a smile probably perfected by Eve while she polished the forbidden apple.

He had planned to bide his time, express his interest, jerk it back if need be.

No need. Yolanda was every half-breed boy's wet dream.

seven

Though her heart had gone out of it, Cameron kept her afternoon appointment with the last architect on her list. Fortyish, he sported an Arizona tan and spoke with a local drawl. As the other two had done, he declined her offer.

But he supplied information she had lacked until now.

"It's all very interesting," he speculated, running a hand through his hair. "I submitted one of the original bids for redoing the Salt River, you know."

She hadn't known. There had been no reason to. Until now.

"I wouldn't touch that hotel now with asbestos gloves—not after all that razzle-dazzle on television. I have to live in this state." He rocked placidly in his ergonomically correct chair, grinning. "Wind Dancer is the big voice on the Navajo tribal council." His grin and tone displayed irony, reverent mockery, if such a tribute existed. "I wouldn't want to go up against him."

A spurt of adrenaline shot through her veins—the tribal council governed the Navajo Nation. And Wind Dancer was the big voice?

No wonder he's so willing to wait me out. So damned cocky.

Gripping the chair arms to keep from shooting to her feet, she forced an amiable expression while her nerves sizzled. "The council carries a lot of weight in this area, I suppose."

"A lot. Sometimes subtly, but it's there. Always has been, always will be." He grinned wryly. "Count your blessings. Wind Dancer is the best in the area—architect *and* contractor."

"Don't you feel that's a bit contrived? Conflict of interest, perhaps?" A monopoly, to say the least.

"Apparently whoever hired him to begin with didn't think so. I guess that would be your…uncle?" He shrugged. "One of the Chastains, anyway, according to the press."

She let that pass, wondering if Lukas had charmed her uncle on the phone or in person. Either way, Hayden would admire Wind Dancer's my-way-or-the-highway attitude. "So I can't persuade you to take over the project? No contract has been signed between Wind Dancer and Chastain Properties, Ltd."

"What you're proposing—this Polynesian thing—is tempting. But it'll never fly here, not with our city planners—one who's Indian, another Hispanic, by the way." He shrugged again. "And as I said, I wouldn't want to tread on any moccasins. After all…" With yet another shrug and a humble expression, he left that hanging. "Seen today's paper?"

"I had a busy morning." Her stomach formed a fist; her mind developed a picture of Kai Blackwater adhering to Lukas' concern about the children.

Carefully the architect folded back a paper lying on his desk and passed it to her. A manicured finger indicated a column in the Valley and State section. It bore the byline Aaron Wallis.

According to Wallis, an elderly Apache named Apenimon, who wasn't quite a chief, had reason to believe the ground beneath the Salt River was sacred. The words "mystical wisdom, burial, and ceremonial dances" were mentioned, along with "unhappy spirits." Apenimon—and apparently Wallis—held the opinion any construction failing to honor Native America was taboo. Using non-Native American construction crews on the land would result in something called *ti'dahwiizhdoonih*, which loosely translated meant 'they will be punished'. That warning wasn't to be confused, however, with something called *ti'ddahooniih*, meaning 'they are having a hard time'.

Cameron reasoned "they" of the first part to be Chastain Properties; "they" of the second part to be the Native American…Indians.

Nowhere was Wind Dancer's name mentioned, yet she sensed his presence so strongly she half expected him to step off the page. His connection to the Apache, Apenimon, was a mystery, but the strands of information in the article were woven too smoothly to ignore.

She placed the paper back on the desk. "Interesting."

A grave nod. "I hear Larry King is trying to get an interview with that old chief."

"He's not a chief." Unless Aaron Wallis had botched his research.

"Whatever. Next thing we know, Apenimon will be on Barbara Walter's most-wanted interview list." He rocked, eyeing a silently blinking desk phone.

She could imagine Walters wearing pink bouclé-wool and empathetic expressions, seated across from Apenimon—or worse, Lukas with his heart-stopping virile beauty—swaying the rest of America toward the Navajo plight. "Should she succeed, I'll be sure to watch."

He grinned, still having fun with her, then sobered. "Why not go with the flow? Build your Polynesian hotel over in Palm Springs. The building code there is more lax. Your hair could turn gray while you try to get a permit here."

"I've had that pointed out to me before." She stood, shouldering her bag.

Minutes later, in the back of an under-cooled taxi, the architect's words echoed in her mind. His advice grappled with lingering surprise over Lukas' tribal council connection and his competitor's belief that that connection would sway the planning commission.

Deductive reasoning, or maybe intuition, told her the now-notorious land was just that. Land. Nothing more. A stretch of once-empty desert the Indians might have staked claim to before moving on to Northern Arizona. Had the ground been hallowed, they would never have vacated. The Indians would never have allowed the original Inn to be built.

Nevertheless, stubborn spirits—hers or theirs— could provide the media with a feast.

ॐ

From behind the bar, Lukas watched through the lobby window as Cameron parked a Ford Taurus station wagon in VIP parking…She had treated herself to a new car, leased, he would bet. Shiny and black as a lump of coal, inside and out.

Sluggishly, she got out, locked the door, dropped the keys into that mammoth purse bearing the imprint of a stranger's initials, and entered the building. Scottsdale Fashion Square shopping bags dangled from her hands. Her hair straggled out of a severe bun. She had wilted, mocking her alert, ready-to-arm-wrestle look when she had stormed out of the inn to confront Kai that morning.

Limp as his niece's rag doll, she appeared as defenseless, but a hell of a lot prettier.

By way of his column, Aaron Wallis had plunged deeper into the spirit of the tale, sooner than Lukas had anticipated. By noon, the full-blown story had made national TV news, complete with the children and Kai's march, and Apenimon astride a bony spotted horse, wearing his almost-chief regalia.

Gloomy scenes from the rez contrasted with those shot in Scottsdale like rawhide contrasted black pearls. As Cameron entered the hall leading down to her pitiful office, the dispirited slant of her shoulders made him wonder if she had seen the coverage.

Minutes later the bar phone rang. His gut tightened with asinine anticipation. "Salt River Bar. Wind Dancer."

"It's Cameron." Hesitation, then, "I need to talk to you."

Searching his mind for a clue about her announcement, he could not settle on feeling triumphant or defeated. Neither could he lose the image of her dispirited face when she had come into the building. He stretched the cord to remove a dirty glass from the lined bar and replace it with a foamy beer. "The whole town is here, drinking and watching the fate of the inn on CNN." Turning his back, he tucked the phone between his chin and shoulder for privacy. "But go ahead. Talk. I'll listen."

"In my office."

"No way to manage that. I'm the only one here."

Weighty silence filled the line. "Close the bar when happy hour ends."

The directive rankled him. His best contacts often came from dinner hour, loners who had nothing to do but drink. "Are you sure you want that? It will cost you revenue."

"It's only a matter of time until the bar will be closed for months." The reminder came in a resigned rush. "Two hours are nothing…in the scheme of things."

Good point. He lit a cigar, inhaled and lowered it to the ashtray. If she wanted him in her office, she either planned to fire him, from both jobs, or sign the renovation contract. "How about seven-thirty?"

"I'll be here."

When he appeared at her office door, she glanced up from some leather-bound tome spread on the desk. Drawing closer, he saw the book was an album, most of the photographs bearing a faded brown tint. Very few black and whites. No color. Her full mouth was too tight, her brow furrowed, an expression he sensed had nothing to do with him. She closed the book and placed it on the floor, leaning against her chair, safely out of sight.

Exotic perfume and sadness hovered in the room.

She stood ceremoniously. The beat-up locket, dangling against sepia-toned skin, caught his eye.

"Come in. Sit down." She replaced the top on a jar of Reese's Pieces and pushed the container aside.

Her hair glinted beneath the ceiling light. Combed to one side with a criss-crossed part— tousled, kind of tangled, as if she had just woken up. The thought provoked a lusty image he preserved in the back of his mind. He would reclaim the rendering later to explore and indulge in, a luxury fast becoming a bothersome but entrenched pattern.

She had changed clothes. Instead of the pants and tailored shirt from earlier, she wore a dress, the same hot-pink color that shot through the steel-blue sky when the sun dropped behind the Estrella mountain range each day. Soft and wrinkled—linen, maybe—it hung loose from her shoulders, grazing her hips, almost touching her ankles. More suited to the local climate than what she had worn before and probably part of the cache in the shopping bags she had lugged from the car.

He waited until she sat down, then took the mock-leather visitor's chair, sitting erect, elbows braced on the chair arms, boots together on the tile floor. "Closing the bar almost caused a riot. I'm lucky to still have my hair."

She didn't look empathetic. "This won't take long." Neither did she smile.

Damn. The CNN coverage had been overkill. On the other hand, that phony old chief would probably live ten years longer after seeing himself on the super-screen TV dominating too much space in his hogan. Lukas waited. How would he explain this setback to the tribal council? He had gambled and lost. Now that the casinos were prominent in their lives, they would relate. Accepting defeat was a different matter, though. He wanted this project, craved it like a celibate man craving a woman—as he had begun to crave *this* woman. Still, if need be, he would go over Cameron's pretty head to Hayden Chastain, force him to honor their man-to-man verbal agreement.

Actually, there had been no agreement on the inn's design, he reminded himself.

While fingering the locket, Cameron leveled those dark almond eyes on him. He patted his pocket for a cigar but, seeing her ashtray was clean, folded his arms over his chest. She almost surrendered a smile, but he had a feeling she was fresh out. Her reticence involved the photo album, he would bet. Either that, or she disliked firing people.

"You should have told me you serve on the tribal council."

So that was it. "Why would I have told you?" And who *had* told her?

Color rose in her cheeks. Her brows knitted, forming a now-familiar crevice. "You could have saved me the trouble of trying to hire another architect."

Her trying did not surprise him. Her failure did, however. "Seems they would all want the job. I do."

"But you want it *your* way, not mine." Her eyes fired, narrowed.

He made sure not a facial feature wavered. He scarcely breathed. "Is that what the others told you? Their way, not yours?" If she answered 'none of your business' she would be right. He supposed what he wanted was confirmation that his refusing to build her fantasy hotel was more than selfish, ethnic pride. He liked thinking his noncompliance had something to do with authenticity in design and honoring his skill, his business sense.

"That's not at all why they refused. They saw no hope of getting the plans approved, due to your connections and the weight the tribal council carries with city planning." Her left hand fiddled with the locket; the right tapped a staccato rhythm against the desk surface with a pencil. Her eyes pegged his. "It's all political, something I recognize the futility of challenging."

He would like to hear more about her and politics, but her rigid jaw line kept him quiet on the subject. "The council will like hearing how influential they are."

"Something you, as the *big voice*, already knew, of course." She slapped the pencil on the desk.

More like something he had counted on. But *big voice*? Where had that come from? Who in hell had she talked to? "I want the job. If being Indian helped for once, so be it."

She eyed him as if measuring his face for a Halloween mask. "Were you behind that demonstration this morning?"

He had expected that. "Did you see me marching?"

"Whether or not you marched has little to do with my needing to know. I asked that woman—"

"Kai Blackwater."

A frown moved from her mouth to her eyes. "She said she acted alone."

"But you chose not to believe her."

"She wouldn't look me in the eye."

He laughed, more relieved than he wanted to be. "To meet the eyes of another is considered confrontation in the Navajo culture."

She paused, as if mulling over his disclosure, then, head tilted, her gaze filled with challenge. "You have no problem looking me in the eye."

He wished to hell that was true. He could look her in the eye, then think of what he had seen, the rich-sable intensity, for hours after. All through the night. But it didn't stop there. The invasive thoughts, if he shared them, and lately his dreams, would color those smooth cheeks crimson, surely lower her haughty eyes.

"When I left the rez I soon learned *bilagáanas*—Anglos—equate eye contact with trustworthiness." Cameron wasn't exactly Anglo, but she had mastered their customs. He supposed her declared distrust was a way of clinging to dignity, something to hold over his head, a genuine *bilagáana* trait. "And you have nice eyes," he heard the other less sensible, hungrier Lukas say. To hell with the vexing cultural muddle. She had beautiful, sad eyes.

"Save the charm, Wind Dancer." She sank back in the chair, hands clasped at her waist. "You have the job, provided you'll omit that ridiculous fire pit in the middle of the lobby floor."

His heart jolted with surprise he fought to restrain, while he visualized her waving a white flag, stipulating a dislike for the hell of it. To show who had the upper hand. "The fire pit carries out the authentic design," he said.

"This is a hotel, not a hogan." Her mouth tightened, eyes glittering.

"It will be home to a hundred people every night. People like to gather."

"I don't want the smoke or the danger of a child falling into it."

"Venting and safety measures are drawn in."

"Omit the fire pit, bring the contract in tomorrow, and I'll sign it."

He nodded, conceding victory. For now. The next year raced through his head as hours on a clock or days on a calendar. Illusive images the pale brown color of her album photos, and each one included this mysterious woman.

Cameron Vickers was both vulnerable and brave. As much as she wanted her dream hotel—for whatever reason—giving in had taken more guts than holding out. Of the two of them, she was the stronger. For him, giving in or giving up had never been an option, never entered his mind.

"I'll do the job CP Ltd. deserves," he said, beginning his humble gratitude speech. "To assemble a crew will take a while, but they will be the best."

"Native American, of course."

"Do you have a problem there? If so, you are not in the minority." *Pun intended.*

"I'm dealing with it. In fact, I've hired Desert Scene Public Relations to plan a gala, announcing the contract has been given to a Native American firm."

"I'll buy a tie." He got nothing in return for his smile.

"At the party, we'll talk about the original hotel and show your renderings, how they're in keeping with history."

He liked the way she pronounced *about*, the same way she said, *out*. More like *oot* and *aboot*. Canadian inflection, he knew, but catchy as hell. He attempted to get his mind off her mouth and onto her disclosure as she continued.

"Desert Scene plans to hire a local dance group for ceremonial dancing—all politically correct, of course." Her pretty mouth dripped bitter honey. "I hope their approach doesn't offend you."

"I'll live with it." She had worked her little ass off since stopping at the bar wanting to know if he had new drawings for her. If the PR firm screwed up the dancing, Apenimon and the council would give him hell. "It won't be the first time I have been mortified by my own people. It won't be the last."

Her face flushed that rosy tan color, unique to her. She seemed to be forming a rejoinder, only to reject it in favor of diplomacy.

"By signing that contract we're forming an alliance. I don't have to tell you that." She had given this thorough thought, he realized. Now her determination showed in the tilt of her strong chin, in her posture, erect as a battle flag. "The only thing we have going for us is our common goal. Each of us wants to rebuild this hotel. I could have held out until the furor died and started over with another architect." Her tone wavered a little with that calm gaze flicking away, charging back before she plunged on. "But in view of my priority, I'm going along with your bluff."

He found the bait too tasty to swim past. "What priority?"

She fell stone silent, as if she didn't intend to share. But then she did. "I want to complete this project without a moment's delay. I don't want to remain here one day longer than necessary." She paced toward the door and then returned to the desk, but kept standing. "Kowtowing to your single-mindedness puts me that much closer to my goal, and—"

"Single-mindedness?" *Kowtowing? Not Cameron Vickers.*

"Concerning your design preference versus mine."

He gazed at her, not wanting to revisit the subject. "And?"

"I'm trying to convince myself that anyone who feels so adamant about a job is the best man for that job."

Damned straight. He stood. "My people thank you for the vote of confidence." He fought to rid sarcasm from his tone, but she eyed him skeptically.

"Do you ever think of anything else? Other than how your people fare?"

"Rarely." Now that he had come to his senses.

"Commendable." A brow quirked, but at last she offered her hand. He took it. A jolt coursed through him almost as jarring as the surprise she had dealt earlier. She felt it, too. He read it in the quickening of her eyes, witnessed it in the way she stared at their hands, tawny and bronze skin blending to execute what should have been a benign handshake. Ritual old as time, suddenly made new.

At last she tugged.

Their eyes locked; he took his time letting go.

"I'll see you in the morning." She sat down and busied herself with straightening a flawlessly neat desk, her throat flushed, hands trembling.

"You coming out to the bar before dinner?" *Let it go, Wind Dancer. Why tempt yourself with a woman you can't have. A woman you don't want, other than beneath you.* "I won't cheat you." Despite his effort not to, he smiled. A friendly, appeasing gesture. One he had found dependable through the years.

Thank God, Cameron Vickers continued to be immune.

"Not tonight. I'm tired. I'll have a sandwich brought to my room." Her eyes remained lowered. Unreadable.

Driving away from the hotel at midnight, he glanced toward her closet-size office and saw the light still burning. Either she continued working— mourning over that photo album, maybe—or she had forgotten to turn out the light. He doubted a woman so intense could also be forgetful.

Cameron had a problem that went far beyond architectural style. Not exactly sure where she was coming from, he nonetheless sensed he had been there. The look in her eyes had to do with rejection, loss, self-doubt. Grief. It involved her craving for Canada. He had been in that spot, too. Craving to go home. The day he had driven back across the Arizona state line, he had wanted to kiss the red earth. He understood this woman without knowing what he understood.

Fiery, focused Cameron Vickers was hurting.

She riled him the way no woman had since Suzanne. And look at that outcome. Helplessly, his mind dissected the past once more, sorting, chastising, playing what-if and might-have-been games, a return journey down the road of chance. A road that had inevitably led to reality. He was Navajo.

Growing up, he had been constantly reminded his existence had edges, that his skin color and tribal connections constructed boundaries that kept him from knowing a world beyond the reservation. He had been eight years old when the Presbyterians, Pastor Dennis Stanton and his wife, Laura, set up a reservation mission. Along with Anglo church every Sunday and every Wednesday night, he discovered videos, big screen television in the rec room, historical and travel books unavailable at the reservation school. His world broadened.

For four years he sought and obtained favors from the Stantons, innocent desires, like playing with their Anglo-blond twins, eating "Yankee" food at their table, once a month lunch at Little America in Flagstaff, if his grades warranted. The Stanton family represented adventure and worldliness. They had lived in exotic, foreign places Lukas could not compare to this drab, mundane, poverty-ridden restrictive world.

Once the Stantons had converted a majority of the reservation population to Christianity, they declared the church well established and announced a new assignment. Lukas had to look up their destination, Senegal, on the library globe. He felt a part of his world being chipped away until Dennis Stanton performed a miracle by persuading Lukas' mother—his father had been dead a year then—to allow him to accompany them, to witness a world other than that of the reservation. Following a year's commitment in Africa they were to return to Boston for a month's hiatus before their next foreign assignment. Lukas would then be given a choice of staying with them or returning home.

Tucked between the Stanton twins, Steven and Suzanne, onboard an interactional airliner, Lukas left his reservation life behind. A twelve-year-old child that day, wide-eyed and eager for what lay ahead, he considered himself impervious to hurt. But as children do, he and his pretend brother and sister grew up. Lukas discovered himself unaccepted in the Stantons' world.

Hurt had taught him to stay with his own kind. A beautiful, foreign, part-Anglo woman with troubled eyes and raging zeal to leave Arizona didn't qualify.

☙

The lighted hands of Cameron's bedside clock embraced midnight. She sighed an audible surrender, threw back the covers and crept to the bathroom. Loud as a hammer blow, the click of the light switch split the silence. Blinding light replaced darkness.

Behind her, Mikela stirred on the bed, then resettled. Eyes closed, Cameron rummaged the medicine cabinet for the pill she had talked herself out of earlier. She placed it as far back as possible on her tongue, palmed water into her mouth, and swallowed. With her wet hand, she caressed her throat where the pill had lodged. Red, throbbing panic rose behind her eyelids, then gradually ebbed as she sensed the drug's slow passage. Moments now…minutes at most…and the headache would subside, along with her revulsion of the remedy.

Her fingertips moved to her temples, pressing. She waited, breathed, waited.

Starting over, coming to Arizona, had been her hope of curing the pain, overcoming her aversion to the medication. Instead, the malady and loathing remained.

How much blame for the ailment could she attribute to Lukas Wind Dancer?

Eyes closed still, she saw him sitting across from her tonight, unable to mask satisfaction at her defeat. Or had her bitterness seduced her imagination? Had he tricked her with his claim of sacred land? Or was she suffering habitual paranoia?

Once again, she reasoned out her decision.

Nowhere in all the imposing media hype had she heard or read a phrase other than *"could* be sacred." But given the state of racial awareness in the U.S., the possibility needed no proof. Had she, representing Chastain Properties, adamantly followed her planned course, CP, Ltd. would have emerged as a heartless conglomerate swooping down from Canada to pursue profit and disregarding the human rights of the indigenous underdog.

Hayden wanted the issue closed, and, for now, she was beholden to her uncle. To stand her ground, *sacred* or not, would have prolonged controversy. Quashing her dream of a Polynesian hotel, giving in to Wind Dancer's dictates, pained her. When she reflected on his circuitous victory and their revealing handshake—she felt the jolt still—working with him for a year loomed troublesome, if not impossible. Yet, sacrificing her own desires would expedite the goal foremost in her heart and mind: returning to Vancouver and all that awaited her there.

Leaning against the sink, she forced open her eyes and pushed back her hair to examine the scars high on her forehead, crowding her hairline. Another, fine and jagged, nestled in an eyebrow. These visible wounds had relinquished their raw anger, grown cold and white. But in the middle of this lonely night, the scars forged on her memory seared her soul.

I love you, Jarrid. I never imagined this could happen to us.

Shutting out her reflection, she snapped off the light. She would wait out the night, welcome the dawn from the patio, a rapidly developing ritual.

Blinded, except for the clock dial, she made her way across the room, fumbled with the door lock, then slid back the door to the walled patio. Behind her, the bed shook. She heard a soft thump on the floor, then felt furry warmth and static electricity at her ankles.

Skillfully, she scooped Mikela up, preventing yet another attempt to escape.

eight

Chuey scrunched down into Lukas' spa, deep enough for the almost-too hot water to close over his shoulders and fend off the October night's chill. A chlorine smell filled his nostrils as the current roiled around his throat. Some where in a palm tree, a freakin' owl hooted. Scary as hell if you believed that Navajo legend crap about owls and sure death. He guessed he believed it, a little.

He sank to his chin, his middle back against a jet in the Jacuzzi wall. Heaven.

Across the small space, Yolanda eyed him over a wineglass, her look challenging in the dim lighting around the pool.

"The first Jacuzzi rule I learned was, no glass in the water," she chastised. "Guess we're not supposed to get the water dirty. You know, if we—like—cut ourselves." Her grin fell a shy bit short of wicked.

"Rules are made to be broken." He retrieved a delicate, long-stemmed glass from the edge of the spa and tapped it against a nearby Carlo Rossi jug. "Bottoms up." He only sipped, more bluster than daring, aiming at sobriety. Tonight was payoff, and he wanted to be able to recall the details.

She giggled, draining her glass. When she reached for the bottle on the deck between them, the tops of her gleaming white breasts cleared the water She had removed her bra without discussion, but kept her panties on. Chuey wondered how much debate getting rid of those would take. Didn't matter. Things that came too easy were sometimes not worth having. Or so he'd heard.

"These are the wrong kinds of glasses." She held hers out, examining it like a bug under a microscope. "Red wine's supposed to go in short, fatter ones."

He shrugged. "Another big-deal broken rule, I guess. Tastes the same." They drank in silence until he asked, "What was the second?" She stared, sipping. "The second Jacuzzi rule you learned? What was it?"

"Jacuzzis and liquor are a bad mix."

Like liquor and Indians, according to history. He braced his hands behind him on a bench running around the inside of the spa, stretched his legs until his toes caressed a firm, silky thigh. "So you're telling me you're not having fun."

Another giggle, but throaty, tormenting. "I meant mixing liquor and body heat. It can cause…heat stroke."

Partially right. Not heat stroke, but a fatality in the making. He swirled the ruby liquid in the glass, then sniffed it. "This is not liquor. It's cheap wine."

"I noticed," she pouted. "Seems like we could sample some of Lukas' stock. He'd never miss it." She swirled her wine. "He doesn't even drink."

Lukas' floor to ceiling wine rack, enclosed in a kitchen nook, crossed Chuey's mind. "He collects. Kind of an investment." He was actually trying to buy up the world's stock, hoard it out of circulation. "Besides, that'd be stealing. I don't steal."

"Never?" The challenging gape again.

"Once."

"What?"

"Some CDs and stuff, when I was a greedy little kid." He drifted back. "Lukas found out and put me through hell and too much embarrassment. By the time I begged forgiveness from the store owner, and worked off the value of the loot, I turned honest."

"We're stealing his house and his pool." She dribbled water across her shoulder.

"We're just borrowing the pool." He didn't know where he'd take her, when the time came, but no way their dripping bodies would end up inside the house. He looked around, contemplating the lawn, a chaise lounge where their clothing lay, a thick rubber floating mat. Maybe they'd just stay in the water, stay warm. "I clean the house." Uncle Bro worked hard for his trappings. Chuey respected that.

She sat down, forcing water over her breasts, holding the wineglass aloft. "Why doesn't he drink?"

"He does sometimes." He edged toward her a bit, then toyed with the jug on the deck, the solid bottom clanking on stone, creating wet circles. "Booze has done a number on our family." Yeah. Like wiping out his granddad. Costing him a mother, leaving him a sister who existed in oblivion. "So he's conservative, I guess you'd say."

He'd seen Lukas drink, a lot right after he came back from Chicago. Less and less in the five years since. But sometimes still, if he was mad, or disgusted. Or sad. Like self-punishment, maybe. Chuey suspected that for Lukas drinking was like taking a dare, standing too close to a cliff edge, or chancing brackish water. "He's told me some drinking stories."

"Dirty stories?"

He laughed. Her one-track mind still caught him off guard. "Scary stories. When he went to architectural school in Chicago he worked part time as a beam walker. You know what that is?" She shook her head. "Companies that build sky scrapers hire Navajos to walk the beams once they get so high no one else will do it—or can do it, maybe." Once again the fact whirled in his mind, still making no sense. "We're supposed to have some kind of special balance and no fear of heights."

She held her glass in one hand, inching along the wall with the other until she was less than a foot away. He got a whiff of her hair, damp but still smelling of whatever shampoo she used. Something with strawberries. Raspberries? *Nice.*

"So?" She cocked a brow. "If it's a natural skill, what's the big deal?"

This girl had to learn reverence. "He was going through a pretty wild time. Used to show up early on a morning after he'd been partying all night, walk

those beams when he had no business being there."
Lukas' eyes had held some kind of wonder when he'd
shared the story while driving them to the rez one day.
Kind of like he was talking about some other crazy
redskin who'd lived in his body back then.

Yolanda set the glass down, raised her hair off her
neck with both hands, offering him a gratuitous peek
at her nipples. "Maybe he has a death wish."

Chuey thought of the unframed, wrinkled photograph he'd found while putting Lukas' clean jockey
shorts away. A blue-eyed blonde. Thin and frail. Pious
and prissy. "Maybe he did once. But he got over it.
He's now the great hope of our people. Plenty to live
for."

She lifted herself easily, buoyant in the water,
straddling him. Her arms circled his neck and she
leaned back, thrusting her pelvis against his belly.
"You meant great *white* hope. There was a Broadway
play called that about a hundred years ago."

"He look white to you, smarty?"

"He looks dangerous to me. Kind of mad." She
bent and nibbled his ear. Wine splashed, then dribbled down his back. "Is he gonna bitch if he comes
home and catches us?"

"Catches us what?" He ran his fingertips inside the
band of her panties.

She laughed in grabbing-for-breath style. "Playing
cowgirl and Indian. Does he do that, too? He acts
pretty stuffy, like he's too good or something." She

seemed to consider. "Except for Cameron. He'd do her, I bet."

Chuey stood, pulling her body onto his, wrapping her strong legs around his waist. "No way. He only plays Indian and Indian. He's suffering from an old war injury." He worked his hands up her ribcage until the sides of he breasts filled his palms. "Why the heck are we talking about Lukas, anyway?"

"Yum. Wind Dancer war stories." She licked her lips, ran her palm down his ribs, around his waist and up his back, molding against him, stage whispering, "Let's hear those." Her tongue danced inside his ear.

"Later. I don't want to blow all my charm on the third date."

And, yeah. Lukas would be pissed if he came home and found out the cowgirl in his pool with his nephew was a paleface. Very pale now that she was fully disrobed.

But, then, Uncle Bro had been burned. *He* didn't play with fire anymore.

❦

Toward midnight, Chuey turned off Southern Avenue into the Mesa Community College parking lot. He parked beside a burgeoning manzanita bush, across the lot from where Yolanda had left her Mustang, doused the lights, got out and rounded the car to her side. When he'd first pulled the chivalrous-gent routine, she regarded him as if he'd grown a second head And wings. This time she waited, even saying "thanks" when he helped her out and closed the door behind her. The sound of their footsteps, hers doubling his in number, drowned out in the traffic buzz on Southern.

"It's early." He pinned her against the driver's door of her car, arms on either side, palms pressed to the convertible roof. Close, but not touching. "You already had enough of me, cowgirl?"

She smiled. "I have to work the breakfast shift. If I'm late Cameron debits my paycheck." Her hands settled on his hips, drawing him against her.

"You're pretty hung up on that job."

"I need it. Some of us can't sleep in." She had pouting down to a ball-breaking art form. "I don't have a rich uncle, like you."

Rich? Spiritually, maybe. He wasn't big on hand-outs, for sure. Chuey earned every favor. Lukas' teaching him the work ethic had been the biggest favor he could have done him.

He shrugged. "I'm just bitchin' to make you feel guilty. I've got a seven a.m. anatomy class. So you're good for me, woman. You get me home in time to study." After a perfunctory kiss, he opened the door. "Get your ass in the car, Calamity Jane."

He tucked her in, closed the door and leaned down, his face close to hers in the open window. This time *she* kissed *him*, her hands on his face, fingertips tracing his bone structure. A long, slow, deep offering. She smelled like chlorine and Juicy Fruit.

"Get going before I change my mind," he warned.

"Or before you change mine." She smiled a dare.

Chuey straightened and slapped his hand on the roof. Dust rose from the cloth top. She started the car, raced the engine, and backed up, then roared out of the lot and into the street, brake lights never coming into play. The red Mustang threaded into traffic, backend dropping as the car gained momentum.

Racy. The girl, not the car. And not just talk.

On their two prior dates, a movie and a rock concert, she had insisted on meeting him instead of being picked up. He had wasted no time wondering if she lived in a hovel she was ashamed of, or had a rabid Rottweiler, recalling instead her comment about her asshole, racist brothers. She came off as too mature to live at home, possibly with one or both of her brothers. Whatever the case, she didn't want him showing up at her door. He'd chosen to screw the mystery. Let sleeping dogs lie.

Maybe it was the wine. The sex. But tonight he no longer felt apathetic. *Dammit.* If she was ashamed of him, screw that, too.

By the time he crossed the parking lot and slid behind the wheel of the Toyota, truth stung like snakebite. It was fear she felt. Not shame.

Fear for him.

nine

A week after Cameron's surrender, the Salt River Inn's lobby throbbed with festivity. With the poolside dancing ceremony ended, an Indian wait staff provided by Desert Scene ambled about serving champagne from slender, stemmed crockery. A crème de la crème crowd nibbled fry bread fragments and engaged in conversation at a hushed, low-grade fever pitch.

Cameron watched the sun falling away behind the Phoenix skyline. It bathed the shabby lobby in warm, soft light, a godsend. As the sky turned from blue to purple to cerise, it lit Lukas' renderings better than any gallery lighting could have done. Near the champagne fountain, Chuey, scheduled to ceremoniously wield a jackhammer against the crackled driveway at the end of the evening, chatted animatedly with Scottsdale's mayor.

Across the room, Lukas held audience for two attentive females: Dos Gringos' bartender and the local TV anchor who had sprung the sacred-ground story. In the tux that Desert Scene had requested he wear, he resembled royalty. A red cummerbund replaced his silver-buckled belt, accenting his narrow waist and wide shoulders. The smoky-black tux fabric complimented bronze skin and dark hair, which, held in place with a coral-studded silver band, hung to the center of his back. A cache of Indian jewelry adorning his hands and the squash blossom he wore in lieu of a formal tux tie shone in patina light. The smile he gave his companions vacillated from somber to jovial, reflecting complex emotions that left his eyes unreadable. Phillip Vickers, exquisitely costumed for one of his thousand-dollar-a-plate fund raisers, handsome as any man she knew, hadn't compared with Lukas' long, lean elegance, the virile mystique he exuded.

Exotic. Once more the term vibrated, then settled in her mind. Dark, engaging, charming, and off-putting, in turn. He presented an enigma she felt equally compelled to solve and obliged to flee. The first moment she had climbed onto that barstool, a whisper of curiosity had turned to attraction. Awareness had reeled into heady sensation when they joined hands a week ago to consummate an agreement she still felt forced into. The wisest plan lay in avoiding him whenever possible, not subjecting her starved body to the soul-stirring jolts brought on by his nearness. Rather than risk complication, she would complete her task and return to Canada, where she hoped Jarrid missed and wanted her back as much as she craved being with him.

Lukas Wind Dancer could be no more than a means to an expedient goal.

Turning from the sight of him, she almost bumped into a miniature, gray-haired man wearing a frayed jacket and sporting a crooked Mickey Mouse bow tie.

"Cameron Vickers?"

"Yes." She changed hands with her lime and soda, offering a handshake.

"I'm Aaron Wallis. I write a column—"

"The *Arizona Republic*. I've been reading it." Since that day in the architect's office when Wallis' account of the land squabble had so eloquently defined her defeat. "Your column influenced the route we're taking with the Salt River."

"Glad to hear it." He grinned, and the tips of his ears wiggled. "You don't want to mess with the *chindi*, you know."

Ghosts. Anna had informed her of their existence while refusing to even open the closet where the office supplies were kept. Cameron had labeled the refusal as stubbornness. "Do you know that for a fact, Mr. Wallis?"

"I took the old chief's word for it."

"He is not—"

"A chief. I know." He held up a hand, agreeing. "But he's regal as one, even in the midst of that waste-land they call the reservation. What a character. He's not Navajo, but he speaks it, so he was a code talker in WW II. Believe me, he's got some stories to tell." He took a sip of champagne, then smiled, eyes mischievous. "I guess you know the old guy is Wind Dancer's grandfather?"

The playful words delivered a full-force shock. Heat blazed her throat. Her toes went into a spasm in her spike-heeled sandals. *Nepotism.* "Did he tell you that?"

"The old man did, when I went to the reservation. I didn't get much out of Wind Dancer, but his gramps gave me enough material for a month of columns."

An imaginary vision of Lukas as a child flashed strobe-like in her head. Then as a wayward teen, a randy college student. Finally she settled for recall of the man in her office a week ago, humble, grateful. *Deceitful.*

Apenimon, the media star. She had been trying to score a goal with half her team benched, while Lukas had needed only one player. "Of course I know about their connection. Native Americans are a clannish bunch, wouldn't you say?"

He eyed her curiously. "They're called Indians around here, and aren't all ethnic groups clannish? It's a blood thing."

Was that the crux of the lifelong curse stalking her? Mismatched blood running in her veins? "I'm sure you're right. Will you excuse me? I should check on the caterer."

With a polite smile, she left him there.

Outside the front entrance, the media gathered for Chuey's eight-thirty performance with the jack-hammer. She checked her watch. Twenty past eight, Arizona time. Earlier, in Vancouver. Dinner hour, if Jarrid's routine had not altered. Enough time

remained for her to say goodnight, if she could penetrate the layers of red tape and walls of scrutiny
erected around him.

$\widetilde{\mathfrak{G}}$

In her room, perched on the side of the bed, she
toyed with a dangling earring, the phone pressed
tightly to her ear, savoring Jarrid voicing his love for
her.

"I love you, too, darling. Time is passing quickly,
don't you think?"

"Not here. " *Petulant.* "How can it be for you?"
More accusation than question.

"I'm taking the positive approach, sweetheart.
We'll survive this."

The voice in her ear dissented. "I miss you too
much, Mom."

As her mind charted soothing agreement, the
sound of footsteps in the hall brought her head erect.
Lukas stood in the doorway she'd left ajar, a champagne flute in each hand. Soft light beyond formed an
aura around his dark, lean body. She had difficulty
believing he'd trailed her to her room when they had
scarcely spoken in days. Suffering a sense of invasion,
a stab of guilt related to her son being on the phone,
she also gave in to satisfaction she could neither
welcome nor fully understand.

She placed her palm over the phone's mouthpiece.
"What is it, Lukas?"

He held the glasses aloft in a mock toast, but braced a shoulder against the doorjamb. Whether intended or not, his gaze held sensual invitation.

Her heart pounded her chest wall. End the conversation with Jarrid or relinquish the opportunity to set Lukas straight? Certainly she wouldn't be celebrating with him.

In her ear, Jarrid called her name.

"I'm here, darling. I have a visitor."

"Who?"

"It's just business." She glanced toward the door. "I left a hotel party to call you."

Lukas made a gesture toward leaving, cocking a questioning brow. She shook her head, stopping him, the movement too frenetic. Too revealing, to him, and to herself, for her own comfort.

"I have to go, Jarrid. Goodnight, sweetheart. I love you," she whispered, reluctantly relinquishing their connection to the pressing business at hand.

Placing the receiver in its cradle, she pressed it there with both hands for a moment, holding onto his face. His voice His disquiet. Until Lukas' presence shattered the spell.

Rising from the bed, she looked about the close quarters, the one chair in the room, the clothing and lingerie she had worn earlier lying on the bed. Visible through the bathroom door, the vanity displayed her collection of cosmetics. Her lacy robe hung on the back of the door, reflected in the vanity mirror. A feeling of exposure—entrapment—moved over her.

Lukas was big, intriguing, unrelenting. A determined man, she now knew, who exuded sex with every breath. She wanted to feel anger toward him, a sense of betrayal. Yet, beneath her raveled feelings, loneliness and confusion welled in an upsurge of pleasure, then ebbed, replaced by guilt as seductive as sin.

"Come in." She moved to stand at the end of the bed.

He stepped inside, permeating the space, filling it with warmth and scent and purpose. Extending his hand, he offered the drink. She took it. Her eyes meeting his over the rim, she made a pass at sipping before he could mouth a toast. Not for a moment could she risk forgetting that Lukas Wind Dancer was a master trickster, bent on having his way.

"There's not much room in here…as you see." She made a vague hand gesture. "We should go out by the pool."

"Raining," he said quietly, without expression. "The party is back inside."

Raining in the desert? She listened to the patter on the windows, barely discernable. Comforting, yet disturbing. The room grew smaller, warmer.

"Nice dress." He looked her over, head to feet, lazily appraising her and the yellow-splashed-with-red mock sarong. The skirt and his scrutiny ended high above her knees. "Good color." His lack of a smile deemed the praise more genuine. Carnal, to be exact.

"I should have chosen pueblo sand, in view of the occasion."

He did smile then, humoringly, and much too charitably to suit her.

"To Salt River." He held his glass suspended in the toast she had dreaded.

She stood fixed, wordless.

He tried again. "To our joint efforts." And again. "To our union."

She sipped without clinking glasses to complete the toast. He looked as if he had been backhanded before he apparently chose to ignore the slight. Settling onto the end of the bed, she indicated the chair.

"Thank you for bringing champagne. You watered it down, I suppose."

He spilled over the chair in places, his long legs extended, feet slender and elegant in fine black shoes. He wore the tuxedo as if to the manor born.

"Would you have honored my toast if I had watered it down?"

Out of character tonight, he had chosen not to avoid the issue, not to condone subtlety.

"I met Aaron Wallis tonight." As she expected, Lukas sat mute, deadpan.

She enjoyed his covert curiosity for a moment. "He told me Apenimon is your grandfather."

"Did he?" He took a drink, hiding his displeasure at her news, she surmised.

"Is he?"

"He was my father's father. He lives with my mother." His eyes sought distance, then moved back to her. "My father died when I was eleven."

The raw hurt in his dark eyes set her back for a moment. Neither did she have a father, but unlike Lukas, she could claim no relationship with one, no matter how brief. Empathizing, she was momentarily swayed from confrontation, but only momentarily, before recalling Aaron Walls' face as he cleared up the mystery of the media craze that had robbed her of her dream.

"You were behind all the bad publicity we received, I suppose."

"Bad? I have heard it said that all publicity is good." His smile appeared hard to come by. "Are you a sore loser?"

"You *are* responsible?"

"Guilty."

"You manipulated me, Wind Dancer." She lowered her glass to the floor.

"Things got out of hand." His tone fell just short of an apology.

"I'd like to hear about that."

"It's behind us." He awarded her his ingratiating signature smile.

"I'd like to hear the story for future reference." Now that she was bound to him for the duration of their joint mission.

His hesitant expression revealed that he was unused to explaining himself. Subterranean fire in his eyes labeled him particularly opposed to defending himself to a woman. Finally, he said, "I have a friend at the Scottsdale TV station—"

"The pretty anchor woman, no doubt." The raven-haired, cat-eyed, hawk-nosed, high-cheeked beauty he had spent the majority of this evening with. "Mosi Joseph."

Surprise flickered in his eyes before he squelched it, nodding.

She explained, "I'm an avid watcher of the local news." *Now.*

"She is pretty." His smile was sweet as an altar boy's but sexy as Satan's.

"What part did she play?"

He placed his glass on the floor, then steepled his fingers beneath his strong chin, eyeing her. Was he finished? Had she pushed him too far? She had every right to—

"She met my nephew, Chuey, at the Famous Door Bar." An eyebrow raised in amused contempt. "He told her the sacred ground story—trying to impress her, *enit*?" He shrugged, but his eyes ran to ebony liquid, negating the dismissive gesture. "I guess she was short of news for the next day. She told the story. The Navajo Nation watched her while they ate fry bread and drank Starbucks coffee."

Not the lack of news, but Mosi Joseph's intrigue with Lukas, the zest Cameron had observed earlier, had determined the story's schedule. She tried to keep the high emotion she was feeling—unidentified at the moment—hidden.

"And Wallis?" The honey on the fry bread, Lukas' unjust desserts.

He shifted in the chair, crossed an ankle over a knee, the casual posture and formal dress rendering him more exotic than ever. Silence lingered, except for gentle rain and the humming bedside clock. He owed her more, even if he had to purge it from his cunning soul. She was determined to outwait him.

Mikela emerged from beneath the bed, stretched and preened while eyeing their visitor. Cameron patted the bed in invitation. Ignoring her, the cat slunk across the minute space and rubbed Lukas' pant leg languidly, purring suggestively. Lukas bent, scooped her up and nestled her against his chest, disregarding the fine suit. As Cameron watched his hand caress the cat's head, sudden sensation spilled over inside her, widening like ripples on the surface of deep, deep water. The erotic reaction, detested but undeniable, settled in her midsection. Palms behind her, pressed to the mattress, she leaned back, willing her breathing not to riot when his gaze honed on her extruding breasts. His eyes raised, proclaiming they could settle their differences here and now, on that bed, if she was willing.

She sat forward, crossing her legs, hands in her lap. Just when she was ready to break the silence, he spoke, belying the message she'd read or imagined.

"Wallis picked the story up from the Scottsdale paper and researched the firms who had bid on the Salt River project. That led him to me. I agreed to talk to him." He quieted again, either recalling or rehearsing. "When he asked me to verify the story I indicated he should speak to Apenimon, the one who claimed to have inside knowledge. As I said, things—"

"Got out of hand," she interrupted, tasting something too close to bitterness to distinguish otherwise. "I don't know if I'm mad as hell, or impressed with your cleverness." A generous term. Only concern for finishing the renovation quickly kept her from being amused by his tactics, from laughing aloud in his handsome, somber face. "Either way, I consider your strategy underhanded."

He waited until her eyes met his, then latched on, snagging her in his gaze. "You have a right to believe what you choose. This job is important to me and my people." His smile lacked merriment. "But you saw that on television."

Rising from the bed, she crossed the room, feeling his eyes pierce her back. At the window, she looked out onto the parking lot, bleak asphalt crammed with expensive cars and four-wheel drive vehicles. She peered through the rain-shrouded glass for a moment, then turned around. "I assure you I don't believe your story."

"Which part?" Barely audible.

Scarcely any part. "About the land being a burial ground—sacred."

"My grandfather's story," he reminded her. "He believes it, and I have ceased to question him."

"As long as you understand that I don't." She folded her arms at her waist.

He stood, dumping Mikela gently into the chair. His air of finality gave Cameron a quick and fiery jolt of regret.

"Understood." He grinned like a sinner who had no plans to repent, adding, "Whatever that has to do with the price of adobe and jack hammers."

She wasn't fast enough to stifle a frown, but any rejoinder would unravel the subject again. Instead she bowed to curiosity. "Your father…he must have been young. What happened?"

"Too much firewater made him slow to react." A cold edge of irony crept into his voice. His eyes narrowed; his back became ramrod straight.

"To what?" she asked cautiously.

He patted his pocket again, this time coming out with a cigarette-sized cigar. His fingers formed a shield around it. "He was clearing desert land for a snowbird housing development in Scottsdale. He never saw the rattlesnake that bit him."

God, those dark, disturbing eyes. Smoky mirrors in which she viewed her own hurt. She took an abrupt, voluntary step forward before stopping short of touching him. "That's awful, Lukas."

"Enit?" A muscle quivering in his hard jaw evolved to a soft smile. "It happened a long time ago."

The comment vibrated within her. His eyes betrayed the old adage that labeled time a healer. The passing years had been no salve to her own hurt. Seeking an end to the vulnerable moment, she suggested, "I suppose I should go back to the party. Protocol demands we say a formal goodnight."

"Who is Jarrid?"

Caught off guard, she took a quick, sharp breath, but found steadying her erratic pulse impossible. Raw and primitive grief overwhelmed her. She chose her words carefully. Stalling. "I read somewhere that direct questions are bad manners in the Navajo culture." She tried leveling him with a reprimanding glare.

"I ride a cultural fence." A verbal shrug. "I saw how talking to him made you feel." And then he had seduced her with his eyes.

"And just how was that?"

"Sad." A pause. "Who is he?" His voice was soft, but firm, final.

"None of your business," she quipped, rocked by his accurate interpretation of the call.

Turning to the dresser, she leaned close, checking her lipstick, smoothing a hair strand behind her ear. Rather than her face, she saw reflections of her life and was hurled through the following years of marriage to Phillip, then plunged head-on and helpless into the mini-van filled with children. The rain outside the window became the wet Vancouver street. A siren in the distance transferred to her own scream. Grinding metal and shattering glass. More sirens. Lights. Amber and blue, then white, glaring down on her in a stark and frigid operating room. Hushed voices. Classical music. Blame. Deceit. Judgment.

Loss.

"You'll feel better if you tell me." From behind her, Lukas' deep, whisper-quiet voice brought her back.

Their eyes met in the mirror—his sharp, assessing, yet gently urging.

"If I tell you, or if I simply talk about it?" As he had spoken of his father.

"It's your call, Yazhi." His jaw clenched, eyes slightly narrowed.

"Thank you, but talking won't help. Like yours, my sadness happened a long time ago."

Retrieving her evening bag from the bed, she led the way out of the room.

ten

A month later, Cameron stood cradling Mikela, staring out the window of her cubbyhole office, watching the rain. A river of water gushed across the rear parking lot and flooded the gutter. Leaden skies mirrored her spirit, magnifying the effect of the uncommon weather on the time frame she had imposed on Lukas and the Salt River project.

Thunder cracked. Lightning jagged the sky painting the alley an eerie green-gold. Mikela rubbed her sleek head on Cameron's breast, a gesture both endearing and sensual. Cameron slipped her hand between the feline and her body, denying pleasure that could lead nowhere.

Mikela purred in rhythm with the rain.

El Niño. The first and last words reverberating in Cameron's mind each morning on waking, each evening before drifting into agitated sleep. *El Niño.* Loosely translated into "little boy, or male child." How could a child, even a male child, wreak such havoc on a plan that had initially gone so well—once she'd accepted the disappointment of defeat at Lukas Wind Dancer's hands?

With the ease Lukas had hinted at, the city planning commission had approved his drawings within a matter of days. Lukas had used the time to assemble his all-Indian crew, along with any heavy equipment the Wind Dancer Construction Company lacked in inventory. A month ago, a construction office trailer had been moved onto the property. The crew, along with backhoes and jackhammers, had arrived on schedule and begun demolishing a sagging adobe wall at the back of the property, near two private bungalows that were too costly for other than special occasion rental—honeymoons or anniversaries. Or pretentious lovers.

All seldom-used property was being dealt with first, allowing the inn to remain open as long as possible. Having adjusted his hours behind the bar, Lukas was overseeing construction, striding around in cutoffs, sleeveless shirts, construction boots, and hardhat. His appealing attire and understated, yet authoritative, demeanor kept Cameron repeatedly returning to the window to watch, and sometimes paying a *catch-up* visit to the trailer. Early evening to midnight, he tended bar. They seldom spoke. Still, feeling they had somehow formed a bond the night of the party, she drifted into deep awareness of the comfort offered by his constant and familiar presence. Too much awareness.

Two weeks into construction, *El Niño* had descended, its initial persistence evolving to vengeance. Desert washes, which in normal weather rambled lazily beneath main thoroughfare bridges, now raced muddy and wild, overflowing streets, threatening all who dared cross. Even if the crew could report to the jobsite, wet conditions often rendered work too risky to tackle.

Drawing Mikela nearer, Cameron closed her eyes. Vancouver had a long rainy season. Jarrid loved to play in the rain. His yellow slicker and red boots made him easy to spot from the window on the few rainy days she had been fortunate enough to be home. Layered in wool and corduroy beneath, he mimicked a chubby canary infused with a child's energy. Behind her closed eyes, he chased the family terrier through Phillip's dripping rose garden.

Thunder rumbled. Cameron's heart quaked, then eased into a dismal ache.

Merciless memory plodded on, segueing to that life-altering rainy night. Slick streets. Impaired visibility. Jarrid never slept until they kissed goodnight.

How do you sleep now, Jarrid, darling? Who kisses you goodnight?

"Watching the rain won't make it stop."

She whirled toward the door. Mikela winced, growling a warning low in her windpipe.

"Oh…Lukas." Hushed and breathless, his name vibrated in the darkening room. Because of the rain, she had not seen him since her watered-down, before-dinner drink the night before. His freshly showered scent and the sight of his hair gleaming wetly took a slivered edge off her disconsolate mood. He looked warm and dry in a red and black flannel shirt. The black T-shirt beneath deepened the dark cast of his skin. His height and breadth crowded the doorway. Like wanton nymphs, her sensibilities sprang to life. How could a man so recently her adversary create such an unwelcome and yet such a distinct erotic reaction?

Nuzzling Mikela's warm neck, she glanced at the wall clock. Lukas would be taking over in the bar in ten minutes. "The locals tell me this kind of rain never happens," she murmured, tone mordant.

He leaned a shoulder against the doorframe, fingertips in the back pockets of new Levi's. A flash of lightning reflected on his silver belt buckle. "I have seen it before."

"El Niño?" She dealt him a skeptical look, agitated by his apathy.

"Winter rain." He glanced at the window. *"El Niño* was here in '93. I'm sorry to say I wasn't."

She deposited Mikela on the desk and ran the fingers of both hands through her loose hair, starting at the scalp. His eyes trailed her motions, as though he were memorizing them. She lowered her hands. "How can you be so complacent?"

"Why waste energy? It's rain. Something I have no power over."

A rod lodged in her spine. "I have no power over tooth plaque, but I don't have to like it."

Smiling, he dislodged from the door, lowered a haunch onto the corner of the desk, and lifted Mikela.

He let her long body hang from his hands, his black eyes staring hypnotically into her blue ones. Cameron had an urge to retrieve her cat. An urge stemming from guardedness or envy?

Instead of reaching for her, she complained, "Mikela hates the rain, too."

"Enit?"

She leaned against the desk, close enough to stroke Mikela. Woodsy, earthy cologne mingling with male body chemistry roused her senses, then settled into familiarity. Heat radiated from his body, contrasting with his tranquil demeanor and the somber eyes that watched her as if seeking some needed clue. Finding the look unsettling...yes, hypnotic, she strove for indifference. "She tries to run away when I let her out. She's almost scaled the patio wall twice. I have to watch her every moment."

"She wants a social life." His hand, sleek on top, toughened in the palm, worked the loose skin and pelt beneath the cat's chin. "Females are like that."

Cameron felt as if the only thing sacred to her in this place was being judged, her territory being invaded. "No, they aren't. Only males do that—tomcats." She couldn't look away from his hand, moving down Mikela's back now, caressing her rump, ruffling fur on its return to her head. A tendril of heat wound itself through Cameron's lower regions, then settled into an ache. "Male cats are known for prowling," she asserted.

"They seek a different pleasure." A sensual glint moved into probing eyes. "If Mikela were a *tomcat,* that wall wouldn't hold her."

Her cheeks scorched. "What does this have to do with the wretched rain?"

"I believe you brought it up."

"I brought up Mikela's trauma. You brought up her sex life."

He shrugged, smiling. "It's a male thing, *enit?*"

"Maybe you should focus on what's important here."

"Maybe I am." His brash smile waned, and his eyes turned dusky. "Rain is a gift from the heavens to the earth. The *Diné* dance to make it rain, not to stop it. This year, *El Niño* was watching and listening."

She wrenched Mikela from him and crossed back to the window. "You're infuriating. Do you know that, Wind Dancer?"

Behind her, he laughed, the sound too soft, too intimate a reaction to her assault. He struck her as being without temper, incapable of being provoked. Her insides churned continually, nerves rioting, spurring her toward confrontation. But he refused the gauntlet.

"Is it me or the weather?" His words barely carried over the pelting rain.

She faced him. "It's you. We're falling farther behind every damned day, and you don't care. I do. Scottsdale and the Salt River are not my life."

"I care."

"Then do something."

"What?" His brows hiked, furrowing his marble smooth forehead.

What, indeed? Would she have him fume, curse, turn belligerent, making the conditions worse? "I don't know. Make plans for catching up when the rain stops."

"What makes you think I'm not doing that?" Did his mouth actually tighten? Had she struck a nerve?

Having no argument, she continued complaining. "Until it stops, do something inside where it's dry. Anything."

"Your guests will stampede if the jack hammers start at six in the morning."

His warning sparked a dread she had been warding off. Hearing her apprehension voiced took it from likelihood to reality. Now that CNN was paying twenty-four hour homage to *El Niño,* reservations had decreased. Some had been cancelled. "If the rain keeps up, we won't have any guests."

"That will solve the problem." The comment amounted to one of his familiar verbal shrugs. "We can move inside with a clear conscience."

Should she slap him or beg to be reassured? He appeared big enough, confident and wise enough to solve any problem. What would it feel like to walk into his strong arms, place her cheek against his soft shirt, have him soothe away her anxiety? But since he neither agreed with nor even understood her concerns, how could he banish them? Could one person *ever* do that for another?

"I'm strongly considering closing the inn, so we can do just that. Move inside to work."

"Wait a little longer. Maybe the rain will stop."

"Don't you watch television?" Exasperation hung in her voice, souring her stomach. What did he do in all this downtime, all these dark, lonely days when construction was delayed, when she was in the hotel and he stayed away until time to work the bar? "The national weather bureau is predicting *El Niño* to go through next spring."

"They are only men with computers."

He fingered a wrapped sample of Reese's Pieces in the bowl, picked up her unused ashtray, examined it closely, then replaced it on her desk, eyeing her stoically...*tenderly?* Or did she only crave and imagine that?

"You should be for closing the inn, moving inside," she persisted. Uneasy with how intently he watched her, her throat warmed beneath his gaze. "Your people you claim to be so concerned about would have work," she pointed out. "Surely you care about that."

"Then the people working inside the inn would have no work." Most of whom were Indians. "Which is worse?" His shoulders rose, then lowered slowly.

"There's no answer." She gripped her arms, feeling a sudden chill.

"The answer is to wait. To trust. To believe in your ability to overcome."

"Oh, God. No preaching, please." She rolled her eyes and ran her fingers through the hair at her temples. "I can't wait. I have too much at stake."

"What?" His eyes narrowed, boring into hers. An entreaty perhaps, a character trait foreign to the Lukas she knew.

"It's personal. You wouldn't understand."

"Try me. If the reason is good enough, I'll ask the *Diné* to dance backward."

She shook her head, determined not to laugh cynically in the face of cumulative tragedy. *Tell him?* Share her emptiness, her aching? Rant? Rave about Phillip stealing her son—not his—by tampering and deceit? Only the knowledge that Phillip, in his selfish, misguided way truly loved Jarrid, kept her from sobbing before this relative stranger. Instead, she declared, "I'll wait another week. If it's still raining, I'll refund any remaining room deposits and close the inn. Any action is better than none."

"That's seldom true."

God, he's arrogant. A damned shaman. "You're entitled to your beliefs, Lukas."

"And you to yours. But in the end, only your decisions will matter."

He stood, bringing attention to his long powerful body, causing her to suddenly marvel at, rather than resent, his stoic nature. A man so big, with harnessed strength so intrinsic it seemed to rise from the earth, could change the world, hold back the rain, reinstate the sun.

She persuaded herself to smile. "Thank you for the philosophy lesson. I'd love to debate longer, but you're on duty, and I have a killer headache." She waited for him to precede her, then closed and locked her office door.

He seemed in no hurry to leave. "Come to the bar when you feel better. I'll serve you a phony drink." His eyes issued a deeper, more profane invitation.

"Maybe." She relinquished a smile, pocketing the key.

"And congratulations." It sounded much too somber to be celebratory.

"For what?"

"For realizing *El Niño* is not a license to smoke." He ambled down the hall, tossing back his I've-got-you-pegged smile over one shoulder.

She watched until he turned the corner, glad he was gone, yet wanting to run after him, remain in his company. A useless, senseless longing. She and Lukas were at different ends of a spectrum, each focusing on a goal, but approaching it so differently that attainment would be a miracle. He wanted to honor and gain honor for his people. She wanted to return to Canada and gain custody of her son. Lukas' stoic, accepting demeanor opposed her innate, take-charge mode of operation. In the past, her strategy had worked, taken the stigma off her femininity. Her accomplishments had won her praise in the industry and pried notice, if not admiration, from the Chastain family.

Briefly, she visualized living the way Lukas lived, adapting his philosophy, then rejected the image as impossible. She would have to be born into his culture. Too many years of swimming against the tide, working for acceptance, striving to be loved for her achievements, had formed a character impossible to alter—not that she felt she could afford to change. Revamping the inn within Hayden's dictates in order to reach her ultimate goal called for strength, not patience. Pondering the months ahead, as if consulting an older, wiser Cameron, she saw the future.

She would be fighting both *El Niño* and Lukas Wind Dancer's passive nature.

eleven

At the Kayenta trading post, Lukas parked his Suburban between a Mercedes bearing gold-framed Louisiana plates and a battered pickup with Arizona plates held on by bailing wire.

"Looks like your typical Saturday crowd," Chuey commented from the passenger side of the Suburban. "Them that's got still rubbing elbows with them that wish they could get."

Lukas shifted into park, killed the engine and eyed his nephew. Chuey's face bore traces of a night with Yolanda. The proof niggled Lukas, left him troubled, but, as yet without the right words to voice his turmoil. "I can tell how much you miss the rez, Run Amok."

Chuey grinned. "Actually I do, you know? That's the damned problem, the reason I don't visit much."

Lukas grunted, familiar with the sentiments of a man straddling fences. Like Lukas and his father before him. And now Chuey, following in their footsteps.

Apenimon remained the only sane one among them.

"Don't get philosophical on me. Save your strength." Lukas opened the door, climbed down, as Chuey did the same. Across the Suburban's roof they locked gazes, Chuey's open and mischievous. "You heard what your grandma said. I'm a man on a mission. I might need backup with Kai."

Chuey led the way, Nikes splashing in the rain puddles on the graveled path that led to the post door. "You're her favorite on the list of potential daddies for that kid. Backup's the last thing *you* need."

Lukas grunted. "Maybe your name could take the place of mine."

Chuey threw a bitter grin over his shoulder "She wants a genuine breed. I don't qualify."

The words rang too true to make Lukas' laugh genuine.

Inside, they parted at the coffee shop entrance, Chuey bent on the breakfast their early Scottsdale departure had cost him. Lukas stood on the perimeter of the gift shop, letting the soft din of mixed accents and intonations, the smell of fry bread and strong coffee, bring him home again. He fingered a beaded vest. It boasted a price tag that could keep a Navajo family in cable TV for a year, yet the artisan would realize little of the post's inflated profit.

From her loom across the room, seated cross-legged on the floor, Kai peered at him through skeins of warp yarn. Stacks of rugs, varied hues and patterns, formed a wall around her. Atop a pile, four-year-old Gad—juniper tree willowy, as his name proclaimed—

sprawled on his stomach. Raptly, he worked the Game Boy Lukas had brought on his last trip to the rez. Four, going on fourteen, Gad would soon tire of the toy.

Lukas placed the vest back on the rack and moved in their direction, accepting and resisting the tug of Kai's black eyes. He ruffled Gad's buzzed, crow-black hair, earning a grunt of acknowledgement, then squatted beside Kai.

"Plagiarizing another treasure, huh?" He ran a finger along the intricate Storm Pattern design, his eyes trailing her flying hands. "Where is the imperfection?" Every rug must have one, since only God could be perfect.

"Imperfections are your specialty, Lukas. I will let you search it out."

His arms were not long or strong enough to spar with Kai. "Sold anything?"

Despite their earlier come-hither message, her eyes now seemed obligated to her skill. "I have a deal working. If I'm willing to cut my commission by half."

His spine barbed. "Tell me you're not willing."

She shrugged rigid, velvet-clad shoulders. A slender braid, blue-black as oil on wet blacktop, hung over one breast. Lukas thought of another tawny-skinned woman, one whose unruly hair harbored red and gold glints. Anglo glints. Stunned, and more than a little troubled, he felt his heart beat in his groin.

Kai's voice, made husky by too many cigarettes and raw mountain winters, grounded him. Faint yellowish circles lived in the patches beneath her eyes.

"I have obligations. No one is giving away food." She coughed, the rattly, ever more constant sound eating at Lukas. She cut him a glance, thunder black as the rug pattern. "No free food since you and your Presbyterians left."

Twenty damned years ago. The woman-child, Kai, had stood in the dusty road with the others, waving while he drove away with the Stantons. She could damn sure hold a grudge. Even if accusatory, her defiant tone gave him hope enough to chastise, "Don't cut your take. Pride is worth more than a full belly."

"*My* belly, yes. My pride is worth nothing when Gad's belly growls."

"Which rug did they take a liking to?" He eyed the stacks, all masterpieces.

She worked in silence, mouth grim, eyes like liquid tar.

"Gad?" Lukas spoke above the clacking of Kai's wooden battens. Gad's head raised slowly, as if his chin were chained to his breastbone. "Which of your mama's rugs—"

"That one." Gad nodded to the rug on the loom, returning to his pastime.

A flawless, rustic beauty. His hairline pricked. "The rich Anglos want fresh kill, huh, Kai? Can't stand to think someone else might have gotten there first."

Her mouth twitched. "They are fools. But their checks don't bounce."

"I'll buy the rug. When will it be done?"

Her hands slowed as she looked at him. "Buy it for your hotel woman?"

He shrugged, gut tensing against the tangled visions her words drew. "I'll show it to her. The inn has to have new rugs. Maybe she will buy all the rest."

"Or maybe you will and give them to her."

Would that alleviate the gathering strain between him and the woman who longed for her other life? His eyes met Kai's, bidding for her silence, nodding to the boy. "I'll take Gad with me. No reason for him to hang around here all day."

"No reason for him to go with you, either."

Her strategy, enticement coupled with resistance, using Gad for bait, dragging him back when Lukas bit, never changed. As of late, wondering how many other men played her game, he had stopped trying to win or even the score.

He shrugged. "No reason that would prove out in a DNA test."

Her head jerked up, eyes narrowing. Slender nostrils flared as though she caught a whiff of smoke…before fire. "Chuey will come for him." Her eyes moved guardedly around the room, letting Lukas know she had seen them pull in. "He told me."

"When?"

She shrugged. "He's a good babysitter."

Close enough to Gad's age to relate, short enough on ambition to devote his soul to games. "Run Amok makes promises he forgets to keep. He's here for breakfast only."

Surprise rose in her eyes, turning to a look Lukas could not quite read.

"Truth is, I like Gad's company." He smiled, appeasing, confessing, "Mama sent me for him. It's Apenimon's birthday, and she's cooking a big spread. Cake. The works. My assignment is to bring back ice cream and Gad."

For a mere breath Kai's shoulders sloped, her eyes seeking the door of the coffee shop. Then pride and stubbornness reinstated the rod in her back. "If he wants to go."

Apparently listening closer than Lukas knew, Gad slid off the rug stack and scrambled for his jacket on the floor. A spindly arm embraced Lukas' thigh.

"I'll tell the restaurant to bring you lunch, Kai." He gave her skinny frame pointed scrutiny. "What sounds good to you?"

"Birthday cake." Her eyes flashed. The weaving boards clacked.

Lukas laughed. "Mama will send some home with Gad. How's that?"

A hike of her dark head. Punishing silence.

"It's my rug now. Not the Anglo's. Do you understand that?"

Ignoring him, she gave her son a soft, dismissive glance and returned to weaving. "I understand more than you know." Her voice was barely audible.

Lukas placed a hand on the boy's head. Gad lifted his moon-shaped brown face, his darker-than-death eyes expectant, curious, devoid of judgment. "Go find Chuey. *Enit?* Tell him we're leaving." Watching the swaying fringe on the back of the boy's jacket, he squatted again beside the mother. "What do you believe you understand, Kai?"

Hands stilling at last, her eyes both pierced and petitioned.

"Again you have chosen to live in two worlds, Lukas Wind Dancer. Lately, you live in this one less and less."

Physically, perhaps, never spiritually. The inn was proving to be more responsibility than he welcomed. The restless innkeeper more than he had bargained for. He lifted one of Kai's tools, examined it and then caught her hand, a finger massaging the calluses on her palm. "If I do, it's nothing personal."

Her tone denied she had heard his own petition. "I understand, too, even if you don't, that you'll be back here with wounds that need licking again. Don't come to me then, Lukas. I have open wounds of my own."

Placing the tools back into her hands, he offered a conspiratorial smile. "I consider myself warned." He rose and looked down at her. "But remind me again when I bring Gad home." Halfway to the door, he turned and ambled back. "Remember, Kai Blackwater. That rug is mine."

As he led Gad to the Suburban, an arm rounding his tiny shoulders, senseless, baseless guilt pricked Lukas' conscience. He meant no more to Kai than she meant to him. He had left the reservation as a child. Since his first visit back as a teen, and on each sojourn after, no matter how much time passed between visits, they had shared their bodies. In contrast to Suzanne's shy, guilt-ridden approach to sex, Kai's eagerness had nurtured his search for manhood.

When he had returned to Arizona to stay five years ago and she no longer felt the need to compete for his attention, for him the carnal edge had dulled. She welcomed him with the lust and indifference of a sexually liberated woman. A woman free of all conventions other than the archaic rituals that kept their people slaves. The fact he was once again foreigner now, his interest in his Scottsdale-based business making him less eager to pay his visits to their homeland than to end them, had created a constant friction that had reestablished a keen edge on sex.

Like his family, like the council who sought his other-world knowledge while detesting his worldly involvement, Kai had joined an uncharted yet unified effort to marry him to the reservation. Their concern and determination was wasted. He *had* grown weary of straddling a cultural fence, and serving on the council provided a way to make up for having left the people to seek the ways of the Anglo world. The lingering pain of that Anglo world guaranteed he would marry a Navajo.

Kai schemed pointlessly.

ॐ

Outside Sarah Wind Dancer's ramshackle house, Apenimon sucked his pipe, rocked lethargically in a cane rocker and regarded Lukas in silence. Holding the smoke in longer than Lukas thought wise, he finally tilted his head and released it at last toward the striated red bluffs of Canyon de Chelly. Predictably, a quiet cough followed, carried off on a sharp mountain breeze.

Lukas closed his eyes, visioning in his mind's eye the distant canyon walls, petroglyphs, sparse sprigs of yucca struggling to survive their rocky foothold. In the chilled, rain-heavy breeze, he imagined a fine sheen of sand tickling his cheeks, smelled the grasses of spring, cooled his mouth with partially melted snow. In the near distance he could hear, for real, the tinkling of sheep bells and barking pups reluctant to relinquish their play for work.

Inside the hogan, his mother bustled in the lamp-light, clearing the last remnants of the feast she had prepared. Strapped into her chair, Chuey's sister, Zoey, muttered endlessly in her lost, imbecilic world, the result of her mother's wasted life. In a lighter vein, a television sitcom droned, canned laughter interspersing with Chuey and Gad's companionable giggling.

Lukas drove his thoughts away into the gathering evening. "I need to take Gad home." Then seek the sanctuary of his own hogan, half a mile away. "Kai will be there by now. Ride with us, Grandpa. Get away for a while."

The invitation vanished in a puff of smoke. "She is a fine woman She would make a good Navajo wife. Her boy needs his father."

Through a cracked window, Lukas studied Gad's profile. "I'm not his father."

"How do you know?"

He knew. After Suzanne had sacrificed their baby, Lukas had kept account of his seed. He never wanted to feel that same loss and pain again. "Kai knows Gad is not my son, Grandfather. She has never pretended differently."

"The boy is Navajo."

For that Lukas felt collective responsibility; shame for his unnamed Navajo brother who had failed to come forward. Still, taking the mystery man's place felt too pat, too planned. The possibility had grown less likely as of late. Pinpointing the reason for his change of perspective brought him no satisfaction.

With purpose, he rose from the spindly cane rocker, a mate to the one his grandfather occupied. Apenimon glanced up, surprised by the abruptness.

"It is time, my son." His words in Navajo held strength, conviction. "Like your mother, I'm counting on you. Your people—"

Lukas held up a palm, no mirth in his laugh. "The whole damned Navajo nation won't self-destruct if I don't marry Kai Blackwater."

"Then who, Lukas? Your nephew also plays a dangerous game. He needs your example." Age granted Apenimon the privilege of hearing what he wanted and speaking his mind. "Do not lead him astray with your Anglo city women. Do not lie with them and risk losing yourself. Keep it for a woman of your kind."

As usual, Apenimon minced no words. Lukas' *ttaajfèè dittidf*—his trousers, or what they covered—could lead him down a troublesome path. But *Anglo?* Not once since the Chicago binge ended five years ago, finally leading him back to home and sanity, had Lukas been with an Anglo. He knew his role. He was doing nothing to alter it. But he needed time. If he only bent without breaking under pressure, the length of that time was his to determine.

Arms folded, he planted his feet in the wet earth, locking his knees, meeting Apenimon's rheumy gaze. "Are you coming with me to Kai's?"

"No. You might want to stay until after the boy is asleep." Apenimon re-fired his pipe, drawing deeply, hacking low in his chest. "I would be in the way."

The very reason he had been asked to go. His grandfather had not lost his cunning.

Most likely Apenimon was right. Once there, he would want to stay. Need to. He had lain with no woman in too long a time. It was natural. Right. Yet tonight, however unwise, he wanted and needed something different, someone foreign. Wanted, needed it more.

Admitting that felt right.

❦

Cameron sat cross-legged in the center of the bed, almost but not quite wielding a brush through Mikela's creamy taupe pelt. Her throaty purr as she pushed against a forearm with her sleek head, willing heartier application, almost lulled Cameron into the same contentedness.

In the mirror across the cramped room, she caught a glimpse of a sage wall and the top of the machine-carved headboard. Her hand slowed…stilled, as she glanced around the generic quarters that summed up her Saturday afternoon.

Wherever Hayden had sent her before, the Northern Tundra, that stint in Ireland, the brief term in Sao Paulo, she had taken personal belongings. Good paintings had replaced hotel offerings. Art books had taken the place of tourist guidebooks. Once there, she'd collected local artifacts and grouped family photographs on cheap veneered dressers and nightstands to take away the sting.

This time she'd brought very little, believing possessions would slow down her return to her son once her time here ended. Surrounded by cold nothingness now, she looked out onto the stark patio. Even as she second-guessed her decision to travel unencumbered, she credited the state of mind in which it had been made.

A nudge from Mikela started the brush and the purring again, as Cameron let rows of Scottsdale art galleries parade through her mind. A painting small enough to fit into a suitcase, maybe? A silver fetish sculpture? Bronze would be better, warmer, more comforting. Ancient pottery, just big enough to hold a few blooms from the bougainvillea growing outside the door, but small enough to slip into that same suitcase at departure? Or one of the intricate Navajo rugs she had seen the day Lukas had forced her to take that walk.

Lukas' image, full blown and imposing, spun out of the less and less resentful edges of her memory and fell into fixed, commanding focus. Loneliness seeped in, festering boil-like in her chest.

Fighting back, she cradled Mikela, left the bed for the patio and lowered the cat to the flagstone surface Immediately, Mikela attempted to scale the wall by way of the flowering vines. Cameron retrieved her and held on. Feline warmth seeped into her, dulling the serrated edges of her nerves. In further search of harmony, she picked a blossom, sniffed deeply, then brushed back her hair and inserted the flower behind one ear.

Why? For whom? Who was there to see her? To admire or make fun?

Curling onto a chaise, she turned her face skyward, eyes closed. The sun beat down, intense. There'd been no rain today, none yesterday, thank God.

Raining in Flagstaff, though. In Kayenta. Canyon de Chelly, too.

She gave in to a wry smile, remembering how she'd woken that morning and clicked on the TV, searching the weather map, as if by rote, for northern Arizona. Then coming fully awake to the reason why, she'd wallowed first in denial, then wonder, before giving into curiosity and envy for his wanderlust, his continually returning to Navajo country. Now, lying in the gentle Scottsdale sun, pressing Mikela to her breasts, she indulged herself again.

Lukas Wind Dancer. His docile demeanor agitated her. His acceptance of all that came his way—even *El Niño*—as Mother Earth's plan, his claims that time would balance all, baffled and intrigued her. His petitioning the gods, then waiting to see if they'd heard or cared, remaining calm when the rain continued, proved the futility of patient petitioning. In her life, only what she forced, not what she desired, ever materialized.

She'd witnessed his gentleness, but she'd seen his passion when it came to having his way. Witnessed him turning a deaf ear, setting his jaw and sights, willing to have nothing if not what he believed to be right. She could never outguess him, nor rile him. Never, whether by power or feminine wiles, had she obtained the upper hand.

Yet she had come to resent weekends when construction halted. She dreaded Friday nights when after serving only God knew why and how many watered drinks, Lukas climbed into the white Suburban and drove away, headed for the reservation. Returning to everything and everyone awaiting him there.

What would making love feel like, taste like, with a man like Lukas—*with Lukas?* Would his graceful motions and thought-out, deliberate speech characterize his passions as well? Would he be that deliberate in bringing her to completion? Would he hold her, talk to her afterward and listen? Care? Or would he be fiery, focused only on physical pleasure, determined to achieve the best for each of them, as he often claimed to be his aim?

He's doing that now. Today. With someone else.

Lukas was holed up in some cozy cabin making love to the rain's rhythm, probably, as she lay imagining, clutching a pitiful animal who wanted nothing more than to escape from her. While she lived for Mondays, in his weekend wanderings, he probably gave her no thought.

If she allowed it, Lukas Wind Dancer would drive her mad.

❧

In the waning afternoon, she stood outside Faust Gallery on Scottsdale's picturesque main street, admiring the displayed Anglo and Native American art, which again brought Lukas to mind.

She envied the way he claimed a part of two cultures, positioning himself in both the progressive and traditional worlds. Had he learned to live with the differences without compromising his own views? Did he wear a mask, play a part? Was he as peaceful as he seemed, or a better actor than she? Unlike her, he *knew* his two cultures, while she had always felt like a stranger in her own world.

Across the street on Dos Gringos' patio the drone of Saturday voices, a different pitch on weekdays, beckoned. She turned, catching the eye of the female bartender Lukas had waved to the day they had strolled here. Conviviality tempted her. She was in no hurry to return to the barren room from which she had taken temporary leave.

She out waited a passing car, crossed the street, and slipped onto a welcoming stool.

Lukas' friend's eyes registered surprise, then recognition. "How you doin'?"

"I'm fine, thank you." *I desperately need a cigarette.* "And you?"

A brow formed a V, invitation to order. End of conversation.

"I'll have Chivas and water. Just wave the scotch over the glass, please."

The woman, handsome in a worn and weathered way, spared a knowing smile. "You got it." Returning with the scotch, she asked, "Want to run a tab?"

Could she risk it? Though the drink was weak enough to have little effect, she already felt spied on, violated. But could she face her empty room? Dismissing the Cameron-is-an-alcoholic myth that muddled her thinking, she made herself comfortable, resting her elbows on the rough hewn counter. "Yes, please. A tab."

Lifting her drink she sipped, smiling, embracing the loneliness of a crowd.

twelve

At midweek, Scottsdale's weather still held. The continuing blue skies and unrelenting sun gave Cameron reason to believe that God, in holding *El Niño* at bay, had adopted an attitude of mercy. The desert stretched and preened. Streets and sidewalks gleamed at dawn and, bathed by two weeks of rain, palm fronds glistened in the soft breeze.

Early on a liberating Wednesday morning, she treated her bruised psyche to a few hours at the under-sized pool. With a towel tented over her face, she dozed off in a balmy cocoon and woke in sizzling heat. Despite her inherent tan, her upper back, thighs and calves had singed. She shrugged into a terry robe, a cold shower beckoning. After that, she'd treat herself to an afternoon inside the cool Scottsdale Interior Design Center.

🍂

Scorched air charged from her newly leased station wagon when she unlocked and opened the door. Suddenly light-headed, she staggered slightly, caught the open door and glanced around the inn's parking lot, feeling foolish and spied on.

From the rear of the property, hard hat in hand, Lukas watched. Though she felt his scrutiny, bright sun prevented her from reading his expression. She turned her back, sensing his continued observation. Leaning into the car, she turned on the ignition and lowered the automatic windows. As she waited for the interior to cool, footsteps echoed behind her.

Vexed, she pivoted, prepared for today's Salt River debate, on whatever topic arose.

Lukas' piercing gaze, dark and soulful, threw her off guard.

He wore bush shorts and a khaki shirt tied at his waist, unbuttoned. Frayed armholes replaced ripped out sleeves. A long strip of khaki, still brandishing the buttons of a missing sleeve, circled his forehead, capturing the sweat that ran from his loosened hair. The silver cross he seemed never to be without gleamed against his sweat-slick, bronze chest.

"Good morning." His greeting faded against the nerve-fraying background of a bulldozer diligently scraping up piles of crumpled concrete. "Finished sunning?"

So he had watched her there, too, even though she had thought she dozed incognito.

"I'm probably finished forever…in Arizona." She glanced at a burnished glow ringing the noon sun, then momentarily closed her eyes. Standing here in blistering heat was the last place she wanted to be. But Lukas had something on his mind. His taciturn manner of cocking his head, watching her through narrowed eyes, had become recognizable. She pressed the back of her hand to her upper lip, then shaded her eyes. "No one told me this place is a hellhole."

His sweat-laden brows flicked, then settled in a straight line. "You're used to a much cooler climate. Your blood will soon thin and you'll be more comfortable."

"I won't be here that long." She only slightly regretted her peevish tone.

He fell into silence, a cheek muscle pumping. She smelled cigars, sweat, and something not yet expressed.

"What is it, Lukas?" Something expedient or profitable, she hoped.

Bending down, she turned the key further in the ignition. When the fine new engine kicked to life, she dialed the temperature and fan to maximum cool, raised the windows and closed the door. He stared as if she had stuck her hand in a bed of rattlesnakes.

"Whatever you have on your mind, could it wait?" she urged.

Crossing his arms, hardhat dangling from his fingers, he stared down at her. The bright sun forged a golden aureole around his head and shoulders, casting his face in deep shadow. An alien, persistent, thrumming infused her, like rain falling on a metal roof, at first pattering gently, then increasing to a soft frenzy. Never had she seen a man more imposing, or more soul stirring.

Unable to sustain the gaze, she focused on the bulldozer, a reprieve.

"You'll burn the engine up if you let this car idle in the heat," he said.

"It's already burning. The car's an inferno."

"Black." Lips, beautifully formed and full enough to be swollen, grew taut. A bronzed brow crept into V formation.

She stared dumbly at the car, then at him. Damned if she would ask what the color had to do with—with anything. She knew only that his nearness had far too much to do with her agitation, her craving to shrink the space between them.

"This is not a desert car, Yazhi."

"It's November—winter, for God's sake." Even if hotter than Hades.

"Winter will pass. If you think today is hot—" He opened the door, shut off the motor, left her mouth *and* the door gaping. "Dandy Doug's Ford." One quirked brow turned the comment to a question.

Her mind spun before seizing his meaning. "Yes. I got it there."

The day she had gone to see the architect, as the cab had passed the dealership, on impulse, she'd directed the driver to turn in. An hour later she had driven away in the shiny, black station wagon she deemed perfect for her Scottsdale tenure.

"Leased?" he prodded.

Sweat oozed onto the back of her neck, down her spine. She nodded, folding her arms at her waist, one hand gripping the strap of the burdensome bag.

"From a 'skin?"

Skin? She stared, at a loss.

"Indian? An old Pueblo named Alton Pivane?"

Her recall reeled backward, latching on. How could he know that? "Where is this interrogation leading?" She pressed her hand to her chest, where sweat had begun to pool between her bra-less breasts.

"In Anglo, Pivane means *weasel.*" He pitched the hardhat on the back seat, made a hand gesture toward the passenger seat. "Take a ride with me."

They were both soaked. Most likely, by now she reeked as badly as he did. No civilized place would welcome them, provided his proposal included such.

"I'm on my way to the design center," she hedged, adding, "I have an appointment." A miniscule, off-white lie.

"This won't take long." He caught her arm, urging her forward. Current shot through her, culminating in his eyes.

As though she were handcuffed, he lightly placed his hand on her head and maneuvered her into the car. He bent to tuck his big, rangy body behind the wheel, leaving her no choice but to scramble into the passenger seat.

On the half-mile trip, crammed with a Mercedes and Lexus horde that shuffled south on Goldwater Boulevard like rich refugees fleeing paradise, he kept silent. Studying his chiseled profile, his relaxed driving manner, she struggled to quiet the erratic reactions his nearness created. Even as she grappled to understand them.

Did she sense or imagine tension in the close quarters? Distinctive, vivid as a sensual nightmare? Was she that starved for attention? So in need of physical contact that sitting next to a man—alien and off limits—could send her reasoning into exile, eliminate common sense and good judgment? Her raw response was unfamiliar, unexplored. Provoking.

Without warning, he looked at her, and she jerked her head forward. In her side vision, he followed suit. She reached, adjusting the cooling vent for a direct hit, praying the warmth on her throat fell somewhere short of raspberry-red.

"Still hot?"

His voice held a tactile quality that allowed her to see the earlier look in his eyes, a look mirroring her thoughts. Her inner thighs grew moist. Heat rose in her breasts. She shook her head, eyeing her hands. "I'm fine."

"*Enit.*"

Not certain if he spoke agreement or question, she withheld an answer.

Moments later, he swung the wagon decisively into a space facing Dandy Doug's showroom. Paralleling the day two weeks ago when Cameron had exited the cab, the "skin" at issue lounged in the window, shoulder braced against the expanse of glass.

Recognition of the car—and probably Lukas—waved across his wrinkled-parchment face. An unctuous smile iced up en route to his lips. "Is that him?" he asked.

"I leased the car from that man, if that's what you mean."

"That's what I mean, Yazhi." Lukas formed a mock pistol with his joined hands, leveled it in Alton Pivane's direction and crooked a finger, as if pulling a trigger. "Son-of-a-bitch," he breathed, his voice as soft as his eyes were hard.

She sensed an undercurrent having nothing to do with her car. "Why do you say that?"

"Navajos are not held in high regard by Pueblos, and we return the favor."

How that involved her, she was not certain, and not accustomed to seeing or hearing him express emotion, his passion surprised her. Favorably. "What are we doing here, Wind Dancer? Returning the car? Getting her money refunded?"

"You'll see." He kept Pivane fastened in a glare.

So damned cryptic. "Whatever—" She had asked enough unanswered questions. "Trust me, I can take care of it myself."

"I doubt that."

"Damn you. You think I'm a woman, and cars are—"

"You are a woman. But not an Indian woman. In this case, it wouldn't matter if you had facial hair and

cojones." His eyes slid over her slowly, spreading heat
on everything they touched. "Trust me."

She stiffened. "I made the initial deal, don't
forget."

"Forget?" He laughed, the soft sound filling the
car, turning his stern face amiable. "Not in this lifetime." His hand went to the door handle. "Are you
coming with me or staying?"

She considered. He might be laughing now, but
the harsh expression he'd brandished while pulling his
mock trigger warned that his amenability could be
short-lived. "I'll wait here."

No feigned disappointment. "Tell me your favorite
color."

Abruptly, she understood. "Sky-blue." An involuntary smile leapt to life. "Canary-yellow. Apple-
green."

"But you settled for black." His tone held skepticism. Or was it pity?

"An economics thing." Her hand traced along the
black, plastic dash, the pseudo-leather seat. "I wanted
cherry-pink."

"No pink. Not for a tough-as-cactus woman like
you." His grin only faintly resembling his more
familiar, heart-stopping smile, he opened the car door,
admitting a rush of heat. "I'll bring the papers for you
to sign. Leave the air on."

"And burn up the engine?"

Brief hesitation. Another grin. "You can wait in
the showroom."

He offered his hand to assist her back out the driver's door. The last time their hands had locked in a common handshake, she had lain awake all night trying to analyze and hold onto the jarring effect No sense in taunting trouble twice.

"I'm fine," she murmured. Exiting the passenger door, she joined him on the sidewalk, eyes drawn to their reflections in the showroom window. What a curious couple they were. She in her hot-colored, tropical shopping costume, the flower in her kinky hair drooping, while he resembled a legionnaire. A virile, avenging warrior, worthy of an endless ticket line at any movie box office.

Inside, a chrome and leather lounge chair provided a perfect view of Lukas and Pivane in the glassed pigeonhole office he had lured her into for his non-refusable offer. Between announcements on the intercom system, she even caught snatches of conversation.

"...you took advantage of..." Lukas' deep, almost too-quiet voice.

"...close out...price was right." Pivane, anxious, a bit wheedling.

"...snowbird...she knows no better."

"...seemed savvy to me."

"...makes the *Diné* look bad...all brothers under the skin."

An occasional glimpse of Lukas' face revealed none of the irritation he had displayed in the car. He appeared stolid, but resolved. Pivane's head repeatedly shook side to side, then gradually began nodding like a mechanical toy as he stole glances at Cameron. When they passed through the showroom, then disappeared through a rear door, neither man acknowledged her.

How did she feel about that? she pondered. Having a man right her error was new. The feeling proved so foreign that her discomfiture and relief sifted into confusion. Hearing a light peck on the window behind her, she swiveled in the chair to see Lukas standing amid cactus and ocotillo, motioning with his fine, dark head for her to join him. A different Taurus occupied the space where Lukas had parked earlier.

She placed a six-month-old copy of *Car and Driver* on a nearby table and strolled through the door held wide by a sheepishly grinning Alton Pivane.

Lukas offered her a set of keys and opened the car door, eyes somber, mouth trifling with a smile.

She paused, looking back. "What about the new papers?"

"A busy woman like you has no time to hang around and sign papers. Especially twice. He will bring them to the inn." He cocked a brow, motioning toward the car. "This was the best choice of what Pivane had left."

Pearlescent-grey with pseudo-saddle interior. Never before had she owned anything so drab. She deemed it meek enough for Camellia, far too tame for Cameron Vickers, however. Her mind raced over a palette of might have-had colors before she managed a reply. "It will clash with my tropical wardrobe, but I'll adjust." Could that be concern clouding his eyes? Dark as they were, who could tell? Moved by the look, she conceded, "It's perfect, actually."

Wondering if his chivalrous act obligated her, she accepted the keys.

thirteen

Rain freckled the windshield, then turned to drizzle as they neared the inn. Not a good omen, Lukas knew. Between his shoulder blades, tension gathered and tightened, the cost of an idle backhoe troubling him. He gambled a glance at Cameron. Detecting that signature crease marring her otherwise smooth brow, he resolved to downplay his own anxiety.

"This shower will cool things off," he said as they entered the lot and she swung the tight, new-smelling wagon into her reserved parking slot. "Nothing to get worked up about."

Glaring at him, she jammed the gearshift into park. Her hand went to the key in the ignition without killing the engine. "It's another damned deluge, of course, and they're already quitting." She nodded at his crew scurrying around in the distance, adding, "But what gave you the idea I'm worked up?"

With a *gotcha* grin, he touched the telltale furrow. Her skin felt feverish, matching the look in her eyes and the shock running through his finger. His hand. Up his arm. For the first time—the slant of diffused light, maybe—he saw a scar jagging through one dark brow. Their eyes locked until she tilted her head away, her hands going to her temples, pressing.

"Headache?"

She nodded, moaning a little.

"The heat," he offered, though the temperature had begun to drop.

"The rain," she countered, adding in a murmur, "Indirectly, anyway."

That admission assured him she wanted this project over with, wanted away from here so badly that any hint of delay made her physically ill. He thought of the phone call he had overheard the night of the party, her unrest afterward. His mind drew faces he had never seen, emotions he could only guess at, reasons unknown, all the while striving not to care.

Resting her head against the seat back, she closed her eyes. Thick, black lashes formed a shelf over rounded cheekbones. At her temples, her skin blotched beneath manipulating fingertips, tiny tangles forming in her hair. He resisted an urge to pull her hands away, hold on.

"You okay, Yazhi?"

"I'll be fine…in a moment." Eyes closed, her hand lowered to the big bag beside her, rummaged, came out empty. She grimaced, as if caught in a bad dream.

He touched her shoulder, a risk, based on how she had pulled away a moment ago. No resistance now, so he left his hand there, fingertips just painfully shy of the smooth skin at the neck of her dress. Her breasts pressed firm against the thin cotton fabric, nipples forming gentle but distinctive mounds. Too hot for underwear, his mind chanted. She was restless, disenchanted. He sensed her blood boiling in her veins. If it failed to cool before spring, when temps went into the triple digits, he would lose her then.

Lose her? What the hell was he thinking?

He glued his gaze to the battered locket lying between her breasts. It lifted and lowered with her shallow breathing, while steadily accelerating rain formed a noisy, not quite opaque curtain around the car. Noting the pebbly plane of her arm, he nudged the cooling system down a less noisy notch.

Her body jerked, eyes flaring open. She had left him for a moment, returning wary, contrary and resistant. Thank God for her aversion, although lately his gratitude for his and this woman's lack of harmony rang phony as hell.

When she reached for the bag—probably to search more thoroughly for whatever it was she needed—she knocked it onto the spotless floor mat at his feet. Most of the contents spilled out. While he intuitively retrieved a vial of pills, his mind selected, discarded, and filed for future reference the remaining items. Among them, tampons and a flat, round plastic container of…birth control pills. So she was the cautious type, in that respect. He also spied an unopened pack of Virginia Slims Menthol, and one of those little booze bottles the airlines gave out and liquor stores kept next to the cash register. Dark. Bourbon or scotch.

Even though the seal was unbroken, his gut coiled. Cameron had not been on a plane in over two months. Hayden Chastain's anxious face and voice hovered in the back of his mind.

"This what you need." He held the pills out to her, along with an opened but capped bottle of designer water. Two more bottles nestled in the gaping bag. No wonder the damned thing was big as a bulldozer and about as heavy.

She thanked him in a hoarse whisper.

Shaking a capsule into her palm, she stared at it as if contemplating poison before finally easing it between her lips, capturing it with her teeth. She uncapped the bottle, placed the pill further back and drank. He watched her throat move, then convulse before she clamped her palm over her mouth and clinched her eyes. A tiny, hot-looking tear squeezed through. The medication had looked too harmless to cause such reaction. Finally, she opened her eyes and gave *him* a lame smile.

This would-be-tough woman was fragile as a moth.

"I should go in." Righting the bag, she eyed the items scattered around his dusty boots.

"Damn. That pill must be a miracle drug." He offered an unreturned smile.

"No, but I'm expecting a call." She made a move to gather the spilled items.

"Wait for the rain to stop." He angled sideways in the seat his bare leg interfering with her recovery mission. She drew her hand back, but sat leaning forward, ready, their knees almost touching, hers tawnier, smoother. Much nicer.

He caught the locket in his fingers, rocking it on the thin chain. She reared backward. He held on. Either she would relent or break the chain. Challenge oozed out of her body, not her eyes.

With his nail, he flicked the edge near the opening, brows raised. "What's in here?" He kept his voice quiet, his tone offhandedly curious.

"It's personal." The pulse in her throat throbbed like a wounded bird's.

"You have a lot of personals in your life." He slid the trinket sideways on the chain, slid it back. "You keep an inventory on that computer of yours?"

Sparing him a guarded smile, she changed the subject. "I suppose I should thank you for saving me from the black blob—even if I was unaware I'd erred."

So, she remained as prideful as she was pretty.

"Next August you'll be more aware. Your thanks will mean more to both of us." For the sake of levity he could not feel, he added, *"Enit?"*

"I prefer to think I won't be here then."

He used his fingers to count off the months in stage whispers, starting with November, ending on the last finger by pronouncing a triumphant, "August." They had agreed he would have a year to finish the project. After that, according to the penalty clause in the contract, he would owe Chastain

Properties a stiff fee for each day he ran over, to be deducted from what they owed *him*. "You'll be here. How much does that bother you?"

She stared into the rain-shrouded distance, her gaze so closed he felt she shunned him. He released the locket and reached to the floor, coming up with a wallet-sized leather binder. In his side vision she lurched, then settled back, caught wanting to steal it from his hands. Opening the binder, he found what he had suspected...and the clue he had hoped for. Photographs. Brown tones all, as if allowed to gently weather and fade, their subjects preserved as much in memory as on paper.

He held the case up, opened to the last photograph. "Who is this?"

"My brother." She sounded captured. Resigned.

"Blond hair," he mused, curiosity raging now. A hail, hearty and beautiful Anglo. Younger than Cameron. Slender. Tall, Lukas would wager, with light eyes if the photo's shading could be trusted. He glanced up. "Name?"

"David...Johnston. He died in a skiing accident." Her teeth found her lower lip. Her hands slipped together, fingers interlocking, turning white. "Last year."

Way to go, Wind Dancer. "Sorry." *Damn.*

She nodded, smiled, granting him license to go on. He held up a second picture, still flipping from the back. She reached, but he moved it just enough.

"Lukas, this is a real invasion—"

"Of privacy, I know, but rain makes me nostalgic."
"He held it up again, eyes inviting, full of assurance, he hoped. "Who is she?"

Cameron sighed softly. "My mother. She was four-teen then."

Virgin-blond hair, not bleached. "Pretty. Like you. No resemblance, though."

This time when she reached for the case, he released it. His heart beat like an assaulted tom-tom, but he held himself back. Bidding for her trust. Willing her not to tuck the photos away in the bag, wondering why he cared so frigging much. He watched as she thumbed through, then turned the case toward him. Two women, one dark-haired, the other gray.

"This is my mother at my age now. And her mother. We have the same brows and chin structure—at least that's what people…" She trailed off, thumbed some more, then closed the case, pressed it against her breasts and fixed her stare beyond his shoulder. "The rain is stopping."

"Not quite." He paid her the honor of checking, then waited for her to look at him "Show me the rest, Yazhi." Maybe then, after sharing, she would hurt less.

She offered no fight when he took the photos back, searched and found what he had set out to discover. He revealed the prize, heart stumbling a few steps. "Is this Jarrid?"

"My son. He was four there. He's six now." Though her voice snagged, it held gentleness, almost awe. Her face got lost in unrestrained sorrow.

Her son. Relief—over something he either didn't recognize, or refused to admit—tangled with sympathy, even as parts of the puzzle began to fall into place. "Do you have his picture in the locket, too?"

She shook her head, eyes lowering. "There's no picture in it."

Let it go, Wind Dancer. For now. No way could he do that. His eyes questioned.

"The locket belonged to Jarrid's…great grand-mother." The pulse in her throat moved. "I'm saving it for him to…for Jarrid's daughter."

Preserving heritage. Easily understood.

He studied the photograph. Claiming the dark-skinned child as hers was unnecessary. Same padded cheekbones and lips, perfectly proportioned nose and almond-shaped eyes. Same overly curly hair, worn in a retro Afro Lukas figured was hard to tame. He had gotten his trace of Anglo blood from her, Lukas surmised. He found it difficult to reconcile the beau-tiful child with the mother's haunted eyes, though. Too many puzzle pieces still missing. But haunted she was. No damn wonder she hated it here, but he now knew that her ordeal had less to do with him and their being tossed and tied together than he had suspected.

"I guess he'll be coming to stay with you." Her expression said otherwise, but finding out why not dogged him. He padded the inquiry with, "You two would be comfortable in one of the bungalows."

No answer.

"Or you could cut a door through and use—"

"No." Emphatic, an angry edge to it.

Punctuating the word, she bent and began scooping items back into the bag, her breasts pressing against his knee, the locket hard and pronounced. His sex tightened, thickened, began to swell. He sat rigid, wanting to help, but riot wanting to give up the warmth of her body. Only when she straightened did he gather the remaining items and hand them to her.

"Jarrid won't be coming to Scottsdale," she said with less venom.

"Why not?" Either she would tell him or close and lock the door again.

She chose to ignore the question. "I'll be moving into the bungalow alone."

He waited.

"I'm closing the inn, Lukas, so you can begin working inside."

Had she made that decision as he pilfered her personal belongings and tortured her with pictures of her child? Had his concern and whatever the hell else was behind the intrusive act brought this on? In her throat that tell-tale pulse throbbed. She frowned, one hand prowling up to massage a temple.

She suffered too much stress for a woman, especially one as fragile as he was discovering her to be. Her life should be spent in wide-open, serene spaces, bearing and rearing children instead of pampering a stand-in Siamese cat. She should be worrying about no more than cooking fish or fowl for a man who could take her to ecstasy each night, then begin all her days with a kiss and a promise to take care of her.

Cameron Vickers should have been born Navajo.

She turned the key in the ignition, quieting the engine, quelling the soft flow of air from the dash. Her hand on the door handle, she paused, looking as though she owed him more. "I've been watching the long range weather forecast. I've even consulted weather experts, or at least that's what they claim to be. The rain—" She released a bitter sound that barely qualified as a laugh. "*El Niño* is here to stay. Until next summer, they tell me. I can't just waste away here waiting, Lukas. There's more to my life than—" She probably recalled she had made that speech to him before, in one form or another. "As you said, we agreed on a year. It's not fair to you or the *Diné*— *your...* tribe... I mean—to have to—"

"I know who the *Diné* are, Yazhi." Touched, he smiled, hoping to ease her soul-searching. "I understand your decision." And he admired her grit, the research she based it on. The woman who had arrived here two months ago would have acted on sheer agitation and retaliation against a force she could not conquer.

"What's this new tact, Wind Dancer?" Her eyes narrowed. "Aren't you going to give me a nature-is-God sermon?"

"Not this time."

"I'm grateful." She smiled, her eyes lighting for real this time. No politics, no placation or salesmanship. He felt he was looking through layers, getting a peek at the real woman. One he could like too much if he didn't keep a tight rein.

"Looks like I'm through for the day." He painted regret he didn't feel into the words. "I'll help you move into the bungalow, if you need me."

She paused, seeming to consider. "Housekeeping will do it."

Too damned independent. "Then I'll make you a drink to celebrate your decision."

"Real or phony?" She peaked a brow as expertly as he had seen it done.

"Depends on if you think the decision should be celebrated." The damned, nagging warning echoed in his head. She showed no signs, but still…

She cocked her head, considering. "I'm glad to be off high center. So…a real Bloody Mary, lots of celery. Thanks to Alton Pivane, I missed lunch."

As they pushed open the lobby door, Anna rushed from behind the desk. One look at her flushed face and wild eyes and adrenaline shot through Lukas' veins.

Beside him, Cameron tensed. "What's happened, Anna?"

The girl's mouth opened, closed Her gaze drifted, returned, then settled on the tile near Cameron's feet.

"What is it?"

"Mikela," Anna said so softly Lukas half-read her lips.

"Mikela what?" Urgent now, demanding. A hand grasped Anna's arm.

"It was Doli—the new maid. While she was sweeping your patio…" Anna's mouth froze. Her eyes remained cast down.

"She left the door open?" Cameron breathed, shooting Lukas a desperate, pitiful look before her eyes pinioned Anna again. *"Did* she, Anna?"

The girl nodded "She climbed the wall—Mikela, I mean. There's blood—"

"Anna." Lukas gave her a quelling glare.

"We looked everywhere," she summarized.

Her troubled eyes darted in the direction of the restaurant where Yolanda, Chuey and the kitchen staff stood to one side. Across the lobby, housekeeping had gathered, the culprit, Doli, tucked in the center. Two separate lines of allegiance had formed, their common denominator helpless panic.

"We can't find her." Anna shrugged granite shoulders. "She's gone."

fourteen

Cameron passed through the patio door and approached the wall Mikela had at last conquered. Random stains, faded to russet by the rain, marred the stark white adobe. Cameron's legs locked before sprinting forward. She snaked out a finger, but before she touched the marks, a large, dark hand seized her wrist.

"Bloody paws," Lukas said. "From climbing. She will have tender feet, but no real harm done, is my guess," he reasoned softly. Beyond his shoulder half the staff, Doli among them, crowded into Cameron's room, watching, listening.

Lukas nodded to where the stone patio floor met the wall. The flower bed, barren in that spot, was trampled as nearly as a ten-pound feline could trample. Cameron envisioned Mikela jumping, scrambling for a foothold in the plaster wall, toppling back. Her foremost conclusion—Mikela had felt like a prisoner in her temporary quarters—culminated in understanding that left her almost paralyzed, stunned by sudden loneliness. Heartsick. That left her a breath away from following in the bloody footsteps, from abandoning ship, screaming defeat.

Through her numb state, she sensed Lukas' hand on her shoulder turning her in the opposite direction. Stoically, he indicated the tangled bougainvillea stalks snaking out of the bed, meandering up the wall. Dazed, she groped for meaning.

"She climbed the vines," he mused. "I'm surprised it took her this long."

Spikes of anger rimmed Cameron's hairline, singed her cheeks. "It didn't happen before because *I* watched her. I always held her when the door was open." Tears clogged her throat, thrust against her lashes; she pivoted away, teeth digging into her bottom lip. Shame and fear that he would witness her weakness swamped her with determination. "I have to look for her." Her mind spun, grasping. "No, I have to stay here. In case she comes back."

Lukas' hands squared her shoulders, forcing eye contact, his eyes riveting. Then, ever the realist, he led her to a wooden gate, released the iron latch, and pushed the barricade open with his work boot. As if he'd read her earlier thoughts of mutiny, Lukas' arm loosely circled her waist while she leaned forward, peering at a twenty-foot drop.

"She would come back, Yazhi, but the wall is too steep for her to scale."

Her body sagged. His hold tightened. Temptation to turn into him, burrow in his arms, seek shelter he hadn't yet offered, nearly overwhelmed her. *Drop the mask. Stop hiding your weakness. You need him.*

But would he shun her?

Behind them a murmur rose, ebbed, died as she stepped away. Had the sloe-eyed voyeurs, with their damn mystic powers, interpreted her useless longing?

"We will find her." Lukas' voice seeped out of a fog. "Was she wearing a tag?"

"Always." *Engraved with the Vancouver phone number.* Who could have known the two of them would be banished to this hellhole? If Phillip got a call about Mikela, his gloating would reach across the miles. If he told Jarrid, and he would to further discredit her, Jarrid would doubt her loyalties even more. She couldn't risk that. She hugged herself, craving Mikela's taken-for-granted warmth and soft-ness. "She's never been outside. The traffic…"

"I doubt she will go near the traffic. She's scared, holed up somewhere."

His brows crimped together, mouth grim. "I'll look around, ask questions."

Pride reared its ugly head. "It's not your problem. It's stopped raining, so you have work to do." She lowered her arms, raised her chin, staging a too-late show of strength. Motioning with her head to the gathering behind them, she murmured, "Take them with you. Tell them the show is over."

His gaze quickened to raven black. "You are hurting, but keep the faith, little one. To bite the hands that might feed you is unwise."

His reprove stung, but weighted grief, along with doubt that help would materialize, kept her silent.

☙

When the phone rang the next morning, Cameron had an intuitive feeling the call wouldn't be routine inn business. Like an old-fashioned cartoon, in her mind's eye the instrument vibrated and leaped a few inches off her desk. She glanced at the clock, running her hands through hair she herself had cropped off the night before, then adhered to protocol.

"Cameron Vickers. How can I help—"

"Cam?" Only Hayden used that name, a residue of her childhood.

"Good morning, Uncle Hayden." She settled back in the chair, smoothing the prickly hairline at her nape, as if he eyed it, appraising her through the wire. "You're up early."

"So are you. I tried your room first." A pause, then, "It can't even be dawn there." Not quite a question, yet not casual enough to mask curious concern.

Yesterday, she had waited out the dawn, sleepless, exhausted, before rising, showering, going to her office. This morning, the second following Mikela's defection, the room had been an isolated cell. She'd left there at three a.m., but the office had provided no comfort, other than a means of keeping occupied. "Early morning is good for catching up before the inn wakes." In a week's time the little hostelry would slumber un-invaded, except for the wrecking crew.

"Wind Dancer tells me you've run into a problem."

Her body pitched forward in wary suspicion and anticipation. "You've been talking to him?"

"Why not? He works for Chastain Properties. Not to your liking, but I did win *that* debate." Pseudo humor tinted Hayden's reminder.

"He's reporting directly to you?" A sense of betrayal crept in. Illogical, perhaps—disturbing, definitely.

"Let's discuss your problem." Recrimination now, just short of accusation.

She drew a fortifying breath before admitting, "It's been raining for weeks, and we're seriously behind on the projected schedule." An agenda paramount to her. Her hand shot back to the hair that still seemed to belong to another, fingers raking through. "I'm closing the inn on Sunday, moving the construction crew inside." Her nails scraped her scalp. "Is Wind Dancer opposed to that?" If so, he should have said that in unsubtle terms. A nagging voice reminded her that he had, actually, when she'd first mentioned closing down. He had stated his objection in a silky sermon about nature and the *Diné*. A homily she had chosen to reject.

Hayden pulled her back. "I was talking about Mikela running off. That problem."

"Oh." Pain shot her throat, broadening it at the back, nearly suffocating her.

"What do you think chances are of getting her back?"

Her head pounded at the thought of gauging percentages. "I've run ads in both papers and hung reward posters in the surrounding area." Every spare moment she had walked downtown Scottsdale asking questions, coming up empty hearted. Mikela seemed to have vanished. "I'll keep trying."

"I know how you miss Jarrid, Cam."

No, you can't possibly know that. Or he wouldn't have sent her here, requiring that she earn redemption. He wouldn't make her wait.

"I know how you depend on that cat to take Jarrid's place. I suppose a doctor would call it attachment transference." Another awkward, question-masking statement.

"I'm not drinking, Uncle Hayden." *I'm not an alcoholic, but you don't want to hear that futile argument. Again.* "If that's why you're calling."

A long pause. Was he analyzing her voice? Dissecting her words? Reading her thoughts across the miles? "I'll have to take your word, won't I? But I don't have to remind you—"

"No." Remind her of their agreement that she would prove Phillip's accusations false by revamping the inn, proving as well that she could function reliably and was capable of raising a child. In return, Hayden would vouch for her, help her get Jarrid away from Phillip. Hayden Chastain held her fate in his hands. What if she told him that despite Phillip's obsessive love for Jarrid, he hadn't fathered him, but that he half believed he was the father simply from being with her while she carried and delivered the child? Would Hayden believe her, and if so, would he continue to neglect her need for her child? "You don't have to remind me. I think of little else."

A phone rang in his background. The smell of coffee brewing in the kitchen wafted through her open door, setting her stomach to roiling. She counted dust motes framed by sun breaking through the window that overlooked the rain-washed alley.

Hayden broke the silence. "You're closing on Sunday, you say?"

"Yes." Faces filed through her mind. Anna. Yolanda. The cooks, Cleveland and Jim Jay. Housekeeping—nameless for the most part, but familiar. "It's not an easy decision."

"But you did make it."

A commendation? Watered down praise? "I've refunded room deposits. Sunday is our last day. I'm throwing a small party for the staff that evening."

He chuckled. "That's amiable, I'd say."

"They'll have jobs when the inn reopens." Doli's sad yet defiant countenance popped into her mind. Bitterness rose like bile. "Most of them."

"I'm sure you know what you're doing, Cam." A hand muffled the phone, just long enough for her to examine his off-hand accolade. "I have a call. We'll talk later."

The line went dead in her ear.

When Cameron spotted Lukas' white Suburban turning the corner, she stepped out the door of Dandy

Doug's Ford, but halfway to the parking area she recognized the driver as Chuey, not Lukas. Stunned by irrational disappointment but striving for a show of indifference, she stepped off the curb, waving acknowledgement to Chuey.

Almost before he had put the gear in park, he was out of the truck and rounding the front bumper, racing to open the passenger door. As she approached, he hastily swept a deflated Burger King bag off the seat, inadvertently dropping it on the driveway. Shriveled fries and empty ketchup packs littered the concrete. After retrieving the mess with a grin, he tossed the bag onto the back floorboard. With a hand to her elbow, he boosted her onto the high passenger seat, then slammed the door and retraced his steps.

Immediately, she caught the residual scent of Lukas' small cigars. His hardhat, a red paisley bandana stuffed inside, graced the back seat. Classical music loud enough to override the blast of the cooling system filled the worn truck interior, immaculate except for Chuey's clutter.

Settling behind the wheel, Chuey reached to adjust the over zealous fan and lower the stereo volume. He cocked his head, eyeing her. "You like this high-brow music? Lukas does. So when I get a chance, I listen, trying to figure why."

"I enjoy it." Knowing Lukas did also surprised her pleasantly, which she took time to examine.

"You have a favorite?" Chuey shoved the gear into reverse, shot backward. Cameron's head jerked when he all but peeled out of the drive. "Sorry." His perpetual grin spread, adopting a look of chagrin. "Do you?"

She braced against the seat, anticipating the approaching corner. The tires grazed the curb as he turned. Were she not privy to Run Amok being his nickname, she might suspect him of imbibing. "Do I what?"

"Have a favorite."

"Oh…Haydn, I suppose."

"Don't know him. Uncle Bro's a Mozart freak." He opened the center console and let her view a row of filed cassettes. "A few John Cages thrown in. He calls those experimental, which he usually doesn't go for—experimenting, I mean. Anymore, anyway."

Except for the music, they rode in silence for a block before he asked, "Any word on your cat? What's her name? Michelle?"

"Mikela," she half whispered, heart seizing up, the music abruptly mournful.

"Oh, yeah. One of those new age African names. Maybe she'll come back."

Contrary to Lukas' sober nature, Chuey grinned continually, as if everything he said—or life in general—constituted a joke he wondered if she were getting. He had a dimple to the left of his wide mouth, teeth that rivaled Lukas' in perfection, and sable hair intent on forming waves at his nape. A comely copper-skinned boy, as appealing as a fattening candy bar, he also possessed a sweet bad-boy charm that failed to daunt her disappointment at his uncle's absence.

"I could have taken a cab, but yesterday Lukas insisted—" Maintaining his pattern of detached concern in Mikela's absence, he had offered to meet her when she dropped off the wagon for routine service and take her back to the inn. "Where *is* Lukas?"

"He ran up the hill. To Kayenta."

"Excuse me?"

"Gone to the rez. Tribal business. That, and Kai's on the warpath again."

"He literally *ran* up the hill?" She visualized Lukas sprinting in loincloth and moccasins, bronze skin glistening in the sun, hair flying behind him.

Chuey laughed. "Probably could, but he caught a puddle jumper to Flagstaff and got a ride from there. When tribal stuff crops up, color Lukas gone."

Irritation reared. She touched her fingers to her temples, drew them down, managing, "Nothing serious I hope."

"Gang trouble."

"On the reservation?" She thought of crowded, drug infested cities, certain parts of Phoenix she avoided, based on Channel 3's accounts and those of the *Republic*.

"Yeah, Lukas says they're reverting back to our past." He glanced at her. "You know. When renegade Indian bands roamed the plains, looking to wipe each other out. I'm not as empathetic as him. They need their butts kicked." Deciding not to challenge a yellow light, he slammed to a stop. Cameron's seatbelt slashed tight across her chest. "I'd have gotten mine kicked, or worse, if I'd acted like that."

"Your father must be very strict."

"If you mean strictly gone, you're right." His grin vanished, as his fingers drummed the wheel. "Never knew him, but Apenimon could still kick butt back then, and Lukas was glad to take up any slack once he got back from Chicago."

Based on his sudden somber look, she decided not to explore her curiosity about his mother. "How long ago was that? Lukas' return from Chicago?"

"Five years." No thinking back or calculating. "Except for visits, he was gone from age twelve on, adopted by the Stantons—sort of. Missionaries with two kids his age—twins. Toured the world with them. Beats the hell out of the twenty years of reservation life he walked out on. Unless you consider the bottom line."

Cameron waited, wondering, hoping he would elaborate.

"You need to stop somewhere before the inn? Run any errands?" He stole a glance. "I'm out of class till tonight. Just doing some clean-up on the construction site."

"No thank you." She wanted out of the truck alive. "You mentioned Kai," she ventured. "Is she all right?"

He shrugged, still smiling. "She's trying to organize a sit-in in Flag, some place that sells pottery and pockets the profit, cheats the artisan. Lukas thinks she's cutting off our noses to—Well, never mind what he thinks. Kai's fine."

True to his nature, Lukas preferred not to rock the canoe.

As the inn came in sight Chuey said musingly, "You know, Ms. Vickers—"

"Cameron, please."

"I know my uncle has a way with women…"

"Does he?" Her hairline spiked, but she laughed, which he ignored.

He swung the truck into the parking lot, one tire hanging over the drive spewing rocks. "I wouldn't get too attached."

Caught off guard, she flushed miserably. Was the whole damned tribe mystical? "Thank you, but your concern is wasted on me." She used an acerbic tone, but rather than risk meeting his eyes, she stared out the window at the construction crew eating lunch in the shade of an undernourished palm.

"That's good." Looking dubious, he pulled the truck to a stop beneath the porte-cochère and eased the gearshift into place, suddenly docile. "Want me to take you to get your car later? It shouldn't take long to service it."

"No, I'll take a cab."

Her hand grasped the door handle, but stalled while her mind grappled with Chuey's warning. Even as she struggled not to pursue the subject he elaborated.

"About Lukas…What I said…" He rubbed his chin.

"It doesn't matter. Nothing in his private life concerns me."

"He's promised."

"Engaged, you mean." Since her vocal cords had taken on a will of their own, she tried for damage control with an insouciant, schoolteacher tone.

The jaunty smile returned. "Not yet, but he's made some kind of vow—"

"It's none of my business." That should be plain enough. *But damn!* As if she looked into a mirror, her feigned disinterest glinted in Chuey's dark eyes.

"He's promised himself he'll marry within the tribe, or at least in some tribe. He spends time over by Window Rock, too, where his daddy's people— Apaches—live. Sowing wild oats." With a forefinger, he massaged a worn spot on the wheel. "Personally, I'm betting he'll end up with Kai, if they can put out the fireworks. Some people think that Gad—her kid—is—Well, he looks like him anyway. Same great nose and chin."

She waited. Neglecting to draw a breath, she entertained visions of the beautiful boy who'd trailed Kai at the demonstration as if she were the pied piper. Even though Kai had denied a connection with Lukas, Cameron's intuition, a sense of Kai having a hold on Lukas, had evolved into conviction. She'd been right.

"Anyway," Chuey said, releasing breath, "Lukas and Kai don't see eye-to-eye on much other than Gad."

"That sounds ominous." She couldn't bite back the words.

"It can be. They fight over her getting him back to the rez to stay, since Kai swears she'll die and be buried there." He stopped, gauging for effect. "All this marrying Navajo stuff hangs on the twenty years Lukas was gone, and how guilty he feels about it now."

"Why are you telling me this?" She spoke around the surprising constriction in her throat, the brine gathering in her nose. "It's none of my business."

"You're right, and Uncle Bro would kick my butt for talking out of school." The tantalizing smile beamed. "So maybe you could forget I mentioned it?"

"It's forgotten." She jerked the door handle up. "Don't get out. I'm used to taking care of myself."

She puzzled over the incident through the morning, convinced the conversation was more than idle chatter. While Chuey had hinted at protecting her, she sensed Lukas' welfare was at the core of his nephew's concern. More enigmatic was the fact that once he'd broached the topic of Lukas' marriage plans, Chuey's zeal to give information had rivaled her eagerness to get it. Had he detected in her the underlying attraction to which she had refused to grant honest consideration before now?

Vexed by Lukas' absence, she stared out her office window watching the backhoe break and scrape up concrete on a rare, rainless day. If Lukas would rate the havoc *El Niño* was leveling on the construction schedule only half as important as the reservation—an obsession she now understood—she would rest easier at night. At the moment, no matter how pressing his reservation business, or Kai's current change-the-world effort, a phone call from him seemed in order. The desk phone remained ominously silent, however, driving home another point.

Considering Lukas was *promised,* denying her attraction to him had proven wise.

fifteen

On the fourth day of Mikela's absence, as Cameron toweled off following a morning swim, construction noise from the bungalows in back of the inn caught her attention. The commercial logo on an unfamiliar truck urged her to veer in that direction to investigate, wrapping and tying her terry robe en route.

When she appeared in the bungalow doorway, construction halted. Sawdust floated on the air, the clean, sharp smell rushing out to her. Paint cloths draped the furniture.

"Mornin'," a grizzled, balding man offered as his companion's hammer halted mid-air. "You lost?" He grinned tolerantly, eyeing her wet hair and robe.

A new hole gaped in the wall separating the two bungalows. Alongside, a carved door leaned against the wall, minus hardware. "What's going on here?"

"New door." He made a half-hearted movement to return to work. "Noise bother you?" Loading his mouth with nails, he passed through the gap into the other bungalow, then peered around the unframed opening, brows raised.

"Who ordered this door?"

The men exchanged looks, then glanced off into the middle distance. The one who had not spoken positioned a long, thin strip of wood to the edge on the gap, took a nail from his mouth, and drove it in. *Dismissed.* The friendlier of the two asked if she'd found the temperature of the pool water to her liking.

"I'm…Cameron Vickers. I manage the inn." She raised the robe collar around her throat, finding the heavy cotton as scratchy as her mood. She spoke above the hammering. "Who ordered the door?"

"Can't say. I was just told to install it." The gray-haired man touched the younger man's shoulder. The hammering stopped. "Got the papers in the truck if you wanna see 'em."

"If I may." She led the way outside. The order on the clipboard retrieved from the truck cab answered her question. *Lukas Wind Dancer.*

Needlessly, she glanced around the parking lot. Saturday. Noting Lukas' later than usual start, she had watched the Suburban pull away that morning, reservation bound, taking his reason for ordering the door with him.

She handed back the clipboard. "Will you finish today?"

"It won't get painted. No Michelangelos hanging around."

"Make sure there's a heavy lock." Painting could come later. Now that she d resigned herself to Mikela

He half saluted, beaming like a bishop. "Yes, ma'am. Locks on both sides. His an' hers, we call 'em."

She failed to see the humor.

❦

Near nightfall, a rap on her room door interrupted packing. When she opened the door, Lukas peered past her, eyes focusing on the burdened bed.

"I thought you d gone—" She hadn't quelled her surprise soon enough. His gaze quickened, afire with…satisfaction?

"Anna called me. The weekend bartender couldn't make it." He braced a shoulder against the doorframe, hands in the pockets of pants that fit his slender hips and long legs as if they'd been sculpted instead of tailored. A leather bob tie, heavy with onyx and…jasper, she decided…rested against an impossibly white shirt. His hair, luxuriant and loose from the usual braid, hung beyond his wide shoulders, outgleaming even his highly polished boots. He smelled of cigars and wood-spiced cologne.

Wherever he'd gone earlier, with whomever, it was nowhere near the rez.

She held onto the half-opened door. "Tending the bar is a moot point, really. Since we're closing tomorrow."

Did his faint grunt signify agreement or argument?

"Anna also told me you're moving." When she nodded, his eyes narrowed. "Have you given up on Mikela, Yazhi?"

"Not entirely."

Throat tightening, she stepped back into the room, neither issuing nor denying an invitation. Without hesitation he entered, closed the door and crossed to the bed where her luggage lay open, one piece filled, the other half empty. Picking up a bottle of perfume, he removed the cap and raised it to his nose, eyes meeting hers as he sniffed. She watched, mystified, as he applied a dribble to his wrist beneath his shirt cuff and sniffed again. Did his smile edify or ridicule? How would she ever know? After wrapping the bottle in loose tissue from the bed, he placed it into a bag, then lifted a sandal, rubbed a thumb languidly over a strap, face solemn, eyes seeking hers. Again he smiled. Softly.

Absurdly, she felt he'd touched her—with hands strong enough to win battles, gentle enough to heal, with eyes wise enough to read her soul.

He's promised.

She struggled to recall they'd been speaking of Mikela. "I've been leaving food in the area below the wall every day." The empathy in his eyes gave her strength to add, "I'll keep doing that, hoping a coyote doesn't eat it."

Or ravage Mikela. Oh, God, why were they even in this godforsaken place?

She turned toward the dresser, eyes seeking the sweating glass she'd left there when she'd answered the door, the pack of unopened cigarettes. The ice had melted, leaving the contents even paler than in the beginning. Hating her obliged impulse, she explained, "I'm having a brandy while I pack."

"With ice." He cocked a brow. "Different."

Her cheeks warmed with invalid guilt. "It's difficult to just wave brandy over the glass," she said, feigning levity. "Luckily I found a bottle of soda."

He chose not to meet her eyes, unnerving her more than if he had nailed her with accusation. But why would he? He knew nothing of her so-called weakness or agreement with Hayden. He neither knew, nor cared to know, anything about her.

"I'm almost finished packing." Obligation nagged. "Then I'll order dinner."

"Good idea." He didn't look at her, but his casual tone assuaged her guilt.

Uncertain of his reason for being there, she slipped into an increasingly familiar tangle of emotion. Agitation and contentment. After searching his face and getting no clue, a business air seemed crucial. She crossed to a nightstand, opened it and scooped out contents she had not had the heart to sort since moving in two months before. As she turned to the luggage, an object slipped her grasp and tumbled first onto the bed and then the carpet.

Quickly, gracefully, he retrieved the small, dog-eared, gold-edged cardboard folder. Heart hammering in rhythm with the sudden pounding in her head, she made a too-late move toward him. Dizziness threatened as she watched him open the folder, study the photograph and the inscription on the flap. His eyes lifted, boring into hers, rife with question. "Camellia Chastain?"

"Lukas—Give me that." She held out her hand. "Please."

Her heart beat in her ears, encroaching on the eternal silence before he handed over the photograph, then glanced at the bedside clock with an expression of finality. "I will help you move. I can be late taking over the bar, or you can wait until I finish there. Your choice."

Damn him. Damn his revered and despised insolent, take-charge demeanor.

"You don't need to help." Now that he'd seen the picture and knew too much, she wanted him gone. "I'll call a bellman when I've finished packing."

"You make choices easily, Yazhi." His smile had a forced edge. "And too quickly, maybe."

"I don't want to impose." Or begin to depend on him.

"Right," he grunted, his gaze sharpening.

Bent on ending the debate, she turned away, going to open the door. She followed him into the hallway, knowing the question had to be asked. "The door— the new one in the bungalow…Why did you do that, Lukas?"

"Jarrid." This smile came easier, appeared genuine.

"Jarrid?" Her scalp tightened, increasing the pain behind her eyes.

"In case you change your mind and want him here."

His thoughtfulness jolted her off guard. She shook her head, sucked her bottom lip into her teeth, closing her eyes for the fraction of a moment allowed. "You misunderstood. It's not that I don't want him here." *God, I do.* "It's just that—" How much was she willing to tell? How much did he expect in return for his thoughtfulness? No reason existed to share. Sharing wrought complications.

"In case things change, then, Yazhi." He spoke so softly, she found herself reading his lips, marveling at the shape, the fullness, the tenderness they emitted.

Before she could shape a reply, he left her there, aching and relieved.

❧

Hurting. The certainty of it haunted him like vindictive *chindi* as he tended bar, dogged him like his shadow through the late night as he made his way along Interstate 17, across the Mongollon Rim and into Canyon de Chelly.

She had been hurting for a long time. He would guess that her pain had begun when she was Camellia Chastain, the bleach-haired, tawny-skinned girl in the picture with a darker-skinned boy with too-curly black hair. His almond eyes were darker than her own, jet, as nearly as Lukas could tell from what the age-yellowed carnival booth photo revealed.

No Anglo blood there. He thought of the boy, Jarrid.

Camellia Chastain & Lee Tutuila. Vancouver 1994.
Penciled youthful script, faint from years of frequent
handling. What kind of name was Tutuila? Whatever,
he had to be Jarrid's father. Yet the name on back of the
picture he'd seen last week, while they waited out the
rain in her car, had been Jarrid Vickers.

Jarrid *Lee* Vickers. Comfit's son. Camellia and
Tutuila's son.

How much did that dark boy in the picture with
her—a man, now, just as she was a woman—have to
do with Jarrid not coming to Scottsdale? How did he
relate to the spiritless look in Jarrid's mother's eyes
when she spoke of her son. How much of her pain
settled on Lee Tutuila, and how much centered on all
that Lukas did not know about her?

As he turned the wheel, guiding the truck off the
highway and onto an unpaved, rutted road, he caught
a whiff of her perfume. He raised his wrist to let the
cloying, too-sweet scent fill his nostrils, saturate his
mind as he drifted back, beyond her room. Beyond the
perplexing photograph. Beyond her pain.

Morning glories.

In Mobile, the unforgiving South, morning glory
vines had twisted like lustful snakes on the weathered
fence around the Stantons' parish-house yard.
Trumpet-shaped blooms draped the barrier like a
casket blanket made of flowers. Every morning, in
warm, muggy, foreign Mobile, he woke to the aroma.
Every day he left the sweet smelling safety of the room

he shared with Steven and faced the cruel redneck prejudice of his schoolmates.

Redskin. Cochise. Geronimo. Their faces ran rigid with pleasure as they spewed the names, eyes hungry for his pain. And when they learned of Arizona and the reservation, they had erroneously found a new label. *Sand nigger.*

Tonight the voices rang in his head, in the red bluffs lining the road he traveled, reminding him of how Steven, whom he had believed to be his white brother, had changed as he listened to the jeers, as he faced, and finally accepted, his only choice. To join the Anglos. To shun Lukas, making him odd man out. In the dark beyond the truck's lights, he saw Suzanne's tears of sympathy, recalled how sweetly she had given herself to him, seeking to heal his pain behind the dead vine-shrouded fence on a cold October night.

In their familiar way, Dennis and Laura Stanton had soothed, counseled, explained away the ridicule. "People, especially Godless people, can be cruel. You must forgive." Although the words went unspoken, he knew he was Dennis and Laura's token minority, blatant proof they loved all of God's creation. Loved his brown skin, black hair, *heathen* ancestry.

Until they discovered he loved and wanted their daughter. And she him.

As he struggled to quash the memory Lukas turned onto a second dirt road, shifted into four-wheel drive and began climbing Defiance Plateau. A few miles to go, time in which to clear his mind, to regain peace.

And then Kai's warm, welcoming bed.

He pulled the truck to the roadside, killed the engine, doused the lights and made his way by memory in the darkness to a stream winding beside the road. Pines rustled in a damp breeze, melding with the ripple of shallow water against smooth rock as he squatted, rolled back his sleeve and scrubbed his arm with frigid water.

His jaded recall, his bitterness, the loss of his child, had nothing to do with Cameron Vickers, the half-white woman. Nor with Camellia Chastain, the pretend blonde girl Cameron had once been. She and her too-sweet perfume had nothing to do with tonight's decision to stop punishing his need by way of Kai's bed. He would forget her once he…

Then why in hell did he crave the smell of her perfume? And crave her?

He rose and stood feet apart, bracing in the muddy soil, eyes cast to the sky. Gradually, as the dawn broke, different reasoning broke the surface of his mind.

Back in the truck, he made a U-turn, heading back toward Scottsdale.

The following night, Chuey pulled his Toyota in behind Lukas' truck, which was parked a block down from Doli's house in the night shadows of a scraggly olive tree. He left the car and slipped into the passenger seat of the Suburban, brushing the cold rain from his denim jacket. The quick way Lukas turned toward him bore a mark of urgency, a palpable kind of gravity. He felt it so strongly that he hugged his frigid hands between his knees, bracing for his uncle's reaction to the truth.

Tolerance for traitors was not one of Uncle Bro's virtues.

Chuey took the plunge. "You were right, Luk. Doli let her out the gate." He waited for a reaction, then ventured, "How the hell d'you know that, anyway?"

Lukas grunted, the closest thing to an answer Chuey would get. In the pale light of a street lamp, he watched a hand grip the steering wheel, loosen, re-grip. But Lukas' eventual reply came as a surprise. "That cat hated being locked up."

So Lukas viewed Doli more as a rescuer than a thief. And as damned gone as he was on Cameron Vickers, he might be losing his hard edge.

"I couldn't find out much else," Chuey offered. "She does have kids. Two." Skinny and bright-eyed, glued to a television too lavish for Doli's Salt River Inn salary. "But I didn't see a cat or smell any trace of one."

"Modern technology." Lukas, always a man of few words, grated out.

"I'm a 'skin, remember? They haven't created a machine that can doctor cat litter enough for me not to smell it." He spared a grin that went unacknowledged.

"How did she act? When you told her you would take her home?"

For two nights in a row, Lukas had tried to give Doli a ride home from the inn, but the woman had found an excuse. "Nervous as hell. I thought she'd refuse me, too, out of feeling guilty, maybe. You know, for letting the cat escape. She didn't talk much in the car, but she invited me inside, made me some kind of tea, and then she just spit the story out, like I was all of a sudden her best friend. Said she let Mikela out on the patio and couldn't stand the way she was clawing at the wall, trying to get over." In the silence, he ran the scene he'd just come from back through his mind. Doli's refusal to meet his eyes, her insistence the kids stay silent. "When I mentioned the cat had never been outside, that she was an easy target for a truck, she asked if we'd found road kill anywhere. Like she was pointing out we hadn't." He mulled that over. "You know, to make *me* feel better. Maybe."

Lukas faced forward, his arms circling the wheel, fingers drumming now on the cracked leather dash. Stewing. "Someone waited in that ditch for Mikela."

"Gimme a break. How would they know to be there?" A week had passed. The cat was history.

"You tell *me* how they knew?" Lukas invited, scarcely more than a murmur.

Chuey felt the ire, but felt his uncle's concentration More. A chafing. "I haven't had my basic P.I. course. You go first."

A car passed, tires singing on the wet pavement, then turned in a drive two houses away. Light flooded a sandy, grassless yard as two kids burst from the stucco bungalow and greeted the male driver. Chuey looked away, longing.

"I checked housekeeping's schedule," Lukas said. "Doli cleaned that room every day after she was hired. I would have to guess that out of sympathy, she let Mikela onto the patio every day. Not just the day she disappeared. Either she told someone to be there that day, or she called them from the room to come to the area under the wall."

"I dunno…" Unconvinced, he tried to frame the suggested scene.

"A twenty-minute walk from this neighborhood. Ten in a car." Lukas fell silent, then spoke as if confessing. "I checked Doli's file. Her cousin is a night prep cook at Salt River, lives one street over from her. She recommended Doli to head of housekeeping, so Doli owes her for the job. The cousin has no children, but her husband is a paraplegic. Bound to a wheel-chair."

Chuey imagined wheels grinding in Lukas' steel-trap mind, slapping out puzzle pieces. "And he could use some company." Chuey fitted a piece into place. "But the cripple couldn't leave the chair, or bed, to walk a dog."

"I see it that way." Lukas' tone rejected the *cripple* tag.

Chuey jabbed Lukas' rock-hard shoulder. "I gotta tell you, chief, that's bullshit speculation. Sounds like a Tony Hillerman plot."

"Does it?"

Conviction in Lukas' voice denied his question. Chuey's skeptical laugh evolved to possibility, then belief that snaked up his spine. Lukas had deductive powers Chuey had been cheated out of by his Anglo ancestry. "I guess you have the address of this cousin."

Lukas fished a scrap of paper from his shirt pocket. He squinted at it in the dash lights, then started the engine, looking at Chuey, his hands draped over the wheel. "Thanks, Run Amok. The rest I need to take care of myself."

Wordlessly, Chuey got out and stood in the rain watching the truck pull away.

Cameron Vickers had pushed Kai Blackwater to the background. Easy to see that Uncle Bro had a new focus in life and only half a right to hold Yolanda—or any Anglo woman—over Chuey's head. Interesting development. Would Lukas go with his heart or follow his *ttaajieedittidi*—what his trousers housed—the danger their grandfather raved against? Or maybe Lukas' pain had eased enough to let his heart and his *manhood* merge again?

Either way, free to follow Lukas' lead, Chuey couldn't lose.

sixteen

Lukas opened the entry door onto the darkened hotel lobby. Stirred by the outside breeze, fronds on the ailing pot palms clicked like dry bones in the emptiness. His boot heels echoed solidly on the cracked tile floor as he crossed the dim space and peered down the short corridor leading to vending machines, linen supplies and what Yazhi liked to refer to as administration. A dim light spilling out of her closet-size office pulled him in that direction.

She raised her head when he appeared in the doorway, but so slowly it might have been tethered to the spreadsheets on the desktop. A tarnished halo of light framed her hair. A slight frown got short-changed by the curious look she gave the writhing burlap pouch dangling from his hand. Then her eyes met his. He leaned against the doorjamb waiting for an invitation to enter—other than the one in her gaze.

"I thought you'd gone." Her voice was throaty unused for awhile. She massaged her temples with her fingertips, then glanced at her watch. "I saw *your* truck leave an hour ago."

Confirming his notion she had been keeping close tabs on him lately.

He smiled as he switched hands with the pouch and shuffled his shoulder to the opposite side of the doorframe. "I thought *you* would be in your flannel nightie by now, watching *El Niño* on CNN."

She massaged the back of her neck, looking tired and a little defeated. "I have figures to go over and letters to write." She chanced a covert glance at the Pouch. Her gaze ran down his length and lingered a moment before meeting his eyes again. "I see it's still raining," she murmured.

"Enit." Navajo for it damn sure is. His damp braid hung doubly heavy between his shoulder blades. Water spotted his faded Levi's and boots like wet freckles. Deciding to go on what he saw in those dusky eyes, he entered the room and rested a haunch on the edge of the desk, lowering the pouch to the floor. He picked up a discarded Reese's wrapper, crushed it into a smaller ball and tossed it in the trash can. From the desk paraphernalia, he selected a letter opener and drew circles with the point against the denim molding his thigh. The movement drew her eyes like a cat drawn to fish. "Maybe you were right," he speculated. "And we *should* be building a beach hotel, since the canal is flooding right up to our doorstep."

His daring to broach the forbidden subject brought a tight twitch to her mouth. Her brow knitted before she smiled. "You arrogant bastard." She rocked back in the small scale executive chair. "What's in the bag? A damned rattlesnake?"

Picking up a pen, he drew an upside down happy face on the leg of the threadbare Levi's. Then he added short, spiked hair. Her new hair cut still jolted him every time he looked at her, granting him license to ask, "What happened to the island princess mane?"

"The heat." She looked a bit guilty, then smiled dismissively. "Is it day-old fry bread?"

"Something better."

She frowned.

"I see you find it hard to believe anything could be better than frybread."

Sitting up straight in the chair, she patted her abdomen. "I've got the added pounds to back up my sentiments."

Which added to her appeal. Rounder hips, fuller breasts, no more sunken cheeks. Anywhere. "Maybe you had better leave off the honey." He cocked a brow.

She mimicked him, one heavy brow arching. "Maybe I'd better practice abstinence."

His sex bucked a spastic rhythm, as if it had never been ridden.

The brow hiked higher. "What's in the bag? Contraband?"

Damned close. Considering. He picked up the pouch and moved to her side of the desk, leaning there, legs extended, ankles crossed. "Take a look." He offered her the bag, feeling the weight inside shift.

She retreated a trace. "I don't trust you, Wind Dancer."

Not since his suggestion they have a glassed-in, live rattlesnake display in the future lobby. "You will." His gaze seized hers and held. "Eventually." He placed the bag on her lap, wondering if the live warmth would seep through to give her a clue.

She hesitated for a moment, eyes boring into his with accusation, then loosened the string tie at the top and peered in, breathing, "Oh…" Thick, coffee-colored lashes lowered onto her cheeks for an instant before her eyes flew open. Had she been saving those glistening tears until just the right time to twist his gut? Cheeks reddening, she blinked frantically as her hands shot into the bag. She whispered, "Is it Mikela?"

"As nearly as I can tell." A little scruffy, and smelling feral from not being pampered. But that speck of black fur behind the right ear branded her.

In the silence, Cameron drew the long feline body from the bag and cradled it against her breasts, stroking pewter-blond fur. "Oh, God. It is. How in the world did you find her?" Her mouth against the cat's bony head muffled her words.

"How in the world" was a long story he hated recalling and refused to share. A deed made worth-while by her smile when she gazed up at him. A different kind of expression, as if he were a snake she had just watched shed its skin. Off balance with the look, uncertain where to file it, he straightened to full height and slipped his fingers into his back pockets. When she rose, they stood inches apart, so close he detected and wondered about a gathering of crooked, hairline scars high on her brow.

Still cradling Mikela, all that separated them, Cameron rested a hand on his forearm, as if testing the water. Her touch was soft, tentative, cool. The flowery perfume, less potent after a day's wear, threatened his senses. Mikela purred, soft and rhythmic, while outside a car turned the corner too quickly in the rainy night. Cameron's hand moved upward to his shoulder, pressure increasing for a moment before she stroked his jaw. The tender touch invaded his soul.

"How can I thank you, Lukas?" Her eyes had gone luminous, languid.

She was doing a damn good job with no direction. "By trusting me to want what's best for both of us." Believing he wasn't the enemy. Pulled by a power he neither wanted to nor could resist, he turned his mouth into her palm, tasting.

Salty. Musky. Delicious.

In that moment, he sensed barriers toppling. She wasn't Navajo. Being with her like this was asinine, nothing right about it. But when he opened his arms, she came into them without hesitance, the feline booty molded between their upper bodies. She lifted her face and he pressed his mouth to her cool forehead. *Salty. Silky.* He kissed her closed eyes, encouraged by her not-quite-suppressed moan. Neither did she resist when he took Mikela from her and lowered the cat to the floor. Instead, she tiptoed, her arms about his neck, thrusting her body against him. He sat on the desk, scooted back and drew her between his spread thighs, striving to not jump the gate by exposing his growing erection, when what he wanted more than his next breath was to be inside her. Old guilt, predictable as it was troublesome, reared its head. A kiss. That's all it would be. He wanted to taste this only-half-white woman, satisfy his curiosity.

Nothing more. Nothing less.

He damped her slender hips between his knees, reading her eyes, making sure she wanted to take that same step. Confident of the answer, he drew her against him. Beneath the sweater, her unrestrained breasts were full and firm against his chest, her back fragile within the circle of his arms. He ran his hands into her hair—as coarse and resilient as he had imagined—cupped her face and sampled the generous mouth that had once seemed damnably cold, and now tasted sweet. Woman mixed with chocolate and peanut butter. Warm and alluring.

She drew back, raising her palms to his chest, eyes cast down until she slipped her arms about his waist and opened to him, razing another barrier. Tilting back her head, he took her mouth, feasting, drawing them across that risky bridge at last.

A bridge on which he must journey back to reality at a saner, less gluttonous time.

seventeen

Cameron hugged Mikela close, hovering beneath the shelter of Lukas' jacket as he walked her back to the bungalow in the slow, steady rain. The comforting scent of wet denim and flannel failed to offset her confusion. Reliving his kisses, she tried to separate gratitude for Mikela from a purely carnal tug that, despite her wariness, had gathered consuming strength.

She wasn't sure she had ever been kissed like that, for the pure joy of it, instead of a prelude to sex. She had sensed, then witnessed his erection, but he had kept control. Beneath the wet clothing, his body had burned, his hair glistening and smelling of wood smoke, his mouth tasting virile, yet clean and moist.

Never had she wanted to kiss any man as much as she had Lukas, and once she had savored him, satisfying all curiosity, months of constraint shattered. She had wanted to climb onto the desk and coax him on top of her, just as she wanted to stop now, sink onto the soggy grass and feed the hunger.

The longing frightened her. There could be no more kisses. Eventually he would want sex without commitment; she would want that, too. Making love could bring nothing but hurt. She wasn't Navajo. He wasn't pliable. Their natures—her take-charge eagerness, his wait-and-see passivity—could never meld or complement. Other than a tugging erotic undercurrent, they were polar opposites.

Was she simply starved for sex, starved even for something as mundane as attention? Or because of the divorce, did she feel the need to prove her desirability? Either possibility scared her. Could she be drawn to Lukas because she felt that down deep they were somehow related in some askew fashion by dark-skinned heritage? Was she trying to carve him into a replacement? Force him to play a role?

At the door, her eyes sought the lock cast into shadow by their joined bodies. Slowly her fingers moved over the indention as if reading Braille. She hesitated to insert the key. Once the door opened she must face a decision. Give in to wanting him, or continue in limbo?

"Let me get it." One arm sheltered her with the jacket as he reached with the other. His braid looped a shoulder. She caught the scent of wet hair as his fingertips brushed the back of her hand, then circled to her palm, finding the key, inserting it in the lock.

Her skin warmed, heat shooting to her hairline. She twisted the key. The door swung open. "It sticks sometimes." Her voice gave away the lie, then betrayed her again. "Are you coming in?"

In the soft interior light settling on them, rain glistened on his face and splotched his shirt, his eyes revealing nothing. "Should I?"

Now she had to either back up or play down the invitation. "For a moment—to see how comfortable I am here."

As they squeezed through the door in unison, he eased the jacket from around her head and shoulders. Only after he'd closed the door did she allow Mikela to spring to the floor. The cat scampered beneath the bed as though she'd hidden there every day since Cameron moved in. Lukas leaned against the door, arms crossed, observing.

"You don't know how relieved I am to have her back." She offered a smile, which he returned.

"Do you have what you need for tonight?"

She supposed her confusion showed, for he added, "Food? Cat litter?" A brow cocked. "Cat nip?"

The last made her laugh. "Fresh out of cat nip, but I kept the rest on faith."

"Good move." His lazy and thorough gaze roamed, taking in the surroundings before returning to her. Holding eye contact, he crossed the room and sat on the side of a bed, his body denting the feather mattress she had added to inn stock. He bounced a bit as if testing the bed, lay back and propped on an elbow. Hugging a new, ruffled pillow, he cocked a brow. "Homey."

Her imagination noted, then settled into a heated, throbbing pang at the delta of her thighs. Frantically, she sought a way to not expose her need. Her longing.

"I'm settling in." She tried pushing her mind backward to focus anywhere but on the sensual undercurrent of his voice. She had bought the feather-mattress pad, a new comforter and the pillows at Nordstrom that afternoon, after enrolling in a fencing course at the community college. She had also stopped at the Chamber of Commerce for a membership application. Considering *El Niño's* promise of a long, cold, empty winter, she'd driven by a few churches, scouting the times for mass. If she was trapped here, she might as well *live* here.

Mired in soul searching, she'd even verified the nearest meeting place of Alcoholics Anonymous before recovering her lucidity, reminding herself the damage Phillip's accusations had leveled didn't make his claim true. She didn't need to fix what had never been broken.

She had Mikela back now, and as of the last few minutes, a marked life change she hadn't yet categorized to deal with. A change capable of provoking or soothing her discontent.

Lukas swiveled, reaching for the novel she'd left lying on the nightstand. His jeans strained across his haunches and thighs. She looked away, then back quickly, sick of trying to ignore his masculine beauty. A drum beat in her ear as he read the book's title and flipped pages before looking up.

"Last of the Mohicans?"

Her mind whirled, settled on, "Research." His eyes questioned, obligating her to add, "Sometimes I feel outnumbered."

"By Indians." Not a question. He fell quiet, eyes sullen, evidently struggling with his reaction. Decision made, a smile nudged the corner of his mouth, waved across his lips. He pitched the book and rose from the bed. "That was written long ago, about different people. Fiction. Try reading Sherman Alexie's *Reservation Blues*. Or go see *Smoke Signals.*"

Pulse rioting, she stood her ground as he came toward her. "Are you saying the hero in *Mohicans* didn't save the heroine's life?"

"Only that it would be impossible today, given the regressed state of the Indian." This smile proved reticent. "Go to the reservation if you're curious."

"I prefer fantasy."

He laughed. "Damn straight. It's easier. Before you got here, I counted on you being homely and wearing combat boots, not being beautiful and braless." His eyes rested gently on her breasts for a keen, telling instant. "Life is one big surprise, *enit?"* He grasped her chin and gently turned her face to catch the light. A thumb caressed the eyebrow in which a scar cowered. "Who did this to you?"

Her heart hammered, surging with memory. "The scars are misleading. It's not what you think."

"How can you know what I think? Tell me about this, little one." His fingertip traced the scars at her hairline.

She eased away, holding his gaze, heart hammering. "Why do you call me that?" At five eight, size ten, she could not be labeled petite. "It hardly fits."

"You are fragile, Yazhi. A long, slender reed threatened by the wind."

Her cheeks singed. So much for her bluff so much for getting the last word. "Poetic."

She turned away, a hand motion sweeping the space. She had rearranged the furniture to form angles and traffic patterns, softened the room with plants, pink bulbs in the pseudo-Old World lamps, a fringed throw over the one good chair. He eyed the watercolors she'd hung above the bed, examined her signature there without comment.

"Would you say I've changed things for the better, despite my fragility."

Ignoring her question, he said, "And the other side?" He nodded to the connecting door, then eyed the silver-framed photograph of Jarrid that graced the dresser. It loomed over other family members cased in smaller, hardwood frames. "Have you changed your mind about Jarrid coming here?"

"I'm not privileged to change my mind." The words erupted, quick and heated. She attempted a softer, less revealing tone. "Phillip—my ex-husband—has custody of Jarrid. I've asked—I'm hoping he'll be allowed to visit over Thanksgiving." She had waited two days for Phillip's answer, growing less confident as time wasted.

Lukas leaned against the dresser, hands behind him, ankles crossed, settling in like an examiner. "How did he get custody?"

Nausea gathered at the back of her throat as images replayed behind her eyes. The day the judge had ruled, she had fought like a tiger, climbing past her defense team, and Phillip's, to claw his face, help-lessly giving credence to claims of incompetence and alcoholism, saddling her with a contempt of court citation. "I'm sorry Lukas, but that's none—"

"What kind of man would take away a woman's child?" Contradicting the question, his eyes held blatant, tactless curiosity for what she had done to warrant the separation. Or did she imagine that, negating any concern than his tone indicated?

"I had a situation to work out." Circumstances forced on her through deceit and false witness. She massaged, then gripped, her upper arms, nails biting through the sweater. "Phillip is a politician, very good at what he does. His life centers on serving the people who elect him, but he gets caught up in causes. He throws away close relationships to serve ideals."

His eyes quickened with an empathy she couldn't quite place. But then a multi-faceted expression played on his face. Pain? Regret? A migraine-sized frown settled there. Somehow, she had struck close to home. But how when she had spoken of a virtual stranger? And what had happened to her reluctance to share her past?

"But he doesn't discard all close relationships. He holds on to your son," he reminded, then jolted her with, "Who is Lee Tutuila?"

Her hands moved to her head, fingertips pressing her temples, eyes closing to shut out his face and the sudden, debilitating pain. She heard him move. His hands closed around her wrists, lowering her hands with a gentle tug. She opened her eyes and stared into his—dark, mired in fathomless depth. Unsatisfied.

She felt queasy. Her head throbbed. "How do you know about Lee?"

"The night you moved in here I saw the picture of the two of you Remember? The one missing from the dresser now." He waited. "None of my business. *Enit?*"

She shook her head, even as she heard herself confessing, "Lee is Jarrid's father. No one knows that but Phillip and me."

A dark, heavy brow shot upward. "And Lee, I hope."

"He's dead." War rockets imploded behind her open eyes, fireworks gone awry, but gradually soothing darkness crept in. Cool, absolving relief. "He died before he ever saw Jarrid. I can't tell you anymore, Lukas. A kiss doesn't give you the right to ask." *Nor me an obligation to share.* She waited to see if he'd accept her refusal.

He smiled. "Maybe not, but it made me want to know more. You'll tell me when the time is right."

When they stood at the door, Mikela slipped from beneath the bed to rub against Lukas' leg. Buffing her head against the instep of his boot, she purred concern for his leaving. He picked her up and ran his bronzed fingers through her fur. "With the inn closed down, you are alone here, Yazhi. Are you afraid?"

"I have Mikela back now. Security patrols at midnight, and just before dawn." Of course he knew the schedule, had arranged it. But revealing to him her unrest, the sleepless nights when she lay awake listening to every sound, would admit yet another weakness.

"Are you lonely?"

Silently, she watched the answer to his question swim in his all-seeing eyes.

He glanced at his watch, a man with a mission, one keeping her from that decision she had feared making. "I'm at Dos Gringos every night now. If you feel like being cheated by the bartender—"

"Why?"

He shrugged. "You gave me a reputation to live up to."

So he's still not forgiven me for that, and probably won't. "I mean why are you working there? When we closed the inn, I assumed you'd spend evenings—"

His eyes flashed amused interest, stopping her cold. "Doing what?"

"Driving to the reservation." *Or meeting someone halfway there.*

"To assume, Yazhi, is to make an ass of you and of me." Sparing a smile that deprecated the maxim, he placed Mikela on the floor.

"Apparently you haven't abandoned your bartending mission," she commented. "You've only moved it to Dos Gringos." Whatever the calling embodied.

A hand rose to stroke her cheek, and her heart leapt. His eyes held proof of his own struggle to share or remain secretive, before the caress died, and his hand lowered to the doorknob. "If you need me, you know where I'll be."

He opened the door and slipped into the rain.

వ

Wrapped in the luxurious feathers, unfulfilled desires churning within, she examined what had passed between them. Somehow, faced with Lukas' apparent caring, in revealing what little she had about Lee she had felt the first inkling of wounds beginning to scab over.

Yet, she knew if she fired comparable questions at him, she would receive even fewer answers than she'd given him. Vague, philosophic replies at best.

Lukas Wind Dancer was as paradoxical as a locked door bearing an enter sign. A door guarding useless treasure. She *needed* him like she needed another bad memory. Yet while his presence comforted her and stirred her blood to boiling, it brought an ache to the apex of her thighs and the secret cove of her soul. An ache that made her aware of his strength, though she suspected much of the strength he emanated was little more than intractability. Stubbornness. Or had she read that theory somewhere and leveled onto him some ethnic cliché?

Still, he exuded strength in his convictions. She longed to burrow into that power, escape the constant urge to prove her own ability to him and the world. But, again, even their convictions were polarized; she could no more afford to relinquish or adjust hers than he could. His kisses were favors he chose to dole out en route to an additional mission. Chuey had warned her, and with good reason.

Lukas would marry within his tribe, strengthen it, and serve his people.

When she completed her duty at the urn, with Hayden's help, she would reclaim Jarrid. In Samoa, they would seal their heritage and begin a new life.

Only hurt can come from getting involved with— The ringing phone shattered her thoughts. The new comforter rustled around her as she reached to answer, her mind a crazed mixture of hope and dread.

"Did I wake you?" As always, the voice was detached, a business air better suited to midmorning, and tinged with a trace of cultured French accent.

"I've been waiting to hear from you."

"I had to give it some thought." A promising or damning statement.

"Why? I made a simple request. I've talked with Jarrid and he wants to—" *No. We've been over that. Of course Jarrid has made his wishes clear to Phillip.* "Why are you dramatizing this?"

A moment of lethal silence and then, "Perhaps because I'm remembering the little hospital drama where you were the star. Or the one in the court-room."

All during a campaign. "I refuse to rehash that. There's no comparison." She had begun to tremble with pain. "It's Thanksgiving. A perfect time for a visit."

"We don't celebrate Thanksgiving, Jarrid and I." She heard the click of his Dunhill lighter, the intake of smoke, activating an indelible scene on her mind. "Neither do you, Cameron, unless you've converted to expatriate status."

"I mean it's perfect, Phillip, because construction will be shut down for four days. I'll have time on my hands—" She strove for the proper plea, one to grant him less pleasure. "The Flagstaff ski slopes will be open. We've had so damn much rain that the snow in the mountains—"

Why would he care about the rain? Care for how it was threatening her every goal? He'd see her utterance as whining. Hear it as fearful dread of spending time alone, as needing a crutch to fend off the urge to drink. Like waking from a bad dream, she had to remind herself that his inferences were a lie, a counterfeit malady with which he'd infected her.

In the next desperate breath, she heard herself touting the desert she had hated three months ago. "This is magnificent country. We'll take a Safari Tour. They're well organized and safe. And I can get tickets for the Coyotes—the Phoenix hockey team." More dreaded silence. "Let him come, Phillip. I miss him desperately, if that's what you want to hear." *He's mine, part of me. I long for him.* "He misses me. I haven't asked you before, but I have the right—"

"A right you relinquished for your lover."

Her breath snagged.

"I've decided it's not wise, darling," he said patiently, contradicting his earlier barb. "Besides, he's too young to travel alone."

Consumed by mind-miring disappointment, she cut to the bottom line. "Then I'll come there. He can stay with me at Hayden's. You can check on him every day. Every hour." She sucked in breath, waiting. *Damn you, Phillip.*

"Come if you like, but I'm afraid Jarrid won't be here." Sudden decision echoed through the wire. "I'm taking him to…St. Moritz. If he's to ski, then he should have proper surroundings. I'm certain the rest of the family would delight in seeing you, however."

"How can you do this? How can you keep my child from *me?*"

"As I recall, darling, your judge's name was Forsythe. Not Vickers. Perhaps you would prefer to argue your case with *him*. Again."

"Rest assured I plan to, but that does nothing for the Thanksgiving break."

"I fail to understand your obsession with an American holiday, Cameron." In the background she heard voices. The housekeeper, the cook. Then Jarrid. "I must run, darling. It's far past the boy's bedtime. Good-bye, for now."

"Wait! Let me talk to him." In her mind she saw the phone being lowered. "Phillip, I want to explain to him—" The line buzzed in her ear.

She sank back into the covers, cradling the phone against a new down pillow, eyes clenched, head throbbing. Again her mind whirled through the approaching holiday. She searched for schedules and commitments, finding them for others, none for herself. The inn would be cold, empty, deserted, devoid of even the constant ripping and tearing of the crew. Devoid of faces, bodies, demeanors and intents she'd come to anticipate, to reluctantly revere. She reached for the phone and dialed.

"Phillip Vickers here."

"I'll go to Europe. When you know your dates and accommodations, call me, and I'll meet *you* there." Of course he'd be at the palatial Chastain Hotel on the slopes, the one he favored above all. "Jarrid and I will be under your eye every moment."

"You don't understand." Indulgence colored his Tone. "I've been too busy lately, organizing the new campaign. I'm taking him on holiday in order to spend time with him. Your presence would interfere."

"We'll spend time together—the three of us. He'll like that. It will feel like family to—"

"Cameron, you give me no choice. I've...met someone. She's Swiss. I'll be taking this opportunity to allow the two of them to become acquainted. Your being there wouldn't do." He paused. "I hope this doesn't cause you too much pain."

"What about Jarrid, Phillip? What about his pain?"

"Jarrid is a veteran of hurt, darling. A survivor. He was well sired."

She placed the phone in the cradle, went into the bathroom, rummaged the medicine chest and swallowed the pills. Then she wrapped the new comforter around her and left the bungalow for the cold starry desert. Following a sleepless night on a chaise beside the icy pool, for the first time in months, she walked to mass in the rainy dawn.

God help her. For now, Phillip had the upper hand.

❧

Lukas drew a pillow over his head, shutting out the hum of the overhead fan but failing to close out the ancient memories and new images that had kept him sleepless. The memory was old trash that coiled his gut. Still, he probed it like a tongue poking at a sore tooth, because each time he did, his recall slid from there into kissing Cameron Vickers...or Camellia Chastain, maybe.

Camellia: An East Asian bloom with shiny leaves and showy flowers.

He had looked it up in the dictionary. For some reason, Camellia had been neglected—no sun, no water—evolving to Cameron, the parched rendition he'd taken into his arms. Beneath his mouth, she had sprung to life. He still tasted her, felt the pliancy the searing warmth, smelled her luscious scent.

Memory bearing Suzanne's face threatened. He crammed it down in favor of conjured images of having the half-Anglo woman beneath him, basking in her gentleness while bringing her strength to submission. In turn, he wiped out that picture, ripped away the pillow and sat up in bed, his sex heavy with greed.

He sensed her being at odds with a culture she'd been thrust into, but she would return to it to claim her child. And even if not, the *Diné* would never sanction a union between them. His council position offered the opportunity to further the good of the people, to purify, not diversify, his race. Making love to this woman would invite needless pain, a truth he must not forget. Or ignore. Only by keeping his distance could he maintain rigid control over his lust.

He owed that to her, to her son, and to his pure blood sons yet to be conceived.

eighteen

Cameron faced Yolanda across her desk, intrigued by how the soft winter sun shafting through the tiny window showcased her youthful beauty. The same mini-skirt Yolanda had favored—or a black one, anyway—struck mid thigh, but today black fishnet tights covered her long, muscular legs. Cameron tried not to stare at the extremely high and clunky shoes she wore, all the while wondering how the girl kept from tumbling sideways when she walked. Body piercing had apparently come into her favor since the inn had closed. A row of glittering studs fanned up the rim of one ear. A diminutive. silver crucifix graced an eyebrow.

Unemployed still, Yolanda was there to request a job reference, but was, for the moment, caught up in Cameron's spiky hairstyle. "That's just short of radical." She grinned at her own joke. "You don't look like an island princess anymore. You know—Hawaiian. Or Tahitian, or whatever."

Cam's heart caught in a regretful little tremor. "Samoan."

Yolanda shrugged. "Well, whatever. It's radical, and I like it."

Cameron tried returning to the subject. "I hoped you might go back to school when the inn closed."

"No chance. I need bucks. I've got to move, and the money I'd been saving for an apartment deposit went for new clothes for job interviews." She kicked her foot forward, giving Cameron an unwelcome view of upper thigh and pink panties. "These alone—" She motioned at her shoes. "—took most of my stash."

Cameron nodded without pointing out the unsuitability of the shoes for work.

Hands on the arms of the chair, Yolanda leaned forward. "I have to move, Cameron—Miz Vickers. I have a little sister—fourteen—and we live with my brother. His wife works nights so…It's a little house. Over on Indian School. My sister and I share a room, and Dwaine and Carol—that's my brother and his wife—sleep together, and that's it. No more beds." She paused, sucking in breath, fingers whitening on the chair arms. "But Eddie—my other brother—he's younger than me, but older than Polly—keeps moving in and out. The bed in our room—mine and Polly's—gets crowded, if you know what I mean."

Cam's stomach lurched. She felt herself nod without true knowledge.

"I need to get Polly her own place. Well, with me, I mean. I've still got that little telemarketing job at Desert Cellular, but I don't get to work that much."

"Have you filed for unemployment compensation?"

"Yeah—yes, ma'am. I got one check. When the next one came in, Eddie got to the mail before me. It went for drugs—pot, anyway."

So horrific was the tale, so harried the delivery, Cameron began to wonder if she were being bamboozled. "You don't have to accept that. Have you spoken to…Dwaine?" Yolanda nodded. "…about this?"

Again she nodded, sucking her bottom lip between her teeth. "They're kind of a team. Even if Eddie is the baby brother, he's bigger than Dwaine, and Dwaine sucks up. You know, like, spoils him. Besides, since I was part time here, too, the unemployment checks are pretty puny." She sat back and re-crossed her legs in the opposite direction. "I thought maybe Chuey would help us out—"

"Chuey Run Amok?" A shiver of concern inched along her spine.

Yolanda smiled. "Is there another Chuey? We've been…dating. Kind of on the quiet, so if you won't say anything…anyway, I thought we might get a place together. He's got the funds, gets them from Lukas. School tuition and walking around money. But Lukas keeps a tight rein. He's not happy about us—me 'n Chuey, I mean. Chuey'd get his butt kicked if he left the dorm."

"Do you really think Lukas has that much control?"

"Like, duh…for sure, and I guess he thinks *I'll* screw up his little half-brave." She laughed, the sound dying short of registering in her eyes. "And since

Chuey's so hot to go to med school…He's weird, sort of. Lukas, I mean."

"Oh?" Cameron hiked an inviting brow, anxiety trickling to the forefront.

"Did you know he's a beam walker?" Judging by her rapt expression, the girl was spellbound by Lukas Wind Dancer.

"I'm not sure what—"

"Guys who work high up in big buildings. Only Navajos can do it, according to Chuey. Some kind of mystic gift." She wiggled her hand in the air, humming, "Doo doo doo doo. Doo doo doo doo," the *Twilight Zone* theme of a different era, then took a deep breath. "And he says Lukas did it drunk, or hung over anyway. Like a death wish kind of thing, you know?" Her brows arched. "Weird."

Cameron did a quick inventory of the Phoenix skyline, entertaining images of Lukas' purported balancing act. "No, I didn't know that, but I'm…impressed…that he has the gift." *Not the insanity to do it.*

"And he's saving that gorgeous body for Pocahontas or somebody." She shrugged, her ice-blue gaze drilling Cameron. "Too bad, 'cause I'll bet he's hung." She grinned conspiratorially. "Don't you?"

Cameron only knew that every time she even recalled Lukas' kiss, her heart raced, her nipples tightened, and her body stirred restlessly in her lower regions. Feeling she was being baited now, she withheld comment on his anatomy.

"Talk about a racist. What a waste that whites aren't good enough—" She seemed to be struck by a revelation. "I'll bet it has something to do with him being on the tribal council. That's a big deal to them, you know. Kind of like our city council, I guess. Whatever…"

Despite her reluctance, Cameron took the bait. "What do whites have to do with Lukas sitting on the tribal council?"

"Oh…Chuey says if he—Lukas—-marries a white woman he can still live on the reservation, but he can't be on the council. And to him the council rocks. Indians are weird, but they're okay, I guess. Men, I mean. Chuey sure is." She took a breath. "And racist or whatever, Lukas probably likes you all right, 'cause all dark-skinned people were Asians, way back somewhere. I learned that in school."

Cameron clasped her hands in her lap, hoping to conceal their trembling. "Racist is a strong word, Yolanda. And Lukas is entitled to his convictions."

"Yeah, and he knows everything. Like might makes right, you know?"

She knew, but it failed to irritate so much, as of late. She also suspected Lukas' actions toward his nephew were grounded in concern, not power.

"He spent years in Chicago, Chuey says going to school and whoring around. That's where he walked the beams. He's connected there, too. Big time. I think that's got a lot to do with his total bossiness."

"Connected?" Yolanda nodded and Cameron prompted, "How?" She knew of only one meaning for the term. It fit Lukas about as well as three-legged pants.

"You'd better ask Chuey. I probably wasn't supposed to mention it."

"I hardly think he's connected in the sense you mean." When the girl shrugged, far from listlessly, Cameron urged, "But you're convinced he doesn't approve of the relationship?" A troublesome sense stirred in the back of her mind, a feeling close to self-protection.

"For sure. It's a Romeo and Juliet thing. Chuey's sweet, fun, if you know what I mean. I like him, but my brothers don't care that he's gonna be something—a doctor. He's Indian, so they hate him. So…" She shrugged.

Voluntarily, Cam's hand raised, as if to brush the image of Lee Tutuila, the similarity in the situation—never for one moment could she have considered introducing him to her family—from behind her eyes. A cold, jagged rock settled in her stomach. She tried to ignore the flicker of apprehension coursing through her. "And how does Chuey feel?"

"Oh, you know. He won't cross his uncle. I don't cross Eddie and Dwaine."

Still, they were not deterred from *dating*. A quick and disturbing thought. "How did he accept you asking for help?"

"Us moving in, you mean?" She smiled. "He's a real healthy boy. He'd like going to sleep and waking up to the built-in action. All I'd have to do is hold out on sex for a while—" She studied her stubby, black-coated nails, shrugging. "You know."

Yolanda was reading beautiful and randy Chuey like a book, or believed she could. In the home environment she'd described, she had perfected manipulation.

"You won't say anything about this? To Lukas, I mean?" the girl urged.

"Your indiscretion is safe with me."

Yolanda stared "Ma'am?"

Apology tinged her sheepish smile.

"I won't mention it." Cameron swiveled in her chair toward the computer, preparing to write the needed letter, then looked back over her shoulder. Renderings of Polly in a crowded bed—if she even existed—filled her reluctant imagination. "How much would you need for an apartment deposit?"

Yolanda chewed her bottom lip. "About five hundred if I get a cheap place."

"Would you accept a loan? From me?"

"You'd do that?"

Easily able to see the girl's mind whirling, Cameron nodded.

Yolanda shrugged. "That'd be cool." A moment ticked by. "Thanks."

Cameron wrote a check, then endeavored to compose a fail-safe referral letter. Afterward, she stood in the undersized, shoulder-high window watching Yolanda leave the inn, her steps more rushed than jaunty. She got into an old model convertible with a tattered top and, like Chuey, deposited a bit of rubber on the drive when she pulled into traffic. The lingering scent of her tangy cologne accompanied the scene replaying in Cameron's mind.

Exactly how had she phrased the tale? Cameron had gotten the impression that *Polly's* bed was crowded, Yolanda's main source of concern. Did that mean unopposed intimacy was taking place between Yolanda and Eddie? Or had Yolanda assumed her objections went without stating? Either way, given the current climate of social disease, how did that affect Chuey? Cameron turned toward the phone. She had promised not to tell only Lukas.

She crossed to the desk, dialed information and asked for Children's Services.

nineteen

Cameron stood gazing into the window of a Fifth Street gallery, listening to live music in the distance. She classified the tune as a rowdy Mexican polka. As though manipulated by marionette cords, she turned and began walking toward the sound in the balmy night. Laughter and animated, open-air conversation drowned out her footsteps as she rounded the corner onto Craftsman Boulevard.

She paused in the shadow of a paloverde tree, transfixed by patio lanterns beckoning mid-block. Their red-amber glow mimicked an earlier sunset that had been magnificent enough to roust her from the bungalow, out to a movie, and later onto the tourist-filled streets. A crowd a bit larger than the one she'd seen while driving past last night, and the night before, filled Dos Gringos' patio.

Lukas was there, working. She had to talk to him. It might as well be now.

For the first time in weeks, she fought desire for a cigarette. The back of her throat felt scratchy and dry. She smoothed the creases in her linen slacks, draped her sweater over her shoulders, knotted the arms at her breasts. She felt in her pocket for the lipstick and fold of bills she'd placed there. Just in case she mustered the nerve to go through with this.

Waiting on the edge of the crowd, she watched the bar until the perch she favored became available. When she slipped onto the end stool, she drew an interested glance from the man next to her. The aroma from the nachos in front of him lit a gentle fire in her empty belly.

She kept her eyes on Lukas. His raven hair, bound at his nape with rawhide, swayed between his shoulder blades. A black T-shirt strained across his upper back as he worked, simultaneously filling two frosted mugs with beer. Graceful as a juggler, he grasped the mug handles in one hand, tossing the empty bottles into a receptacle a few feet away with the other. When he turned toward his patrons, he caught her in a sweeping solicitous glance. His dark head gave a jerk, his lean body quickened, shooting a frisson of satisfaction up her spine.

He's surprised. Pleasantly so.

She relived the loneliness of the past two evenings when she'd driven by without stopping and then returned to the desolate inn, the empty bungalow.

"What can I get you?" He maintained the distance, hiking his chin, voice raised over the spirited din. His casual tone denied any of the emotions she'd detected earlier.

"Margarita." She raised her voice in turn. "Frozen. No salt."

She watched his efficacious movements. Measuring, adding ice, stabbing the blender switch. As the machine whirred, her mind's eye replayed the way the muscles in his forearm had contracted when he'd reached for glasses on a high shelf. Precise movements, gentle and graceful for a man of his stature and strength. As gentle as his arms had been when he held her, as purposeful and thorough as his mouth on hers. A helpless, hopeless, irrepressible sensation, a quiver evolving to a spasm settled in that no longer deniable secret center of her groin.

He placed the sweaty, stemmed glass before her, draping a towel over his shoulder, then folding his arms. The V-neck of his shirt revealed the silver cross hanging just below the pulsing hollow in his throat. "No salt," he murmured.

She raised the drink and sipped, her eyes holding his across the glass rim. She took a second sip. "No tequila either."

"I warned you." He awarded her his *gotcha* smile.

"You warned me. You just didn't scare me away."

"No?" His smile died, his mouth tightening a fraction.

She twirled the glass, ran her finger around the rim, lifted and sat it down. "I couldn't sleep, so I went to a movie and did some window shopping. I heard the music."

"Loneliness is not a crime, Yazhi," he said softly. He switched the towel to the other shoulder, refolded his arms and widened his stance.

"I haven't seen you for…a few days. At the inn."

"I was there 'Making hay while the sun is shining,' as Apenimon says." He took a small, crooked cigar from his back pocket, stuck it in his mouth and talked around it. "Thanksgiving is coming. We'll have no crew then. The roof is getting heavy from too much rain. We spent two days siphoning off water."

"I knew you were there, but I thought you'd come into the office. I wanted—needed to talk to you."

"You have my cell number. Call when you want me."

So he *had* been avoiding her. "Fine."

"Talk to me now, if that's why you came. To talk business."

She glanced around. "It's noisy. And you're busy."

He checked the turquoise studded watch on his wrist. "We close in an hour. I'll walk you back."

"I'd like that."

He seemed to examine her declaration, eyes clouding as though reading a letter filled with bad news. Evading his eyes, she feigned interest in the late night revelers. He moved away to deal with the clientele She spent the time till closing captivated by his affable manner that so contrasted his sober nature at the inn. But for her, his eyes were so dark and soulful, his gaze so piercing, that she found it unnerving to glance up and find him watching her in turn.

☙

Their footsteps echoed as they strolled the streets in the tranquil night, his boot heels soft and solid against the sidewalk, the wooden heels of her sandals clacking like lazy castanets. They rounded the corner on Stetson, bringing the Waterfront Project into view. Giant earth movers hulked like sleeping predators on the sandy soil. Into the memory-laden silence, she interjected, "We've made this walk before."

"Maybe we'll make it many times."

Him, perhaps, unless his marriage altered his life drastically, as Chuey predicted. But when her time here ended, she never intended to stroll these streets again. "I saw you working in the lobby. Laying out a pattern of some kind on the floor." When he nodded, she challenged, "It's not that damn snake display, is it?"

"No snakes." They waited out a passing car, then stepped off a curb into the street. His splayed fingers touched and lingered an instant at the small of her back, leaving a cold void when he took his hand away. "I'm ready to dig the fire pit."

The announcement nettled. She searched for a congenial reply, but tact went down in defeat. "I don't want a fire pit. You know that."

"It's authentic design."

Déjà vu rankled. "We're not talking Fountain Head. It's a damn hotel. A commercial endeavor. Nothing else."

"You'll like it. Trust me." He smiled with further grating tolerance.

"That's not the point. We had an agreement when you signed the contract."

"I doubt you'll fire me now over a hole of fire in the floor."

She doubted she would try firing him again if he torched the whole damn place. "That's not the point."

"What is?" He stopped walking. Hands on her shoulders, he turned her.

"I badly wanted a Polynesian hotel, Lukas. You manipulated me out of that. A damn fire pit is flaunting your victory in my face." The words floated away, the night air providing a cool, crisp veil of pettiness.

"When you see how it mesmerizes your guests you'll forget your loss." His smile made her feel like the spoiled child she'd never had the luxury of being.

She shrugged out of his grasp and began walking. The inn came into sight, dark and uninviting, shrouded by the copse of palms hovering at the entry. "I won't see the guests fall under your spell. I'm not staying once the refurbishing is done."

He stiffened as if probed by an ice pick. "If you're not staying, then agreements must mean as little to you as you claim ours did to me."

How did he know she had originally agreed to stay, once the inn was open again? Agreed to stabilize it before hiring new management? Did he also know she'd been agonizing over a way to convince Hayden to release her from that part of their pact? After the last phone conversation with Phillip, sensing his cold, hard cunning, she couldn't risk the odds of him losing the next election. He'd have nothing to keep him in Canada, every reason to run from defeat, taking Jarrid with him. But Lukas couldn't know that. And if he did, it could neither better nor worsen her impasse.

They entered the drive, which shone like molten tar in the spotlight mounted to the inn's roof. Lukas veered in the direction of the bungalow, but she took the path to the pool, and he fell in step. She sat on a chaise, unknotted the sweater, slipped it on, and buttoned it. Then she reclined against the chaise back, curling her legs to free a space in unvoiced invitation. He paced to the edge of the pool, fingertips shoved in his back pockets, staring down, his powerful form limned by the moon glazing the cloudy desert sky. She knew that could she see his face, he'd be brooding. He belonged miles from here, at the edge of a mountain lake, in the company of a woman suited to him.

He squatted suddenly, dipped his hand in the water, then shook it, and wiped it on his jeans. "Too cold to swim."

"It's too costly to heat when I'm the only one using it."

He swiveled in his crouching position. "You'll heat it for Jarrid, though."

She eased the sweater up around her throat. "He's not coming." She sensed his quick reaction, readable for once. His pity made her throat seize.

"Why the hell not? It's Thanksgiving."

"We don't celebrate Thanksgiving." She searched desperately for a way to escape revealing the extent of her pain. "From what I've read and seen, neither should you."

"I shouldn't, and I don't. I'll use the four days to complete a set of drawings I've promised." He rose, crossing to sit on the end of the chaise. His hand rested lightly on her calf. "I'm sorry about your son, Yazhi."

She nodded, tearing as her teeth damped the inside of her lower lip.

"Give it up." His hand moved to her ankle, resting lightly on bared skin. "You said it yourself. It's a damn hotel, a damn career. What is that, compared to your son? Go home."

"I can't. I never wanted this kind of career. I wanted to be an artist, but I'm here, and it's all part of a master plan. If I fail—"

In a distant ocotillo bush a cricket celebrated. The security van's lights flashed across the drive, signifying midnight. Lukas waited, his hand searing her flesh.

She grappled for a way to make him understand, enlist his valid efforts. "I'm concerned, Lukas, about our schedule. I have been all along, as you know."

"This is what you wanted to talk to me about." She nodded. "I have my own concerns, Yazhi, and my own deal with your uncle. But I can't stop the rain. The best we can do is—"

"Make hay when the sun shines." For the first time she sensed mutual aim, hope of true partnership. She sat up, breaking away from his touch. Drawing her knees up to her chin, she wrapped her shins with her arms. "Tell me about your deal with Hayden."

"It involves a bonus for bringing the project in under budget. I have the money earmarked." He looked perplexed, a rarity. "I know rain is a gift of Mother Earth, but every time she gets generous, it screws up my chances a little bit more."

She stared at the cold water, his talk of finances allowing her to realize she'd been wise to sacrifice her daily swim and forgo the exorbitant expense of heating the pool.

"Whether my deal with Hayden Chastain pans out or not," he added, "the inn won't suffer, but my people will."

He had earmarked his life for his people, as well as any excess money from the inn. Her scalp tightened with the sensation of coming in second. "*My* concerns affect the rest of my life."

"Mine, too, since the *Diné* are my life. Now," he added softy, and then, "but you go first, little one."

An open palm gestured invitation to air her concerns so they might be pitted against an ever-growing list of his missions. Her anxiety clashed head-on with untenable desire for a man promised to a nation.

She swung her feet around and tried to stand. "Compared to your lofty goals—"

His hand, a bronze band clasping her wrist, stopped her. "I have two aspirations. Pride in my work and satisfaction in serving my people. That may sound loftyto you. To me it's no more than hard work and staying focused."

"And a mission," she reminded, anticipation turning her words to a whisper.

"To tell a secret can dispel its power." A jaw muscle knotted over clenched teeth. His penetrating gaze measured her trustworthiness, and then turned acquiescent. "Because my father was drunk, that snake bite killed him. He was barely older than I am now."

She understood his reluctance. She'd been reading, studying. Naming the dead man as his father, lamenting his passing, defied Navajo tradition.

"My sister…Chuey's mother…was a drunk. Because of that, I have a niece who is a vegetable. My mother lives with the consequences beneath her roof every day. My sister died drunk delivering a white man's baby. Chuey. My mother grieves for him. I stalk him like a starving wolf watching a fat rabbit, looking for signs he will follow his mother's path." Momentarily, he fell quiet. "Sometimes what is closest to me is hardest to see."

She waited, attempting to form a conclusion from the pictures he painted.

"In the bar here, and now at Dos Gringos, I can spot firsthand who is drinking too much, who might get behind the wheel of a car, wipe out a life and change many others in the space of a minute." His mouth turned grim, jaw clenched. "Behind a bar, I have the power to say no."

From the beginning her imagination for his so-called *mission* had known no limits. Now the weight of discovery settled like boulders. "You hate alcoholics."

"Alcoholism, not alcoholics," he said quietly.

Hate the sin, love the sinner.

"I could have worked any place when Salt River closed. I picked Dos Gringos because sometimes a brother who's just cashed his paycheck wanders in off the street. If he's out of line, I confront him. If the problem warrants, I urge him to get counseling, or counsel him myself if he refuses. It's that simple, Yazhi."

"It's far from simple." She settled back, her head against the raised chaise, eyes closed. Memory tumbled backward, then catapulted forward. "And apparently you've cast me in the role of the needy, from that very first day to the drink you made me tonight."

"Habits," he said softly, dismissively. "Your turn, little one. You said you need to talk to me. Talk."

Wanting to believe his explanation, she plunged in. "We have to push the crew harder. I can no longer afford the time I allotted for myself here. The delays are stretching it out even more."

"Go home. With the inn closed, what's the point of staying? You can't scare back the rain. I was hired to oversee construction. I'll do that if you're here or not."

"I can't go home. I'm serving penance. I'm on trial." She avoided his eyes, their unasked questions. "We either have to push this crew harder or hire more men. We can run a twenty-four hour shift. When it doesn't rain, the day crew can work outside, continuing to replace the roof, maybe." They were stranded midstream, the half-replaced roof covered with tarps, awaiting enough dry days in a row to continue. "A night crew can work inside where it's lighted."

"Eventually the electricity has to be turned off so the wiring can be replaced," he reminded her, then drove home a headier point. "If I hire a night crew, my deal with your uncle is dead. That bonus money is promised."

That word again.

"Then push this crew harder. Tell them they can't take Thanksgiving off." She combed her hair with her fingers. "Why in hell would they want to celebrate having their country ripped away from them, being doled out Godforsaken land, having their children in schools hundreds of miles away—"

His laugh quashed her diatribe. "You've been to the library, I see."

"Work with me, Lukas. That's all I'm asking. I have to get back to Jarrid."

"Serving penance for what? What kind of trial?"

Had he even heard her petition? "What does it matter? I respect your reasoning. Do the same for me." She sensed him waiting her out. "Jarrid was taken away from me because…I had an accident. It was raining. I was driving and—" She froze, sorting through memory, selecting what she felt obligated to reveal. "Two people were killed. One of them was a child."

Her throat seized, tears scalding at the brink of her lashes. She swallowed once, then doubly hard when he took her hand, his touch gentle, as if he held an injured bird. "Phillip and I—We were having problems. He was in the middle of a campaign. My accident, the unfavorable publicity, was like waving a red flag in his face. He used it to get Jarrid away from me."

"What judge would take a child from his mother because she screwed up a political campaign?" His eyes demanded more.

A deluded judge. "That doesn't matter now. I came out the culprit. All my life I've been trying to prove myself to my family, to earn their respect. They all sided with Phillip. Even Hayden, and he's the one with all the power." Searching his face, finding no clue, she plunged on. "What matters is Hayden's given me another chance. if I complete this job—if I prove I can take care of myself and Jarrid—he'll help me get him back from Phillip. Chastain Properties has a hotel in Samoa. My grandfather built it before I was born. Hayden will deed that hotel to me, and I'll be free of my family."

"Your beach hotel at last, huh, Yazhi?" His tender smile made her ache.

"I know you've thought all along I was obsessed. I am, but with reason. They tell me—My father was Samoan."

Abrupt cognition lit his eyes. She had revealed too much.

"Let's hear about that, little one."

"Why? It has nothing to do with what I need from you."

"I'll let you know if I believe that after you tell me about your father."

Should I tell him I've never met the man, never seen him? That I don't know his name or anything about him, other than he could be any one of a pack of Samoan beach boys my white mother lay with in her seventeenth summer, assuring I'd forever be more tolerated than accepted by my pompous family. Would Lukas care that after a wasted trip to the island to search for a man even my mother can't identify, I made the decision to find a new life.

"I'm taking Jarrid to Samoa to live, and to find our heritage. That's all you need to know."

"Except for why you have to prove you can take care of yourself."

"Damn, Lukas. Do you want blood?" With her arms she formed an X across her chest, hands tucked into her armpits, shivering suddenly. Prompted by his silence she began again. "When the police came to the crash sight, they found an open bottle."

"Were you drunk?" His tone was too gentle for the question.

Somehow she held his gaze. "According to Phillip, I'm guilty. So you were right to water down my drinks. One of the people killed was in my car. A man." Hot tears spilled over, distorting his face.

He looked as if he'd just drawn an ace. "The dead man was Lee Tutuila."

"Yes."

twenty

Lukas withheld the censure her haunted eyes sought. Who was he to pass judgment? Unlike him, she had kept her child, at least for a while. She was fighting like hell to get back to him, while seed for his own sons waited to swell the belly of an unknown woman. No matter how unorthodox Cameron's methods, or why Lee Tutuila had been with her that night, she had suffered. She would find no condemnation in him. Beyond satisfaction for the slow unraveling of the mystery, he felt no more than sorrow for her grief.

He stood, drawing her up and against him. She was thin again, even more so than when he'd kissed her a week before, as though her desire to leave him and this place was consuming flesh and bone. He buried his hand in her unruly hair and pressed her cheek against his chest. The contact traveled downward, curling in his gut, then lowered, tightening, thickening. His heart began pulsing in his loins. "It's hard to think of this place without you, little one."

She tilted her head back, her eyes holding defiance and a gentler hint of pain. With a soft rush of resolve, she said, "You have your own plans, Lukas. There's no room in them for me."

Knowing she might want there to be room left him feeling clubbed in the middle with a two-by-four. "How do you know that, *asdzani?*"

"Chuey told me. He's very protective." In the scarce light, her gaze skittered away. "*Promised,* is how he referred to your status."

"I didn't realize you and Run Amok were that well acquainted." His hairline tightened, began to tingle.

"Protective of you," she reiterated in a resigned, gut-gnawing tone. "But he's clever enough to pretend he's concerned about my feelings."

"I'll kill him."

"Then you'd *lie* about it…being promised?"

"I've considered it, since you and me in bed occupies the majority of my thoughts these days. I'd be lying if I denied *that."* He lowered his hands to the outward tilt of her backside, pressing her against the hard proof of his confession. Her body stiffened on a sharp breath. He eased his grasp, working up her rib cage until he felt the warm pressure of her breasts against the heels of his hands. Her arms circled his waist, one hand catching the tail end of his braid. She yanked it lightly, pulling his head erect.

"Omission is a lie, too, Wind Dancer." An errant breeze smelling dangerously of rain ruffled her hair. "You're guilty of that, because you knew I was beginning to want you, and you did nothing to turn me away."

Her words ran along his backbone, tightening his shoulders. A mirthless smile surfaced. "Well, no matter what you think, nailing you is not something I set out to do." His contrariness alone should have guaranteed failure.

"Nailing me?" An eyebrow raised in contempt, her gaze sharp as a machete blade.

He whispered against her ear, "Even now I'm trying to repulse you."

"You're failing, and I'm not sure I can forgive you for how I feel." Her mouth moved against his neck, prickling his skin.

Fighting back a groan, he trifled with visions of taking her back to the pool lounge, stripping away her clothing, along with his hated restraint, sating his need. Feeding hers. His palm grasped her chin, fingers bracketing her jaw. He raked his tongue across her pursed lips. She opened to him like a parched plant accepting water, eager and heady as the goddamned ghosts of the morning glories on the Stantons' back fence. Braced by that memory, he ended the kiss, stepping back. The separation stung as keenly as if he'd gone under a surgical knife.

"You don't want a reformed runaway Navajo, Yazhi."

She stared into the near distance, arms at her sides as though they'd become useless. "There's a theory, Lukas, that prehistoric Asian tribes crossed the Bering Strait to settle this country, that Native Americans are their descendants." She fastened her gaze on him.

"I'm Asian, so we aren't so different as you believe."
Her soul-splintering argument held a sing-song
quality, a shield-like reservation, giving him the out he
needed.

"You *have* been to the library." He scavenged the
rubble in his head for a smile, then interjected his own
Argument. "I might be the right color, but in your
South Sea fantasy, I'd be a desert gecko trying to swim
in salt water." He paused then reiterated, "Out of
place."

"It's not a fantasy. I'm making my own destiny."
She turned away, eyeing the bungalow in the distance
until he caught her hand and turned her back.

"How much did Chuey tell you?"

"Not nearly as much as your gecko sermon just
told me."

"I've lived in the white man's world, Yazhi, and
loved a white woman. Navajos are people of few
words, but not of shallow feelings. Even now, I live
half in, half out of the *bilagáana* world, but I won't
always. On the rez, I *know* the dangers. I run no risk
of getting blindsided."

Her eyes shifted to him, skeptical, accusing. "I'll
interpret that as your damned philosophical way of
saying you got hurt, and now're bitter."

"I was burned. What kind of fool would lie down
in fire twice?" A long brittle silence followed, during
which he shoved his hands into his back pockets,
willing himself not to reach for her. "You're hurt, too.
You're running."

"Too bad we're running in different directions, isn't it, Lukas?"

She turned away again, the curve of her body in the white sweater and pants an erotic etching against the dark pool water. He felt the rain in the air, whiffed the undeniable scent. No defense against it existed.

"I'm trying, Yazhi, but I'm not made of stone. If we do this, the consequences will hurt like hell. For me, anyway." He turned her again, holding her by the shoulders. "But if it's what you want, if you can sleep with me knowing what you know, planning what you're planning, say the word." He caught her wrist, pressed the back of her hand against his fly and held it firmly in place. "Because I want you more right now than I want to breathe."

Infinite silence fell, broken only by her shallow breathing and the soundless drumming of his heart, before she said, "No. I've gone that way before. It's not what I want, ever again."

Not sure what answer he'd sought, he stared, memorizing her face, the swell of her body, her smell. Commuting to memory her voice issuing her refusal to cross the line he'd drawn, lessening, but not ending futile pain. Fat, wet dollops began to pepper their shoulders, splatter on the Pebble Tec deck at their feet, underscoring the words, "I can't ask the crew to work Thanksgiving, but I'll do what I can to rush the job, to help you get away—"

"Not to get away from you, Lukas. To get back to Jarrid. I have no choice." If she had held on to the disclaimer would it help him want her less?

"To get you there faster, then. You have my word."

"I had your word on the fire pit."

"This time we're talking about your life, Yazhi. And mine."

Wordlessly, he cupped his hand behind her head, rested the other on her hip, and drew her to him. He feather-brushed his lips over her hairline, then her scarred eyebrow before joining their mouths. He kept the kiss soft. Non-invasive.

Chaste enough to leave him aching when he walked away.

తి

What little Cameron had told him tonight, he sensed she had pulled from Canyon de Chelly depths. Like her, Tutuila was Samoan. Lukas' gut sensed prejudice, the reason she had never had her family's respect, the reason she had married Phillip Vickers and not Jarrid's father. If she had spent her life bending backwards for a family who had never seen past the color of her skin, he and Cameron had just enough in common to make their situation hopeless. For a brief spell he had let himself believe they had their profession in common. But her confession that she toiled at her career under protest, wanting to be a different person, reset their boundaries.

Between them existed no more than a fragile promise, paper-thin and capable of drifting away on a hot desert wind or dissolving under *El Niño's* torrents. They were archetypal male and female, the sun and the moon, fire and rain, caught in lust, magnetized by differences that would become a battle ground, once the lust was given its head. Maybe she understood that, believed it. Did she also know how much he wanted to cover her, enter her, plunge so deeply that color lines blended into the sepia tones of the pictures in her album? But he would not.

Because he loved her, he would never allow himself the joy of making love to her.

twenty-one

Chuey slumped against the front of Lukas' white sofa, a wrist hooked limply over a knee, fingers of his other hand worrying a snag in his cutoffs.

"I wanted to take you, babe. I can't now. I told Cameron I'd do what she wants, and I'm gonna show. So, get over it."

"But it's Big Head Todd, Chuey." A deep sigh elevated Yolanda's breasts. "I can't believe it." She gave him a pouty look, extending her muscled legs in front of her on the Navajo rug. She sipped wine from a clear plastic cup, shuddered and wrinkled her nose. "I hate this cheap stuff."

He ignored the jibe. "Big Head's old news. You'll live." He seized her hand, working the delicate bones in the back. "Give me a break, okay?"

"Polly's never seen them. You know how much I wanted to take her."

His eyes fixed on her cushiony lips, lapis eyes adorned with a silver cross pinned in her eyebrow. He'd have liked dragging her through the concert crowd, pissing off Anglo guys. "I promised, so I'll get the tickets for you. Best I can do."

"I want you to go, too." She crushed a darkly stained cigarette in the mayo lid he'd fished out of the trash, then laid a hand on his bare leg. A finger brushed his fly. "It's Thanksgiving, for God's sake. You should've told Cameron no."

"After the way you set me up, saying no wasn't an option."

"I just went to see her for a referral. *She* asked all the questions."

"If that's true how'd she know to pump me about Lukas and Chicago? He'll kill me if she gets around to quizzing him about his degenerate days."

"Jeez. All Chief High and Mighty did was walk beams. What's so—"

"That's not all he did, and you know it. I never should have told you about the women. You got her attention. And how else would she know about him being *connected?*" The same anger he'd felt when he learned Yolanda and Cameron had conferred crept back under his collar. "Trust me, babe, now we *are* talking about me getting killed."

Her brow crimped. "I never mentioned Suzanne Stanton or him whoring around. I mostly told her you're not interested in moving in with me." She removed her hand, rubbed her own thigh. "I covered your tight brown ass instead of setting you up."

"I'm interested." The tip of his finger turned the snag in his pants into a rip.

"But you're not doing it. Right?"

"You don't need me to, now. You weaseled the deposit money from her."

"I need your body." She smiled. "Anytime I want it."

"You've got that. You needed someone to come up with the cash. She did."

"I've gotta pay it back." She sucked in her bottom lip. "Besides some of it's already gone, and I haven't found a friggin' place yet."

The heel of his hand smacked his brow. "Crap, Yolanda. Lukas finds out you gypped her he'll have my balls, never mind my scalp."

Her chin hiked. "I've got bills, and Polly needed some things."

"Yeah, like a fast exit outta there." The pictures she had painted raced through his mind like a coyote after a roadrunner. "That settles it. I'm working Thanksgiving, 'cause you're getting out of there, and one of us is paying back the loan. Find a cheap place and use what's left of the money for a deposit."

"I need some of it for gas to get to Tucson. You promised Polly the concert, and I'm not gonna let her down."

"Your priorities are screwed, you know that, Yolanda?"

"So are yours, Run Amok, if you work Thanksgiving, instead of spending it with me."

"Like I said, babe, what choice do I have?"

"I don't want to fight, Chuey." She checked the Timex on her wrist. "It's almost three a.m. and I have to be home before Polly wakes up. Besides, if she didn't do her homework tonight, I'll have to do it for her, and if I'm bummed over you, I won't feel like it. Okay?" Her hand stole to the waist of his cutoffs, tugged on his T-shirt. "I want us to do it on this sofa. It's so big and soft it's radical." The hand lowered playfully. "Make me happy, okay, Chuey?"

"Not on this sofa." He jerked when her hand tightened. "You're wearing makeup."

"I'll wash my face. I love this couch."

"So does Lukas. He's not gonna go for any stains, so watch that wine, Yolanda." The cup was tilting, but that wasn't the stain he alluded to.

"We'll put down towels." Her tongue bathed his ear.

"What if *I'm* bummed?" He eased her hand up. "It happens, you know?"

"Get over it." Bounding from a cross-legged position, she began circling the room, loading her arms with fat candles, still holding the plastic wine cup. Scarlet liquid sloshed ominously. She formed a circle with the candles on the granite lamp table, and looked around. "Where does Geronimo keep his matches?"

"Put the candles back. Lukas can tell if one thing's been moved." When she reworked the arrangement heedlessly, he warned, "We're not lighting those."

Her smile indulgent, she went to the purse she'd left on a chair and rummaged, coming up with a book of matches she tossed to him. Chuey shook his head, getting as far as his knees before she caught the hem of her crop top and peeled it off. She wore the bra he liked best. Black, see-through, with under wires pushing her breasts up and out. Her hands stole to the front hook.

"You light the candles." She unhooked the bra. It fell apart in the middle, the straps remaining on her shoulders. Her hand played around her pierced belly button before lowering the zipper in her shorts. "For me. Please, Chuey?" She stepped out of the shorts, shed the bra, tossed them on the floor near the sofa.

Coaxed by the thickening in his crotch, he gave in and lit the candles. The carved, decorative pillars flared, fanned tall by the breeze from the door he'd left cracked to mask her cigarette smoke. She awarded him an appreciative smile. Heading for the bathroom, purse in hand, tight ass swishing in pink bikinis, she directed over a naked shoulder, "Turn off the lights," then promised, "I'll hurry."

Chuey peeled off his shirt and dropped it on the arm of the couch. He was reaching for the light switch beside the front entry when he caught the movement outside the window. His hairline spiked before the barbs ran down his spine.

Holy crap! Lukas!

But no way. He would have pulled the Suburban into the garage, the rumble and creak of the overhead door giving a warning. Lukas had run up the hill in the middle of the night, ticked by some damn thing, from the way he'd sounded on the phone. He'd be homing in on the res by now, due back tomorrow. Or else Yolanda couldn't have talked him into this.

Footsteps echoed on the flagstone porch.

Security. Damn. The guy was thick with Lukas. He'd blab for sure.

Heavy, angry fists pounded the door. Chuey winced, darting a glance down the hall, willing Yolanda to stay put.

But since when was making out a crime?

He'd charm this guy, explain how they had no place else to go, other than the car. Get his sympathy, maybe. Make him an accessory to the crime.

Drawn by more pounding, Yolanda appeared in the bathroom door. He motioned her back, mouthing "security," then opened the door.

"How you doin', asshole?" A skinhead look-alike, minus a uniform or badge. He had backup behind him, not as big, but definitely unfriendly. More like hostile.

Chuey's brow dampened. *Asshole?* "You talking to me?"

"You got a woman in there, Injun?"

The sweat iced up. Yolanda's fears, warnings about her brothers, culminated in one gouge of memory. Sudden understanding pounded his brain.

"Eddie, right?" And the one in the shadows, older but smaller, the way she'd described him, was, "Dwaine? That you?"

Chuey felt Yolanda behind him, heard her ragged breathing. Mind pictures that Eddie and Dwaine had seen for real through the window—her strutting down the hall, nearly naked, purse in hand—blasted him.

"You're a friendly bastard for an Injun," Eddie allowed. "She said you were. But you weren't friendly enough not to sic the state on us, huh, buddy?"

What the hell was Eddie talking about—the *state?* "'Scuse me?"

"What do you want, Eddie?" Yolanda voiced his real question, then followed with, "How'd you find me here?"

"We found the number you left with Polly." Dwaine moved alongside his brother. "My buddy at the police department matched it with this address. Get your clothes on, yo, and get your ass home. This little powwow's over."

Chuey flinched as Yolanda latched onto his arm, her breast warm and firm against his skin. The sofa pillow she clutched was failing to perform its job. Suddenly conscious of his own near nakedness, he looked around for his shirt. It lay half on the sofa arm, half on the lamp table, too far away. He folded his arms across his bare chest, unfolded them and made an attempt to close the door. A work boot the size of Rhode Island blocked his effort, the toe digging a dent in the carved alder wood door Chuey had waxed just that morning.

"Not so fast, asshole." Eddie edged closer, wedged a shoulder against the door and pushed through, Dwaine on his heels, minus the enthusiasm.

"Call security. Do it, Chuey. Eddie'll hurt you." Yolanda shoved him.

"Damn right. She knows I mean business, don't you, bitch?" Eddie caught his arm, swiveled him around. "You screwin' my sister, redskin?"

Adrenaline coursed his veins. "I was about to." *Dumb, Run Amok. Damned dumb.*

Beside him, Yolanda gasped, started to whimper, shaking her head furiously.

"Let's just take her and get the hell out of here, Eddie. She wasn't gonna make the guy rape her. That's for damn sure."

"You called Children's Services on us, Injun, got them nosing round the house. They're gonna take our little sister 'cause of you." One finger drilled Chuey's chest, the nail jagged and sharp. Chuey staggered.

"What's he talking about, Children's Services?" He caught the cognizance on Yolanda's face, relief and dread tangling in his brain. He hadn't called, but that didn't matter. Even if it took his getting killed, Polly would be out of there. From the look on Yolanda's face, he realized she'd long ago given up on help for herself.

He felt sick, soiled, wanted to retch. He should have seen the signs.

Dwaine's hand damped his sister's wrist. "Let's go, yo. Don't get Eddie riled. You know better."

Even though she planted her feet, Dwaine dragged her toward him. Writhing, she bent from the waist, kicking him with the high-heeled brogans she'd had no time to take off. She doubled over, her teeth sinking into his forearm.

"Goddammit!"

Dwaine bellowed, letting go, shoving her. Chuey stepped in to catch her. They tumbled backward into the sofa, swayed into the lamp table going down. Candles tumbled, rolled, one onto his shirt. More dropped to the floor, hot wax hissing out flames. In a back cavern of his mind, Chuey prayed they all would be snuffed out.

The bra caught fire first, popping, sizzling. Fueled now, the candle flame burst into larger leaps of red, yellow, blue that spread onto Yolanda's white gauze shorts.

Chuey let go of her, dived for the disaster. Eddie lumbered in. Catching the blazing garment on the toe of his boot, he launched it onto the sofa. Chuey lunged. Candles rolled across the Navajo rug Kai had spent months weaving for Lukas' thirtieth birthday. Tears rushed up, choking him, blurring his vision. The boot moved backward, swung down and up again, catching him in the chin.

Yolanda screamed.

His head hit the table. Her face, the scream, faded. The room went black.

౿

The rising sun painted Gad's dismal room golden champagne. The gentile light masked his features in long-passed babyhood innocence. Gad snuggled in a pile of rough blankets, face and dark head scarcely visible. Lukas stood at the end of the bed, a hand resting on a rough cedar foot rail. The bed had been a birth present from Chuey. Hewn and carved in a high school woodworking class, in a different era of innocence. While the rez hummed with speculation back then for the swelling in Kai's belly, Chuey's eagerness for the coming child had far outweighed his curiosity about the father.

Chuey's feelings for Gad, a peer in a world of fatherless boys, never waned.

Lukas placed the trendy and extravagant toy he had brought—a Furby—on Gad's bed and swiveled toward the sound of soft footsteps…Kai, barefoot in a worn cotton gown, a blanket about her shoulders. Her frail appearance mocked the robust woman she mimicked when disguised in velvet and buckskin, silver and pride. A cough rattled her chest, quaked her shoulders. Concerned for the drafty surroundings Lukas waited her out, empathy wracking his own body.

"The lock is still broken," he pointed out. Rusted, hanging from its hinge like wrenched tendons. She had slept soundly, pallet spread on the dirt floor of the hogan's lean-to, secure in the smell of a dying fire, fried meat and isolation. "Did I scare you?"

She choked off a cough with a cupped palm. "Not so much time has passed that I don't recognize your Footsteps." But too much time, according to the look in her eyes.

"You cough still." Nothing. "It's gone on too long, Kai."

She shrugged away his warning, crossing to stand beside him. She still had the fever, too. Searing. At close range, she wheezed. A reedy, wavy sound.

"You drove all night," she said in Navajo. Not a question. She could always read what his eyes concealed. Through scent, body language, unspoken words.

"Enit." With Cameron's taste, his craving for her, weighing down the night.

Kai plucked the stuffed toy, turning it in her hand. "You came to bring this. Not to pleasure me."

In a past time he would have gone straight to the pallet, made silent love to her, intent on not waking her fatherless child. That had been a different man.

"I couldn't sleep, so I drove. I've rescheduled your tests, and I'm driving you back tomorrow, checking you into hospital. No arguments."

Face stoic, her dark, callused hands kneaded the fur trinket like bread.

"Chuey found it on the Internet." He nodded to the stuffed animal. "It talks, tells all your secrets if you're not careful." The smile he vied for never surfaced. "He charged it to me, then skipped lunches to pay me back. He asked me to drop it off."

Her mercurial black eyes went luminous, then clouded on the boy. "Gad counts the days till Chuey comes. He didn't make the mission team again. He thinks Chuey can fix his game. Make him into Michael Jordan."

"He probably can, or die trying."

She smiled tolerantly, placing the toy back on the bed. "Gad is too short. Practice will never change that."

"As a boy I was short, they tell me. So was Chuey. Gad's time will come."

"If not, he may lose faith in his idol." She glanced up, reiterating, "Chuey."

Lukas slipped an arm around her shoulders, felt her thinning hair, silky beneath his arm. He steered her across the cold hogan, out the door onto the porch.

Frost-laden air nipped the hem of her gown as she balanced against him, one foot atop the other. Her toenails were painted dark purple, the color of an aging bruise. On the concrete step sat two Carlo Rossi jugs. Filled with black dirt interspersed with colorful marbles, they housed spindly cedar branches. A child's garden, Lukas surmised, hoping the bottles had come from the dump, not the liquor store crowding the rez's border.

"Chuey said you're scared about the tests."

She hugged herself. "Like the child he is, Chuey talks out of school." Again she spoke Navajo.

"Bring Gad. When the tests are over, stay with me for a while."

"I'd be a kept woman. I'd owe you." She spared a measuring smile. "I'll find another place."

"Suit yourself."

"I will, Lukas. I no longer suit you."

He pressed his lips to her hair. "Do you need firewood before I go?"

"It's Gad's job. He'll be up soon for school." She hacked and swallowed, eyes burning with effort not to cough.

"I'll send someone from the post to fix that lock and the broken window." He nodded at the dented bucket in the center of the floor. "And the leak."

"Go, Lukas. The world waits. I've been given my share of you."

He forced a laugh and kissed her brow. "You're in fine form, Kai."

He backed the truck into a half circle at the edge of the yard, then headed forward. In his rearview mirror, she tended the dead plants with water from a rusty coffee can, her figure growing smaller as the distance widened between them.

He had to find a way to take care of her and the boy. The first step, even though she'd fight like hell for her independence, would be to move them into his hogan for a while. Hers badly needed repair, dangerously cold in the winter, a sweatbox in summer. His mother and Apenimon could keep an eye on them, make sure Gad attended school regularly, and encourage her to go for treatment when she needed it. Seek a solution other than the *hataalii* healing rituals she clung to so tenaciously. Her cough echoed in his head, tying his stomach into a cold knot.

The phone in the console whirred, imploding his thoughts. He let it ring again before a sixth sense guided his hand to the instrument. "Wind Dancer."

"Oh, Lukas! Thank God!" Exasperation and relief wrestled for upper billing in Cameron's tone. "I've been calling! I left a message."

He had seen a notation of a missed call on the cell's screen, but ignored it, in no mood to talk. Now he allowed his mind to wander where it insisted, guided by the sound of her voice. He glanced at the dash clock. Cameron didn't rise this early. Had she been up all night, nursing thoughts similar to his own? "I've been out of range of the phone."

"Where are you?"

"The rez." He sat at a crossroads now, not knowing which way to activate the turn signal lever. Not knowing if she'd had a change of heart since they'd talked by the pool, decided to throw consequences to the wolves. Not knowing, sitting at this juncture of his life, if he was deciding the same.

"You have to come back."

"Why, Yazhi?" *Have you changed your mind. Will I change mine?*

"I'm sorry to be the one to tell you."

His heart hammered. "Let's hear it."

"Your house—I saw the fire on the news this morning, and—" She fell quiet then exploded, "Lukas, your house caught fire. It's badly burned." She stopped.

Gripped by fear, he counted his heartbeats.

"Chuey was in the house."

twenty-two

Cameron watched Lukas sift a pile of ashes with an iron poker, one of the few items in the living room area that had withstood the heat.

"What was it…before?" she ventured, deeply moved by his rounded back, shoulder muscles bunching beneath his shirt, the incline of his proud head, the way his hair hung on each side of his neck, onto his chest. "The ashes?" They covered his boots, soot dinging halfway to the knees of his time-bleached Levi's.

"A Navajo rug."

"Valuable," she concluded.

"One of a kind." With athletic grace, he bounded up, tossed the poker into the fireplace and jammed his hands into his back pockets. "Kai destroyed the pattern when she finished. An act of honor to the recipient."

His words brought feelings in which Cameron took no pride. She studied her toes, black inside her sandals, her ankles dusted with sediment. "I'm so sorry about the fire, Lukas." The words were beginning to sound lame. Redundant.

He nodded. Again. As he surveyed the damage, dark eyes that had at first clouded with disbelief, took on comprehension, acceptance. "These were possessions, trappings of monetary value only. Anything of worth, other than the rug, I keep on the rez."

Miraculously, the door to the studio at the far end of the hall had been closed. Though sprinklers had activated throughout the house, the room was intact, his files unscathed in metal cabinets. But from his interpretation of "worth," she questioned the significance of the saved study.

She was reminded of her perspective when she'd come to Scottsdale from Vancouver, merely passing through, bringing along nothing of import. She could easily see this had been a beautiful house, but a means to an end, a place for Lukas to serve his own penance.

He bent to retrieve an empty, half-melted bottle from the floor. Turning it in his hand, he studied the singed label. "Tell me again about Chuey."

"He's all right, Lukas. Really. It's just that watching them load him into the ambulance scared me. That's when I began trying to call you—when there was no mention of you, other than being the homeowner." She relived her confusion and dread, taking a breath. "But I went by the hospital. Chuey's fine. He has a gash on his forehead and a minor concussion, and he inhaled a lot of smoke. They were releasing him by the time I arrived. He'd called a friend to pick him up." She offered a smile. "He's sick about the house, and he's not looking forward to facing you."

He pounded his palm with the misshapen bottle. *"Enit."* Thinking in Navajo, as she had come to recognize, he spoke so softly she had to read his lips.

Her concern overriding any sense of intruding, she followed him from the shell of a room. He moved down the hall into the bedroom she had inspected earlier while waiting for him. Nothing was burned, but the firemen had entered through the terrace door, spraying water liberally. Muddy carbon saturated the room and its furnishings, casting a surreal, ghostly look. An elaborate weight-lifting machine that explained long muscles and a granite-hard body hulked in a corner, its chrome appendages wet, glistening in late day sunlight blazing through a window.

The acrid smell of smoke stung her nose, made her eyes water. "Your clothes are ruined, I'm afraid. Water and smoke damage."

He grunted. Still holding the bottle, he strode purposefully to the door of the walk-in closet and peered in. Either he doubted her or craved misery.

"You need time to regroup, Lukas." Once more she rehearsed words in her mind, examining them, trying to believe they were only charitable. "Come stay with me. I've thought about it. I want you to."

Over his shoulder, he gave her an appraising glance. Quiet scrutiny. A simmering smile appeared, then settled into a hard line.

Apprehension skittered spider-like across her nerve endings. Motivated by his challenging look, she examined her willpower and resistance capacity.

Her breath sounded like a tidal wave in the silence. Finally she managed, "I was offering you the other bungalow."

"That's generous, but I'll get a cot and set it up in the studio."

She pretended to ignore his refusal. "Jarrid won't be coming—or if that miracle occurs, he can stay with me. The empty bungalow is the perfect solution."

"Is it, Yazhi?" One dark brow arched. "I'm not so sure."

A flush spread up her throat before igniting her face. "We made our decision last night, Lukas. The fire won't change that. Yes," she affirmed ."I'm sure."

Was she? Or would it be the most hurtful mistake they could make?

༅

Standing in front of the charred shell, examining his agreement to move in with her, Lukas watched Cameron's taillights glow at the stop sign, then disappear around the corner. He stowed the empty, half-melted wine bottle in the Suburban and crossed the street to the security guard sitting in a logoed pickup Truck. The man was his age, brawny and friendly. Rather than adopting the attitude that Lukas lived in the wrong neighborhood, he seemed awed and a bit envious of the accomplishment.

"Tough luck, Wind Dancer. But you can rebuild. You're in the business."

Lukas nodded. "I guess you know Chuey was here."

"Yeah. I was first on the scene. I called the fire department, helped him close doors, hook up the water hose. Otherwise, the whole place woulda gone."

"What else?"

"You talked to him yet?"

"Not yet. He's hiding out." Lukas forced a conspiratorial grin.

"That big blonde was here." An antipathetic edge crept into the man's voice. "I seen that beat-up convertible." Lukas waited. "I seen another car, too, on my rounds. A couple doors down on the wrong side of the street, back wheels angled out from the curb like the driver got out quick with someplace important in mind."

"What kind of car?"

He shrugged. "The kind a guard gate would keep out, a gate like I been bitchin' about you guys needin'. I shoulda paid more attention, got a tag number, but at the time—It was a big old model, a boat. Chevy I'd have to guess. Couldn't get it outta my mind, so I made a quick round on the next block. When I come back your place was blazin,' and that convertible was gone. Other car, too." He shrugged again, his grin crooked. "Damn kids was partyin'. When the cat's away the mice will play."

Mind pictures of Yolanda, followed by shadowy made-up images of Chuey and her, even though understandable, plagued Lukas. Chuey's raging hormones, his incessant need to cross the color line, had almost gotten him killed.

"Damn shame with Thanksgiving on you. You got a place to stay, I guess." The guard's crooked grin resumed. "I seen that woman leavin'. Looks like you're squared away." The lewd gaze labeled Cameron's tawny skin just dark enough to pass muster. "But you might get some looters in here. I'll keep an eye on the place."

"Thanks. I'll vote for a guard gate at the next homeowner's meeting."

"There you go."

"I'll be in and out of the house over Thanksgiving weekend, using the studio. If you remember anything about the other car—"

"You got it, chief."

Lukas' spine spiked. He pushed down the reaction and clapped the man's shoulder. "I'll talk to Chuey, too. Get to the bottom of this."

"Tell him I said them pale face chicks are fiery numbers." He leaned forward, turning the ignition key, chuckling at his pun. "Tell 'im they're too hot for him."

Precisely what Lukas intended.

❦

Chuey sat on the side of his dorm bed, Lukas on the twin across from him. Their large, rangy bodies cramped the room. Under questioning, Chuey had admitted to Yolanda being with him, but refused to admit to anyone else being in the house when the fire started. Lukas was supposed to imagine scenes involving drugs and orgies too sinister to reveal. Chuey didn't do drugs, and his fixation on sex, a means to a nameless need, excluded sharing.

From the nightstand, Lukas picked up a small, carved coyote statue, painted a farcical bluish color. He turned it over in his hand, the situation at hand tumbling end over end in his mind. In Navajo legend, coyotes were a sign of witchcraft. A Navajo guilty of an evil life became a coyote after death. He ran his thumb over the carving forming the snout, wondering if he believed the legend, and if Chuey did. Wondering why he thought of it now. He stuck the trinket in a drawer.

Chuey bent forward now, elbows on knees, staring at his Nikes. In the sun from the window, his short, spiky hair formed a roan helmet for his head. Tears ran down chiseled cheeks and dripped unchecked onto his Grateful Dead Thirty-Year-Tour shirt. As far as Lukas knew, his twenty-year-old nephew had never been within screaming range of the Dead.

Lukas needed Chuey's grief and shame like he needed a second penis.

"Hey, Run Amok." Somewhere in his pity he discovered a tough tone.

Chuey's head shot up, eyes lambent with surprise.

"The goddamned house is insured."

A dark, callus-free hand swiped tears. Against his brow, an oversized Band-Aid gleamed like whalebone.

His wide mouth fought a feeble grin, revealing perfect teeth. "That's sacrilege, right? Since when do 'skins go for insurance? I thought we danced for our good luck."

"Since we walk in two worlds."

The grin died.

"I don't want your soul, Chuey."

"I'd give it if it'd wipe out the fire."

Chuey's father, God burn *his* fetid soul, must have been an actor. Or a drama coach. "I want a promise." One he had never bent to solicit. A promise he had waited for Chuey to grasp on his own. "Stay within your tribe. It's that simple."

"The house would've still burned last night if I'd had Pocahontas' great-great-granddaughter there." He rose and stomped to the window. Anger slanted the broad shoulders he jammed against the sill. "I was thinking with the wrong head."

"Any descendent of Pocahontas would have stayed and helped you put out the fire. It's an Indian thing, Chuey." Chuey's back went ramrod straight. "I hoped you would figure it out from my great adventure with the *bilagáanas.* But you want your blood spilled as mine was. I would say it's your choice, if that could happen without hurting your people." His own bitterness, which Cameron had homed in on last night, was the prize Lukas had brought back to the Navajo world. A heavy enough burden for him and his people. But Chuey's bent for risking his life was not acceptable.

"Who are my people, Lukas?" The voice came from far away, deep inside.

Me, dumb ass. I'm the fourteen-year-old who found you. I cut the cord binding you to my dying sister. I breathed life into your lungs, dribbled water into your mouth, carried your naked bilagáana-*red body to refuge. I'm your damned people.*

"Just by being alive I've already contaminated the tribe," Chuey said.

"Not you, Chuey. Your mother did it." Ainii was her name. But Navajos didn't speak the name of the dead. Still, many nights Lukas woke with the name Jordan, that of his and Suzanne's dead baby, silently screaming in his head. "You have the power to wipe out her errors. Once you finish school, you will be a psychologist. Return to the rez and cure your people. Love is the only healer on earth. It's a gift from God."

Looking absolved, Chuey turned, his smile beautifully vulnerable. "Nice sermon, Uncle Bro."

"Give me names of the people there when the fire started," Lukas prompted.

Chuey shook his head. "No names, and don't call in the Chicago connection on this. Okay?" Lukas grinned, amused by the childish fascination his nephew held on to. The smile died when Chuey elaborated, "I'll even that score. Somehow."

Fear and pride, hot and fierce, clamped Lukas' chest in a vise. "Be careful, *askii.*" He was indeed still a boy, struggling now to be a man. "Use the right head this time."

Outside the dorm, Chuey stood watching as Lukas backed the Suburban away from the curb. Then he raised a hand and stepped forward. Foot jamming the brake, Lukas dragged his work jacket over the mangled bottle on the seat.

Chuey clamped a hand onto the door, fingers extending into the open window. "Where are you staying, Uncle Bro, now that I've burned you out of house and home?"

"Cameron offered me the empty bungalow."

Chuey's eyes held a look Lukas couldn't read. "What about Thanksgiving?"

Only four days away now. "I'm pretending the first one never happened."

"You going up the hill? You and Apenimon could smoke a war pipe and cuss pilgrims while you pig out on fry bread." The playful grin could be staged.

"I've promised a set of plans for Monday. I'll work on them in the studio. Except for the water from the sprinklers, it came out in good shape."

After a too-long silence, Chuey slapped the door and stepped back, solemn.

Lukas pulled away, cradling the bottle in his lap, headed for research in the nearest liquor store. Something about that charred bottle struck a curious chord.

૱

Cameron tossed in the tangled sheets, pounded the pillow and buried her face there. Seeking sleep, she employed a childhood ritual of counting red-coated Royal Canadian Mounties astride black horses. As minutes wasted, rather than dimming, the images glared in her mind. She scrunched down in the feathers, drawing the blanket around her bare shoulders. Its warmth seeped into her, relieving her chill, but doing nothing to dull the serrated edges of her nerves.

She sat up and stared at the clock. Mikela purred contentedly at the foot of the bed. Rain pelted the tile roof in gentle but agitating cadence, filling Cameron with a sense of loss underlined with hopelessness.

The room lay deafeningly still. The night grew deeper. Darker. Quieter.

Then she heard footsteps. The strides were measured, and even in boots, light as a skilled hunter's. Footsteps she had come to recognize from lying there the past three nights, torn, yet resolute, listening for Lukas' return from Dos Gringos.

Her heart slammed against her ribs, her senses revving. She envisioned leaping from the bed, flinging open the front door before he could unlock the adjoining bungalow and enter. Before he could once more honor the choice he'd given her, the choice she'd so adamantly made. She seized a pillow, hugged it to her heaving chest and buried her face again to keep from crying out his name.

A lengthy interval passed between his halted footsteps and the door creaking open. Had he stood, staring at the carved twin panel of wood separating them? Did he sense she waited? Did he feel the torment?

A sliver of light appeared beneath the door that divided the rooms. She crept out of bed and crossed the floor to press her cheek against the wood grain, her hand on the unlocked knob. She had but to turn it, only to knock on the second door.

If we do this, Yazhi, the consequences will hurt like hell. His words echoed in her chaotic mind. While praising his wisdom, his strength to hold on to their agreement, she damned her weakness for wanting him.

In darkness, she made her way to the bathroom, splashed her face with water, then turned on the light. Staring at her mirrored reflection, she groped for her bearings. Suppose they made love? Suppose he fell in love with her as she had with him? Would he still honor his pledge to finish the inn as quickly as possible and set her free? Could she chance him stalling to keep her there?

Water began running on the opposite side of the thin wall, gently at first, and then full force. The sound of the shower door closing rushed a new set of images to her churning mind. His hands running over his own body, the mass of black hair streaming wet and heavy down his back. Closed eyes, dense jet black lashes plastered on prominent cheek bones.

Fire leapt in her belly, rushed downward, settled into a throbbing ache.

What would life be like with a man like Lukas? A man so strong-willed, wise and responsible. Loyal and loving from what she gleaned of his relationship with his family. A man whose greatest ambition was contentment within himself.

In her life she'd known two men, both highly ambitious. When she and Lee had met at Concordia University in Montreal, his life focus was to be the most outstanding football player ever to play there. Later, playing pro ball for the Calgary Stampeders, he'd lived to break all league records, and to go back to Samoa a rich hero.

Phillip's political aspirations had known no bounds, and he had punished her mercilessly for casting a shadow on his ambition. He punished her still.

She had merely fit into the plans of each man.

Ethnic differences had written Lukas' life creed. Rejection had framed her own *She* knew the grief of being judged by skin color. Her son was a little brown boy growing up in the white man's world, just as, according to Chuey's sketchy story, Lukas had. Only *she* had the power to change that by taking Jarrid to a place where his skin would be the criterion, not the exception, where he would establish rather than continually confront society's culture.

She turned off the light, shutting out her haunted eyes, closing the door on the sound of running water, killing her erotic visions.

❧

At four a.m., drawn by the same sliver of light, Cameron slipped a robe over her nakedness and rapped lightly on Lukas' door. Sharp as rifle fire, her knock echoed in the stillness. Then came interminable silence, as though he waited for her to ask permission to enter. Or maybe he slept. After Lee had been killed, she had slept with a light for months, fighting an aversion to stifling darkness.

She turned the knob and eased the door open. Mikela whisked past her ankles and into the room. Classical music whispered from the clock radio beside the bed. Lukas glanced up as she entered, removing delicate wire-rimmed glasses she'd never seen. The strong bones framing his sober eyes seemed more prominent tonight. A tinge darker than his skin shadowed the hollows at his temples. This unfamiliar, more vulnerable version of Lukas Wind Dancer jolted loose a tenderness she'd yet to feel.

He sat at a small round table. Barefoot, he wore only frayed jeans, zipped but unbuttoned. A standing lamp had been moved from across the room. It lit architectural drawings spread on the table and shimmered off his sable hair, transforming his flat, corrugated belly and hard chest to molten bronze.

Lukas Wind Dancer, a panther-like man. Dark. Sleek. Beautiful.

"You should be asleep." Barely a whisper, his voice carried on the background of music and droning rain, sending a heated glow coursing through her veins.

Donning the glasses, he turned his attention back to the paper before him, lined up a ruler and made a quick, emphatic stroke with a mechanical pencil.

"So should you." Tightening and retying the belt of the robe, she crossed the room and slipped into the spare chair at the table. She ran her fingers into her tangled hair, lifting it away from her face. "You've been up all night."

"Sleep and I are not on familiar terms." His eyes devoured the paper.

"Is something troubling you, Lukas?" *The same desire raging inside me.*

Silence. She puzzled for a moment.

"Are these the promised drawings?" She extended a hand, an index finger stroking the paper. He nodded. "What happened to working on them tomorrow?" *Thanksgiving.* She had depended on that. Any alteration on his part could prove troublesome.

"Change of plans." No elaboration or apparent concern.

"Another secret mission?"

He looked up, eyes narrowed fractionally. The corner of his mouth twitched before his lips tightened. "More sudden than secret." He shed the glasses, leaned the chair onto its back legs, a thumb hooked inside the waist of his jeans, a leg extended close to hers. He drummed the pencil eraser against the table. "Kai is staging a four-day woman-and-child sit-in at the tribal zoo in Window Rock." His smile held resignation.

She cocked a brow, struggling to hide her envy of Kai's ability to command Lukas' attention. A senseless reaction when his distance and preoccupation were actual boons to her own pending scheme. "Why?" *Is the woman tireless?*

He shrugged. "She wants traditional ceremonies held there to show respect for the animals, or she wants the zoo shut down, the animals released into the wild." Catching her puzzled look, he grunted softly. Then looking as if it pained him to do so, he explained, "Bears. Cougars. Snakes. They are sacred."

"To Kai."

And to me, his eyes said. "Our people are divided on the zoo issue. The tribal deity is now involved. I want to be there as a go-between if one is needed."

To protect Kai. And Gad, whom Chuey believed to be Lukas' child.

She freed her gaze from his, turning the drawing and scrutinizing it, adhering to an unidentifiable sense. "This is something special. Am I right?"

"To me, yes." Indolently he twirled the glasses. "But beauty is in the eye of the beholder." Indian jargon for: The subject of the drawing is not for you to know.

She heard herself voicing the thought she couldn't drive from her mind. "You said you had loved a white woman." His eyes appeared to darken. "I'd like to know...Will you tell me? Will you share your hurt with me?" Perhaps the pain, his for telling, hers for listening, would free her to share in turn.

Pattering rain laid a background for low strains of Mozart. "It happened long ago to a different man."

As if it burned her fingers, she dropped the drawing, attempting to rise. His hand grasped her arm and held her in the chair. Their eyes locked

"And it meant too much to you to discuss with me. Isn't that what you're saying?" She loathed the tremor in her voice, the stinging in her throat.

"Why do you want to know, Yazhi? Why do you care?" His gaze moved to where her nipples strained the robe fabric, lowered to his crotch, raised to her eyes. She watched his full lips carve words. "Are you here to cancel our agreement?"

The un-mussed bed drew her eye, followed by visions of rising, taking his hand, leading him back to her own bed where she had writhed for hours waiting for sounds of him. She opened her mouth to speak. Mikela rubbed her ankle, mewing softly and plaintively, restoring abrupt reality. "You lied, Wind Dancer. You *are* made of steel."

He frowned. "This is your idea. If I bother you being here, say it."

She pried his fingers loose and rose. "No, you're welcome here. And you have my word." Her heart pounded in her throat. "I won't bother you again."

She scooped up Mikela, exited the shared doors, closed hers and locked it.

twenty-three

A plump-bodied quail pecked at the adobe sill of Cameron's office window. Vivid sun formed an aura around its perky topknot, lending a quality as surreal as the rainless day, warming the cramped space. Cameron stared out the inadequate window, marveling at the change in the weather, and took pleasure in the sound of work coming from the inn's lobby.

Had she been able to predict that Chuey and his bedraggled helpers from the Phoenix Rescue Mission would have had sun for the entire four day holiday, they could have been dispatched outside, even if their time was wasted, bailing water off the laden roof.

So much for hindsight. Their inside work had expedited her goal, a means to an end. A few more days of the sun she had prayed for at mass this morning and the roof would dry, then be replaced *El Niño* had tired of tormenting her. She felt it in her reviving spirit.

With or without Lukas' cooperation, she would survive—triumph.

And just as well. She had heard nothing of him since the troubling scene in his room. Today, Sunday, he would surely remain on the rez as long as possible.

For no discernable reason, the chandelier she'd found at Faust Gallery and hung to brighten the Office swayed overhead, capturing her attention. A lovely extravagant whim she'd leave behind, because like a Navajo spirit born of the desert, Mexican tin would corrode in Samoa's salty sea air. A theory based on Lukas' sage rejection.

Leisurely, she turned a page of the album on her lap. Working her locket back and forth on the chain, she studied the last photos Jarrid's saintly nanny had sent. Stolen treasure.

He's growing too quickly. I'm missing so much of his life.

She turned pages backward, seeking one of the two photographs of Lee she owned, this one as a child, near Jarrid's age now. The two could be one and the same, each bearing the strong, primitive, exotic beauty that had attracted her to Lee. Jarrid had her finely shaped Chastain nose. Otherwise he was solely Lee Tutuila. If only he could have seen that before he died. Had they planned the reunion for a different night, so much could be different today. So much…

Her memory, gauzy now, segued to that life-altering night. The board meeting. The one glass of superior cabernet she'd allowed herself at dinner, the pounding headache, the unfamiliar, untried prescription she had taken, seeking enough relief to drive.

Following Lee's untimely call, she'd driven too fast. The drugs had left her shaky, too dizzy to risk the dark, rain-slick street. The on-coming mini-van had skidded. Her Mercedes brakes had failed. Phillip had been notified, and later that same night, revealing his true nature and veiled resentment, he had exacted revenge.

In a less obvious manner, his reprisal seethed in the present.

Backing up her earlier thoughts, the timbers above her head creaked and groaned. She all but felt the kindred distress, imagined the huge beams shifting and resettling. Again, she whispered a silent prayer for sun.

Her first warning came as a loud *whoosh* Goliath might have uttered had David managed to kick him in the stomach. Before the thought could fully register, reality played out in an interminable, thunderous crash, followed by profane masculine screams. Her industry award plaques slid from the walls, crashing onto the tile floor. Mikela howled, jumping from the dancing desk to scurry from sight. The chandelier swung crazily, dropped, and shattered.

Silence.

More ragged screams turning to blasphemous prayers.

Cameron bounded from her chair, the album tumbling askew. She tripped over her discarded sandals, then raced barefoot down the endless hall. Terror shot through her body like a blowtorch, winding her. She rounded the corner into the lobby and stumbled to a stop, paralyzed.

"God—" Her pulse pounded in her throat, her mouth too dry to pray aloud.

Chalky gray film belched up from the jagged concrete floor. Brackish water thundered through the sky-framing gap in the ceiling. The tarp Lukas had used to cover interrupted repairs drooped into the ruptured roof like boneless vulture wings. The urge To bolt raged. Covering her mouth, she breathed through her nose, forcing an accounting.

A body was visible in the rubble. Oh, God, there'd been three men. Where were the other two? Oh, God, Chuey! She gaped around frantically.

"The old guy's okay. He ran off."

Cameron wheeled toward the hoarse whisper. Chuey was sprawled on his front, facing her, a massive beam pinning his legs, holding him half in, half out of the wreckage. Her feet turned to burdensome webs, her tongue to stone. She staggered toward him.

Brow furrowed, eyes darting frantically to his helper, Chuey motioned her away, rasping, "Over there—Chauncey. He needs help."

The injured man, Indian, soft-spoken and reticent, grateful for the cash she'd deposited in his hand at the end of each day, lay silent. On his back in obvious agony, eyes closed, lips moving soundlessly. Blood oozed from a wound in his scalp. A dark fist closed and opened rhythmically. She gasped a breath, moved to his side, and sank to her knees. Thick, warm fluid seeped between her fingers when she pressed her hand against the wound.

"It's all right. You'll be fine." The inane words rocked her like a dynamite blast. "I'll get help." *The phone.* Yes!

On all fours, she crawled to Chuey's side and roughly rummaged his clothing. His eyes flared in surprise. Or pain.

"Your phone." She knew he had one. She'd heard the jaunty, customized ring throughout the day, heard him talking, laughing. *Oh, Jesus.* "Where is it?"

Amidst a moan, he hoisted onto his elbows and fumbled in the chest of his blue work shirt. He produced the tiny cell phone, a link to mercy. "I'll do it." He coughed, choking slightly. "I'll call."

Refusing to imagine a reason for the cough, she rejected the possibility of more than Chuey's legs being crushed. He had to stay quiet, still. She lunged for the phone, clamped it in both hands, hysteria nipping the edges of her mind. With surprising strength, he wrestled it away from her.

"I'm okay." His voice had weakened as if their wrestling match had sapped his strength. Dialing, he nodded toward his injured peer and urged, "Help him."

She crawled back to the man. Inching forward she saw his eyes were open now, large and staring, whites grotesquely enlarged. Unknown debris caked his hair. No part of his visible body moved. Not a twitch. He neither whimpered nor cried out. Chuey's voice

droned in her ear, petitioning 911, giving details, the
address. She heard him dial and talk again,
murmuring low for too long a time. Would no one
help them? The sun was going down. Soon it would
be dark and cold. All of the inn's blankets had been
donated to shelters.

Hands trembling, she began flinging debris aside,
digging through rotted insulation and tarpaper, soot
and scraps until she unearthed the limp body.
Rimmed by a stark-white line of pain, his lips stood
out in his face. They had ceased praying. His teeth
were clamped, but bared. Straining, ignoring the
possibility of further injury, she lifted him, formed an
X with her crossed legs and wedged them beneath his
shoulders, making a makeshift pillow. She nestled his
bloody head in her lap and rocked, stroking his sweaty
face with one hand. The other reached out to grasp
Chuey's hand and hold on, as though he were a life-
line. Her eyes sought his. He smiled, managing a
thumbs-up sign. She thought of Jarrid. She'd never get
him back once Phillip heard about this disaster. He
would blame her. Hayden would believe him, not her.

Don't die. Please, God, don't let this man die.

Outside the inn a car door slammed, a heavy
urgent thud. Her head jerked around. Too early for
the paramedics. Chuey had barely hung up the
phone. But help, thank God. A door opened.
Footsteps in the entry Familiar. Revered.

Lukas. Her heart pounded, then seized with relief,
joy. Dread.

When he stood before her, her body began to shudder. Where had he come from? Was she trapped in a nightmare or a dream?

Lukas scanned the scene, her, the man she nursed, the wreckage. Never had she witnessed such open emotion. Disbelief, disgust, fear. For once he hid nothing. His eyes, charred knife blades, pierced her sharply, his gaze deep and jarring. While her body burned with regret, her mind scurried backward to what she might have done differently. She had regarded Lukas' warning of the over-burdened roof as obstinacy buried in a sermon praising Mother Earth's gift of rain.

Spotting Chuey, Lukas uttered a quiet cry. Minimal wide steps put him at Chuey's side. He sank to his knees, hands seizing, shoving on the broad beam. Nothing. With a mighty cry, arms straining, back muscles bulging, he lifted and flung the beam aside, then laid both hands on the backs of Chuey's legs, his eyes closed, face lifted. Breathing raggedly, he spoke plaintive Navajo. Chuey answered in their shared tongue, struggling beneath Lukas' hands, attempting to sit, to smile.

"No." Lukas roared. "Don't move."

Chuey froze, burying his face against a bleeding arm. Never having heard Lukas raise his voice, Cameron cringed. The man she nurtured winced, in turn. She prayed to stay calm, bending to croon in his ear a lullaby once reserved for Jarrid. The metallic and salty smell of blood filled her nostrils. She tried not to gag.

Lukas ripped off a rolled bandana that had held back his hair and bound Chuey's arm above the cut, grimacing as he lightened and tied. He swiped at Chuey's blood and wiped it on the sweatshirt he wore, then lowered his head into his hands. A mass of raven hair masked his face, but not his grief.

Chuey's feeble assurances contrasted with the wail of a distant siren. Cameron closed her eyes and clamped her lips, breathing deeply, fighting a dizzy fog.

From his squatting position, Lukas swiveled, lips rigid with suppressed fury. His eyes fixed on her bloody hands, seemingly for the first time. In his face, disgust tangled with emotion she failed to identify before his indiscernible gaze snapped to hers. Severing the connection, he rose. Hands jammed into his back pockets, he paced away, stared up into the hole, paced back glaring at her, whole-hearted wrath restored.

"My brother is dying," he said, voice husky, eyes haunted.

Navajos, except for those who had adopted Christianity, hated death, viewed it as the enemy, held aversion to dead bodies. According to her cache of research books, existence in the hereafter appeared shadowy and uninviting, marking death and everything connected to it as something to be avoided. Lukas' own repulsion said as much. She tried to focus on this new vulnerability that so contrasted his strength, converging her thoughts on anything but the devastation around her.

Her eyes locked with Chuey's. His were dulled, but they assured her Lukas had spoken of the stranger in her arms. Their Navajo brother. She shook her head, hiking her chin. "He won't die as long as we don't give up on him." When she pressed the bloody head to her breasts, Lukas' eyes fired with something other than fear. "I don't give up easily, Lukas."

The siren's agitating whang neared, increased to deafening, whined, died. Doors slammed. After an eternity footsteps pounded on the asphalt drive, across the tile and through the entry door. Two paramedics braced, waiting for direction.

"Over here." Lukas' voice held familiar quietness now. Resignation.

Warily, he stepped over her burden, knelt and pried her hands loose and held them in his. His touch, suddenly tender, jolted her into searching his eyes. As the man was lifted off her and loaded onto the stretcher, Lukas tugged his shirt from his jeans and wordlessly worked to wipe the drying blood from her hands. She averted her eyes, struck by the deftness of his large hands and their gentle strength. Sinful, help-less desire roiled from her groin to her heart.

&

Outside, they stood without touching as para-medics maneuvered Chuey's stretcher across the drive to a second ambulance. Splints guarded his legs.

Glucose dripped into a vein. An orbiting globe atop the ambulance cast an eerie glow on the darkness, painting Lukas' strong profile a sickly blue. He stepped to the back of the van before the doors closed, spoke to Chuey in Navajo, then addressed the attendants.

"Take him to Phoenix Indian Medical Center." Brooking no argument, he pivoted on a boot heel and strode toward the Suburban.

Cameron raced in his wake, night air stinging her cheeks, pavement cold and rough beneath her bare feet. Anticipating resistance, she followed to the driver's side and wedged her body between Lukas and the truck door. Stone-faced, breath ragged, he stared down at her. Behind them, the wail of Chuey's ambulance waned to silence. An owl cried out in the desert night. Lukas flinched at the sound.

She sucked up resolve "I ride with you, or I drive myself. I don't want to do that." She trembled. "I'm upset. I shouldn't drive, but if I have to I will."

"Stay here." His arms crossed his bloody chest, stance widening, blocking her escape even as he refused. "You don't belong. You have done enough."

"Go to hell, Lukas. I'm going to the hospital." Ire overriding guilt, she shoved him and wheeled away, striving to remember where the Taurus was parked.

He caught her arm, spinning her back around, an angry mist passing over his eyes. "Why?"

A million reasons collided in her head, leaving her mute For the last hour, since the roof had caved in, while she functioned in a mental nether land, her fighting spirit had sustained her through the worst. She hadn't crumbled or broken apart, and she wouldn't now beneath his judgment. She sent that message with her eyes.

Slowly, each finger releasing in turn, his grasp Eased. "Get your shoes," he grudged. "Or they will think you're Indian."

෯

As he drove, too fast but cautiously, his fingers extended and flexed, curled back around the wheel, gripping as if he might yank it from the dash. A jaw muscle spasmed while his exquisite mouth clamped tight.

"Lukas."

He held up a hand, its blood-crusted back toward her. "Not now."

"Yes, now." He shot her a disbelieving look. "How did you know—"

"Nothing mystic." His acerbic tone stung, reminding her of Chuey's second phone call, informing her he'd been nearby after all.

"Don't blame Chuey for what happened. If that man dies—"

"That brother. *Shilah.*" He stared straight ahead.

"If he dies, it's my fault, not Chuey's."

"Damn straight."

Her head began to throb with the zeal of an abscess. "My plan made sense. They could even have worked on the roof. We've had four straight days of sun—"

"And three nights of rain, Chuey said, in case you slept through it. That much weight stretched the tarp to the limit." The floodgates had opened on his reticence. His glance became a glare. "What I want to know, Cameron, is how you rigged this behind my back?"

Cameron? Not Yazhi. He might as well have slapped her. "You told me you'd be in Window Rock. With Kai."

"Kai called off the sit-in," he gruffed.

Her mind whirled. "Why?"

"Priorities. Answer my question."

"I was panicked over our schedule…I couldn't let four non-productive days pass. Chuey was my only chance." To make hay while the sun was shining. "I bribed him."

They sat out a red light, his fingers drumming the wheel, eyes narrowed. "Bribed him, how? With what? Chuey only does white women." The light turned and he jammed the gas.

So he was still riled over Yolanda and the fire. If not for her concern for the injured and dying, her reluctant empathy for his pain, she might have spit in the face of his innuendo. Her pledge of secrecy to Yolanda—obsolete but still a vow—echoed in her head. "How is between the two of us…I blackmailed him, actually, and that's all you need to know."

Silence lingered. A loss of words urged her to bide her time.

"Deception is the nature of the beast." His voice sank to steely quiet, but instead of stirring resentment, the characteristic sermon left her feeling restored.

"I can't deny I went behind your back. I'm desperate, Lukas."

"I told you I'd do all I could." His hand flexed, regripped the wheel. "You don't trust me. It is that simple."

"I can't afford to trust you." Nothing about the situation was simple. "Our priorities are too different."

With a grunt, he swung the Suburban into a parking lot and sped past a glaring emergency sign. Commandeering a parking space, he rammed the gearshift into place. "Then I will have to watch my back with you. Count on it." His hand grasped the door handle and jerked. The overhead light blinked on.

"I'm so damned exhausted from fighting you, Lukas." Something in her words, or maybe the frustration in her tone, halted his exit. She ran her fingers into her hair, massaging her aching temples as he waited, poised on the edge of her claim, like a sleek cat ready to plunge. "I've fought you from the first moment I laid eyes on you. I'm sick of it."

"But there is more fighting in the goddamned story than what you speak of. Right?"

His meaning probed another wound, reiterating her point "Right! And we'd be just great in bed. Wouldn't we, Wind Dancer?" She bent to don her shoes, addressing the floor. "We'd spend all the time when we could be making love wrestling for the top position."

As she worked on buckling the intricate ankle straps, she slowly became aware of the burdened silence, and overly aware of his presence. His smell, his size, his heat. The air shifted, roiling with a new kind of friction. Straightening, she stared across at him, meeting his eyes in the dim but tell-all light "Lukas…"

He had twisted his shoulders into the corner formed by the seat and door. One arm draped the wheel, the other ran along the back of the seat. Silent, he stared as if memorizing her face for a quiz he planned to ace in the future.

"I don't think we…I didn't mean it that way," she said. "Not really."

"If you stood on your head in bed, Yazhi, I'd find a way to make it good for you."

Without waiting for the reply clogging her throat, he opened the door. In silence, they entered the emergency area and approached the desk. Uncommonly gruff, Lukas identified himself, demanding to see Chuey.

A desk nurse eyed his bloody clothing, her gaze running to Cameron for a long moment. She nodded, murmuring, "Down there," and returned to her paperwork.

At the end of the hall, two men wearing surgery scrubs stood with heads inclined, speaking in hushed tones with a woman in a hospital-issued robe. Prompted by Cameron and Lukas' approach, the trio turned expectantly. With a small, feral cry, the woman stepped forward and into Lukas' arms.

Across his shoulder, Kai Blackwater's troubled eyes met Cameron's.

twenty-four

From the foot of Chuey's hospital bed, Lukas assessed his condition. One leg and a collarbone broken, the other leg severely lacerated and bruised. Seventeen stitches had closed a gash in his forearm. He slept now, face as childlike as Gad's had been when Lukas stood by his bed a week ago. A bag of clear fluid dangled from a slender steel rack, a tube trailing down, ending in a needle inserted into the back of a smooth, dark hand. The other hand clutched a switch-rigged cylinder capable of intravenously doling out the painkiller in the bag at Chuey's discretion.

Twice, Chuey's brow had furrowed in his sleep, eyes clenched; his thumb had pressed the switch. Considering his injuries had proven minor compared to those of the brother in the room down the hall, in Lukas' opinion, a little harmless but memorable pain might be worthwhile. Chuey had many more loyalty lessons to learn.

Kai slept also, a chair pulled close to the bed, her upper torso draping it, hands splayed on Chuey's chest as if to cover as much of his body as possible.

Warding off the goddamned evil spirits that had already wreaked havoc.

Lukas stepped closer, eyeing Kai's dark head resting against the white sheet, recalling the fuss she had made when Chuey came from surgery, her refusal to leave him. Lukas had somehow convinced the staff to move her from her own room to the empty half of Chuey's. From there she would continue her stepped-up series of tests.

Seeing her in the hall as he and Cameron arrived had caught him off guard. Speculating on how in hell she had known Chuey was under the same roof snaked a cold breath down his spine. Lately, news of her health, her political unrest and any plans to abate it, had funneled to Lukas through Chuey. The two seemed fused in mind and spirit, connected at the hip. Connected, anyway, without question. He turned to stare out the window, hands in his pocket .

And then there's their liking for the same goddamned cheap-ass wine.

Whatever. Healing had to be the main focus. Chuey waking up and finding Kai there, instead of having to face Lukas' wrath so soon, might go far toward that purpose. He considered that license to leave the room and look for Cameron.

She was absent from her post outside Chauncey's room. Lukas peered in from a safe distance, then turned away from the sound of the wheezing machines and the smell of death. The waiting room down the hall, littered with Styrofoam cups, candy wrappers, and magazines lay deserted.

"She left." Forcibly, the desk nurse broke concentration on a droning TV.

Lukas checked the clock above the nursing station. Most of the hell-of-a-long-night had passed. "Did shesay where she was going?"

"She asked for directions to the chapel. Later, she used my phone to call a cab."

He mulled over his surprise and a feeling he had to label as disappointment. "How is the man in 213?"

"Hanging on. We're looking for family members. Any clues?"

So they still expect him to die. His hairline crawled, making the braid suddenly tight. "None. But I'll find some."

☙

Lukas killed the Suburban's headlights before pulling in at Salt River and parking beside Cameron's wagon. Turning off the engine, he stared at the bungalow in the near distance. A picture of the destruction inside the inn, his fear before he realized Cameron was not among the injured or dead, repeated in his head like a ritual chant. He would carry to his grave the sound of her crooning, the sight of tears streaming down her cheeks, her rocking body, the lack of prejudice in her anguished almond eyes as she cradled Chauncey's bloody head against her breasts. Love and lust had pierced his anger, twisted his gut and heart. The feeling barraged him still.

Led by a drawing in his groin, his eyes sought the bungalows beyond the windshield, through thick Palms. Anger resurging, he looked away to the inn.

From day one, he had pegged her impulsive nature. The damage that would throw construction severely into arrears, a certain-to-come government inspection, possibly a brother's death, could be blamed on her aggressiveness. Her penchant for living and operating on impulse.

On the other hand, she *was* capable of acting without haste. *Plotting.* Having known for days when he would be gone, she had leisurely spent the time planning to deceive him, and involved Chuey in her scheme. She was a woman with an agenda that did not include or consider him. This fiasco proved it. She fought him at every turn, considering all fair in love and commerce.

Gradually, Jarrid's face—dark guileless eyes, too-curly hair—settled in his mind, denting the edge of resentment, softening the perimeter of his pain.

He left the truck and unlocked the inn's entry door, stood in the darkness, surveying the damage for real. The fire pit, half filled with water and debris, caught his eye. Cameron's hate for that symbol of his victory had led him to half consider filling it in, cheating design integrity. Tonight he vowed to complete it and render the breach between them insurmountable.

With his boot heel he scraped through the dark residue of Chauncey's blood and then kicked at the beam that had mangled Chuey's leg and shoulder. Its resistance brought memory of Cameron's body running rigid when she spotted Kai in the hospital corridor. Her eyes had held pain, loss, then renewed determination.

Cramming down his useless deliberation, he strode to the pool, stripped away his bloody clothing, and sliced into the icy water.

෯

From the window of the construction trailer, Lukas stared at the stiff back of the OSHA inspector crossing the inn's neglected grounds. He stopped in front of the entry to make additional notes on a clipboard, then continued to the parking lot. Before his government-issued vehicle pulled into the street, Cameron was out of her bungalow. Shoes in hand, a magazine shielding her head from an afternoon rain, she ran toward the trailer. Inside the door, she dropped the flimsy shoes and stepped into them, breathlessly fitting straps behind her heels. Lapis shadows stippled the golden skin beneath her lowered eyes.

"What did he say?" The first words to pass between them since the hospital last night, when Kai's presence had closed her tighter than a tomb.

"Just what I expected." He shoved a citation into her hands. A bureaucratic demand for safer working conditions inside, new tires on the back hoe, the seat tightened, an outside water fountain installed for the crew, the trailer moved another five feet in from the property line. And more. *Too much more.* A staggering fine capped it off. "Construction is stopped until we comply with this."

Her eyes skimmed the page, then misting, lifted to his. "Oh, God…"

"Enit." He stomped to a pot of scorched coffee on a side bar, setting the trailer to vibrating. "He probably stayed awake all night making this list in his head, before he even looked up the inn's address." The name Wind Dancer Construction would have guaranteed that. If Lukas had learned anything about construction in the past three years, it was that more was required of him than of his competitors.

Indians had to do it better.

As he poured coffee no human could ingest, she murmured, "I have to call Uncle Hayden." She might have been speaking to herself.

"He knows all about it. CNN picked it up—from Channel 3, I guess—and went into their archives to rehash you and me squabbling over the inn last fall."

Her narrowed eyes and pinched mouth assured him she was still pissed over their nationally-aired feud. *"You've* been talking to him." Her tone hinting accusation, she worked her battered locket back and forth on its fragile chain.

"First thing this morning. It was my job to fill him in." And hers, but she stood to lose flesh and blood instead of earmarked bonus money. "He is surprised he hasn't heard from you." He hooked his gaze into hers.

Her lips clamped, eyes closing, then prying open. No words came. He had smoothed it over with her uncle by assuring him of her concern for the project and Chauncey, but now the baser side of his nature kept him from setting her mind at ease.

"I'll handle this." He pulled the list from her hand and tossed it on the desk. "It will take time we don't have, but—"

Alarm leapt into her eyes, quelling the speech. She shot her hands into her hair, then lowered them to briskly rub her crossed arms. The trailer was cold, but he was wearing jeans and a heavy shirt, not a damned all-but-see-through dress. He tossed her a denim jacket from a hook on the wall. She shrugged into it.

"Lukas…"

He could easily detect her concern and unspoken questions. "When I talked to your uncle I gave *El Niño* the blame." Where it would fit if the ire raping his reasoning ever let up. True to pattern, Chuey just by being Chuey, had already eased off Lukas' crap list on which Cameron Vickers remained.

"So we're partners in deceit, now," she said softly.

Deceit. A familiar bedfellow. Learned first hand from Suzanne, and now this divisive woman. If it had taken this disaster for her to consider him a partner, how far would his edited report to Hayden Chastain go toward earning her trust? Why did he care?

Knowing the answer to that rendered his resentment wasted.

"He wants to talk to you. Seems you have a visitor coming in a couple of days." He saw startled imaginings of her son in her widened eyes and regretted he had to douse their fire. "Michael Preston. Your uncle said you'd want to know."

Again she looked surprised as she nodded vaguely. He had hoped for an explanation, but deserved nothing. Still, shelving the subject proved difficult. "What have you heard from the hospital?" he asked.

"I've just come from there."

He nodded, crossing his arms, bracing a haunch against the cold steel desk. He had checked by phone every hour, but he wanted her rendition.

"Chauncey's vital signs have steadied. They've located some of his family in—"

"His people."

She flinched. "They're in Gallup. They hadn't heard from him in years and didn't know where to look." She struck a pensive look. "He has no insurance...of course...since he agreed to take cash for his work. It's not fair for his expenses to fall to his people." She had not missed a beat that time.

He debated on letting her fume, but the furrow between her sad eyes won him over. "I've alerted the insurance company. He had a verbal contract with you. He's covered by workman's comp."

"Then maybe what happened is a kind of blessing." She took a deep breath, her hopeful eyes seeking his, then finding no encouragement, skidding away. "Don't you think?"

His laugh sounded hollow and bitter, even to his jaded ears. "You might have a hard time selling the blessing theory."

"I sent money for them to come here."

"Bribe money?" *Let up, Wind Dancer. Admit it. You love this clueless woman.*

She turned her perfect profile to him, staring out the open door, sheeted now with rain. The downpour pelted the metal trailer roof like drumfire. Visions of the feather bed back in her bungalow almost crowded out those of Chuey lying in his own blood beneath that beam. Lying immobile now in a blue-flowered hospital gown, casts holding together his leg and shoulder. A crucial ASU semester gone.

"I left a book and candy for Chuey." She might have been reading his mind.

"Still sleeping, huh?" He knew differently, but af hovering dilemma had to be dealt with.

"Kai was with him, so I didn't go in." Her own thorny issues tangled behind burnt-copper eyes, then escaped in words that seemed to prick her lips. "What is she doing there? Is she…ill?"

"Ask Kai. She sics bad spirits on me if I talk out of school."

Her blue-hued hands tugged the pockets of the Coat. Ignoring the idle electric space heater in the corner, he toyed with temptation to take her in his arms and warm her out of ever deceiving him again.

Hopefully, self-flagellation would ground him, restrain deluded visions of any future they might share.

"Is that where you were this weekend? With Kai?" Wounded eyes probed.

"A great opportunity for you. *Enit?*" *Goddammit. Ease up on her.*

"Yes," she half whispered, eyes dulled. "I lead a charmed life, Lukas."

Removing the jacket, she held it out. When he left it dangling from her hand, she crossed the trailer, hung the jacket on a peg and started for the door.

Stay and fight, Yazhi.

Without a glance, she went out into the rain, her head high. He watched her unfaltering steps and squared shoulders, memorizing the way the drenched dress clung like a drowning man to her rounded buttocks.

Did she deserve an explanation? Deserve to know the one common ground between Kai and him had been sex? A tie Kai's mind refused to sever. Sex, the same insatiate hunger he purposefully allowed Cameron to believe tied him to herself.

Should he tell her that after five years of watching scars form he was unsure if he had ever loved *the white woman* she had begged him to speak of, or only loved the way she had fed his need back then?

Lukas closed the door on Cameron and the rain. *Better to let sleeping dogs lie.*

Torn between need to both punish and forgive, emotion still far outweighed by carnal craving, he kept away from her, working with the crew by day to right the inn's damage. He pulled extra night shifts at Dos Gringos, inventing ways to stay away from the bungalow till near dawn. Avoiding Cameron like the *chinde*.

On Wednesday evening, as he toiled alone at shoveling debris from the fire pit, she appeared like a revered apparition. He sensed and smelled her an instant before a faint wind from the door leading to the pool fanned his naked back. Her heels clicking off slow but decisive steps on bare concrete ended his useless parry.

Bracing himself he turned, leaning on the shovel.

She stood with one arm loosely wrapping her middle, one foot cocked on a spiked heel of the flimsy sandals she had worn the night she labeled him a thief. The other hand clutched a midget's handbag and a hot-hued floral scarf that should be covering deep cleavage revealed by a dress near enough to the gold-brown hue of her skin to make her look nude. A pair of piano-wire-thin straps held up the dress. Perfect black pearls, paired with the abused locket, rose and fell with the pulse in her throat, as if she had run the distance between the bungalow and lobby.

She wore *war paint,* subtle yet suggestive enough to win any damn war. Her nails, usually clear and tipped in white, glistened, a bruised copper color.

While he waited for her to break the impasse, results of the inventory he had taken ravaged his intellect and surged blood to his groin.

"I thought you might consider all that trash that ended up in there an omen." She nodded at the shovel resting in the pit, voice resonant on the quiet. Light from the falling away sun turned her spiked hair to warmed cinnamon.

"I consider it a challenge," he mouthed around the unlit cigar in his mouth.

"Issued by *El Niño?*"

Issued by a headstrong, impetuous mutineer. "Closer to home than that."

Her body adopted fight mode, mouth clenching. "Maybe you're getting your divine signals confused, Wind Dancer."

"Not a chance." He kicked a hunk of timber with a work boot. Brackish water splattered onto his cutoffs, trickled down a bare leg. "Cameron."

All animation left her eyes, her creamy shoulders going slack. Why in hell did he not feel more triumph in hitting the bull's-eye?

Resignedly, her face droll, she announced, "The hospital called while I was getting dressed. Chauncey has been taken off the critical list."

"And you're on your way to see him with Winstons and Wild Turkey."

Her jaundiced stare eventually veered to the fifty-gallon drum of sand he had shoveled and hauled from the desert in the middle of last night. But she kept her visible curiosity to herself. "Actually, I'm having dinner with Michael Preston." She paused. Indecisiveness hovered. "Business," she declared, as if he had inquired. "He's one of the family attorneys. He has papers for me to review."

In these days of electronic mail, fax, and couriers? Lukas grunted. Then sensing she had more to say, he ripped a bandana from around his brow and mopped his chest. Waiting.

Her eyes traced the sweaty wake as she segued into her purpose for being there. "The latch didn't catch...on your bedroom door. The wind blew it open."

So her door *had* been unlocked, standing open in invitation on the opposite side of his not-quite locked door—just as he had sensed. Only one of many reasons he had spent minimum time in the room.

"Mikela ran under your bed, she said softly. "I couldn't coax her out, so I came to ask you to watch for her...when you go in later. She's still looking for any opportunity to escape."

Like her mistress.

"No problem." He retied the bandana, seized the shovel and heaved a load of soggy slag within inches of her feet. He succeeded in keeping his eyes on his work, not on her, as her heels clicked retreat on the pavement.

He continued shoveling until a vision of her across the table from a stranger—to him, anyway—smiling allegiance, face lit by candlelight and wine, immobilized him. An urge not felt for months nagged in his gut, tickled the back of his throat, even in the face of argument. What Cameron Vickers chose to do and with whom was not reason enough to throw over conviction.

Then reason ran out.

He lit the cigar his mouth clamped and stalked to the stocked bar.

twenty-five

At a corner table for two in the Phoenician Hotel dining room, memory of Lukas' solemn face and fiery eyes lodged in Cameron's mind so strongly that the image almost rendered him a third party. So much so that when she signed the check with a flourish of finality, offering to walk Michael to his elevator, he looked reprieved.

"I take it you have some place more important to go."

She smiled into her brother's amiable blue eyes. "I'm planning to visit a sick friend, actually."

He reached for her chair as she rose in suggestion of leaving. "Well, I don't know how cowboys and Indians do it, but a Royal Mountie would see a lady to her car."

"You always were my *valiant* brother."

She handed over her car check as they left the dining room. They talked hushed family gossip as a valet attendant raced purposefully into the balmy evening toward a palm lined parking lot. Michael lit a cigarette, dropped the gold lighter into his pocket, and exhaled.

"How come you're not lighting up, fast and furiously? You haven't had a cigarette in two hours." He considered, brow arched. "Maybe in the ladies' john?"

"No…Don't think I haven't thought about it. Especially in view of your mission. But I've quit—or at least I think so." She smiled. "One never knows."

"Woman of steel." He took a deep drag, turned his head to exhale, then crushed the cigarette with the toe of a sleek Italian loafer. "Interesting auto. Blends with the desert elements," he observed as the Taurus approached the curb. Eyes taking her in, head to toe, his tone labeled the wagon too tame for her tastes. "That scarf is you, all right, but I'm positive the dress is borrowed."

She wound the scarf about her throat. "Why do you say that?"

"I remember your penchant for tropical colors."

"I'm going through some changes." She heard herself voicing at last what she had only feared and fought heretofore.

Draping an end of the scarf over one shoulder, he mused, "I guess changing your name was a forewarning of things to come."

She cocked her head, smiling. "You're suited to your trade. Observant and outspoken—just like David…was." Assailed by memory of their dead brother, she held his arm as they stepped off the curb in the direction of the waiting car. "You're actually more like him than I ever realized. And you're resembling me more as you get older."

He tucked her between his lanky form and the open car door. "Any family resemblance is unlikely, since we three had different fathers—and had them briefly, I might add." His smile evolved from teasing to caustic. "And each of us saw very little of our mother."

Somewhere in her cache of bruised memory, she found a sympathetic smile for him. For herself. "I never had a father," she reminded him. "Not even briefly."

"But still, after your mystery dad no other man measured up for Mom."

"How would she know, Michael?" *Since she has no idea who my father is.* His rueful expression prompted an apology. "I'm sorry you felt you had to come all this way to bring me the news, but I loved seeing you."

He tapped his briefcase "Confronting this required eye contact. And we got the unpleasant business handled." When she held his gaze, he prompted, "You're sure you're okay with it?"

"I trust your judgment." She hugged him, tilting her face to his kiss. "You'll take Jarrid my note?" His nod gave her strength to enter the car. "Tell him I love him." Her hands grasped the wheel. Her throat gripped back tears.

"Done. But he knows it." Smile grim, he slapped the car dismissively.

She pulled away and down the hotel drive, his words repeating in her head.

You're sure you're okay with it?

She tried picturing a stately mansion, rolling lawns, solicitous, white-coated attendants. Only one image materialized: her once-beautiful, heartbroken mother, suffering for an unwise, long-ago indiscretion, locked away, bound in restraints. A prisoner of her youthful folly.

❦

Cameron shed her shoes and in her stocking feet crept silently down Phoenix Indian Medical Center's tile corridor. Now a familiar and tolerated figure, she barely drew a detached wave from a charge nurse engrossed in a phone call.

As usual, Chauncey slept. A robust, dark-skinned male relative filled a faux-leather recliner, head lolling on one shoulder. Canned television laughter provided background for his sonorous breathing. Cameron tiptoed to Chauncey's side and watched the silent but even rise and fall of his frail chest, then raised her eyes to the constant drip of intravenous feeding. She placed the backs of her fingers to her lips, touched them to his cheek, then left as quietly as she had come.

In his room down the hall, Chuey sat propped in bed, naked but for boxer shorts and his casts. She knocked on his open door. He looked up anxiously, scrambling for the sheet, his infectious grin inviting her in. She approached the bed with a tall cup of Starbucks mocha latte, which she had discovered he loved.

"Cool. Thanks."

She kissed his forehead, noting the gash he had received the night of the fire was fast forming a scar, and that his coarse sable hair was days past the close cut he favored.

He worked at getting the lid off. "Decaf, I'll bet."

"Of course." She twisted a strand of hair in her fingers, bringing a wince to his gray-brown eyes. "Should I braid this while I'm here?"

"I was hoping you had scissors in there." He nodded at her small bag, then glanced at the wall clock. "You're out late. But nice of you to dress up for me."

She drew up a chair, sat, slipped her shoes on, and attempted to tuck the dress about her legs. "I dressed for Chauncey, since he always ignores me."

Chuey grunted a laugh. "Trying to scare some life back into him, huh?"

She tapped his heavily autographed leg cast with a fingernail. "Is this new?" *Yolanda.* Carefully printed, with elaborate scrolls added to the letters "Y" and "D."

"Don't touch it," Chuey warned and tried to lean out of range, but the leg cast kept him anchored from the waist down.

"Is her signature that sacred to you?" Concern knotted Cameron's stomach.

"The ink's still wet. It might smear and blight the real artwork."

While his cynicism surprised her, it wasn't a disappointment. "How did she know you were here?" Had he called? Or sent her a mystical message?

"She read about the fiasco in the paper. I am a media star—Chauncey 'n me."

She smiled. "I *thought* I saw her in the parking lot when I arrived." She waited for his nod, then added, "A man was with her, though, so I wasn't sure."

"Yeah." He pressed one palm against the mattress and grimaced while dragging his body to a more upright position. "Dwaine."

Cameron's mind sorted through Yolanda's story. "The not-so-evil brother."

"Evil enough." His brow creased. Diverting his eyes, he placed the coffee on the rolling nightstand.

"What did they want?" she asked tentatively. She had no right to know, but his branding Dwaine "evil enough," pebbled her arms with apprehension.

"To smoke a peace pipe." The look she gave was not severe enough to warrant his next rush of words. "Dwaine was at the fire—Eddie, too. The three of us got into it over Yolanda. If the fire hadn't scared them off, I'd be tenderized buffalo."

His confession stunned her. While she sat mute, trying to comprehend, he retrieved the coffee and sipped thoughtfully.

"I shouldn't of had Yolanda at Lukas' house without him knowing about it."

"Or any girl." She adopted an authoritative but kind tone she would use to teach Jarrid, should she ever have that privilege again.

"Having Pocahontas there would have been okay with Lukas."

His satiric grin was a disturbing reminder that in Lukas' eyes, she, a non-Indian, also failed to measure up. "Does Lukas know about Dwaine and Eddie?"

He shrugged. "Not much gets by him, but if he knows, he's keeping quiet. Probably waiting for me to come clean."

Instead, Chuey had chosen to tell her. She felt claustrophobic, cornered in an undersized, windowless room with a locked door. "You have to tell him, Chuey. Or I'll have to."

He swigged coffee, set the cup down and massaged the leg not housed in a cast.

"Chuey?"

"I'm working on a deal. I wouldn't have told you if—"

"Lukas hasn't forgiven me for the accident. I won't deceive him again." She had done it for Jarrid, yet her duplicity had worsened her dilemma.

"Right. I'll take care of it." His eyes took on a haunted look. He was no longer the cavalier man-child who had picked her up at Dandy Doug's only a few weeks before. Knowing she was partly to blame filled her with regret.

She stood, reluctant to leave him, but suddenly eager to be away from the secret that bound them. Dutifully, she asked, "How is Kai? I assumed she'd be with you." In which case she would have peeked in and tiptoed past.

His dark eyes shifted away. "She went back up the Hill. Tests are over. She'll probably organize the damn sit- in again."

"Are the test results back?" A gleam of hope and an aura of dread plagued her.

"You'll have to ask Kai." This smile was uncharacteristically somber. "She's a banshee at guarding her privacy."

His disclosure rang familiar. Forcing a smile, she kissed his brow again. "Good night, Romeo. Sleep tight with your secrets."

Both of which, unquestionably, would involve her and impact her life.

☙

Chuey lay sleepless far into the night, mulling over the new twists in his life, and how his decisions would affect the people involved. Gradually, he was discovering that accountability was hell.

As he'd told Cameron, Yolanda and Dwaine had offered a deal. They would turn Eddie in for starting the fire. To save Dwaine's ass, Yolanda would swear he was there as a failed mediator between Eddie and Chuey. Not knowing if the last part was true or false, Chuey had reserved argument. In return for their offer, Chuey would contact Children's Services and call off the bloodhounds, who had returned to the house a second time, sniffing deeper, barking louder. Dwaine swore he would come up with the apartment deposit

Yolanda had squandered, once the state lost interest and he knew Polly was safe.

Dwaine's offer tumbled around in Chuey's head, banging out a question of just how *safe* Polly would be in Yolanda's care. And since he had never squealed on the trio to Children's Services, how in hell could he stop the process? If he knew the caller's identity, maybe he could cut a separate deal. He had no friggin' idea where to start looking…well, maybe one, but a definite long shot.

And then there was Kai. The general assumption was that people didn't get what Kai had anymore, but those immune people didn't sleep in Kai's leaky hogan, exist on her God-awful diet, smoke unfiltered cigarettes and drink that dirt-cheap wine she liked.

He forced himself to rethink that. He knew better than to blame her lifestyle. She had a virus, pure and simple, a parasitic leech, draining her, dragging her down to useless despair.

Since Lukas had managed to get her moved into his hogan, she could let Grandma and Apenimon watch over her—her and Gad, thank God. But regardless of what he had told Cameron about Lukas and Kai, Kai's living arrangement was temporary, and TB wasn't. Trying to scare Cameron away from Lukas had been for Kai and Gad's sake, and maybe it had worked. Or maybe Lukas' red-ass actions since the roof cave-in would do the trick, tip Cameron off to what life under Uncle Bro's thumb entailed. But who was *he* to waylay Cupid?

Let's call a spade a spade, Run Amok. Who are you to play God?

Lukas was in love with Cameron Vickers. Figuring that out didn't require a psychology degree. Lukas' behavior damned near screamed it any time Chuey caught them within smelling distance of each other. Or when they weren't, and he fell into those long, brooding silences, brow wrinkled, mouth grim. Considering Lukas' cockeyed convictions regarding the tribe, he might never do a damn thing about loving her, but he deserved space and a clear head while he worked it through. And his concern for Kai and Gad would muddy the water.

Chuey could fix that. Everything he was and hoped to be, he owed to Lukas.

To Kai, he owed his life.

Night air stinging her shoulders, Cameron stood at the end of the pool watching Lukas' powerful arms slice the water with incisive strokes. He halted directly before her, and without hesitance placed his hands on the pool deck, hefted up and out of the water. With predator-like intent he moved forward, wet and bare as Adam in Eden. Classical music wafted out from the lobby to the terrace, while thunder menaced in the distance, followed by a rip of lightning on the horizon. His athletic silhouette gleamed like burned copper under the shadowed moon. He smelled of chlorine, yeasty beer scent, and purpose.

Her abdomen muscles clamped with visceral reaction. She looked around frantically for a towel or his clothing. Sighting none, she jerked the silk Hermes scarf from around her neck and held it out to him. He used it to blot his flowing hair, his disregard for its value jolting her.

"How was business?" He drew the scarf through his hands as if it were a lasso. "Did it leave you satisfied?"

While she pretended to ignore the innuendo, a million questions bunched into one mundane statement. "I thought you'd be at Dos Gringos." She had even planned on taking Michael by there, introducing them, but Lukas' earlier' frame of mind had deterred her. "That water has to be—What are you doing out here?"

"Waiting for you. We have business of our own." His tone held an irascible quality that was rapidly becoming familiar. "Unfinished business."

Unavoidably, Yolanda's apt speculation on his anatomy vibrated in her mind. She jerked her eyes back to his face and found his own glittering dangerously. "You're naked." Except for the silver cross.

"Damn straight. I believe in expediency."

She would have laughed at the pointed remark, but his hands reaching out, finding her dress straps with wet and cold fingers, muted her. On second impulse, she attempted to back away. He held firmly to the straps. She felt the fabric strain. His next words stunned her.

"Did you sleep with him?"

"Who?" Her mind whirled, then settled on his meaning. "Of course not."

A thumb raked over her mouth, roughly, smearing the lipstick she had reapplied at the hospital. "Did he kiss you?"

Her hairline spiked. Anger kept her from setting his mind at ease. "You're off base. Besides, it's none of your——" His hard, narrowed eyes stopped her cold. "It's late," she ventured. "We'll talk in the morning."

This time his grunt that normally could mean Anything spelled unqualified refusal. He hooked the wet scarf around her neck and tugged, drawing her forward, his cold, rock-hard body already warming.

She braced her palms against his slick chest. "Lukas——" She searched for reasoning. "You've been drinking."

"Just enough." He grasped her wrists and lowered her hands, pinning them between their bodies, against his growing erection.

"Just enough to manhandle me?" She forced slack into her fingers.

"Enough to know what I want."

He found the zipper beneath her arm. Its release whispered loud as an angry sea in the still night. A hand slid inside the chemise dress, splaying against the small of her back. His fingers brushed the upper curve of her buttocks, then traced the cleavage so low that she drew a sharp jolting breath. He withdrew the hand and moved to a breast, not grasping, but cupping her gently.

Half fear battled whole anger. Yet she became aware of an inconvenient bunching inside her, a heated tidal wave in that mystical place she could never name. Never had she wanted a man as much as she wanted him, and never had desire been more unwise. "Lukas…We should talk." She held her head out of range of his seeking mouth. "I don't want to do this."

His laugh was soft, his eyes hard. "The hell you don't."

"But you don't. You made that clear. You spelled out the consequences."

"The devil lurks in details, Yazhi." His voice had turned soft as a caress.

Heart hammering, she tried again. "This is not like you—going against what you know will only—"

"Right now it is." Before she could step away, his hand caught her wrist. "Later I will nurse my regrets."

With deft, one-handed dexterity, he unhooked her bandeau bra. It grazed her body beneath the dress and fell at her feet, the soft sound echoing on the pool deck. Then swift as thought, he did the same with the dress. The straps skimmed her arms, then her hips…the garment pooling around her ankles. She stood before him in nylons and shoes. Sucking in breath, arms forming an X over her chest, she backed up. Her feet snagged in the dress. He righted her before she stumbled, jerking her tight against him, his skin taut, silky and searing.

She fought a mounting craving. "We have to talk, Lukas."

"No more talk." His sex pulsed, matching her heart rhythm.

"You're scaring me, damn you," she rasped. "Is that what you want?"

"No," he mumbled at last. He released her, hands going to the band of her hose, fingers gentle on the indentations of her waist. Still, his gaze speared hers.

Again she glanced around frantically. Her eyes seized on the chaise lounge where only a few nights ago they had so calmly discussed and decided on abstinence. Tonight, she faced a craving, caged beast straining to be released. Yet once released, a beast could create injury. One of them had to uphold their agreement made at a saner time. Even knowing this, consumed with the anxious danger of risking everything, she craved to free him and to free her own longing.

"Take off your shoes." He rolled the elastic band onto her hips.

His command evolved to heady visions, seductive enough to produce doubt of her sanity. "We can't do this. Not here. Security—"

He used his warm, yeasty mouth to seal her protest, conveying intent that rapidly became her desire. Fighting logic, she clung to him, running her hands into his wet hair. Holding the kiss, he effortlessly scooped her up, strode toward the open lobby door and across the disheveled space. None too gently he stood her down, knelt and began peeling off the panty hose.

When she realized she stood on the edge of the *fire pit,* ire shot through her veins.

"Wait!" She squirmed determinedly. He held one bare leg fast, working to free the other of restriction. She went rigid. "Not here." *Damn him!*

The words hung on the balmy air. In one smooth, continuous movement, he stepped into the pit, grasped her waist, swung her down, and rendered them prone onto the fresh sand bottom. She raised on her elbows, but he pinned her gently, nuzzling her temple, then her mouth. She fought the sinking sensation that battled her vexation, the grainy bed scouring her shoulders and buttocks, the backs of her thighs. She wedged a palm beneath his chin, seeking his eyes in the faint amber light seeping in from the terrace.

"I hate this damn thing, and you know it. I won't do it *here.*"

A powerful leg looped her hips and he lowered his face to the pulse rioting at her throat. His tongue explored the indention, then moved to flick an ear lobe. "Here," he whispered, the edict husky, his tone tenderly decisive. "Then you won't hate it."

While his eyes impaled hers, a hand seared a trail down her body, ending between her thighs. His fingers twined her pubic tuft before he pressed upward against her mound with the heel of his hand. He fitted his Mouth to a breast, teeth nipping, tugging so slightly the ethereal sensation could be imaginary. Her insides liquefied, pooled and whirled under his touch. She bucked off the sand, biting back a moan Reminding herself where she lay, she determined not to appease him. His fingers glided between her secret folds and then into her, a gentle intrusion. She strove against being lured into a warm miasma haven, struggled to hold back, to deny herself pleasure on this despised bed.

His fingers sank deeper, stroking, expertly manipulating.

"Take me…somewhere else, Lukas." Her voice sounded on the charged air, foreign and weak.

His warm, deeply invasive kiss turned her objections to moans, sending her onto a foreign plane from which she watched her hips thrash the sand, pump against his hand. She plunged into pleasure so dense, heat so fierce, that it spiraled through her and sprang outward to the tips of her fingers and toes.

"It has to be here." His urgent whisper singed her ear. A finger homed in on the crest of her vulnerability, working skillfully. "Trust me. I will take care of you, Yazhi."

She knew the briefest instant of defeat before cognizance drowned in a pool of frantic passion, controlling her mind and body, overwhelming any other emotion. In the vast, wrecked lobby, she whimpered in his coaxing embrace. His mouth sealed her to him; he swallowed her protest and passion. Her body arched. She shuddered mightily and shattered. Her very being cast off into space, a trillion tiny pieces whirling outward before they floated downward into infinity, never to be possessed again.

She lay rigid, her breath breaching the parched air, unable to believe she had submitted so quickly, making it so easy for him. Wrenching away, she sat up, arms on her drawn up knees, face buried in her hands, her body trembling. Behind her, he was still. Then she sensed his body curling, felt his heat, smelled his distinct and primitive maleness. He pressed his mouth to one shoulder blade, the other, to her middle back, then kissed her low on her spine. She froze and then thawed, running liquid, voracious.

Resolute.

Swiveling, she pushed him backward, straddled him and grasped between their bodies, attempting to settle onto him. Effortlessly and carefully, he rolled her over on the cushion of sand. She clutched her knees, but he drew her beneath him, spread her thighs with a knee, and entered her. She winced at the tightness abstinence had rendered. But desire created a moist path and she parted, her legs circling his hips. He imbedded his engorged sex with a series of small, possessive thrusts, each drawing a soft moan she no longer sought to stifle, and then he rose to brace on his palms, plunging roughly, rhythmically, his jaw grim. She clenched her eyes, shutting out the clouded, distant look his own held.

Abruptly, he grew still. "Open your eyes."

She shook her head, sand grinding into her hair. He had had his way in this place, and would again, but she would somehow hide her mutinous pleasure. Silence rent the air, interrupted only by their soughing breaths.

"Open your eyes." Softly now, like a tender, coaxing undertow.

Supported by his elbows, he settled his partial weight onto her, the cross dangling lightly between her breasts. Hands framing her face, fingers in her hair, he kissed her mouth and then her closed eyes. Willfully they opened and searched his lean, dark face. Her heart rioted, then ached, as she discovered in his unmasked eyes all that his tormented, twisted creed forbade him to voice. For that moment, he crossed a border, allowing her to know his secret feelings that turned his commitments to burdens.

Her mirrored feelings leapt to life. She reached, pulling his mouth to hers, rising to his penetrating kiss, sucking him in, offering her body, spirit, and soul.

His hips resumed the rhythmic stride, each plunge deeper, more powerful, until her body found his tempo, met and matched it. Then he buried so deeply within her that she wondrously imploded, taking a second joyful, solitary journey to the outer edge of reality, returning to the man who held her. "Lukas, you—"

"Now," he whispered.

One final, emphatic thrust cast him into his own spasm. Abandonment moved in waves across his face before his body turned rigid, shuddered, and ran slack. Their mouths and bodies still joined in an ebbing tremor he carefully turned them. Wet and spent, she lay in his arms, their gazes meshed, and confronted the reality of all they had forsaken and embraced.

And all neither of them was free to voice.

twenty-six

A rain-peppered dawn crept into the bungalow, framing Cameron in ashen light. She sat across from him, legs drawn into the straight-back chair, hair tousled from bed, now kinked by the humidity. Her fingers, tapering into the long, bruised-copper nails, wrapped a mug of black tea he had brewed in the miniscule galley and teased with brandy. Mikela stretched across Cameron's shoulders, head visible on one side of her neck, rump on the other.

Lukas knew Cameron had scarcely slept, and the turned-up collar of a white terry robe underscored subtle blue shadows beneath her eyes. Invasive daylight revealed bare, swollen lips. Contrition stirred his conscience before getting lost in lustier recall. Gradually, he settled on the reality of where the night had taken them. A place from which they could never wholly return.

Not since Suzanne had Lukas allowed morning to find him with a woman in his arms, or allowed himself to make love in his own habitat. His pattern had been to steal away in the night, leaving no question about his reason for having been there, no doubt of his shallow feelings. By sharing the morning with

Cameron, he aimed to prove love with action, not words. He had fought against saying, "I love you," knowing that later, when he could no longer hold her, the phrase would ring hollow. An empty echo that would shape-shift into carnal lies. Neither of them needed that. He hoped to give her something more tangible than words.

Pitching forward, he grounded his chair on all four legs and reached across the table, cupping her nape. A wary furrow formed between her brows. Smiling, he drew her mouth to his and whispered a kiss of silent apology. "Long night. *Enit?*"

"I'm a bit weary," she admitted. "You're a tireless lover, Lukas." Elbows on the table, she studied him above the mug rim, advancing the commendation into an accusatory vein. "And more skilled than I want to think about."

With a thumb, he touched her puffy lower lip, lingering at the corner of her mouth. "There was a time when I had a lot to prove, Yazhi. I believed being with many women would accomplish that." *Any white girl in Chicago who would part her thighs.* But he had guarded his spirit, avoiding involvement, not risking hurt.

Somehow Cameron had penetrated that armor.

Pulling himself into the present, he offered wryly, "I am Indian, so I learned to perform better." Her throat flushed beneath his hand, enabling him to smile, mocking the sullied past and anxious present.

"Being with you followed a long dry spell. If I was too rough, forgive me."

Her sable eyes flashed unasked questions bearing Kai's name, then her lashes lowered onto her cheeks, preventing his knowing if she believed his vow of abstinence. Or knowing if in his greed he had mistreated her.

"Who is Camellia?" At the question, her head jerked up, curls jouncing around her face, the furrow deepening. "Who?" he urged.

She sat back, cradling his hand in hers. "She was once me…She was me last night. But Camellia was too tender, too vulnerable…in my former life. When I could no longer afford that, I took a new name."

"And a new persona." Before, her softness had been her strength. "You're Cameron, now. A tough, take-charge woman." He kept his tone light.

"I'm still perfecting that." She managed a self-effacing smile.

"Did you change your name before or after the car wreck?"

"Lukas—" She shot him a chastising look, exasperation cramming her tone. Rain thrashed the tiled roof, sheeted the windows, closing them in. In the murky light, her eyes grew haunted. "Just because we had sex—"

We made love, Yazhi.

She looked away, lifting her fingers to her temples, tips pressing, turning white. Mikela stirred, then resettled. Listening to the cat purr, Lukas envied her closeness as intently as he craved to steal Cameron's pain, heal her. Free her.

"Headache?" He kept his voice at whisper level.

Her teeth created a jagged white line against her top lip.

"Did you hit your head in the wreck?"

She smiled defeat. "Yes. But I've had the headaches since childhood." Slowly her eyes opened, dull, but resigned. Locking her hands around her raised knees, she hooked her chin there and contemplated her petite, polished toes. "I had just gotten new pain medication. I took it for the first time that night." She looked uncertain, fragmented, then began again in a quiet, resolute tone. "I'd had a glass of wine...at a board dinner. As I was leaving, I got a call. It was Lee. He was in town for a football game." Glancing up, she looked as though she were reentering the present. "Lee played pro ball. I don't think I told you that."

Lukas shook his head, his mind a vortex of reserved questions.

"I went to meet him. To talk. I had a second drink there." She slid the locket along its chain, then back to the center, just below the throbbing pulse in her throat. "I didn't realize the strength of the pills, the effect the wine would have..."

So she was seeing Tutuila while married to Vickers. His gut spasmed. Senselessly, he wanted to believe no other man had heard her guttural groan when inside her, to believe no man after him would bring her to that pinnacle of pleasure he had taken her to, or see

the same feral greed that had glazed her eyes at that
Moment. Afterward, he had watched her sleeping,
supine, radiant, and felt everything he knew to be
wrong was somehow right.

Son-of-a-bitch. Had he known it would be this
way—that he would want her enough to think
crazy—he would have walked away that first day and
let her have her goddamned South Seas Hotel. He *had*
known, but he had hoped he could beat it, maybe slip
away from a bloodletting without scars.

Maybe he still could.

He shoved out of the chair and paced heavily to
the teapot, but before the brew hit the bottom of his
cup, her look of injured surprise at his sudden retreat
hit his heart.

*Let it go, Wind Dancer. She had a life before you.
She'll have one after.*

He turned, holding the pot aloft. "More tea, little
one?"

Relief flooded her face. "No, I'm fine." She lifted
the mug and sipped.

He re-crossed the room, pressed his mouth to the
top of her tousled head, winning a smile, then slipped
back into his chair.

"I suppose you want to hear more," she said.

"Damn straight." He hooked his gaze to hers. "I've
got a vested interest now."

His remark won no smile. "It's difficult to talk
about the child…that died."

Her throat convulsed visibly. Her eyes glistened. What part of this reaction was Comfit's ghost? How much could be attributed to her failing struggle to become the tough and brittle Cameron? Whatever, her vulnerability ate at him like a trapped fox gnawing a shackle.

Taking her hand, he coaxed her off the chair and onto the lap he made for her. Mikela leaped to the floor, then bounded back onto her mistress. Cameron drew her knees to his middle, tucking the cat in. She burrowed her face against his neck and he felt her run soft and pliable, needy in a way he had only craved and never expected. Her musky smell drew images of the night just passed to play through his mind. Twice she had showered, and twice the sight of her damp, fawn-like body had led him to negate her fastidious efforts.

Easing her onto another topic, dragging his mind away from her nakedness under the robe, he urged, "Tell me about the locket. Show me what's inside."

Her hands stole there and opened the trinket without hesitance, revealing a tarnished, bare interior. "It was my mother's. She *says* my father gave it to her, that it belonged to his mother."

He took the locket between thumb and forefinger. "You don't believe her?"

"When she was seventeen she spent a year in Samoa, on the beach mostly. She slept with a whole pack of beach boys—"

"Pack?"

"That's how I visualize it. Her in heat. The pack in pursuit." Bitterness coated her tone. "One of them gave her the locket, but who's to say he was my father?" She frowned, her swollen mouth forming the answer to her question. "She never knew which one he was."

The locket tale sounded like anything but wanton beach sex. He figured it for the only heritage of her father her mother could preserve. Nuzzling her salty-tasting hairline, he whispered, "Were there no white studs on that island for her to lie down with?"

She drew back, shooting him a quick, wary look. "Why?"

"The world is more forgiving of bastard white babies than of brown." He snapped the locket shut, his words ricocheting like shrapnel in his head.

Her smile was wan. "But if I were white, Jarrid wouldn't be Jarrid."

And she would not be Camellia, fragile and branded, trying to be Cameron. "Tell me the rest of it…the crash."

She tried to sit up, but he held her, keeping her vulnerable, knowing the telling would form for her one more layer of healing scab. He waited out her reluctance, watching resignation settle gradually into her eyes.

"I was taking Lee to see Jarrid. As I told you, it was…raining. Some nights when it's raining *here,* it all comes back to me…so dark, except for the blinding lights. When the van skidded across the centerline, I didn't react quickly enough." He imagined the scene playing behind her somber eyes and wondered how much Tutuila's presence had affected her. "We hit head-on. I lost consciousness, and when I woke up…" Again her throat convulsed. Her hand raised to her mouth, then withdrew to rest loosely against his bare Chest. "The area was swarming with police, and they were loading Lee's body into an ambulance—the same one that carried the dead child, I found out later. Phillip was there, too, overseeing the operation—the cutting. He was supposed to be in Toronto. Otherwise—"

She would not have been taking Tutuila to see his son. "Cutting?"

"I had to be cut out of the car." She shuddered. "With that huge machine."

Jaws of life. His hand swallowed hers, pressing it tight against him.

"I felt it even then—the animosity from the police. The heavy-handed questions they never stopped asking, shouting them over the sound of ripping steel and shattering glass." She stopped, easing her hand away, a tough cold edge lighting her eyes. "Considering your intolerance toward drinking, you're the last person I should be telling this to."

"I doubt that." He traced her scarred hairline. "Try me."

"The open bottle they found in the car—" Her nostrils flared, along with the dusky eyes. "Somehow Phillip, or someone loyal to him, put it there."

Raw and primitive disgust sizzled his nerve endings, but he kept still.

"They found drugs in Lee's pocket."

"Vickers again?"

"I don't know," she admitted. "I hadn't seen Lee in years, since before Jarrid was born. I had no idea of his…lifestyle."

The shred of blame and anger he had held in reserve dissolved into a guilty aftertaste. "You loved him once, though. *Enit?*"

Her brow knit. "I was in love with the idea of him, what he was."

"Samoan."

She nodded. "Yes."

His mind shifted onto Phillip Vickers. "What kind of a man would do that?" The question was fast becoming redundant.

"One as ambitious as Phillip." A fingertip strayed to a temple, pressed. "I know now that he married me to get close to the Chastains, because of their name and political influence. The crash—Lee being there— my being blamed—gave him license to end the marriage, but getting custody of Jarrid held his link to the family. They were easy to convince, to persuade to side with him in court."

He waited, sifting the knowledge, attempting to hide whatever the hell he was feeling. Anger? Pity? For damn sure, a futile desire to erase it for her.

"I drank in college," she said. "And for a while after. Until I got pregnant. It was common family knowledge, so they assumed I'd been a closet drinker during my marriage. Somehow, my being a model wife, my outstanding career, meant nothing. Lee being in the car, the bottle and the drugs, said it all."

"Did you use the planted bottle and drugs in the custody trial?"

"I couldn't swear the drugs were planted," she reminded. "And my attorney pressured me not to bring unfavorable publicity on the family and the hotels, saying it would be better for Jarrid's future. He assured me I couldn't lose a custody battle."

Yet she had, and now suffered the consequences.

"That's enough," she said wearily, her voice distant, a hand stroking Mikela. He caught her free hand and pressed his mouth into it, resigned. Then she declared suddenly, defiantly, "Phillip testified that I drank—far too much to be a fit mother. The only counter testimony I could bring—"

"Was Jarrid's." *Son-of-a-bitch.* No way could she have come out a winner.

"When my attorney realized we were losing, he insisted Jarrid testify. I declined. The bastard quit the trial—which did nothing for my image." Bitter reflection filled her eyes. "Phillip was a stellar citizen. The judge—the family—believed him. Even Hayden, but not completely. He gave me this chance." She shook her head, her eyes boring into his, voice raspy. "I can't fail, Lukas."

"No way, Yazhi." He slipped his hand inside her robe, running his palm over a nipple that glowed copper against her supple skin; then cupping her breast, he lifted, kneaded. Her wounded eyes fired. He watched war rage in their depths.

Desire battled grief before her mouth besieged him to take the pain away.

෮

Lukas dialed the Chicago number he had been harboring for almost six years, dialed his own cell number after the pager signal, then waited in the privacy of the Suburban. In less than an hour, the cell rang. "Wind Dancer," he answered.

"Well, Goddamn." A pause. "I thought sure as hell you were dead, a victim of your wicked ways."

Lukas' heart smiled. Memories tangled with need he had vowed never to allow the day he pocketed Donato Silvaggio's card, returned his embrace, and drove away from all they had shared. School. Women. Booze. Wildness for the simple hell of it. It had been Lukas' first in-depth look at the secular world, including his unqualified acceptance by the Silvaggio *family*.

"Some days I feel like a victim," he admitted. "And many times I have wondered the same about you."

Donnie laughed, a guileless sound that so contrasted with the man Lukas knew him to be. "I ran through the women you left behind and stopped whom. Got married. Got a kid and one coming. I cleaned up my act."

"Congratulations. How clean is the act?"

"Figure of speech, pal. I'm the *man* now. Papa's ailing, gone into gardening."

"Like in the movies, *enit?*"

"Just like that, now that you mention it."

"Give your father my regards. He saved my ass more than once." By handing down orders that anytime Lukas showed up hung over he was not to walk Silvaggio Construction's high beams. Or if he showed up drunk.

"The old man always had a soft spot for crazy bastards." Donnie laughed again. "You want the bodyguard job he offered you? I'll arrange a vacancy."

Lukas avoided examining the implied scenario. "Just a favor for now. Checking someone out. He has strong Canadian ties…and maybe European."

"Name your poison, Wind Dancer. I'll deliver it personally."

twenty-seven

For weeks Cameron had dreaded giving the speech the Chamber of Commerce had invited her to present. But in half an hour she had brought them up to date on Salt River progress, how they had dealt with the accident, and announced an expected completion date that might have been selected by throwing darts at a calendar. An hour after the speech, she preened cat-like in the sun on a pool lounge, thankful the task was behind her, but invigorated by the reception. Almost to the point of feeling traitorous.

She had dragged the lounge to the far corner of the pool, putting as much distance as possible between her scantily clad body and the crews working on the roof and inside the inn. Turning onto her back, she stretched her arms above her head, aware of sensitive inner thigh muscles, the tenderness of the area they guarded. She smiled, mentally restating her conclusion. Lukas was a more indefatigable than gentle lover. She was bone weary but surfeited beyond imagination. Gorged.

Still, she had found it difficult to pass up the construction trailer on her way from the car to the bungalow, and then again on her way to the pool—

especially when he had stepped to the door and called out for her ears only, "Try the water, little one." She had found the water and his sacrifice warm as Indian summer.

Thinking about Lukas now created a sudden surge of desire, its intensity jolting. Living in close quarters had left her even more aware that he was imbued with a kind of sensuality and masculinity that made sagacious sexual restraint an impossibility. Envisioning his long heavy hair against her breasts, his marble-smooth skin, size and strength, stamina and resilience, sucked her into a mire of erotic memory. In some ways she'd never had a man before Lukas. He had touched places in her...a depth that made her forget herself, place, time and its demands.

Though he spoke to her in hushed terms of lust, she sensed he felt more and held fast to the notion, pressing it into her heart. His gently persuading her to share had exposed her deepest hurts, releasing and dulling harbored shards of soul-hardening bitterness.

Ripping down the sexual barrier had rendered them blissfully symbiotic. Lukas had redoubled his effort in her behalf, conforming to OSHA, toiling alone long after the crew departed, to set the damage right, blindly focused. His dedication, which would ultimately separate them sooner, cut like a double-edged sword, perpetually lodging a sad sense of loss in the back of her mind.

She dozed restlessly, the mellowing sun forecasting the afternoon shutting down. At last she heard raised voices that grew distant, then thudding car doors, motors firing, the squeak and squeal of rubber on asphalt. Then quiet. Freed, she gathered her belongings and wrapped her hips in her sarong-style cover-up. Shoes in hand, she crossed the yellowing lawn headed for the trailer.

As she drew closer, Lukas' voice came to her softly, and then louder, still characteristically soft but resonant. Her gaze strayed to the empty parking lot. Reaffirming the workmen were gone, she realized she was hearing one side of a phone conversation. She paused, undecided on interrupting or continuing to the bungalow. And then she heard her name. And yet, to Lukas it wasn't her name. *Cam.*

The shock of discovery hit her full force.

Barefoot, she quietly mounted the trailer steps and stood in the open doorway. Mozart, barely audible, drifted from a tiny radio on the coffee stand. With his back to her, Lukas leaned forward in his chair, elbows on the paper-strewn desk top, phone receiver caught between shoulder and jaw, heels of his hands pressing his temples. The loose braid she had formed for him at dawn hung between his thick shoulder blades and down his broad back. An acute sense of sadness and betrayal pricked and clung to Cameron like spikes of a jumping cholla cactus.

Listening now, Lukas offered an occasional, "Unh." The grunt might or might not be agreement. Eventually, he commented, "Sometimes she does, but not much. I still see no problem as far as the inn goes. If I did, I would tell you."

A pebbly cloak covered the skin on her back and upper arms.

He changed ears with the phone, delineating the muscles in the backs of his arms, exposed by the sleeveless shirt, reminding her of how fiercely he had held her grounded, no matter how high she soared. She looked away, overcome by loss.

"What you are calling an agreement, I consider a dictate." Silence, and then, "Did she say that we are— or are you guessing?" A grunt. "Yes, then. I see no reason to lie about that, or anything else." More silence, then, "Cam is holding up. Under the conditions, she's fine."

With an abrupt, emphatic motion that paralyzed her, he rocked back in the chair. But he stared straight ahead as if memorizing the Grand Canyon calendar pinned to the wall. "She told me about the custody hearing. If what she said is true, I'm not at liberty to repeat it. But if it's true, Cam got a raw deal."

Voluntarily, her arms circled her waist, warding off a sudden chill in the warm afternoon. As though he felt it, too, he swiveled slowly in the chair. When his eyes locked with hers, she thought she glimpsed her own regret reflected there.

"I have to go." No other farewell. He placed the receiver in the cradle and stood.

"Cam?" She mimicked, the name echoing and vibrating in her head. *"Cam,* Lukas?"

Silence. He came forward. She backed onto a lower step. He reached for her, and she drew back as though threatened by a striking rattler.

His eyes searched her face, perhaps gauging the effect of what she'd heard. She searched her soul, doing the same. He jammed his hands into his back pockets. "It seems the name Cameron is too hard for your uncle to get used to."

"So of course you accommodate him." Her mind skidded backward to times when Lukas had divulged knowledge only she and Hayden shared. Then images of her first day at the inn replayed in her mind. Her first night…the stop at the bar before dinner. "*If* what I say is true? *If*, Lukas?"

"Bad terminology." The words were so hushed, she strained to hear.

Her tongue thickened and her throat clogged. She stared at him, stomach growing queasy while the word *if* repeated in her head. "You've been spying on me from the start."

His mouth formed a grimace. "Not exactly."

"Is he paying you an additional bonus to water down and count my drinks?"

"Is that what you believe?" His eyes betrayed nothing.

She searched this stranger's face. Where was the man who had made love to her, held her afterward, coaxed hurts from her, the man she'd welcomed and held inside her? Trusted.

The threat of hated tears scalded her throat. "You pious, sanctimonious traitor."

He flinched. A jaw muscle throbbed. "Have it your way, Yazhi."

"Then show me I'm wrong," she pleaded while wanting to claw him, to somehow penetrate his stoicism, erase his betrayal.

His eyes flickered, burned. He stared at her as if he were attempting to search her soul. Then his gaze shuttered, leaving his face resolute, hard. "I waste my time here."

Having spoken with a soft emphasis more effectual than a shout, he brushed past, his momentum rocking her, descended the steps and headed toward the bungalows. Recovering her equilibrium, she raced after him, grasped his forearm, and managed to spin him around.

"Damn you, Wind Dancer. Don't walk away from me."

His eyes lowered to where her fingers gouged his flesh, nails digging bleached, moon-shaped impressions in his bronze skin. His blacker-than-pitch eyes lifted to hers. In their depths warning and petition warred.

She released her grip and turned her back, her hands forming fists.

Disoriented, she reentered the trailer, her eyes surveying the small space, committing every nuance to memory. His denim jacket on a wall hook, his hard hat beside it. On the coffee counter, a bag of Starbucks Jamaican Blue Roast, the top folded over and neatly sealed, alongside a pack of raisin bagels. A small, unlit cigar in the ashtray bore the mark of his clamped teeth, the tobacco-leaf wrapping stained darker by his mouth. An irrepressible tremor gripped her. How could all she thought she knew and loved now feel so alien?

Anger surged again.

She reached for the phone, Hayden's private number reverberating in her head, but her fingers stalled in the middle of dialing when a file in the center of the desk caught her eye. She replaced the receiver and picked up the multi-copied document, a real estate contract covering Lukas' burned residence. His signature was already affixed. Her eyes skimmed the small-print stipulations that the house had been sold without repairs, at what had to be a fraction of its original worth. Lukas' pained, resigned expression the day of the fire rushed back to her.

His scarred leather briefcase stood on the corner of the desk, a thick, spiral-bound notebook next to it. In deepening twilight, she examined the book, its rich leather bearing the insignia of Scottsdale Air Park. Lifting her eyes, she peered out the door at the bungalows, dark except for the small window of the bathroom Lukas had been using. Tamping down the illusory sound of a shower running and erotic images she no longer welcomed, she opened the book, discovering it to be an aeronautical manual. The theory portion of a piloting course. Stuck between the pages, bookmark fashion, was a snapshot of a black helicopter.

There was more. A stack of brochures depicting the Hole-by-hole layouts and crediting the designers of golf courses scattered around the Phoenix-Scottsdale area—throughout the state, actually. She riffled through the pamphlets, finding golf coupled with Lukas beyond the stretch of imagination.

Baffled, she sank back in the chair, attempting to assemble the puzzle, beginning with his failure—his disinterest—in defending himself against her accusations of betrayal. Her mind spun between the real estate contract and the fact he was obviously learning to fly. And somewhere, somehow, golf was involved. He was getting on with life beyond the inn's completion, and not a trace of that life, not one remote remnant, included her.

But then Lukas had never pretended nor led her to believe otherwise.

She remained in the trailer until he emerged from the bungalow, showered, judging from his gleaming hair, and wearing fresh clothing. Without hesitance or a glance in her direction, he climbed into the truck and left the parking lot.

The empty bungalow lay as still as earth the moment before creation, mocking her. As though bent on punishment, she stood in his doorway taking in the placid room, yet taking care to keep her eyes away from the bed where she'd gone to him in the middle of the night. Her shock waning to belief, she closed her own door, locked it, and went determinedly to the shower.

If he wanted to monitor her drinking, she would make it easy for him.

❦

Sipping a virgin Bloody Mary, saving up for the bogus pleasure of ordering a real one from Lukas, Cameron finally asked with mock apathy, "Where's Lukas?"

"You tell me." Ruthie, the female bartender, cocked a Brow. Tired hands kneaded her bulky waist. "I've been here since noon."

The back of Cameron's neck iced. "He didn't come in tonight?"

"He called, but it's not like him to no show. I figured you'd know."

Denying Ruthie's astuteness, she shook her head. A hollowness in the pit of her stomach echoed her sense of loss. "No. I'm surprised, too."

Walking the lonely streets back to the inn, her mind surrendered to every remembered detail of the strolls she'd taken with Lukas. As she approached the inn, the bungalows that before had merely spoken of quiet, now screamed isolation. Knowing the ruse she'd considered a relationship was over, she unlocked the connecting Door. A clock ticked loudly where once Mozart had played softly. The standing lamp had been returned to its former position, the tea pot and two pottery mugs left upside down on the drain board, the bed stripped.

The scraped-clean emptiness denied he had ever made love to her there.

twenty-eight

Draped half-on, half-off the iron cot in the store-room of his reservation hogan, Lukas stirred beneath a suffocating weight, fighting his way up from the dregs of sleep. His sandpaper eyelids scraped open, solving the mystery of the crushing weight.

Holding an empty wine bottle, Gad straddled Lukas' ribcage, elbows on raised knees, his dark, gray-flecked eyes dubious. "You smell funny." Nothing humorous in the announcement

"Enit." Fighting back a moan, Lukas extracted the bottle from Gad's chubby hand and lowered it to the floor. Glass clanked on glass. He forced his head up to peer over the side of the cot. Two more empties. Reading the labels released another groan. Foggy memory of having chosen the best vintages his Scottsdale stash had to offer wove its way into his muddied head. He made a move to get up, half relieved when Gad failed to take the hint. "Where is your mama?"

"In the kitchen." He picked at an undone button on Lukas' soiled shirt. "Where's Chuey?"

"Won't I do?"

"You smell weird." He grinned forgivingly. "Did you bring him?"

Lukas shook his head, instantly curtailing the movement. "An ambulance is bringing him home today. When you get back from school, he'll be at Aunt Sarah's." The title Lukas' mother preferred from the rez kids.

"Cool." A grin lit Gad's full-moon face. His swinging leg barely missed clipping Lukas' chin as the boy leapt off his chest, dumping him. "I'll tell Mama."

Hoisting onto his elbows, Lukas surveyed the drafty, cramped room, colder than the government's heart. Only a miracle had prevented him freezing to death. But at the moment, rigor mortis appealed more than the sobering up that lay ahead. Memory of walking beams in this condition, before the Silvaggios had nixed that, fell into the miracle category.

Guilty disgust wrapped his gut in barbed wire. Memory of the disbelief, anger, and, finally, resignation on Cameron's face heated to fever pitch.

Following yesterday's outburst, love and resentment had warred within him, each strong enough to cancel the other, leaving numbness in their wake. This morning—much sooner than he had anticipated—separation from her stung like a gaping physical incision.

Suck it up, Wind Dancer. Do what's right. For her and for Kai.

❦

From a lotus position on the floor, legs lapping the front crosspiece of her loom, Kai eyed him critically over the rim of a teacup. "Did you get drunk because of her, Lukas?" Keeping her eyes on him, she set the tea down, then picked up a shed rod. She positioned the tool in fresh warp, preparing to birth a new creation.

After carefully considering the question, he concluded no woman could *make* a man drink beyond reason. "Because of me." He rolled his cup in his hands, gazing into the pit of fire burning dead center of the dirt floor, opting for a change of subject. "You look better. How do you feel?"

With an heirloom-quality weaving fork, she tapped down the laced yarn, then began a new line. "Heat, food, and television are wonder drugs. I'm much stronger."

"Strong enough to take care of a husband?"

"Do I look like the type to wait on a man?" She worked steadily.

"Keep Gad home from school. We'll drive into Flag and get a license."

A shallow cough rattled the taut quiet. "Hunting or fishing?"

Nothing easy about Kai. "Marriage license. I want to marry you."

"The *half-bilagáana* woman can't make you drink, but she can make you marry." She smiled stoically. "Strong medicine."

His stomach churned, head pounding. His hands made their way to his temples. He jerked them down, images of Cameron still haunting. He was every bit the hypocrite she had labeled him. Grunting, he downed the tea and crossed to the stove. Boot heels burying deep in the dirt, he poured water over a new tea bag, dipped zealously, sloshing water onto the counter. He tossed the bag into the trash, leaned against the cabinet, and folded his arms. "You want me to get down on one knee?"

She smiled as if weighing the possibility. "You're in love with Cameron Vickers, Lukas."

"I have feelings for you, and for Gad, that will make it work. I will give you a good life, *aszda.*"

"Where?"

The constant impasse, her theory being that a man walked in harmony only by remaining at peace with himself. And that peace existed in only one place. *The rez.* "Wherever."

She worked silently, then put down her tools and sipped tea. "Suppose you marry me and I die?"

The words, the ease with which she spoke, triggered his own reluctance to speak of death, the dread of facing it. "I would raise Gad in the Navajo way."

"Will you lie to me and tell me you don't love her?"

"I'll get over it. I've had practice."

She took up her tools and wove the batten through the yarn. Her hands did not manipulate as decisively or confidently as he had admired in the past, but she worked steadily again, as if she were alone in the warm, still hogan. "Thank you for your offer, but I warned you, that's a wound I don't want to lick. I want more from a man than pity."

"Navajo lives are dictated by what we are, Kai, not always by what we want."

In their language, she said, "It took you many years to learn that, Lukas."

"Is that a yes?"

"All those years, I waited. Now I'm holding out for a younger man."

His heart knocked in his chest. A vision of the wine-jug flower pots she had transferred to his front porch, along with that of the melted jug he had retrieved from the fire, half-blinded him. Her concern for Chuey at the hospital, Chuey's soulful link with her, Gad's hopeful eyes when asking for him just this morning, replayed like a bad dream in Lukas' head. "Why younger? I'm not exactly used up."

"You are set in your ways, Lukas."

His hairline crawled like a sidewinder.

She grew silent, threading, tapping, threading, while he waited. Then she spoke as if reciting song lyrics. "I am a willful girl in a woman's sick and aging body. I have many causes with too little time. I need a man willing to step away from conformity when necessary to carry on my causes. A man with radical spirit."

"Chuey is a child, Kai."

She worked minus expression while Lukas reviewed the years when he had thought he knew her and what she wanted. When had her wants shifted to Chuey?

All those trips home she had been waiting for *him,* for their coupling. While Suzanne was restrained, always looking over her shoulder and leaving him burdened with guilt, Kai eagerly sought out the bed of an idle pickup truck or a haunted hogan, filling him with a sense of prowess and worth. He knew she had others, and disease should have been a factor, but in his teens he had believed himself invincible. Suzanne had insisted he protect her against pregnancy. With Kai he had flung caution aside and basked in the rush of freedom. God's timing, not man's wisdom, deserved credit for the fact Gad was not his son. Gad's birth and the waning of Kai's and his union had been coincidental. The real change had come when Lukas began lusting for a forbidden woman.

He groped now for some argument to stave off Kai's latest fetish. "You're fanatic about pure blood lines." Just as he was. "Chuey doesn't qualify."

She murmured something about "no fault of his own," and then, gaze cast on the rolling prairie beyond the window, declared, "Neither does Gad."

Though the news rocked him, questioning her now would only sidetrack the issue. "Look at history. Chuey can't take care of himself, much less you and Gad. You'll have another child on your hands. What the hell are you thinking?"

She raised her face and empty teacup to him, eyes plaintive and taunting, luminous as wet tar. "He is a child because you have spoiled him."

"Enit." For *goddamned* sure.

"The matter of time he needed to grow up has at last come to pass, Lukas."

༺

A sensed presence drew Chuey's attention away from packing the few belongings he had collected into the canvas duffel resting on the hospital bed. He worked his wheelchair around, angled toward his visitor, stifling his surprise.

"What'cha doin', Cochise?" Yolanda advanced into the room.

"Blown' the hell out of Dodge." But not soon enough, evidently. "I'm getting out today." And heading home to the rez, which she didn't need to know.

Standing next to the bed, she ran a manicured hand—short nails, no black polish—over the half-packed bag. "L.L. Bean, no less. Friggin' fancy."

"Cameron loaned it to me." He eyed her sleek hair, white blouse, knee length skirt and matching blazer. Her squatty-heeled shoes hid the slender, red-tipped toes he'd always got a rise out of sucking on. *A bygone era, Run Amok.* "You're looking fancy yourself. Going to a funeral? Or preaching at one?"

"Cameron's referral landed me a job at the Scottsdale Princess. Today's my first day." She smoothed a lapel on the blazer. "Wish me luck."

"No problem."

"You still mad? About the fire and all? I thought we might kiss and make up." She searched his face which he was determined to keep deadpan. Her eyes settled on his mute mouth. "I have some news for you."

"Yeah?" He glanced at his watch. "My ride's overdue. You might have to send it by smoke signal."

Only her lips smiled. "Things got worse after the fire. Apparently you never called Children's Services back like we asked you to."

Hell, no. Not after he'd reasoned out who had called them to begin with. He clamped his lips against defense or argument. "How much worse?"

"They gave us an ultimatum. Either Eddie moved out, or Polly and me had to." She hoisted onto the high bed. She wore flesh colored nylons that made her crossed, number-ten-rated legs look nude. Glossy nude. She placed her shoulder bag in her lap, then wrapped it with her fingers. "Dwaine got a loan from his boss so me 'n Polly could get an apartment. Soon as I get caught up a little, I'll start paying back Cameron's loan. I thought you'd like to know that."

"Yeah, thanks. I'm glad." About the loan, but mostly about Polly.

Yolanda's blue eyes dulled. "But soon as Eddie wheedled the address out of Dwaine, he started showing up at the new place."

"Somebody ought to cut his—"

"We told him if he comes around again, we'll turn him in for starting the fire."

"Bet he's scared shitless." Chuey fetched a John Grisham novel off the nightstand and crammed it in the bag, followed by a travel clock.

"He robbed a check-cashing store last week and got Caught. They found drugs on him. He's locked up." Her voice trembled. "Eddie was only five when Mama and Daddy split up. He never—" She shrugged, her smile wan. "I have to stop making excuses. If you want to tell the cops he caused the fire, that's up to you. Dwaine and me have agreed to back you up. But Eddie Won't be bothering Polly. For a while, anyway. And I hear—I've heard that once word gets out in prison about fooling with kids…" She shrugged listlessly. "Well, you know…."

"What goes round comes round, I hear." He jerked the bag's zipper closed.

"I've missed you, Chuey." She leaned forward, streaking a hand through his too-long hair. "Lukas is probably on your case, so if you want, you can hang at mine and Pol's place for a while. But you're probably going back to the dorm, huh? We're close to there. Maybe we—"

"The dorm's out of the picture for awhile." His throat felt scratchy, then tight. "And I've got some other stuff working, but thanks for the offer."

She traced a finger down the bridge of his nose, across his mouth, then pressed it to her lips. "I didn't appreciate you, Chuey. I mean other than your—" She blinked, her chin hiking a fraction. "It's over, huh?"

"Yeah." He fought back old images, embraced new ones. "I guess so."

A movement at the door jerked their heads around. A nurse and an orderly eyed them with matched expressions—knowing and apologetic. Sighing, Yolanda slipped down from the bed and shouldered her bag. The orderly, with whom Chuey had played a hand of gin from time to time, spoke up. "You ready, chief?"

"Ready, cowboy."

As Lukas trudged the half mile of frozen, rutted road to his mother's house, Kai's words reverberated in his head. *The matter of time he needed to grow up has at last come to pass.* And later he heard the proclamation as he helped maneuver Chuey from the ambulance into a wheelchair, wheel him up the makeshift wooden ramp and through the narrow door, his leg and shoulder immobile in their casts. Once Chuey was settled in Lukas' old room, nibbling on fry bread fresh from his grandmother's skillet, and Sarah had finally left them alone, Lukas broached the troubling subject. "I asked Kai to marry me."

The hand that held the bread halted halfway to Chuey's mouth. His eyes flared, then narrowed. "Why? You giving up on Cameron?"

Ever perceptive. "Kai turned me down."

"Get outta here." His tone held more relief than incredulity.

"She wants a younger man."

"Yeah?" His brows shot up, a grin breaking out like measles. "Guess you screwed around too long after all, Uncle Bro." He measured him, squinting, still grinning. "Or maybe it's the hangover. The fact you had to get drunk to propose."

"She wants you, Run Amok, from what I can figure out."

The grin ebbed, but hung on as if beyond repression. "You warned me to stay in the tribe. I figured you'd be happy I was getting around to telling you."

After the fact. "You two need more in common than Carlo Rossi wine."

Despite Chuey's look of surprise then quandary at mention of the wine, he remained steadfast. His emotional gamut pulled Lukas into a realm of revelation and set his mind reeling before it seized understanding.

Chuey's eyes. The full-moon shape, the hood his brows formed above them—Lukas-like eyes, people said.

Suddenly, clearly now, Lukas recalled Gad's face peering at him earlier with those same sadly expectant eyes. Hell, no wonder the same people who marked the resemblance between Chuey and himself claimed *he* had fathered Gad. But Gad's eyes were copper-speckled pewter. Like those Lukas stared into now.

Realization reared. "You do have more than wine in common. Right, Run Amok?"

"So she tells me." The concession in his grin edged into pride.

"When?" How long had Chuey known, when no one else had guessed?

"When I was about fourteen, I guess. Maybe fifteen. I've never put the calculator to it, but we…me 'n Kai had a…thing when I was a kid."

Chuey had misunderstood the question. Lukas waited, accounting for his own whereabouts and loyalties at that time, wanting to know the intricacies of the *thing,* but doubting he was worthy. Chuey shifted in the steel chair, rubbing a smeared signature on his cast as if he wanted to erase it.

"I was going through some stuff," he said. "Kid stuff. Drinking when I could get it, ditching school, giving Grandma and Apenimon trouble. You were back, but you had troubles of your own—drying out. The most you had to give was a threat or a mean look. I started hanging out at Kai's. And you know Kai." He looked up at Lukas and shrugged, grinning. "She introduced me to sex, switched the hell out of my priorities, and saved my ass. Then you stepped in and made me toe the line."

So Kai and I engaged in a kind of unwitting partnership. His heart willed opposite his head, wanting to believe his nephew, even as a child himself, had not cowered in denial all these years while Kai struggled to give her half-breed—no—her quarter-breed child an identity. "When did she tell you about Gad?"

"When I was in the hospital. I guess she thought the time was finally right. I don't want to sound weird, but I always felt close to—loved Gad. We were like— connected." Bronze-gray eyes misted, granite-hard umber cheeks pinking.

Lukas throat broadened at the back, ached ."I suppose you have a plan." Suggestions, self-constructed, self-appeasing remedies, whirled in his mind. He willed his voice to silence.

"We're kinda wingin' it right now. When I'm out of these casts, I'll start working on her old hogan, get it ready for us to move back in." His steady gaze read Lukas' foremost question. "I'll take the rest of the semester off till we see how Kai…" He cleared his throat, began again. "If she makes it, I'll enroll in Northern Arizona in Flagstaff, get the premed classes, and hope I win the lottery eventually. I'll have to work part-time—maybe selling Kai's rugs somewhere." His eyes quickened, as if that had suddenly occurred to him.

"And if she doesn't make it?" The damned, dreaded, feared subject again.

Chuey fell quiet, non-viewable pictures playing behind his eyes. "I'll raise Gad and work…at something. But somehow I'm getting my degree and going to med school."

Lukas' scalp rippled. "You think fatherhood disqualifies you from my help, Chuey?"

He shook his head "It's time I showed what I'm made of, Luk. Past time."

Lukas paced to the window where he fingered the precious art of his mother's hand-woven hop-sack Draperies. His eyes raised to the flimsy, ill hung aluminum rod supporting them, taking in the irony of contrast. Inside, loss gathered, tightening his chest, warring with the relief of freedom. Kai's mystery solved at last. Chuey slipping from his protective grasp. Cameron lost to her *bilagáana* world. His hopeless hope for the two of them dying a cold death.

Staggering changes, all beyond Lukas' reach.

❦

Chuey stared at Lukas' wide stance, the way his arms straddled the window, hands gripping the frame so tightly his back muscles strained his flannel shirt to the limit. His uncle's silences had always reminded him of his fear of God.

Might as well clear the slate.

"There's something else we need to talk about."

Lukas turned, eyes burning questions.

"Yolanda's brothers were at your house the night of the fire. They were hot because—well, because of the usual. You know. But that night Yolanda and me were getting it on, or getting ready to." He recalled their prior discussion. "You know that already. They showed up at a bad time."

Lukas nodded, eyes filled with more exacting questions.

"Eddie, her little brother, caused all the hell. He'd probably have killed me if the fire hadn't scared him off. I've been biding my time, trying to figure how to even the score."

"Like he couldn't finish the job next time?"

Chuey offered a grin. "I was planning to beat him senseless with my crutch, but Yolanda came by this morning to tell me he's in jail. Picked up for robbery and possession of drugs. So…I'm leaving the ball in your court."

After an eternal moment, eyes darkly brooding, mouth grim, Lukas murmured, "Let sleeping dogs lie." Another of Apenimon's favorite homilies.

He crossed to the bed, retrieved his shearling coat from the bedpost. Shrugging into it, he eyed the rusty iron cowbell Sarah had placed on the rough cedar table beside the bed. "Go the hell easy on that bell, Run Amok. Your grandmother deserves more than a nursing career. *Enit?*"

"*Enit,* Luk."

Chuey wheeled to the window to watch Lukas' departure. He stopped in the yard beside a dwindling woodpile and shed the coat. Breath clouding on the waning December afternoon he stood with hands on hips, gazing skyward. Sensing he intruded, Chuey felt an urge to look away. Eventually Lukas hobbled on one leg and then the other to remove his boots, stripped off his socks and struck out in a run across the meadow in the direction of nowhere.

twenty-nine

The first lonely night without Lukas, Cameron tossed sleeplessly until the sound of the ringing phone echoed in the silent bungalow. Michael's voice revved her heart until he assured her the call didn't involve Jarrid.

Her mother was dead of an aneurysm. She tried to grasp the news.

How soon could she come to Canada?

Within her mind, she cried scant tears that burned hot and acrid. Goodbyes between her and her mother had been said and grieved over long ago. Her thoughts turned to Jarrid and hope that with death's sting would come the possibility of seeing her son.

Michael was there when she deplaned in Vancouver. Miracle of miracles, his gently restraining touch rested on Jarrid's shoulder. Cameron dropped her hand luggage to the floor and knelt. Jarrid rushed into her extended arms and pressed his face to her neck, squeezing her shoulders tight. He was, however, reticent about returning the kisses she placed on his cheek, his hair, his brow. He blushed, pecked her lips and lowered his head. As she sent Michaela silent message of gratitude, she attempted to credit Jarrid's action to his advancing age, his transformation from childhood to boyhood. Much too soon.

In Michael's car, Jarrid secured in the rear seat perusing *Fright Train,* the new book she'd brought, Michael repeated part of last night's message. "She went in her sleep. They tried to wake her for medication, but she was gone."

Cameron struggled with the image, recalling all the nights she had tried rousing their mother from torturous dreams. "Is it too cruel to say it's a relief?"

"I've been asking myself the same thing. I've decided that no, it isn't." Michael signaled and changed lanes. "Her quality of life was shot."

"I know." From the moment she had placed her secretly pregnant body on that plane from Samoa almost thirty years ago. From the moment she'd admitted her sexual folly and had begun her penance of shame. "I should have been here—at least visited her after she went into the…"

Michael smiled his empathy. "I've been calling that place a hospital. And how could you know it would happen so soon after she was admitted?"

"Was she…lucid…enough to will her end?"

He glanced at Jarrid, who glanced up at his mother. "Let's not go there. Okay, Cameron?"

"You're right, of course." She gave Jarrid a reassuring smile. Surprised by her urge to cry, she determined not to stroke her throbbing temples.

Hayden had arranged a small memorial service. Family only, ashes in a pewter urn, a large, dated

portrait of Sabrina Chastain Johnston Preston,
flanked by one of her and her three children, taken
shortly before David's death. Cameron's dark hair,
brown-gold skin, full mouth and strong nose mocked
the delicate features and flaxen coloring of her mother
and siblings. As she listened to the eulogies, she
looked around the chapel at her extended family, pale
and regal to the last man and woman. Did they wear
expressions of weary tolerance, or was her imagination
acting by rote? Hugging Jarrid, she reaffirmed her
well-rehearsed escape plan, even as she detested her
cowardice.

Jarrid. *Do it for Jarrid.*

Inevitably, her thoughts segued to Lukas, her
mind's eye framing his face. Chiseled, cast in somber
bronze. His quiet voice echoed in her head, while his
arrant lovemaking that left no doubt of his desire,
spiraled back to her. The sting of his deception ebbed
in comparison to her loneliness, a sense that part of
her being had been gouged away.

Her loss doubled, she grieved in a different realm
of her soul.

Hayden stood with his back to her at the closet bar
in his study. He poured tea from a pot his housekeeper had delivered on a silver tray so heavy she
strained with the burden. Lamplight, soft as Jarrid's
snores as he curled on the sofa, head in Cameron's lap,
formed an aura around her uncle. When he turned,

reaching for century-old brandy to lace his tea—not hers—she caught a glimpse of a thickening middle, a weakening chin. Still, he was a fine looking man, his carefully trimmed pewter-gray mane framing a strong weathered profile, the result of years of skiing and a penchant for hunting. He boasted the indefinable patina of an alliance to old money.

Cameron accepted tea, refusing cream or sugar, a preference she had learned from Lukas. She sipped, returned the cup to the saucer, leaned carefully over Jarrid to place the exquisite china on a mahogany table. The gold cup rim gleamed in the perfect light, inviting memory of rough pottery mugs in the bungalow, the rainy morning she and Lukas had shared tea after a night of endless lovemaking.

Seated across from her, in a high-back leather wing chair, Hayden broke the silence. "I know this has been a shock, Cam. Especially with the service taking place so soon after…But the family was able to gather quickly—even you—so I saw no reason to dawdle."

No reason to prolong the embarrassment that her mother had long ago become to the family. She nodded, harboring her thoughts. "How were you able to talk Phillip into—" She ran her fingertips into the curls fringing Jarrid's brow. *How* seemed suddenly moot. "Thank you, Uncle Hayden. I'm grateful."

"Phillip knows he'll be fine under this roof." His eyes measured her reaction as she struggled to strike a placid expression. "On the other hand, he's occupied in Paris and felt bad about not attending the service, so relinquishing Jarrid for a day or two is compensation, I'd say."

She glanced down at her sleeping child, marveling at the similarity in their skin tones, but envying his composure. His face attested to a depth of serenity she could never recall experiencing. Neither could she share these musings with her uncle. But she was not as successful in tabling more nagging introspection. As hurtful memory surged, she took a gulp of tea, then pushed the cup aside on the table, announcing, "I've discovered Lukas Wind Dancer has been spying on me."

Above the rim of his cup, caught off guard, Hayden silently cocked a brow.

Cameron elaborated, "Spying for *you*. Counting my drinks, to be more specific." His continued silence chaffed. "Granted, I drank once. I'm a different person now. I know you've never quite believed I'm not an alcoholic. Phillip did a thorough job of selling you on the theory—"

"You've been doing a better job of convincing me otherwise, Cam." He leveled one of his flinty stares on her. "I had definite qualms about the make or break situation in Arizona, but apparently the stakes are a high enough deterrent. You've shown great strength in not falling apart when things got rough, at least according to Wind Dancer."

"You've belittled me in his eyes, making it impossible to go on working with him." Memory of the empty half of the bungalows coiled viper-like in her consciousness. Spine icing, she reflected bitterly, "You should have trusted me."

"Maybe so, but years of dealing with your mother's drinking…" His voice wavered. "I know your mission was—is—to get Jarrid back. But Sabrina had children, too. The comfort she found in a bottle was stronger than the well-being of you and your brothers."

The remembrance he launched plagued her. "I'm not my mother."

"No." He rose and went back to the bar where he abandoned the tea and poured a scant splash of brandy into a cut glass snifter. He swirled the amber liquid in the glass, halted it halfway to his mouth, then lowered it with a resigned expression. At his desk, he removed something from the middle drawer, slipped it into the pocket of his stiff white shirt and returned to his chair. "You're not your mother, Cam. The lack of physical resemblance is striking, and I'm sure you've made every effort to overcome any other traits you might have inherited."

"She was cold." She swallowed, waiting for the stinging in her throat to ease. "I loved her. I never stopped, but eventually I realized the futility. To her, I symbolized the shame she couldn't cope with." Yet by conceiving Jarrid with Lee, she had blandly followed in Sabrina's footsteps, then, determined to spare Jarrid guilt she had known, covered her *faux pas* with a lie. That lie had bound her to Phillip, turning her into his pawn.

"She wasn't always cold." Hayden sipped the brandy, then loosened his tie and undid the top button of the shirt. The scent of his familiar cologne drifted to Cameron. "She was joyful once, and it was contagious. She died of a broken heart, because no one—no other man—could measure up to the legend that lived in her mind."

"The legend of my father." She was barely able to wait for his nod. "That's impossible. She never knew—"

"She knew. It's time you stopped believing otherwise." Eyes clouding, he swirled brandy, drained the snifter and cradled it in his hands. "I was on the island with her. We went to private school with the boy…with your father. He was a senior, there on an art scholarship granted each year to a privileged islander."

Cameron scoffed. "He was a beach boy, one out of the pack she slept with. She told me often enough…when she was drinking. I went to Samoa with the intent of finding him." She shoved down recall of the lonely beach strolls, the helpless realization to which she had finally surrendered. "Finally, I admitted he could be any one of the aging men still pandering the tourists. Had she been with me, even she wouldn't have known which one."

Hayden's frown could have announced a festering, aching tooth within his strong jaw. "Cam, listen to me. There was no pack of beach boys. She loved your father—well, as nearly as a seventeen-year-old can love." He held the empty glass up and stared at its diamond facets dancing in the firelight. She thought she saw desire for a second drink in his eyes, renounced, she theorized, in deference to her spurious malady. "She refused to name him," he continued, "because he had received an art scholarship from an English university, and she wouldn't cheat him of his chance. She lied about the number of boys she'd been with so our parents wouldn't suspect."

Cameron sat frozen, hesitant, yet jubilant, to discard a lifetime's belief. *An artist?* She resummoned her skepticism. "How could he let her face that alone?"

"He never knew she was pregnant. Still doesn't. The lie, and not knowing how her life and yours might have gone with him, drove her a bit mad, I think."

"Still doesn't?" Her mind seized on the words. Her heart shimmied.

"I've made a point of keeping in touch, but about you Sabrina swore me to secrecy." From his pocket he withdrew the items he'd placed there, and laid them on the cocktail table. Within her reach. "I've always thought you had a right to know. Your grandparents are gone now, so as far as I'm concerned, any reason to keep the secret from you any longer died with your mother."

and leaned to scrutinize the photographs, one a snapshot of a teen, one that Jarrid might someday resemble. The possibility made her heart ache. The second, a studio sitting, transformed the boy to a man banked by a dark-skinned woman and two adolescent children. Her half sisters—if this tale could be believed. The date on the back signified ten senseless, longing, lost-forever years.

Swallowing the nausea filling the back of her throat, she picked up the photo of the teen, fighting the urge to press it to her breasts. "You want me to believe this is my father." Against her lap, Jarrid flinched, jolted, perhaps, by her harsh voice, the rising timbre. Gently, she stroked his brow.

"I've told you the truth. What you believe, and what you do about it, is your choice. But don't make the mistake your mother did, Cam. You built this man into a legend and then tore him down again. He's neither a god nor a villain. He was simply caught in a web, the way you were. I told you I once saw joy in your mother. I've never seen that joy in you. Maybe now that will change." He rose, returning to the bar.

She stared at his back, his accusation vibrating in her mind. There *had* been a joyful time. With Lee. When she'd felt she had come home. Only he had seen her brief joy, and gradually, over the years, her memory of it had tarnished.

Jarrid was the only reminder.

Hayden turned and rested against the counter, ritualistically warming the refilled snifter within his palms. "I'd also be less than honest if I let you believe Lukas Wind Dancer willingly spied on you."

Her head jerked up. "I heard him talking to you."

"I called him the day you left for Arizona and tried to enlist him to keep tabs on you. To call me at the first sign of trouble. Any news I got, I prodded out of him. From day one he never agreed to anything other than to watch out for you as best he could. I trust he's done that?"

Her whirling mind encompassed, sifted, discarded, accepted. She kept quiet.

"Any conversation you might have overheard, I instigated. Pulling information from him—other than praise—was like extracting wisdom teeth. You're not sleeping with the enemy, Cam. Don't make that mistake."

She chose to ignore the innuendo with a change of subject. "I've been approached by another hotel chain. They're looking to fill a high management position." She heard herself confessing what before now she'd harbored in the nether regions of possibility. A proposition she would not have considered before that afternoon in the trailer. "They've asked to interview me."

Showing no surprise, he offered unfamiliar praise. "They'd be lucky to get you." His gaze speared hers. "But we had a deal, Cam. You finish the inn, show me your mettle, and the hotel in Samoa is yours. Free and clear with my blessing."

She placed the photo she'd been holding on the table before her and retrieved the other, searching the faces of the children for resemblance to her own. "And Jarrid. You haven't forgotten that end of the agreement."

"And Jarrid. But I sense Phillip is up to something. Time may be crucial."

thirty

Cameron returned to Scottsdale, eager to make amends with Lukas, only to discover he had hired a foreman, a weathered man twice his age but equally agile, efficient and disturbingly mute. When she let herself think of the bonus Lukas coveted and the bite Wilson Nakai would cull, guilt nagged.

She managed to pry from Nakai information that Lukas had appeared the day she'd gone to Canada, then left for the reservation the day she'd returned. Since no one had been privy to her agenda, she labeled his schedule coincidence. Although impressed by Nakai's skill with the crew and his daily progress, she was raw with loneliness and worried over Phillip's plans for Jarrid. Eagerly and futilely she anticipated Lukas' return.

Eventually, she cornered Nakai in the trailer. "Where's Wind Dancer?"

Nakai's dark eyes squinted against gentle mid-December sun slanting through the open door. His strong mouth pulled into an immobile line.

"This is his project," she prompted. "He signed on for the duration, but he hasn't put in an appearance in two weeks. Has he abandoned the inn?" *And me?*

After an interminable silence in which her heart pounded, Nakai begrudged an answer. "We're making good time. Especially since we hired a night crew. Just pray the rain holds off till we can all get inside."

"Who's idea was that? Night crews?" No matter whose, the decision would require a second foreman and guarantee her additional guilt feelings.

"Lukas said time is important to you."

Nakai's consoling tone, as well as the amused look in his eye, rang familiar. The pencil he stuck behind his ear disappeared into thick, gravel-gray hair tied back with pink ribbon that would have seemed feminine if worn by a less virile man. On the desk, a tinny, scarred radio played a soporific chant, reminiscent of what she'd heard in the bar that first day. The repetitive *hey-a* soothed, yet agitated.

"I give Lukas a report every day. If *I'm* doing something wrong, tell me." Wise and gentle eyes read her perfectly, negating the possibility of shortcomings on his part.

"Yes, time is important." *Imperative.* She hugged herself, feeling suddenly chilled. "And no, nothing's wrong. You've replaced Lukas quite well."

Back in her office—so empty it echoed—she stared out the token window onto the parking lot, haunted by memory both pleasant and painful.

Sacrifice. The word reverberated in her mind.

Lukas must choose her or his people. She must chose Lukas or the promise she'd made to herself, and an unwitting Jarrid, to find and embrace their heritage.

Lukas had no doubt made his choice. Along with a resigned respect for his decision, she found empathy for her mother's sacrifice in freeing her father, at last believing she could feel her mother's pain. Did her love for Lukas allow her to do any less than free him? Yet within, sheltered in her heart, a desire to know his every nuance, the very spirit and soul of what she would never have, raged.

The longing outweighed pride and reason.

☙

She had always thought of Flagstaff as where Lukas lived his second—now his first—life. Discovering differently surprised her. The lively little city, boasting a wide main thoroughfare banked by cut-rate motels with western names and neon-lit diners, was not the reservation.

Sitting behind the Taurus' steering wheel, she unfolded a stiff new map and traced her finger along Interstate 40 West, then north on Highway 89. The road snaked through a large patch labeled Navajo Indian Reservation to *Cameron?*

Thoughtfully, she tapped the town with a nail, going back to the day Kai had demonstrated at the inn. Because of the name coincidence, a Cameron Trading Post sticker decorating the rear window of Kai's van had lodged in Cameron's mind.

Ninety miles east of Cameron on 160 was Kayenta. Her mind echoed Chuey's once saying that *Lukas had run up the hill to Kayenta on reservation business.*

She folded the map, her irrepressible anticipation crammed with dread.

At Little America, she topped off the Taurus' gas tank while sipping gourmet coffee from a paper cup. A chill wind moaned forlorn blues lyrics in the stately pines. Fallen razor-sharp pine needles whipped against bare skin beneath her longish skirt, her only accidental preparation in deference to the temperature drop between the Sonoran Desert and the Chuska Mountains. Back inside the car, cold and wearied by her foreigner's naiveté, she cranked up the Taurus' never-used heater and headed north out of town.

She passed the Cameron trading post, then catching the one traffic light green, glided through Tuba City and into country vast enough to be intimidating if it were not dotted with what she could only think of as a million Christmas trees. Miles would pass without a single dwelling in sight, then she would top a hill to discover a cluster of frame houses, or maybe trailers, or both, each community boasting its own car graveyard.

Outside of Kayenta, she pulled onto the dirt shoulder. The sight of wide-open, rolling prairie and canyons—like unspoiled backwater in the river of time—made her heart skid around in her chest, leaving her breathless. A bit dizzy. Never had she seen sky this blue or empty. There were no neon signs, billboards, or power lines. No thrown-up-overnight bedroom communities, fast food restaurants, or strip malls. The only blight on the landscape—yet it enhanced rather than spoiled—was a roadside stand hawking Indian blankets. Her alien feeling remained, but she'd played an immigrant role in places less serene and beautiful.

At the Navajo Cultural Center in Kayenta, mentioning Lukas' name won immediate instructions. Taking the road to Monument Valley, she passed through another settlement, a blight of junked-out cars, woodpiles, and stacks of old tires until the landscape cleared. Sensing accomplishment, she squared her shoulders. But reaching the destination along the desolate dirt road she'd been directed to required consulting a sheepherder who gave guidance with unabashed reverence for Lukas. Reluctant to release the tranquil scene of the man and his wooly charges, she watched as long as possible in her rearview mirror.

Eventually, she spotted the regaled *yellow frame house,* aproned by a dirt yard lined with dead flowers nodding brown and withered in the wind. She pulled in beside a rusting pickup truck with a single infant moccasin dangling from the mirror. A fading bumper sticker proclaimed *Fry Bread Power,* while the raised hood revealed a hole rather than an engine. An inward smile penetrated her nervousness, the simple surroundings teasing her senses like fine wine she wanted to gulp, yet savor.

Behind the house, a curious number of bicycles leaned against a small barn with an attached corral where a shaggy black horse braced stiff-legged against the icy wind. Still farther away, down a rutty path, a

hogan, its wooden lean-to contrasting with the traditional dome shape, stood in bold relief against the
blustery afternoon sky.

When she was halfway up a brick path that had
been meticulously laid in sand, the front door of the
house opened. An elderly man, etched infamously in
her memory, watched her approach from behind a
screen door, his predatory-bird stare as appealing as a
skirmish with coyotes in the surrounding canyon
might be. Behind him, a television blared. As she
neared, a savory aroma wafted out the door, triggering
sudden rapacious hunger, reminding her she'd eaten
nothing today but Reese's Pieces.

Behind Apenimon, a woman floated through the
shadows. The television volume lowered before she
appeared, sturdy and handsome, beside her father-in-
law. A splendid claret velvet skirt and blouse contrasted
with a stricken expression, assuring Cameron that her
very existence was legendary here.

The legend had come to unwelcome life on Sarah
Wind Dancer's doorstep.

She stopped deferentially short of the low concrete
steps. "I'm Cameron Vickers. I've come to see
Lukas…if he's here."

Apenimon harrumphed, a look associated with
finding an elusive piece to a jigsaw puzzle settling in
his eyes. But Lukas' mother recovered her manners and
needlessly introduced herself then pushed open the
screen door and stepped back. A hand on Apenimon's

arm bought a stingy retreat. Above Cameron's shoulder, Sarah's gaze fixed onto the lonely distances.

"I have made squash stew. We were about to sit down. Please come in and be our guest." She spoke in a guttural tone, as if reading litany.

A thin but tempting edge of warmth seeped from the dwelling. Beyond Sarah and Apenimon, a woman the size of an adolescent slumped in a chair, head propped on a limp, backward-crooked wrist. This had to be Zoey, Chuey's older sister. The fetal alcohol-syndrome child. A ghostly parody of Lukas' voice echoed. *My mother lives with the consequences beneath her roof every day.*

Risking rudeness, Cameron inquired, "Is Lukas inside?"

"No." Apenimon spoke quickly without mercy or regard to manners.

Pointedly, she checked her watch. "I can't stay, but I need to talk to him." She glanced around, prompted by an eerie sense of his presence, or perhaps only *by* her want. *Her need.* "If you can tell me where—"

"Out back. In the barn." Sarah's gloom melded with resignation. Eyeing Cameron's linen shirt, she commanded, "Wait," turned away, then back, a plaid wool coat in her hand. "Here," she said softly and passed it to her.

With shuffling steps, Apenimon followed Cameron's retreat down the brick path. She kept moving, hoping he would not accompany her to the barn, halting at the end of the path when his feeble voice called to her above the wind.

"What are you?"

Wheeling, she faced him squarely, her spine prickling as if the borrowed coat were a hair shirt. She buttoned it to her chin, jammed her hands into the pockets, his strange, yet crystal-clear, question roiling in her mind. What was she? She could proudly tell him Samoan. She could offer the we-share-an-Asian-heritage story with which she'd tried to bribe Lukas. But Apenimon's condemning eyes raised her hackles, kept her from uttering humble apologetics.

"What?" he prompted. Spurning culture, his rheumy eyes searched hers.

Her chin gave a voluntary hike. "I'm a woman in love with your grandson."

Without waiting for his reaction, she spun on a cold, sandal-shod foot, strode across the arid yard, and thrust through a patch of ankle-high weeds to the barn. At the door, she heard children's voices, Lukas' deep quiet tone, then his laughter mixed with theirs. Her heart hammered, spiraled up to pulse in her throat. She thumbed the rusty latch and pulled back the door. Laughter died, replaced with stark quiet and the sound of wind whipping her skirt, rattling the latch on the open door. She stepped inside.

Afternoon sun spilled through a large, incongruous window in the far wall that framed the meadow, forming a silver aura about Lukas' head and shoulders. Mica rays danced off his hair, loose from his braids, spilling across his shoulders like black water. He showed no surprise, but in his hard eyes the slightest glimmer of light shone, like the sunny rim of a cloud. A grim look of victory—no, relief—or did she only wish that—skidded across his revered face.

Just as his mother had warned, cold overrode the bright sunshine and she was caught up in smells she'd only read about but identified as hay and tack and sweaty horse blankets. Near the big window, nine warmly dressed, jet-haired children shared rough wooden benches and tables that held large pads of paper. Sketch pads, she decided. A tin can filled with pencils occupied the center of each table. She became the rapt focus of the children's attention. Jet eyes, curious and expectant moon-shaped faces. Each empty of judgment.

Lukas stood beside a tall easel, holding a long pointer in his hand, still as a bronze statue on a summit only he could guard. The easel, too, held a large pad, its back to her, concealing whatever it depicted. Mud, or maybe manure, caked his boots and the bottoms of his faded jeans. A black T-shirt peeked from the collar of a coarse wool shirt. She helplessly imagined the garment chafing her breasts through her thin shirt, once this awkward overture ended and she was in his arms.

She ventured forward, stopping short of touching, but within range of his radiating warmth and virility. Close enough to smell wood smoke, to sense sudden adrenaline, and simmering distrust. His silence almost aggressive, he waited out her next move, while her heart rioted like a flock of captured birds.

She shored up her resolve.

"Is the class full, Professor Wind Dancer?" She spared a glance at the tables, then surrendered to the urge to devour him with her eyes, drink and swallow with her greedy mouth, then commit each pleasure to infinite memory.

Removing the wire-rimmed glasses she found so appealing, he solemnly addressed his audience while his dark, immutable gaze pinned hers. "This woman is my boss. I've been playing hookey."

A few quick grins lit otherwise blank faces, until she played along. "If I'm interrupting, please go on with class. I can fire you later," awarded her a round of abashed titters amid a flurry of jabbing elbows.

"We're finished." Face resolute, Lukas slapped the folded-back pages forward on the easel pad, preventing her from seeing what they concealed. "Next Saturday. You can tear off your work and finish it by then." He directed the words toward the children, who scuffed back the benches. Above the sound of ripping paper, he ordered, "Remember. The chalk and charcoal stay here."

With moans, shuffling feet and backward glances the children cleared the barn. Finally, she and Lukas squared off in solitude. The pointer he stored on the metal easel tray echoed like shrapnel on a tin roof. Far into the bowels of the barn, chickens she'd not been aware of till now clucked conversationally, while a

Walkman dangling from the easel whispered strains of a Mozart sonata.

"So *this* is why you make the trip to the reservation every weekend." Her memory replayed a scene of him pulling away from the inn each Saturday morning. The emptiness she'd felt then now echoed anew in her head and heart. "You're an artist. You're passing your skill on to them."

"Architect. I am teaching them to draw. That's the extent of my skill." His rigid jaw set a pulse to throbbing.

She lifted the easel pages, one by one, the paper cold and slick against her fingers. Her mind embraced the spirit and beauty of stark charcoal sketches of the countryside she'd driven through and pastel chalk renderings of the meadow surrounding the house and barn. There were bold, striated-red depictions of the rock canyon beyond. "Remember me telling you my career was not my first choice?" He rewarded her question with silence. "I wanted to study art." *My father was an artist.* "I'm an artist at heart."

His eyes softened a trace. "The college in Flag offers good art classes."

She searched, floundered. "I...don't know what that has to do with me." Eyes hot and luminous, he crossed his arms and widened his stance, locking his knees. "Probably no more than your yen to be an artist has to do with me."

He was smarting from her hurled accusations of spying, maybe even from her suspicions on that first night, wary now, and capable of leveling hurt in return. She hid her pain as best she could, voicing the words crowding her heart. "We have matching souls, Lukas. This proves it all the more."

He eyed the borrowed coat and her bare, blue-cold toes, then with a stab of a finger silenced the radio. "I am sorry about your mother, Cameron."

She swallowed deeply, waiting for leftover hurt from the death and new hurt from his detached manner to ebb. "Thank you. I'm fine with it."

A look strangely akin to frustration hinted he would rather witness tears. "Let's go. It's cold here." A few steps away he turned and gruffed, "Coming?"

She followed him to the corral, huddling in the coat, hands crammed into the pockets. Wordlessly he raised a wire latch on a sagging gate, briefly disappeared into that end of the barn, then emerged with a rusty bucket. He set it on the ground, called the horse—Gaagii—over and stroked its neck as it sniffed out the bucket's contents. When the huge animal began to snort, sling and chomp food, Lukas returned to where she waited outside the fence.

He hooked his fingers over the edge of the gray-weathered boards and extended his arms, braced as if holding on in a storm. One bent knee caused his taut rear to protrude. He turned only his head to look at her, his body stately and slender as the copse of pinion pines framing the meadow. Wind fluttered his hair, putting her in mind of glossy crow's wings.

She had to look away.

She watched the sun, silver sheeted now by high drifting clouds, until she felt compelled to break the silence and his well-cast spell. "Wilson Nakai is making great strides at the inn. You chose wisely, but I'm sure you know that."

He stared into the distance. "My mother's brother."

Puzzle pieces tumbled into place. "He's your uncle?" She mustered a smile. "Well, that explains his overly talkative nature."

The tension in his arms went slack. He turned, leaning against the fence, facing her, and she surrendered to her tangled emotions, foremost among them, love. His unmasked gaze burned fierce with lust, but not hot enough to consume other swirling but readable feelings.

"I know you're angry, Lukas. You have a right to be."

"I can't decide whether to lock you up in that hogan down the road," he motioned backward with his head, painting erotic visions for her, then lowered his voice, "or run your ass off the reservation."

Picturing that, she faked a smile. "What's this? The Navajo Nation's sagest seer, Jay Lukas Wind Dancer, grappling with a decision?"

Reaching out, he lightly raked his thumb across her lips. "Watch your mouth, little one." His sultry warning came out in visible silver wisps on the frigid late afternoon air. When he withdrew his touch she felt naked in the abrasive wind.

"I talked to Uncle Hayden while I was gone. He assured me you were an unwilling part of *his* spying. I owe you an apology, Lukas."

He grunted. "Let's have it."

She waited for a steady voice. "I misjudged you—jumped to conclusions." He nodded, expressionless. "I *am* sorry." He nodded again. Catching his hand, she examined the silver inlaid bracelet he wore, as though she'd never seen it. She pushed her fingers beneath to stroke the thin skin at the underside of his wrist, where veins ran like gorged, blue-blood rivers through a parched brown desert. She raised her eyes to his. "Will you forgive me, Lukas?"

Gaagii munched grain. The television droned softly in the background, while Lukas burdened her with time in which to wonder if her apology would go unaccepted.

At last he spoke. "To have told you I didn't spy would have been only a defense you would not have believed until you talked to him anyway." The wry smile twisting his mouth faded into a soft and sorry expression. "The essence of Navajo life is harmony. Every time you and I disagreed my gut seethed."

Her mind slid backward to countless times *she* had felt that way. Now his admission seemed to cut him from the inside out. "I never knew that."

"To let it show is not the Navajo way." His tone, the intimacy of it, underlined the significance of his reluctant willingness to share. "I couldn't stay and fight you. I care for you too much to put you through that."

But not too much to leave me. "Just tell me you forgive me, Lukas."

"Walk up the road with me. I will show you."

Her eyes sought the distant, isolated hogan. "I'm tired of discretion and denial. Show me here."

He cupped her neck with a warm hand, fingers snaking inside the coat collar. "We have an audience. The rez cops would arrive before I could even begin what I want to show you."

Cheeks warming, she cut her glance toward the house, but he blocked her view by dipping his head and kissing her, a vow of the forgiveness she sought.

"You taste like peanut butter." His tongue invaded a corner of her mouth, then raked over her lips.

She mirrored the action. "It's my new diet. I'm aiming for fat and pimples."

"You're failing." He gave her a long speculative look, then hands on her shoulders, marched her backward until she landed roughly against the fence. He grunted—moaned—either in satisfaction or apology; the light in his black eyes gave no clue. But then he lowered his hands to her hips and pressed his lower body into hers, destroying a need for clues. Over his shoulder she spied a shadowy figure at the window and moved her head out of range of his mouth.

"Surveillance is probably dialing the phone this minute," she whispered.

With a humorless smile, he stepped back, hands on her shoulders. "You have come a long way. My mother has cooked. Not to eat with us would be rude."

A rock-like sensation settled in her stomach. "I've met your mother—and Apenimon. They want me out of here. To eat with you would be rude torture. For them more than me."

He laughed. "*Yisdadiinaat.* They and you will survive."

"But will you?" Her laughter emerged thin, like a sprinkling of shattered glass. "Or will they make it hell for you when I'm gone?"

"There is safety in numbers, Yazhi. For now, we will be together."

ॐ

Apenimon's appreciation for Cameron's love of fry bread did not go unnoticed by Lukas. Neither did the way Cameron—seated close on his left, the unrequited contact, painful as an abscess—opted to speak only when obligated. Mostly, she kept her eyes lowered, as if the air of disapproval could be shut out, like debilitating darkness or wretched weather.

Nor did he miss the abstract way his mother watched her, scarcely eating for fear of missing a chance to weigh and judge. Not cruelly, as Cameron had gleaned from the earlier meeting, but concerned. A veteran now, Sarah was eager to ward off the disaster threatening to invade her household, infiltrate her family.

He, too, watched Cameron, unable to get enough. He had not yet gotten his mind around her coming to him. Certainty of the imminent consequence of her presence, questions of where those consequences would fall, plagued him.

Though she had the same vulnerable look as that first day in the inn bar, today she wore war paint. Applied skillfully, artfully, it was still no match for her sultry, exotic beauty. Her nails were done in the clear, white-tipped way he liked, making it easy to recall them piercing his back, to recall her under him, sleek and hot, as unpredictable and untamable as lightning. Easy to recall her desire to cover him, his continued refusal each time they made love. Her eventual surrender.

He shifted in the chair, his loins knotting painfully. *Doo 'aaníínií baa naashá*. In his head, the damn demon the Stantons had called his conscience chanted. But how could he be *doing something wrong* by having her sit at his mother's table? How could a woman so sensitive and brave, as committed and moral as Yazhi, contaminate a bloodline? Start a family war? Turn a people against a leader?

Glancing up, she caught him in the act of watching. His blood ran thin and watery. His very essence and all his convictions threatened to stream out of him in the strong rush of an unclogged river, sweeping away all tradition in its path, and soaking into Kai's irreplaceable Yeibichei rug beneath the table.

He dropped his napkin into his plate and shoved back his chair. Zoey's head angled up, her eyes unfocused and suspicious, while his mother's eyes came to rest on him, knowing, yet still petitioning.

"Had enough?" Lukas said.

Cameron's scared-doe look turned his heart upside down and left it empty as a robbed room. Given her hurtful history, she deserved to live a lifetime free of the treatment being handed her here. She deserved his guarantee it would not happen again. "Enough stew, Yazhi? Or maybe you would like dessert?" He rose without waiting for an answer.

"I'm fine." She rose in turn, addressing Sarah. "It was wonderful."

"I am taking Cameron for a ride, Shima. Do not look for us before morning."

In answer, he received silence from a grim-as-granite mouth. Resignation replaced the earlier plea in his mother's eyes.

"Ya 'di 'ladinii." Bracing on his cane and the table corner, Apenimon struggled to his feet, warning, *"T' áadoo doo áaniinii baa nanináhí."*

What are you saying? Lukas translated in his head. *Behave yourself, don't do anything wrong.* As if Lukas were four years old, not thirty-four. The admonishment whirled in his head like refuse caught in a dust devil. Gently, firmly, he placed his hands on the old man's shoulders, lowering him into the chair. He spoke Navajo in turn. "You have taught me well, Grandfather. Trust me, as I trust you."

Back outside, he coaxed Cameron away from the Taurus, assuring her the ride he planned could not be done by car. Not even in the Suburban parked back at his hogan. Wordlessly, her expression dubious, she watched him throw a blanket over Gaagii's back and fit him with a saddle and bridle. Her steps unsteady, breath cloudy, she made weather-related small talk as they strolled the rutted, frozen road toward the hogan, Gaagii straggling behind at rein's end.

At the door Cameron balked, answering his questioning look with, "Kai," surprising the hell out of him. The way she had heated up to his kiss earlier denied she knew or cared that Kai Blackwater existed.

He dropped the reins. "What *about* Kai?"

She held the coat collar around her throat with one hand, warming the other beneath her arm. "She's living with you. No house is big enough for two women, Wind Dancer."

"Chuey tell you that?"

"It's a cliché, but it's true. No *man* is big enough for two women either."

He quashed a laugh. "Did Chuey tell you she is *living* with me?"

"Yes, when he was in the hospital. He was worried about her, too." At least she was crediting him with concern while accusing him of cohabiting.

"Since the hospital a lot of water has run under the bridge." A damn flash flood, but he was slowly beginning to dry out. "Kai's place was rotting. She and Gad *stayed* here. Regardless of what Chuey told you, that's all it was."

She shook her head, either disbelieving or not appeased. "If we're going for a ride we should just go. I have to get back soon...to Mikela."

He released the latch, gently swept her up, kicked open the door; crossed the threshold, and whacked the door closed with his boot heel. Once inside, enveloped in the hogan's warm mesquite-scented air, her remaining resistance could be measured in a thimble. Gently, he deposited her on an old tin trunk at the foot of his single bed and knelt before her, loosely resting a hand on her knee.

"Here's a news flash. Kai and Chuey teamed up. Her hogan has been repaired and they are living there. Seems Chuey is a daddy, soon to be a husband."

"My God, a daddy," she breathed. "You mean Gad? That's…incredible."

"Enit?" Her shock—undisguised wonder and relief—gave him the impetus to laugh at the situation. For the first time, the worry in his heart almost eased. Visions of pushing her backward on the bed, burying what remained of his concern within her welcoming warmth, undulated behind his eyes. Instead, he rose, crossed to a chest standing near the screened-off toilet, rummaged a drawer for what he needed. He turned and caught her taking in the room, eyes darting as rapidly as her thoughts, then settling on Kai's loom. The way the corners of her mouth jerked down almost made him laugh again. Her jealousy was heady. *Healing.*

"Kai has not been well. Weak, but she's better now. They will pick up the loom tomorrow." He kept his tone matter of fact, kneeling before her again, taking one of her feet in his hands and slipping a cotton sock over her sandal and smoothing it up her calf. "These will keep your feet warm." He followed suit with the other foot, layered thick wool socks on top, and rocked back on his heels.

"Two pair?" She cocked a brow in that pesky way he sometimes craved in the middle of the night. "That's overly generous."

"Navajo hospitality." The words emerged in bitter irony, his smile dredged from the murky depths of his heart. "Don't worry, Yazhi. I won't let your feet touch the ground."

"You haven't, Wind Dancer, since the day we met." She tugged on the top socks, then fitted her skirt over them and stood. He came up to meet her, and she cocked her head. "But *that* grand treatment was off the reservation. You're not fooling me about hospitality. I just sat through the most torturous meal of my life."

He vowed to erase that memory, starting with a change of subject. "I would offer to show you the rest of the mansion, but this is it."

Taking her time now, she surveyed every inch. Sod walls hung with rugs and no-name Indian art, the hard-packed dirt floor and smoldering fire pit, all surely stirring emotions in her he wished he could read. On one wall, above a desk housing a laptop computer and cell phone, a television and state-of-the-art stereo shared space. Old and new worlds blending together to form his domain.

"Cozy." Her voice came out husky, pensive. Then she reconsidered. "It's nice, Lukas. I can picture you here, but somehow I can't picture you alone."

"I am alone, Yazhi." Alone and celibate when the wind howled and the snow pelted the walls and he lay wondering how much of this life to abandon, how much to safeguard. He brushed his lips across her brow. "Ready to go?"

She would not be put off. "All you need to make this perfect is an Indian princess." Her eventual smile vacillated between praise and derision. "Judging by the awe in the eyes of the people who directed me here, you can take your pick."

"You are right. I can." He refastened her coat buttons. "But I'm afraid I may have been jaded by a Polynesian princess."

thirty-one

Hugging a backpack Lukas had loaded with items from the kitchen, Cameron watched him attach a bulky, cylindrical bundle behind the saddle. He tied the last cord with a flourish, gave a final jerk to the band circling the horse's belly, swung into the saddle, and coaxed Gaagii nearer to the door. Cameron's body jerked backward, her backside banging the splintery hogan door. Grinning, Lukas removed one foot from the stirrup, leaned down and extended a hand.

She shouldered the backpack, tried lifting her foot stirrup-high and stumbled forward. Gaagii shied. A surprised warning rasped deep in his throat. Cameron retreated, feeling her eyes flare as wide as the animal's.

"Whoa, Gaagii. Whoa." Lukas turned his head away, shoulders shaking.

"Damn you, Lukas. Don't laugh. I've never even smelled a horse before."

"Then stand still." He stroked Gaagii's jugular, leaned down again, took the backpack from her and hung it over the saddle horn. "Turn around."

"Why? So you can run me down from behind?" She gasped air. "Let's just go somewhere in the car. Wherever—Or back into the house." An idea that held sudden and vast appeal. "I can't stay much longer any—"

"Turn around, *asdzáni.*"

Lowered to an intimacy as serene as the falling evening, his voice possessed the power to turn her, but failed to quash her fear. The saddle creaked; she sensed Gaagii purchasing ground. Then Lukas' searing hands slid into her armpits and pulled her up onto his thigh. He held her as if she were a weightless fantasy, the arm that curled around her waist as supple as a vine, firm as a vise. He smiled. "You were saying?"

Mute, she stared at the ground beneath her dangling, socked feet. Lukas shifted his weight as his hand lowered between her legs and lifted the right one over the front of the saddle. He flattened his hand against her lower body and situated her between the pommel and the well of his spread legs. She worked at tugging down her bunched-up skirt, aware of how closely he watched her futile efforts. The hand resting on her hip, steadying her, stole to her bare leg and stayed there, causing her nerve endings to dance an erotic celebration that ended between her exposed thighs. A reaction expressed by her ragged breathing.

"*Enit?*" he taunted.

"Extremely *enit,*" she groaned. Laughing, she added, "You savage."

Chuckling, he encircled her arms and pulled on the reins. Gaagii danced in a tight circle, then trotted off across the meadow behind the hogan. They rode in silence, Lukas' breath stirring her hair, until they crested a peak and he slowed the horse. In the near distance, a smoothed circle of red clay formed a crude landing pad. In the center, a small helicopter glistened black and bird-like in waning sunlight. The same one she'd seen in the picture on his desk. Wrestling panic, she assured herself that had he intended this machine to furnish their *ride,* there'd be no need for Gaagii. They could have hiked to this spot.

Feeling him waiting, she voiced her thoughts. "I'll bet there's a story here."

"Golf courses." Warm, sweet breath and scanty information teased her ear.

She pondered the connection as he urged a skeptical Gaagii nearer to the helicopter.

"Building golf courses is the new 'skin industry. Much needed money for the people. They will be built on the reservations by Indian labor. Indians will operate and maintain them, working close to the land."

She tried to imagine this vast, arid land green and lush, trafficked with golf carts hauling soft-bellied men wearing plaid pants. "You mean build them here?"

"In warmer places. Near Sedona. And south on San Carlos and Gila River land." He nodded to the helicopter. "This ugly bird can go between locations, land anywhere. Also, I can fly the *Diné* to Flag for emergency medical treatment they often go without."

Ever the shepherd protecting his charges…

"You know how to design golf courses?" She slanted her head around to view his face, the bigger picture taking over, piquing her for some reason. "You're just full of surprises, aren't you?"

He turned his head away, his profile forming a dark silhouette against the horizon. Although she knew him to be determined in all he pursued or desired, she'd never seen his jaw lashed quite so tightly, his gaze so steadfast.

Finally he explained, "I'm designing clubhouses. Also, I will oversee the labor to build and maintain the courses. The *Diné* will have work to take pride in. I will have work on Indian land, honoring my birthright."

"Honoring your quest for harmony." She fixed her eyes on the sinking sun.

He caught her chin, enabling him to search her eyes while his own remained veiled. "Thank you for understanding that."

"I'm trying, Lukas." Thus far her efforts had failed miserably.

His smile represented a rare, playful offering. "Indian kids will learn to play golf. Maybe we'll produce a Coyote Wooded Lands to make our nation proud on the big box every Sunday afternoon."

He expected her to laugh, or maybe only hoped she could. Expected her to overlook his abandoning the inn, *her* link to harmony, for his people and golf courses—stinging truth, regardless of his reasoning.

"I'll be sure to watch."

They rode on, surrounded by wide views and sage-scented air, an occasional jet-towing a contrail across the voluminous sky. Gaagii's gait spurred a rocking cadence that thrust Lukas' crotch against Cameron's breech. Her awareness and desire grew with his heated, hardening arousal, so evident through their clothing.

"Where are we going?" Her voice came from a removed, wistful plane.

"To a special place." The words vibrated quiet and deep next to her ear.

"A place worth waiting for."

Content to anticipate, craving his promise, she slacked against him, the weight of her breasts settling onto the arm enfolding her midriff. They neared a low rock wall, which in falling darkness appeared waist high, an irregular circle formed of hand-stacked stones and adobe. A makeshift corral, she thought. Imagination failing, curiosity peaking, she broke the silence to inquire.

"Sheep." He said. They rocked on until Gaagii drew abreast of the enclosure. Lukas reined him in to afford a closer look. "A shearing corral."

"Why's the ground so green? And it's…petrified," she observed. "Am I seeing right?"

"Sheep dung, baked by the sun and wind over the years while the pen sits empty." His voice adapted the patient quality she'd heard him use with his art students. "Sheep being sheared here would once have been a common sight. Now chasing the American dream takes people away. Asphalt and air pollution have taken the place of sheep in their lives. More and more, aging Navajo women are forced to sell herds belonging to the next generation." He fell quiet, fingers twisting in the reins. His body tensed, the saddle creaking.

"Our family heritages are falling into the hands of strangers."

"Aging women?" She attempted the same reverence she'd heard from him.

"Women own the sheep. They are passed as gifts from mother to daughter, generation to generation before the daughters have even started families of their own. My mother still has the herd she inherited from my grandmother, but she married young. The handwriting on the wall of things to come is as plain as a canyon petroglyph."

"I hope she's not ill." She had appeared hawk-eyed and hardy.

He touched his mouth to her crown. "She is vital, still. Zoey's mother's death robbed her of her only daughter. Her nieces have gone to the city to be superwomen. Some day Sarah Wind Dancer's heritage will also be lost." A nudge of his boot heels spurred Gaagii to a trot. "So you see, Yazhi, while you fight to find your heritage, my mother fights to keep hers."

Sarah's reproachful looks at the dinner table winged across her mind, the sting no less acute, but the basis, the strength of the convictions, conceivable.

The terrain grew steep, the surrounding landscape considerably more primitive than what they'd journeyed Through. On the horizon a light show ran a color gamut from orange to carmine, to prismatic lavenders, then bowed to early darkness. Silence fell as though they were saving energy for Gaagii's plodding climb, saving breath in place of that he noisily expended. Cameron's cold hands gripped the saddle horn, but she felt herself sliding backward even more tightly against Lukas. Gratified by his erotic reaction, she surrendered to her own hunger, surreal in its intensity.

At the incline's crest, Lukas pulled up on the reins and dismounted, almost simultaneously. He held his arms up to her. "We'll walk from here."

She threw a leg over, sat sideways in the saddle for a moment, then let go and slid into his upraised arms, her body skimming his as he lowered her to the ground. He held the reins in one hand, and her hand in the other, drawing her along as he continued climbing. They halted yards away from a sheer and rugged wall of rock. Wind swirled Lukas' hair like heavy black cord around his face as he unhooked and passed the backpack to her, removed the bundle and unbuckled the saddle's cinch strap. He removed the saddle and placed it on a low rock, leaving the reins to dangle.

"Won't he run away?" Like her words, shuttled skyward on the wind?

"He remembers the bucket of free food. He is lazy. He'll wait."

He retrieved the rolled bundle, and with an upturned, outstretched palm, invited her to precede him. Warily, she followed his instruction until face to face with the boulders, where she paused to catch her breath. Hanging back, confused, she stared through the darkness at the rock wall. Lukas moved forward and tossed the bundle through a hidden crevice formed by overlapping boulders. He followed suit with the backpack, then stepped back, smiling. "You go first, little one."

She examined the tight passageway, understanding why he'd tossed their provisions through. "I can't fit."

"Take off the coat." She stared at the gap, then dubiously at him, until he said softly, "Come." Catching her hand, he angled sideways, sucked in his stomach, tucked his derriere, and sidestepped through, coaxing her to follow. Rough rock gnawed the coat's shoulders and the back of an errant heel, but finally she emerged on the other end unscathed.

Sheer cliffs formed a small box canyon, maybe twice the size of Lukas' hogan, creating shelter from the wind, casting a comforting illusion of warmth. Cottonwoods rustled and gleamed beneath a cloud-laced moon that painted the grass floor mica-sharp to the eye, yet it lay cushiony beneath her feet. Turning toward a gurgling sound, she discovered a small pool nestled into a boulder outcropping It churned like a pot of boiling water, steam rising *in* the night air.

Lukas answered her unvoiced question with, "Underground hot springs."

In her mind's eye, she slipped beneath the current, up to her chin, willing it to chase the chill from her bones. "That scent." Sharp, almost medicinal. "What is it?" she whispered, the quiet, unspoiled beauty turning her into an intruder.

"Juniper. One of Mother Earth's gifts. But the leaves are sharp, so be careful."

Above it all a star-studded sky pretended indifference to heritage, culture, or dashing goals, offering perfect solitude in a special, worth-waiting-for place.

He crossed to the pool's edge, lowered the backpack and unfurled the bundle to reveal a sleeping bag. Her pulse pounded, then quieted, her whole being suddenly filled with anticipation. With uncharacteristic haste, Lukas entered the shadows of the trees, moved in small circles, slightly crouched, raking the ground with the side of a foot. She followed, curious until he began to gather fallen branches, forming a stack in a crooked arm. Wordlessly, she did the same until he murmured, "Enough for now."

Back at the edge of the pool he snapped each limb in two beneath his boot, crossed his legs at the ankles and sank to the ground. Not nearly so gracefully, she knelt and watched him layer the pieces in a criss-cross pattern. From the backpack, he produced a small can of fluid—lighter fluid, judging by the smell when he squirted the wood—and a butane-filled wand. A snap of the wand trigger ignited the fluid with a whoosh and small flames shot skyward.

"I'm disappointed. I thought you would rub two sticks together."

"This is no time for Hollywood tricks." He set the fluid and wand aside and rose effortlessly without touching the ground, then reached a hand down, drawing her up. "My woman is cold."

She looked up into his face where the moon emerging from the clouds played on the sharp planes and angles but exposed nothing. "Your woman?"

"In my heart, yes." Emotion, unheard before, lay raw behind the simple words. He pressed his parted lips to hers, kissing her long and slow, angled against her, allowing her to feel his muscle and soul. A hand drifted to the button holding the coat closed at her breasts. "Take off your clothes. The water will warm you."

Already drawn into a warm fluid place by his kiss, she stepped back, her breath audible as she began to undress, socks and sandals first, then the coat. He watched, taking the coat, placing it carefully on the ground, her shirt on top. She slipped the skirt past her hips, let it pool at her feet and stepped out of it. His eyes on her impugned the chilly air as he folded the skirt loosely and added it to the stack. She unhooked the front dosing on her bra. His reach languid, yet quick, hot as a lick of flame, he palmed her breasts for a heartbeat, then slid the silk aside and down her arms, breath soughing above the bubbling water. His heated gaze trailed her hands as she removed the last item of clothing and passed it to him.

Without haste, while her heart hammered, he folded her panties in half, then in quarters, tucked them into a bra cup and laid them aside. Taking her hand, he guided her into the water, helping her purchase footing. He released her as the rocky ledge sloped into waist-deep depth, so hot that for the instant before she hunkered down, she questioned her endurance.

Her raspy sigh brought a grunt from Lukas, while the moon, fully emerged now, revealed a satisfied smile. He tugged off his boots, then unbuttoned his shirt. Arching his shoulders, he pulled the tail from his waistband, discarded the shirt and peeled the T over his head. His zipper rasped in the night. Peeling off the remainder of his clothing, he pitched it beside the careful pile he'd made of hers. He turned and squatted to poke the fire, staring into its depths for a lengthy moment.

No man should be as beautiful as Lukas. A part of his appeal emanated from his inner strength, she realized, the very ideology she hated: his refusal to settle for less than he believed to be right. Though she questioned his views, she could never fault his sense of convictions.

Nerve endings raveling, she looked away, then back, coveting the firelight's intimate dance on a slender and sinewy torso, on his dark pubic patch, on long thighs, the muscles superbly shaped. His sex swung weighted and dark against his inner thighs as he rose, tossed the branch into the fire and stepped agilely into the churning pool. He submerged onto a bench-like ledge along the perimeter, an arm's length away, groaning softly, creating a quickening in her middle that she hid behind a laugh.

"This is heaven. I'm not getting out until summer. You do have summer, I hope." Swirling her arms in the warmth, she questioned that hope, knowing she would never be here to witness the changing seasons.

"Summer is also heaven." She strained to hear his quiet allegation. "It is nothing like the Scottsdale heat you hate."

"I'm adjusting. I don't hate it so much now." And she loved the fickle sun.

"You haven't seen a Scottsdale summer. It will cook your soul, little one."

Again her mind calculated. "I'll be gone before I have the displeasure."

"So you say."

They settled into silence. Above the water's gurgle, an animal she couldn't name called out, receiving a forlorn answer that echoed off the towering walls.

"How long have you been coming here?"

"When I was a boy, before I left the reservation, I chased a rabbit into here."

"Do you…Have you brought other women?" The menacing question she had had no right to ask, and had vowed she wouldn't, hovered on the night.

Too much time passed. "Would you have me lie to you?"

"I wanted you to tell me I'm the only one."

Again he waited, as if weighing her words. "Why?"

She lifted her face to the moon, his question reverberating behind her closed eyes. "Because I'm in love with you." *It's so much more than being in love.* "I love you, Lukas."

He extended his hand. She took it. He drew her through the water toward him, just short of touching. In the diffused light, his eyes burned into hers. "I have brought no woman here that I loved." He lifted and settled her onto him, fitting her legs about his waist, her arms around his neck. When he spoke again, the words sounded like they'd been dislodged from a guarded stronghold. "No woman before you, Yazhi."

She pressed her face into his neck, torn between rejoicing in and crying over the knowledge of shared love. Hands in his hair, she kissed him, a chaste pledge, but his hand at the small of her back pressed her against him, infusing life into the offering. Lips parting, he drew her in, then encouraged her tongue's tentative probing with his own exploration of leisurely, gratifying strokes.

Water swirled hot and strong around them, while beneath her his arousal pulsed, eager and insistent. His hands cupped her buttocks, lifting her, bringing her breasts out of the water. His tongue ringed the dark, raised centers before he took each one in turn into the wet warmth of his mouth. A flutter in her

belly shot to the notch of her thighs as he lowered her,
secured her legs around him and rose to thigh-depth.
Moon-glistened water sluiced off his shoulders and
onto her breasts. Their gazes locked while the cold
wind nipped their fevered bodies. Leaving the water,
he moved to the spread blanket, sank to his knees, laid
her down and bent over her.

She touched his face. "Tell me again."

"I love you." Gently, he caught her wrists and
kissed the underside of each, kissed her palms, took
her fingers one by one into his mouth. He twisted to
kiss her instep, her calf, her knee, an inner thigh, as if
to favor no part of her body above the other. With his
mouth, he explored the soft indention of her belly, the
muscles in her forearms, the hollow of one shoulder,
as his moist tip pulsed against her thigh. Turning onto
his back, he drew her astride his hips. She leaned
down to seek his mouth and felt him lift her as he
reached to join them together. Her senses lurched,
tangling in surprise and excitement that arched her
body. She sat back, searching his face.

"I want you to have your way, Yazhi."

The quiet, sensual claim pricked her awareness.
Love had taken away her passion to dominate. She
lifted off him, lay beside him, aligning *her* body to his.

"*You* are my way, Lukas. No one ever made me feel
the way you do. I never want to change that." Her
hand at his waist urged him to turn toward her. "I
want to feel your weight on me, feel you making love
to me."

A finger traced her mouth. "You are sure?"

"So sure."

Drawing her beneath him, he parted her legs with a decisive hand and entered her slowly and completely, his gaze holding hers. An immediate sense of rightness passed shock-like through her, the gentle invasion of a shaft of fire, pressing upward to her being, spreading into a torrent of nearly unbearable pleasure. His body quivered into a rhythm, moved against her gracefully, purposefully, his mouth working hers.

Her hips lifted to embrace his full, stirring length. Each thrust created and filled in her a spasm of need and desire until her ragged breath pained her throat and her body ran taut. She moaned, powerless, yet reluctant to journey so quickly into a lonely, visceral realm. But then, her confused desires culminated, imploding in the soft hollow behind her closed eyes. He filled her with molten steel, his groan and her cry of surrender and serenity blending in the cold night air.

thirty-two

The hot pool's rock ledge dug into Lukas' back. He held his position, knowing Cameron was content leaning her back to his chest, arms hooked through his where they circled her, her chin barely above the water. He bent to press his lips to her crown, moving his hands down to stroke her belly, up again to cup her breasts. The eager way she tilted her head, seeking his mouth, stirred his heart and groin.

Just as he had dishonored his vow never to make love to her, tonight in admitting he loved her, he had defied fate even more. Lack of commitment had stopped the telling before, but tonight he silently committed to love her forever, even if she found reason and strength to refuse what he would ask of her.

"Something about you has changed." Her voice carried above the water and night sounds.

Did she have an eye into his mind? He tweaked a distended nipple. *"Enit?"*

"I've been trying to decide. You're gentle, I think. You made love to me gently." She laughed, her breast jiggling in his hand. "I don't hurt anywhere."

"I have lost my anger."

"For what?" She twisted around with a look of disbelief. "For me?"

"I had made up my mind not to love you." Never to love again. Anyone.

"I was never quite that strong." She turned to face him, drawing her knees up, easing his back, depriving his hands. "Some deranged part of me wanted you from the start. But I kept getting the feeling confused with wanting to flog you."

He laughed, recalling that first night in the bar, their tour of Scottsdale the next day, her defeat at the hands of CNN. *The hated fire pit.* Somehow, he would make her grasp his plan, convince her—"You have to come to Samoa with me. We'll build a life. Come with me, Lukas. Unbreak my heart," she urged softly.

He thought of all that entailed. "That's a tall order, Yazhi."

"You're a very tall man." She smiled. He supposed his own smile encouraged her to go on outlining the fantasy. "By the time I'm ready to go—when the inn's done, and I've been back to court for Jarrid, you—"

He pressed a forefinger to her lips, sealing off the impossible proposal. Regret and frustration for his poor-ass timing roiled. "We have been over this."

"Things have changed since then."

Based on his weakness in voicing his love. "Not that much."

"At least we can discuss it. We can build a life there, Lukas. Where no one cares what—"

This time he silenced her with two fingers and a tender smile. She shrugged back in the water, almost tumbling off the edge before he steadied her.

"Talk to me, damn it." Her eyes lit like the fire he had built for her.

"I am talking to you. You're hearing me, but not what you want to hear."

"Fine." She sounded more determined than defeated. "Then this—tonight—means nothing. Or did you lie about me being the only woman you've brought here that you loved."

"It is no lie. But I won't go to Samoa. I don't want you to go."

Throwing him an incredulous look, she made a move to leave the pool, but he caught her wrist. "What would you have me do, Wind Dancer?"

He had not intended to lay out his plan for her under fire. "Stay in Scottsdale. When the inn is finished, run it the way you told Hayden you would."

"That was a temporary part of an agreement he's released me from." She pried his fingers off her wrist. "I can't stay. I have to get my son back."

"Bring him to Scottsdale. Run the inn. Make a life for him there." Once more the plan unfurled in his head. "I will be minutes away. You and I—the three of us—will share that life."

"That would be convenient for you, wouldn't it? You could just land your ugly black bird on the inn roof anytime you felt lusty." Her chin hiked. He hated what the moon allowed him to see in her eyes. "Tell me. Is there some sage Indian adage that covers having your cake and eating it, too?"

"Wanting you—loving you—does not wipe out my concern for my people."

She stood, moonlight casting her ripe profile in relief against the night. "The day Chuey referred to your obsessive concern as *promised* was the day I should have packed and run like hell."

"What about the way you are trying to change history, little one?" She turned to glare at him. "You're a love child. Your father was Samoan, but he could have been Russian. Albanian. Serbian. Wherever the hell the next hotel was being built. You can't wipe out a wanton mother by sleeping in her love bed."

"Damn you." She tossed her head. "You have no idea what you're saying."

He let her go, watching her pick her way gingerly to her clothes, drag them onto her wet body. He didn't follow until she was buttoning her shirt. He pulled the T over his head, worked his jeans over his wet skin, zipped them half way, and went in search of more wood. He returned to find her crouched on the sleeping bag, hugging her knees, shivering so hard he could hear her teeth chatter. He pitched the wood onto the fire and offered her his mother's coat. She shoved it away. He offered his wool shirt. When she only stared at him, he forced her arms in and pulled it together in the front, the breasts that had filled his hands minutes before now forbidden territory. He determined not to give up.

Legs crossed, he sat before her, bare feet tucked beneath his calves. Frigid air braced him, fed his Resolve. "Remember the white woman I told you about?"

"Don't you mean the white woman you refused to talk about? The one who sealed my fate?"

"I'm ready to talk now." Maybe to make her understand, persuade her to give in. In the face of her silence he began. "I left the reservation when I was twelve to live with a missionary family. We traveled all over the world. Suzanne was their daughter." With his naming of her adversary, he felt her body quicken. "I was with the Stantons for ten years. We—Suzanne and I—grew up together. Along the way, when we were really still children." He willed the details from his mind. "We fell in love. She never wanted her parents—anyone—to know, so all those years we hid it."

"Why?" The word drifted out to him, emblazoning hurtful answers he must release from his nightmares.

"Religion, for one thing. She was raised to believe sex outside marriage is wrong. We were too young to marry, but not too young to lust." Once again, deceit coiled serpent-like in his belly. "Racism, for another. She loved me, in her way, but even though she defended my Indian blood, she never forgave me for it."

Cameron nodded, looked away, then back, her teeth pressing her bottom lip.

"After college, we ended up in Chicago, where she worked and I went to architectural school. We didn't marry. She knew her parents would protest. But all that freedom made us careless. She got—I made her Pregnant. We argued. I wanted the baby. She wanted an abortion."

"What about religion?" Her tone fell just short of derisive.

"She panicked. Religion did not cover half-breed babies." He tried to push the picture from his mind. "I kept arguing with her while the pregnancy progressed, hoping she would get used to the idea. Finally she told me she was resigned to being pregnant and she was going to Guatemala, where the Stantons were living, to tell them."

Despite an attempt not to, he tasted their kiss the morning Suzanne had left, relived her rigid posture, her wobbly gaze. He waited for an even tone in order to continue. "She was gone too long. The Stantons had not heard from her. Eventually, she came back, but she had left my son in an abortion clinic trashcan." He managed to shrug, wanting to sob. "So much for equality."

"I'm sorry." Her tremulous tone backed up her words. She stroked a finger across the nylon bag, studying an imaginary flaw, finally lifting her eyes to his.

"She died a week later from infection."

"Oh, God." It sounded theatrical, but her eyes raged with shock and sorrow.

He owed her more. "When you deceived me by setting Chuey up to work on the roof—"

"You compared me to Suzanne." He nodded. Eyes glimmering, she touched his face, cupped his jaw, setting him free to grieve yet again. Then she dropped her hand. "Saggy roofs are not babies, and I'm not Suzanne Stanton. I would be honored to have your baby, but you're hoarding hurt and anger toward Suzanne like money in the bank, and I'm the one who's paying the interest." He nodded again, the truth hitting home. "Let me guess the rest. You feel like you want to spend your life doing what? Making amends? For what, Lukas? Loving her?"

"For deserting the reservation and my people. For chasing a dream God meant for white men, not me. A dream that includes a white woman—any white woman."

"Including me, though I'm only half deserving of the honor."

"Stay in Scottsdale, Cameron."

"And be your mistress?"

He grasped her hands, pressing his thumbs into her palms. "Be there for me. Love me the way I love you."

"I'd be cheating you if I loved you that way I want the world to know I love you. I'm not governed by your skin color." She pulled her hands free and ran them through her tousled hair, then pressed their heels to her temples. "I'm asking you to be with me, instead of hiding you. But you chose to stay in this godforsaken wasteland and grovel in the wake of Suzanne's deluded sins."

Her words beat a drum-like echo in his head. "I was born on this land. Every time I return I feel completed, a feeling older than the *Anasazi*. I can't pull the reservation out of my blood. Would you take me from this to an unknown place?" He pulled her hands down, held them and her gaze tightly. "Try to understand, Yazhi. My heart is in the old world. My head is in the new, knowing we need new ways in order to survive as a people. At times I forget all that when I begin to think *I* won't survive without *you*." He ran his thumbs over her knuckles. "Times like now when I am asking you to stay. Other times I fear you could not survive with me without showing your son what you believe to be your heritage and have chosen to be his. Right now my two worlds have turned upside down as one. You are part of *that* world."

"But only a convenient part tucked away in Scottsdale. I can't do that. If that's what you want in a woman, I'm not the woman you need."

"Somehow, knowing that has not kept me from loving you."

Her brow furrowed, her mouth turning grim. "You say that, but you want to hide me just like. Suzanne Stanton wanted to hide you."

"To keep you from being hurt. To protect you, little one."

Knowingly or not, her nails dug into his palm. "I can do that for myself. And Jarrid. My uncle is offering me a hotel, Lukas. The one I've always craved. He's granting me independence. A chance to prove myself to my judgmental family."

For him, her words painted only distance, a sense of not knowing, of loneliness and longing. "Don't go. Come here, Yazhi. Live with me here." He heard himself voicing the trump card in his plea, the one that would sentence each of them to pain anytime they were out of one another's arms. Any time they faced reality. "I will take care of you and your son. We'll make it work." *Somehow.*

"You saw the way your family looked at me tonight—even Zoey. Why would I trade legacy for prejudice? Why would I subject Jarrid to that when all you have to do is go with us and start a new life?"

"I can think of only one reason."

Her eyes brimmed. She blinked furiously. "Don't use that on me. I *do* love you, Lukas."

"But not enough to do as I ask."

"I can say the same about you."

"Whither thou goest, Yazhi." In his mind's eye, he saw the needlepoint sampler Laura Stanton had moved from country to country, hardship to hardship. The one that hung over her bed. "It has been a woman's role since time began."

She shook her head, fists pressing against closed eyes, elbows on her folded knees. "In these modern times women take care of themselves. I got off track,

Lukas. I fell in love, but I'll survive." She raised her head, eyes full of fake resolve. "I want to go back to my car. Please take me."

"It's too cold to ride. You need fire and a warm bed." *I want to hold you.*

She got to her knees, began unbuttoning his shirt. "I'll find the way alone."

He rose to his knees to meet her. "Sleep with me here. Give that to me."

Her eyes sought his, searched and held. Her hands stilled, then reversed their action. "And to me," she whispered.

He held her through the night, her firm little rear tucked against his thighs, his sex pressed low to her spine, an arm beneath her head, a hand splayed on her breasts. He knew neither of them slept; he felt her body tense each time he moved, heard his rejections and petitions echo in her head, while in his, her refusals and pleas resounded. His past and their separate futures roamed restless on his mind. Gradually they floated upward to memory that unearthed a need in him base enough to overcome his grief. The moon dimmed and dawn painted the gray cliffs with ancient bloodstains. He hardened against her. She groaned softly, caught his hand, moved it down and clasped it between her parted legs for a while.

When she turned to him, whispering, "Help me find the heart to leave you, Lukas," he petitioned God for the strength to let her go.

Lukas leaned down at the Taurus' window, arms resting on the door, hands dangling inside, loosely clasped. He had promised himself not to touch her again. Cameron's hands met at high noon on the steering wheel, semi-circled in opposite directions to three and nine, back to noon, gripping so tightly her fingertips whitened. Her hair, a mass of loose curls, shone like a Chicago matron's sable coat, the circles beneath her eyes only a shade lighter. She was hurting. He felt it.

"Thank you for coming." He swallowed, hard. "It means a lot to me."

She nodded, leaned forward and turned the key. The trusty Taurus kicked in. "You can check on Wilson in person. I've decided—I'll be away for a few days. I meant to tell you, but somehow it got lost in the debate."

"How long?" At least he had stopped himself from asking where.

Her eyes fastened onto the distance, then on him. "For as long as it takes."

He had no right to ask what the hell that meant. He asked anyway. "Does this have to do with Jarrid?"

"I thought you knew. Everything has to do with Jarrid. I keep getting reports—" She clamped down, as if remembering she had chosen to go it alone.

"You should hold off a while longer, Cameron."

Her lush mouth dipped at each corner.

"Advice from me is the last thing you're looking for. *Enit?*" Silence gave him the answer. "Put the inn out of your mind. I won't leave you hanging."

"That's good, because my life—"

He held up a hand, stood erect and stepped back, catching a glimpse of Apenimon's royal purple bathrobe behind the screen door. "Spare me. Okay?"

A shield dropped over her eyes. "Of course."

He slapped the car door with an open palm, Eyeing the sky. The ride back from the canyon had been hellaciously cold. Now snow was starting to fall, and she had refused a coat, murmuring, "No more bogus handouts, Wind Dancer." His mind played with visions of her upended in some icy ditch, freezing to death in the friggin' linen shirt and bare-ass thin skirt. And those goddamned sandals.

"The snow will make it hard to see the road. Be careful, Yazhi."

So much for vowing to carve the name off your tongue, Wind Dancer.

As though she had been cued, she slipped the car into reverse, senselessly checked the rearview mirror and gave the Taurus enough gas to inch backward. "You be careful, too. Even self-made idols are some-times blinded." Then she braked, seeming to soften, her eyes going shiny and regretful. "I'm wrong to expect you…to ask you to leave here and go with me, Lukas. Please forgive me for that weakness. I love you. I'm hurting, or else I wouldn't…have."

Before he could say he understood, she pressed the gas, backed, then drove away.

He watched for miles, until the barren landscape swallowed the Taurus, then led Gaagii to the corral, unsaddled him, and began to brush him down. The horse turned his head to nudge Lukas' shoulder, his low whinny as mournful as his eyes.

"Enit, Goddammit." He rested his cheek against Gaagii's warm rump and stood stock still, his regret intense as a vision quest, painful as a sacrificial sun dance. If he moved, in any direction, he would shatter and never find the pieces.

❦

Windshield wipers slapping snow, car heater on high, Cameron watched the rearview mirror until she was forced to relinquish Lukas' physical and visceral image. She had thought him to be a king, ruling his domain with pride and confidence, whole in his culture, his being. Now she knew differently. Based on his birthright, Lukas knew rejection. From the white family he had craved to emulate, from the woman he had loved who had denied him and scrapped his flesh and blood. Her own mother had given her life, kept and loved her in her hapless way. In turn, *she* had given life to Jarrid, cared for him. Worshipped him. When measured by Lukas' wounds, hers were shallow.

His were deep enough to sacrifice his love for her, hers for him.

Tears blinding, spirit spinning out of control, she pulled off the road and rested her head against the cold window, bidding her heart to accept. To believe.

For Jarrid's sake she couldn't forsake the future by holding onto what might have been.

Gratitude for her glorious sadness rushed in, for the ability to feel love and loss like she hadn't felt since the judge's gavel had fallen like a knife, severing her from her son. She searched the beautiful, formidable landscape, breathing deeply.

Determination to win Jarrid back regained dominion in her soul.

thirty-three

The promised favor arrived by limousine. It occupied the backseat of the spacious interior like royalty. The driver presented it with a solemn air that mocked its plain wrapper, a manner divulging more about him than about his charge. When the car had disappeared over the snowy horizon, Lukas opened the envelope, removed a hand-scrawled note on a sheet of rag-edged linen paper.

Let me know what you want done here. It's your call. Donnie S.

Sitting next to the fire pit on his hogan floor, he read the file, five pages of single-spaced type. He read it again. Then once more, his stomach curdling. Then he burned it, poking the pages into the coals with his boot, wondering exactly what he would actually like to see *done,* picturing, then driving the ultimate solution from his mind. Had Cameron only trusted him, not jumped the gun, she would be fortified. But she had chosen. Her fight for Jarrid, her life, no longer involved him.

It was the way of the Anglo woman. He was a veteran of that gender war.

❦

Cameron watched Phillip's car pull away from the curb. In the Chinatown bar where he'd insisted they meet, the dim light hadn't disguised his grim mouth-set and cold eyes. The demeanor underlined his continued refusal to let her see Jarrid in the week she'd been in Vancouver. Neither had he denied he'd obtained a passport for Jarrid, the one Michael had warned of in a message that had been waiting when she returned from the reservation. Based on the European ski trips to which Phillip had alluded—trips fabricated to dissuade her coming to Vancouver—she'd assumed Jarrid already possessed a passport.

Knowing differently, realizing Phillip deemed one necessary now, pricked a deep-seated sense of urgency.

She'd had no choice but to come to Vancouver.

Destination unclear, she strolled past market stalls, shops and cafes along Chinatown's Keefer Street, sea air kinking her hair, mellow sunlight warming her shoulders. The morning's election poll figures played through her mind. Seemingly, Phillip's incumbency was swaying numbers in his favor. But local television predicted his naturalized Canadian status, compared to his opponent's fifth generation political legacy, would change that by Election Day.

Phillip could lose.

Michael s phone was ringing as she turned the key in the lock and stepped into the foyer. By the time she reached the phone on the bar a voice mail greeting kicked in, followed by a beep and a pause long enough to convince her the caller had hung up. She opened a bottle of Perrier, reached for a glass—and froze.

"This is Lukas Wind Dancer looking for Cameron Vickers." Another pause in which her heart pummeled her chest "If you are there, Cameron—"

Later, she would not recall picking up the receiver. "I'm here."

Another pause, almost as long as the first. After a brief struggle she surrendered her imagination to a memory feast. His mouth running rigid, his umber eyes darkening to jet…maybe he folded his arms…widened his stance. "Lukas?"

"Hayden gave me this number. If I shouldn't be calling you here, tell me."

Or not be calling me at all. Easing the pain of the inevitable. "Michael's my brother. I'm sorry I never got around to telling you." But what would that have changed? She would still be here, and him there. She read this pause easily.

At last he said, "So you've decided to take Phillip back to court now. Not to wait."

Apparently his direct line to her uncle had not changed. "I *can't* wait."

Static on the line—probably poor cellular service in the mountains—allowed her to hear only, "…is it going?"

Badly. I'm so alone. So lonely. "It's going fine, thank you. Was there something you wanted? Is something wrong there? With the inn, I mean?" Mikela brushed her ankles. She picked her up, pressed her to her breasts.

"Explain 'fine' to me, Cameron."

Beyond the twelfth story window a ferry skimmed past Vancouver's skyline, headed for the North Shore. Inside her, his resonate voice touched depths she had intended to close to him forever. "I've hired an attorney—Michael's friend. We're going before a judge Monday—" Two endless days away. "—and petition for a new hearing."

More static. "Sounds like history repeating itself."

Her chest felt tight. Why should she hide from this man worries that were surely revealed in her voice, even over thousands of miles? Wedging the phone between her cheek and shoulder, she massaged her free temple. "No. Everything's under control. But thank you for…your concern."

"I have a number you might want to call."

"For help, you mean?" Silence. "Thank you, but this attorney is highly recommended."

"(312) 666-6000." She thought the bad connection had kept him from hearing her disclaimer. "If things happen not to be as fine as you say, you can decide what action to take after the call."

"I—" What had she failed to explain, or he had failed to understand? She opted for politeness, thanking him and then sensing an immediate fissure. "Lukas?"

"Be careful, little one." The soft-as-a-caress words broke their connection.

❦

Exhausted, Cameron lay watching the clock hands migrate toward two a.m., Lukas' call, his alien and intimate voice, the number he'd given her, repeating in her head. Curled against her backside, Mikela purred softly. A foghorn sounded in the distance. She watched the clock's second hand. At twenty past two she gave in to the curiosity Lukas' urging had provoked, along with a vague sense of significance, and dialed the phone from memory. A guttural, scratchy voice answered, as though the owner had sat by the phone for hours waiting.

"This is Cameron Vickers," she ventured.

"You got a fax machine?"

"Why?"

"If you got one, give me the number, honey."

"Hold on." Hoping not to wake Michael, she tiptoed barefoot into his study and quietly read the number off the machine.

"Good. I got somethin' you need." He hung up.

She sat in Michael's desk chair, feet drawn beneath her nightgown, expecting the fax to click, hum and spew out a mystery clue. When that hadn't happened at hour's end, she returned to bed, burrowing in beside Mikela. Her mind whirled with the week's happenings and the significance of tomorrow, until sheer exhaustion shut it down and she fell off a precipice into sleep.

At dawn, as had become the week's pattern, she woke into disorientation. Her pain resembled the agonized wrench of childhood when her mother had moved in with a new man, and once more she would find herself expatriated. Now, as then, she'd waken with the light falling from the wrong direction, dizzy from the bed being turned the wrong way. The moment she managed to orient herself physically, she returned, as well, with a sinking weight to thoughts of all she'd destroyed by leaving Lukas, Arizona, the desert, the inn. Each morning she felt she was waking to an illness, a long fever she couldn't break.

Until she remembered her son.

On this particular morning, haunted by such acute memory of Lukas' voice on the phone, she focused on coffee smells and the sound of Mikela's claws being sharpened on Michael's Porthalt sheets. She dropped the feline gently to the floor, pulled on her robe and went in search of caffeine and kitty gourmet.

When she appeared in the study doorway, coffee mug in hand, Michael glanced up with trance-like eyes. He separated a sheet of paper from those he'd been rapidly shuffling and shook it at her. "Where the hell did this come from?"

"Was it on the fax?" Arriving after she had given up hope and gone back to bed? She crossed to him, extending her hand for the paper. He jerked it back, his odious expression bringing back the sinister quality of the stranger's voice last night. She demanded to see it. "All of it."

Warily, he complied, eyes disbelieving.

Placing the coffee mug on his desk, she perused the first sheet, reluctant, yet eager to get to the root of his reaction. "Oh…God." As he had done, she shuffled, read, shuffled, heart racing, then raised her eyes. "This is…"

"What? It's what, Cam?"

"Incredible." And surely not true. Yet a glimmer of hope accompanied the thought, an inner sense that it *was* true. Every word.

"You didn't know any of this?"

"I resent you even asking that, Michael."

"Well, you should resent it." Ruffling his longish blond hair, he rose, stretching a body lean and agile from his martial arts fetish. He paced to the window, hands thrust into his robe pockets, then in afterthought demanded, "Where'd that garbage come from, anyway?"

"I tell you I don't know." Voice shaking like the faxed sheets in her hand, she searched for a clue. "There's no number showing where it originated. Isn't there some kind of government thing requiring—"

"Some people are above the law." He took the papers, his eyes brooking no argument, and searched them as she had. "You said you waited up. How'd you know to do that? You must know something you're not telling."

Her mind ran a reverse gamut "I got a call from…a friend. He gave me a number to call in case I needed help with the custody hearing." She took in his nod and corrugated brow. His eyes registered agreement, or perhaps insight that excluded her. "I didn't even write the number down. But in the middle of the night—"

"You called. So you remembered the number?"

She nodded. "I'm not sure I can now, though." At his urging she searched the nether regions of memory behind her closed eyes. "Three, one, two," she began haltingly. "six, six...six." She opened her eyes, throat tight and aching with failure in that moment before she realized where the information came from didn't matter. She finished with a flourish and a shrug. "More sixes and zeros."

"But you *are* sure about the area code?"

"Yes." She could picture that clearly, along with the first three sixes. "But all that matters is whether or not this is true and what I choose to do with it."

"Or whatever the hell I choose to do with it."

"Phillip is the only father Jarrid knows, Michael. Please consider that."

"Chicago."

She questioned him with a look.

"If you're remembering the area code correctly, it's Chicago. I call a client there daily."

She spiraled back in memory to the day Yolanda had sat across the desk from her, chattering innuendoes about Lukas' *Chicago connection*. A glacier chill eased down her spine. "China Star...that bar where they claim he receives his payoffs?"

Michael nodded, one brow arched.

"I met Phillip there yesterday."

He looked stricken. "Tell me you didn't drink with him."

"Drinking was the last thing on my mind." And had been for so long now she found it difficult to believe it had ever been a factor. It seemed a lifetime had passed since she had second-guessed Phillip's accusation. "When I arrived, Phillip was talking to the man that's mentioned in the fax—Wu Chang. He introduced me."

"The guy owns a big part of Chinatown. Lots of tenements and bars."

"Phillip would only meet me if I agreed on that bar. Killing two birds with one stone." The chill spilled across her shoulders. "Dashing my hopes while collecting his payoff."

"No wonder he's got the damned Chinatown vote wrapped up."

"That doesn't make sense if this is true." *It's true. Accept the gift.* Still, she felt sickened by what she'd learned. "He's exploiting their daughters."

"For every girl sacrificed, another Asian family enters the country. Have you forgotten girls aren't a revered commodity in China? Where it counts—with the male population—the biggest voting contingency—Phillip's a god."

"Phillip is a hypocritical monster."

"Tell it to the judge, Cam." He leveled his blue eyes on her. "Or I will."

❦

Lukas replaced the air phone in its receptacle, glanced up at the blonde hostess who was taking drink orders, and shook his head. "Nothing, thanks."

Her smile denied they were strangers. "Pretzels?" He shook his head again and turned his attention to the rain peppering the window next to his seat, Cameron's voice, staticky on the cellular line, resting on the edges of his mind.

Fine, she had said. She was not above lying still. But he had heard her bravado.

He retrieved a book from the seat pouch in front of him, tried to fit his suddenly too-long legs into the space allotted, gave up, and crossed an ankle over a knee.

"Nice boots," the blonde commented from across the aisle, ignoring a toddler's harried mother trying to order orange juice. "They're ostrich, I'll bet."

"Nothing so exotic. Snake."

"Snake's exotic." She swayed away, smiling over a shoulder. He traced a finger over the book title. *Healing Racism in America.* Opening it to the marked page, he re-read the passage he could not shake off. The one that aligned prejudice with an emotionally committed belief in ignorance, triggering guilt that settled on him boulder heavy, leaving a sour taste in his mouth.

In his mind, he saw Cameron's face, the word "fine" echoing in his head.

Fighting with one hand tied behind her back, she had lied to him as easily as when she had deceived him

about the roof. But considering her pride and determination, and the way he had turned a deaf ear on her
that night in the canyon, lying was her only choice.
The second time he had called she had admitted, "I
feel like a one woman army. Phillip hasn't let me see
Jarrid. I have moments when I lose track of what I'm
fighting for."

The number he had given her, the information
waiting there, was artillery to shift things in her favor.
But she was not a woman who would allow a man to
fight her battle.

He had done all he could. Bottom line, the choice
was hers.

Sunday morning, following another sleepless
night, Cameron faced Hayden in Michael's kitchen.
Mikela, Cameron's momentary link with sanity,
draped her shoulder, enjoying a morning spit bath.
Sworn to silence, Michael stared out the window,
shoulders tense.

"It's all in here." Cameron tapped a finger on the
file resting on her lap. Original documents replacing
the papers faxed the day before had been mysteriously
left at Michael s door that morning. The delivery had
been followed by a phone call to alert them. "But I
don't feel I can turn this over to you You'll have to take
my word for—"

"Why for God's sake, if it's as damaging as you
say."

Although her hunch to safeguard the file was deeply entrenched, reasoning eluded her. "Damaging to Phillip, Uncle Hayden, not me." He nodded, raised his coffee, set it down untouched. "But it would be to Jarrid. A stigma he might never live down."

"He's a child. If you're as hell bent on taking him to Samoa as you say—"

"Damaging to the whole family then." She reached further. "Chastain Properties." His eyes fired, then settled. "I'll summarize if you care to listen."

"You know damn well I care. Let's hear it."

"You're familiar with Phillip's legendary humanitarian efforts, all the Asian families he's helped to come to Canada?" She waited for his nod. "It's a guise. When he's approached by a resident family hoping to bring in relatives, he advises them the extent of his help is to obtain visas through his political connections. For financial assistance, he refers them to a man named Wu Chang."

"The Chinatown tenement baron," Hayden said quickly. "He's known for his own philanthropic causes. Phillip's in good company there."

The file scorched her hand "They're filthy imposters."

"Before you throw those kinds of accusations around, Camellia, you'd better be able to prove it." His gruff words failed to match the concern in his eyes, and his use of the name she'd discarded struck a cord she'd almost managed to sever.

"I'm hoping it never comes to public accusation. But according to my source, Phillip and Wu Chang are under-the-table partners with a third man—a Johnnie Lee who runs a whorehouse disguised as a Chinatown hotel."

His back arched as a hand raised, one finger running around the inside of his collar. He loosened his tie. "That's another strong accusation."

She pretended not to have heard. "Some members of the local police departments are among the most avid visitors."

Hayden looked as if the coffee cream were sour. "Not John VanCleef, for God's sake." A department head, an old and close friend…

"His name's not on the list." She met his relieved eyes. "Maybe now, Uncle Hayden, you find it easier to believe me about Phillip planting that bottle."

He grimaced. "Go on, Cam."

She glanced at her watch, gauging when she had to leave to meet her attorney. "This third man is secretly funded by Phillip and Wu to bring the Asian families into the country with visas Phillip supplies. In return, Lee asks for the use of a young girl—very young, and she can come from their family or from anywhere they devise—Lee's not choosy—to work in his *house* for two years."

"Paying off the debt." Michael's voice split the tense air. "Sons-o-bitches."

"This is reading like a bad movie, children. One I've seen."

"X-rated," Michael quipped, turning, striding to the sink for water.

"I'm finding this hard to believe, Cam. Phillip is an odd duck, a bit too *European* for my taste, but I'm inclined to say someone is leading you astray."

"I would have thought that, too, Uncle Hayden. I lived with Phillip all those years, and until the accident, until he showed his true colors, I, too, believed he was some kind of humanitarian martyr. He was a good father to Jarrid, and in his way, a good husband. But he had reasons that never included love or the sanctity of marriage." She hugged the envelope to her breasts, her other hand stroking Mikela. "In here there's a copy of a chain of title proving an off-shore corporation owned by Phillip, and Wu owns the hotel where the brothel operates, as well as other ventures. I also have photo-copies of transactions in a seven-figure joint Swiss bank account that bears the names Vickers, Chang, and Lee."

"That could be trumped up. In this computer age, anything can be." His strained expression ricocheted between acceptance and disbelief.

She opened the envelope and drew out a grainy, black and white snapshot of Phillip, two Asian men, and three young Asian girls crowded into a banquet. One of the girls held a menu bearing the name China Star. She held up the snapshot for Hayden to scrutinize, then passed it to him face down. Phillip's name had been scrawled on the back, along with Chang's and Lee's, and a date only a week past. "I'm sure a good private investigator could verify this if need be."

"So you're holding the trump card. What do you plan to do with it?"

She shook her head, pressed her temples, reeling between power and indecision. "I only know I'm getting my son back. Whatever it takes."

thirty-four

From the end of a corridor, Lukas watched Cameron and her entourage exit the elevator. A white blouse beneath her black suit played up her tawny skin and dark hair, while the past-era, sky-high heels faked a stately, commanding woman.

The lanky blond Anglo, so much Cameron's opposite, had to be Michael. And industry literature Lukas had seen at the inn identified the older man with gray caterpillars-kissing eyebrows as Hayden Chastain. Lukas pegged the man in the gray suit, carrying a too-slim-to-be-helpful attaché case, for Ronald Burns, the attorney on whose expertise Cameron was betting the farm.

Later, from a back row vantage inside the courtroom, Lukas studied the opposing team. Another suit with an officious air—his latest information attached the name Anthony Reardon—his young female assistant, and Phillip Vickers. He fitted this man's face to the report he had burned. Expertly tailored clothing. Smooth olive skin, thick wavy hair. Effeminately handsome.

Lukas' fingers curled into fists.

Even when Michael leaned to speak to her, Cameron stared straight ahead. Lukas checked his watch. It could be over for her in minutes, cutting her risk. Or she could choose to linger in a series of losing battles on her own, disregarding what she'd learned, and chance losing the war.

Lukas listened as the court entertained and ruled on five petitions before the clerk announced, "Vickers versus Vickers. Request for child custody rehearing."

Cameron, Phillip, and counsels approached the bench. The judge shuffled papers, conferred with his clerk, shuffled and read. Shaking his head, Burns leaned to whisper to Cameron while Lukas' gut fermented in helplessness.

Her fingers stole to her temples, nursing pain, he knew, the root of which she had only partially unearthed for him. He willed his spirit to at least steal *this* pain from her, willed her to release it She turned suddenly, as if that spirit had tapped her shoulder, eyes searching until they hooked into the tug of his and their eyes collided. If he rose now, ran the back stairs to the street, and took the first plane to within walking distance of the rez, his intuition had not deluded him; his brief presence would have had…merit. She now knew she was not alone.

The judge looked up, leveling a silent invitation over his horn rims.

Burns spoke up. "If the court agrees, Mrs. Vickers and her family request a private conference with Mr. Vickers." Shards of pent-up breath seeped between

Lukas' clamped teeth. "Without presence of either counsel, your honor."

Lukas grunted low. At least she was holding one ill-gotten ace in the hole.

"You're taking the court's time, Mr. Burns. This could have been done earlier, could it not?" The judge shoved up the glasses, read, peered over them again.

"We were unable to reach Mr. Vickers or his counsel over the weekend, your honor."

The judge looked to Phillip and Reardon. "It's your call, gentlemen."

The two men formed a side bar, heads together Cameron's chin hiked and held as Phillip slanted his hard gaze on her. Inside his head, Lukas counted off the seconds in Navajo before Phillip nodded to Reardon, breaking the client-attorney huddle.

"Fifteen minutes," the judge grumbled, whacking his gavel without verve.

Lukas left his seat, headed for the door.

ॐ

Locked in a crowd at the courtroom door, Cameron peered at the dark-skinned man waiting in the corridor. Charcoal suit, ivory shirt, somber tie and laced shoes. Only the raven-black, middle-of-his-back braid rendered him real instead of a parody of Lukas. She tugged her hand from Michael's, heading blindly in Lukas' direction, almost colliding with a woman carrying a baby.

"How is it going, now?" he asked softly, when she reached him.

She scarcely heard the words above the din, yet the concession in his eyes screamed answers to her middle-of-the-night soul searching. Her hand twitched willfully, a hunger to touch moving through her arms. Was he an angel? Hers? No. He was a man, maybe the first real man she'd ever known. A man acting on what he knew to be right, win or lose. "I can't believe you're here. When we talked that last time—You were already on your way, weren't you?"

The hard stare he focused beyond her shoulder shifted to follow Phillip and his attorneys moving past in the direction of the assigned meeting room. "I think I have been on my way since the minute I tracked you down."

And learned her relationship to Michael.

"Since you read that dreadful report," she said. His eyes affirmed the answer. "You have to tell me where it came from, Lukas."

He folded his arms, his stance widening only slightly on the marble floor.

"I don't care. I'm going to use it." Even knowing, she had to ask, "It's all true, isn't it? God! Thinking how Jarrid's been under his influence all this time, I don't want it to be true. And yet I do, because no judge could rule against me again." Down the hall, Phillip paused outside the meeting room to dismiss his attorneys. The normally intimidating glare he directed at her appeared watered down by uncertainty.

"We're headed for a private meeting now. If that doesn't work, I'll have no choice but to expose him."

"I doubt it will come to that." Did she see in his eyes promises too vague to imagine, perhaps a prediction too ominous to voice?

Michael appeared at her side exuding a sense of urgent curiosity. Lukas' expressionless gaze settled on him as Michael touched her arm. "So this must be the friend."

She introduced them and over their handshake urged Lukas, "Come with me to the meeting."

He eyed the door. Phillip. Michael. "It's your fight. I will be right here."

"If I said I need you?"

"A woman as strong as Cameron Vickers needs no one to fight her battle. You have only to let that strength show."

Hayden stood with Phillip now, his rigid expression somehow conciliatory, convincing her he had delayed acknowledging Lukas in order to keep Phillip calm.

"Time's passing, Cam." Michael touched her arm. "You don't want to blow this." Eyes curious and cautious, he nodded politely to Lukas and moved away.

Clutching the file to her breasts, she sought Lukas' eyes for his answer.

"I'll wait here, but my spirit will be in that room, little one." Touching, strengthening her, as she had sensed in the courtroom earlier.

"If you hear screaming…" With a weak smile, she left him there, glancing over her shoulder for his encouraging smile before opening the door on the waiting test. As she took her seat at the meeting table, Phillip's hard gray eyes swept over her uncle and brother.

"I fail to see the fairness in Michael's presence when I've been denied my own counsel."

"Michael is here as family. My attorney is cooling his heels with yours, Phillip."

The hard eyes darted to the file she placed between them on the table. "I see you've acquired some wild-west terminology, Camellia." His French accent tasteful, he spared her a meant-to-be-disarming smile, lifting the corners of a thin, perfectly trimmed moustache. "Charming. I'd like to hear more."

Her spine ran cold before it bristled. "I'm sure you're wondering why I asked for this meeting—"

"I'm wondering, actually, why we have an audience, darling. Your penchant for voyeurism, I suppose." He quirked a brow, his smile denigrating, but she no longer felt compelled to defend herself. Neither Michael nor Hayden would ever believe his lies again. Her memory spiraled back to that cold day by Gaagii's corral fence, to Lukas' kiss, his laughing promise of *safety in numbers*.

"This private meeting is to give you the opportunity to agree to my request for a new—" Again, she heard Lukas' voice. *I doubt it will come to that.* She regrouped, feeling Hayden and Michael's surprise when she announced, "I've changed my mind about a new hearing, Phillip. I have no more desire to put Jarrid through a custody battle now than I had two years ago."

Phillip torqued a brow. "And just what kind of desire *do* you have, Camellia?"

She extracted documents from the file, laid them on the table and swiveled the top one with a nail. "Take a moment to read this. Basically it's a recap of…" She lifted the edge of the folder, allowing him a glimpse of the contents. His eyes homed in on the stack of legal documents. "We have only a few minutes."

His eyes skimmed the same revelations she had outlined for Hayden that morning, glancing up periodically, then down, mouth twisting. Finishing, he shoved the paper sideways onto the floor, taking the only out available to him. "This is preposterous." His eyes shifted to Hayden, came away daunted. "It's blackmail."

Elbows on the table, Michael leaned toward Phillip. "You recognize blackmail, huh, Phillip? But *we're* not using thirteen-year-old girls like you did. So that puts us a rung above you on the smut ladder, asshole."

"You have no proof." Phillip straightened his tie, retrieved the cast-off paper from the floor and shook it in Michael's face. "These documents are forgeries. I'll have them traced and prove it's all lies."

"You're clinging to the wrong era, Vickers. Computers and faxes did away with warped typewriter keys and finger-printed paper bought at the five and dime store."

Phillip looked blank, yet a bit pale around the jowls.

"Trying to disprove anything would be asinine, Phillip." With the tone of Hayden's voice, more of Phillip's bravado faded, and Cameron realized that until then Phillip had considered Hayden an ally. "Once the media gets word of an investigation, whether instigated by us or by you, you've lost the election."

"So why in hell are you blackmailing me?" Phillip demanded of Cameron.

"When we go back into court, I want you to relinquish custody of Jarrid to me." She braved his glare to reiterate her point. "Here and now."

"You're crazy. You've always been. You're trying to drive a wedge between Hayden and me, ruin me. All because you couldn't keep your legs closed or a bottle out of your mouth."

He started to shove back his chair. Michael leaped forward, catching Phillip's lapel, pinning him in place. Cameron shook her head, urging him to back off. Disgust palatable, Michael sank back beside Cameron, eyes drilling Phillip across the table. Her first inclination when Hayden reached for the file was to hover over it, run with it, protect the only weapon she owned. His gentle touch on her wrist stayed her.

He handed Phillip the tell-tale photograph of him and his Asian partners, accompanied by the young Asian girls. They watched his eyes skim. Deny. Accept.

"That's you, isn't it, Phillip?" Hayden patronized. "With your partners Wang and Lee in the China Star? I understand that's where the payoffs are made."

Phillip ripped the snapshot in two, then four, pieces, stuffed it in his pocket.

Snorting, Michael leaned back, long legs shooting forward to clip Phillip's shin. "Ever heard of negatives, butthead?" He fished Swiss bank records from the folder, rose, rounded the table and placed them before Phillip. Leaning forward, his arms framed the smaller man's shoulders. "Read, don't touch, or I swear..." His gaze snagged with Cameron's.

Finally, Phillip looked up. "Forming a partnership with these men, owning property—no matter what it's used for—is not the hideous crime you're alluding to, Camellia. Maybe I'll take my chances, as far as the election goes."

"Why would you, Phillip? We're dealing with children here. Indigent children of impoverished families. The moment I hand this file to the judge—" She consulted her watch. "You have no chance of keeping Jarrid. Uncle Hayden now knows you for what you are. Any association with Chastain Properties is ended. Why would you want to sully your name—phony as it is—for a lost cause?"

He steepled his fingers, manicured nails gleaming. "What assurance do I have that once you have what you want you won't release this garbage anyway?"

"From me, as much assurance as you require. I'm delighted to say, however, that I can't speak for my anonymous benefactor." Lukas' face, along with one lacking features but belonging to the middle-of-the-night attentive, guttural voice, waved across her mind.

Michael straightened, taking back the documents, granting Phillip breathing room.

His fingertips whitened where they pressed the table edge, his gaze spearing hers. "Touché, bitch. When would you like to pick up your bastard?"

Michael's hand raised, fingers rigid, his palm angled, aimed at the back of Phillip's neck. Another quick shake of Cameron's head and the chastising look she shot Michael prevented Phillip's ever knowing the physical peril he'd survived. She watched her uncle and brother credit the term bastard to Phillip's perverse need for revenge.

"I want to pick him up now." In front of Phillip, she placed papers Ronald Burns had taken the liberty to prepare, documents transferring custody of Jarrid. "I want you to accompany me back into that court-room and sign these papers in front of the judge. I'll never spend another night away from my son because of you."

thirty-five

Once the meeting with Phillip ended, all proceedings returned to legal mode. The attorneys re-entered the courtroom to inform the court of Phillip's decision and Michael assured her the nightmare had ended. Jarrid was hers.

Later, as the cab she and Lukas had hailed pulled into the drive of Phillip's stately home, her stomach fluttering, Cameron reminded herself she had brought Jarrid from the hospital to this house. For four years she had lived the role of wife and mother, an era both pensive and sanguine until it had ended one rainy night in a nightmare of indiscretion.

As she rang the bell, she anguished over not knowing how Phillip had handled his farewell to Jarrid, what kinds of scars might result from a bungled explanation. Surely Phillip lacked the temerity to be present now. She rang again, grateful for Lukas' presence beside her.

Jarrid's teary-eyed nanny opened the door. Phillip stood behind her, his hand on Jarrid's shoulder, proof the nightmare had not quite ended.

Jarrid balanced a child's travel bag on each small shoulder while crystal chandelier prisms painted his dark face diamond white, highlighting his eager, yet unsettled, eyes. He eased his burden off his shoulders and came into her embrace, burying his face below her breasts. She bent to kiss the top of of his head, murmuring greetings and assurances. Then she stepped back.

"Darling, this is Lukas. He's come a long way to meet you." *To be here for me. For you. To make us one again.* "Lukas, this is Jarrid."

Jarrid cocked his head, his hand venturing forward, disappearing into Lukas' grasp. Heart tripping, she sought Lukas eyes. Dark and heavy as thunderheads, as he no doubt remembered the many times she had shut him out with no explanation beyond her goal to reclaim this child. Did the mellow look he wore now signify understanding?

Lukas knelt, easing Jarrid's neck strain. "Your mother talks about you all the time."

Jarrid beamed, looking to her for confirmation she knew he would forever need.

From his squatting position, Lukas shouldered one bag, held the other out in invitation. Jarrid heaved it onto his shoulder, eyes raised to Phillip's, then lowering, as if recalling they were out of good-byes. "Bye, Dad I'll call you."

"Yes, do." The hard edge in Phillip's eyes softened for an instant only before his gaze pinned Lukas. "Just who the hell *are* you?"

Lukas smiled. "A nightmare you have not even begun to shake."

Phillip made a gesture encompassing Cameron and Jarrid. "And what's your part in all this?"

A cheek muscle pulsed in Lukas' square jaw. "My vested interest in your ex-wife and your son."

Phillip's eyes narrowed, his thin lips pinching out, "He's not my son."

Cameron cringed, Phillip's words and Jarrid's recoil ricocheting like shrapnel off the walls of her chest.

Lukas ruffled Jarrid's curly hair. "Your lucky day, *enit*, bro?"

Only Lukas' conspiratorial grin, the easy camaraderie *in* his voice, could have given Jarrid the courage to emit a weak smile through his hurt and lack of understanding.

Just as Lukas' presence had given her strength to fight.

At the airport, vying for seats together, juggling luggage while hustling to an already-boarding plane, Cameron corralling Jarrid, Lukas toting Mikela's cage, Cameron was once again stunned by Lukas' sheer beauty. Not the way the exquisite suit fit him or how the white shirt emphasized his dark skin and raven hair, but the graceful way he carried his height and athletic build. The quiet way he spoke to Jarrid, touching him gently, directing him in a way that left her son feeling self-reliant. Lukas did nothing to command attention, yet as they moved through the crowd scarcely a head failed to turn, or an eye failed to appreciate. Her eyes most of all. While she tried imagining a lifetime without him…a lifetime with him kept superseding that vision.

On board the plane, seat back reclined, plane engines humming in her subconscious, Cameron watched Jarrid sleeping, his head in her lap.

"Some day you have to tell him." From the seat beside her, Lukas' voice jolted her, assuring her of how easily he could read her mind. *Tell him about Lee Tutuila.* His hand covered hers where it rested on Jarrid's brow.

"I know. I will when this is behind us."

He lowered his eyes to their joined hands, to her sleeping child.

"I'm still overwhelmed, Lukas. Still sorting."

Lost in his intense gaze, she placed the two of them in Phillip's foyer again. "Thank you for going with me to Phillip's." She swallowed around the barrier in her throat. "And I'm glad you delayed your flight to wait for us. I wasn't ready to be alone."

He tried straightening his legs, but his boots banged the hand luggage. He grinned and grunted, running a forefinger through Jarrid's curls. "You have about twenty years, little *amá*, before you can even start to worry about being alone."

She smiled, her finger following his, noting Jarrid's frown, his twitching nose. "I have you to thank for that."

"Give credit where it's due." He stared out the window. "To Lee Tutuila."

If he'd tried to hide his wistfulness he'd failed.

"I was referring to what happened with Phillip. I could have never—"

A warm and suede-smooth finger sealed her lips. "I was nowhere near that meeting, Cameron. You chose to stand up to him. To ruin him if you had to. To risk further alienation from your family."

"I still want him exposed. I can't bear to think—"

"Don't lose one night's sleep, little one. It will happen."

A ripple of excitement, one she chose not to explore, pricked her spine. "As for the family, I care only about Michael and Hayden. And Jarrid." *And, how you see me, Lukas.* "You know I couldn't have done it without…the information."

He straightened a crimp in the pillow Jarrid's head rested on, his hand lingering for a time near the small Throat. "It might have taken longer, but you would have won." He raised his eyes in a kind of sad praise. "Or died trying."

"Enit." She tendered a smile from within a joyful, yet apprehensive, spirit.

ॐ

Past midnight they made their way along the path to the bungalows, burdened with luggage. Cameron suddenly discarded her cargo in favor of a nymph-like toe dance, circling off the path onto the dewy grass. She grasped Jarrid around the chest from behind and swung him, their laughter mingling. Lukas watched their play, his mouth toying with a smile.

She blushed, retrieving her share of the luggage. "I missed this place. I'm happy to be back." Her burden thwarted a shrug. "What else can I say?"

Smiling wryly, he admitted, "Nothing that would surprise me more." Again, he led the way, his steps soft and decisive on the flagstone path.

Bedding Jarrid down in Lukas' former habitat stirred a flutter of memory too sweet to banish. Risking a glimpse at Lukas' eyes as he brought a glass of water while she lowered the lights assured her they shared the same images. Their hands brushed as he placed the glass on the bedside table with the same grace and care with which he'd removed her locket and placed it there that first night. A night in their lives when, for her, this moment had been a guarded daydream.

Finally satisfied Jarrid was confident in his surroundings, she whispered, "I'll walk Lukas to his car. You know it's close by, so you won't be afraid, will you?"

He rolled his eyes, he and Lukas sharing a laugh as Lukas bent for a good-night handshake. Feeling a bit like odd-woman-out, she kissed Jarrid and led Lukas away. Leaving the bungalow door ajar, she wordlessly headed for the swimming pool. Her heart lurched as she felt him hesitate where the path veered from the curbed Suburban, then ease into a more temperate rhythm when he matched her pace. At pool's edge, she dipped her hand in the water and smiled her satisfaction.

"I had Nakai turn off the heat." She cocked her Head. "I still have your interest at heart, Wind Dancer." She smiled. "Well, *still* is stretching it a bit."

Lukas caught her hand. Again her heart noted, this time because she expected him to take her into his arms. Instead, he led her to the low diving board. Hands on her shoulders, he guided her to sit, then straddled the board, boots planted to either side on the deck. Much as he'd done on Gaagii, he hooked a hand beneath her knee, swinging one of her legs over so they sat facing.

"Only Jarrid is keeping me from dragging your pretty ass to the fire pit." Moonlight glinting in his eyes colored them both devilish and somber.

"Actually, he's a very sound sleeper. But *I* might put up a fight."

He laughed, then sobered so quickly she was robbed of breath. "I am not as much of a hero as you think right now."

"I'll be the judge of that."

A passing car pierced interminable silence. "I was on my way to Boston the first time I called."

Her mind searched. "Boston...Massachusetts?" He nodded. "I hear its an interesting place. Very historical." *Boston?* Visualizing Lukas there, she wrestled her incredulity to silence.

"Yes." The word sounded far off, contemplative, then he seemed to begin a travel monologue. "Many minorities make up the population. Heavy Asian, I found out, and some Indians are still there." His eyes roamed a million miles, encompassing centuries and tragedies, drifting back like wet gossamer.

"Survivors, I guess, from when the pilgrims came to America."

She nodded, smiled, completely in the dark.

"In architectural school I had a friend who came from there."

"Another connection?"

A brow shot skyward. "Forget you ever heard that term. Never listen to a damn thing Chuey—"

"Actually it was Yolanda who—"

He held up a hand, palm out. "I get the picture."

Smothering a laugh, she nodded. "Fine. Tell me about your Boston friend."

He drew an audible breath "We keep in touch He's from an old line family of architects. His firm does mostly restorations."

Remembering how he favored that—down to the last damn fire pit—she deemed the statement self-placating.

"I have been invited to join their firm."

"What a compliment, Lukas." A safe, amiable, non-revealing comment.

He nodded. "I have accepted. With stipulations and conditions."

Despite her vow to stay calm, even indifferent no matter what he told her, her mind ran a wild, infeasible gamut, and her mouth sagged open. "What?"

He surrendered a mirthless smile. "Which part did you fail to grasp, Yazhi?"

Any of it. She searched for a reply that would conceal her alarm. "Why in the world would you ever agree to...to move to Boston?" His gecko-in-water speech echoed in her head.

"I think of it as mutual territory," he said quietly, a bit gravely.

Understanding glimmered. "What stipulations? What...conditions?"

His hands caught hers now, on the rough board, between their spread legs His fingers clamped too tightly, but she judged him unaware *"Á deejí sááh,"* he whispered, then translated huskily. "I realize how wrong I have been to hold my people up as superior— it was racism, nothing else. And I was wrong to expect...to ask of you what I asked. You were right to refuse." He pressed his mouth to her brow, whispering, "You *are* too much woman to be my mistress. My condition for accepting the Boston offer is you marrying me and living there with me."

The sting in her throat moved up, smarting her eyes.

"Will you, Yazhi?"

She lined his face with her palms, leaning in until their upper bodies touched as lightly as stolen breath. Her mouth found his more than receptive. "I love you, Lukas. I'd be honored to be your wife."

He vowed huskily, "I'll love you. I'll love Jarrid like my own son."

Heart aching, she kissed him again, then inched back to see his face. "But no way will I live in Boston with you."

She classified his body lurch as involuntary. He shifted on the diving board, one knee doing a Saint Vitus' dance. After a brief moment in which she feared he might get off and kneel before her, he resumed his travelogue. "I drove through Boston neighborhoods. Anglos don't seem to be a heavy majority—in some neighborhoods, anyway. But, then, *you* are Anglo…"

She watched his throat move as he swallowed, regrouping, revealing a new and different Lukas Wind Dancer. One not afraid to let his feelings show. "People say the public schools are better than in some other cities—Phoenix for one. And because it's on a bay, it's cooler than here in the summer." He fell quiet, perhaps running out of accolades. "We can start over there, Yazhi, on shared ground. Build our own culture from our love. Put behind us any hurt that—"

"You would do that for me? Leave everything you believe in here? What about the golf courses and jobs for the people? You'd give up being part of that?"

"To have you, I will. I love my people, but I love you—"

Her turn to damp a finger across his lips. "I want your mother's sheep."

His turn to say, "What?" with a skeptical smile, one brow cocked.

"That was quite a speech you made about those damn sheep, Wind Dancer. Not to mention the accompanying body language." Memory of that ride to the canyon whispered a fluttery romp that migrated into a low, sheltered ache. "Since then, aside from Jarrid, I've been unable to concentrate on anything but getting my hands on those sheep. Marrying you and living *there* is the only way it will happen. I apologize for the circuitous route I took to figure that out."

Dim light painted his smile reticent. "I'm not sure even that would do it for my mother."

"Then you'll have to convince her that I'm her best bet. I'm counting on you." She kissed him, her tongue teasing the corner of his mouth, withdrawing at his quick response. "We'll keep having sons until we get a daughter for me to pass the sheep on to. I may taint Sarah's heritage, but I'll never let it die."

"I'll be sure to make that point when I try to con her out of her sheep."

"Good thinking. And another thing, Lukas..."

"Let's have it, Yazhi."

"Since I'm half white, there's half a chance you'll be removed from the tribal council. But here's what I say to that." He waited. "In Boston—or any other asinine place you might come up with—there'd *be* no Navajo council, but if this one banishes you, it's their loss." The crease between his brows prompted her. "But I have faith that you'll find a way to keep those savages in line from the sidelines. The way Apenimon has done with you for all these years."

"The way he tried to do," he said softly.

"Thank God he failed."

He laughed, eyes going moist and shimmery by moonlight. Drawing her close, he pressed his face against her neck, a hand stealing up her back beneath her sweater, then down, fingers edging low within the waist of her slacks.

"Lukas."

"Hmm?" The caress moved around to frame the sides of her breasts.

"The reservation is not a godforsaken wasteland. I know that hurt to hear me say that." She'd had too many nights with the regretted words reverberating in her mind. "It's so barrenly beautiful, so serene and Enveloping. I think I was scared. I won't be scared with you."

He straightened, his hands staying their ground, and studied her face, so long that she felt a stir of trepidation.

"You seem…stunned," she ventured. "Are you?"

"Oh, hell, no." His smile held irony. "I spent a week psyching tip for Boston while you were doing the same for the rez. It takes some getting used to."

"It didn't take me a week. I knew by the time I reached the interstate that morning I left you." She cocked her head. "I think you baited me with the art classes in Flagstaff."

She would almost label his expression skepticism. "What about Samoa? I thought you'd walk out of that courthouse and book two seats on the next flight."

She feigned surprise. "Is that how I impressed you? That I'd leave the inn unfinished? Uncle Hayden didn't have to honor his promise, but I'll make good on mine. Now that I have Jarrid, I'll even run the inn for a while, as I should."

A brow peaked. "What about the heritage you've been preaching about?"

"I've learned something…" She gave him a patronizing smile. "…that's taken the edge off my *trying to change history.*" He listened quietly, eyes bright and encouraging as she shared all Hayden had confessed regarding her mother and father. "Knowing my father's identity has taken away the frantic need to find him, or to make up for not being able to find him. I'm not sure it would be right to disrupt his world by surfacing after all these years."

"To take one's time is always wise." His hands moved to her face, heels cupping her chin, long lingers caressing temples that for once threatened not the slightest ache.

"I'm realizing that what I've been craving can be found in our love."

"I'm happy for your new peace, Yazhi, but what about Jarrid?"

Her concern deepened. "Are you trying to change my mind?"

He kissed her softly, almost chastely. "I want you to be sure. I'm talking forever here. Not a trial run."

"I've been wrong all along. Some of the other things you said in that canyon…brought that home to me. I have the right only to love Jarrid. I can't make him more Samoan by taking him there. When he's a man, if he wants to seek his own heritage, he'll have my blessing. The two of us and our love will sustain him."

"Tell me I'm not on a vision quest gone crazy." He touched her hair, ran his finger along her cheekbones, across her mouth. "Tell me I'm not hallucinating from too many days in the sun with no water."

She worked her way onto his spread legs, wrapping her own around his hips, then lowered her pelvis and Pressed. He awarded her with a ragged catch of breath. "Feels very real to me, Jay Lukas. What do you think?"

His far-from-chaste kiss explored, probed, plundered, as if to unearth the truths he declared he needed. Satisfied only when her soft whimper became a groan, he released her with a carnal smile. "Let's see how sound Jarrid sleeps."

He lifted her off him and left the board, drawing her along. Near the bungalow door he announced as if reminded, "I'll build you a great house. Windows. Floors. The works."

"I can make do with the hogan. But that damn fire pit may have to go."

He laughed. "For your son then. I'll build a house for Jarrid."

Catching his arm, she faced him. "My son has had Houses. He's lived m the finest. But he's never had the most loving gift of all. The teaching of a man like you. You're decent and wise and loving, Lukas, with a servant's mindset. Promise you'll teach those qualities to my son."

"To all of our sons. I will do my best, little one."

"By the way." She balked on the bungalow steps. He turned expectantly, brow hiked, smile tolerant. "Until the inn is done—"

"Enough for now." Gently, decisively, he urged her up the steps and through the door.

She cocked an attentive ear toward the adjacent bungalow. Confident Jarrid slept, she began unbuttoning her sweater. "Until I make it to the rez for the duration…"

He shed his coat, unknotted the tie then hands at her waist, drew her against his arched body, nuzzling her neck. "Sounds like a stipulation, Yazhi. Maybe you're starting to live up to your own tough image."

Or starting to relinquish it.

"Until then, Jay Lukas Wind Dancer, golf course connoisseur and fearless Navajo leader…" She raised her mouth to receive a deep stirring kiss, returning it in a silent pledge. "…till then, please feel free to park your ugly black bird on my roof every time you feel lusty."

2008 Reprint Mass Market Titles

January

Cautious Heart
Cheris F. Hodges
ISBN-13: 978-1-58571-301-1
ISBN-10: 1-58571-301-5
$6.99

Suddenly You
Crystal Hubbard
ISBN-13: 978-1-58571-302-8
ISBN-10: 1-58571-302-3
$6.99

February

Passion
T. T. Henderson
ISBN-13: 978-1-58571-303-5
ISBN-10: 1-58571-303-1
$6.99

Whispers in the Sand
LaFlorya Gauthier
ISBN-13: 978-1-58571-304-2
ISBN-10: 1-58571-304-x
$6.99

March

Life Is Never As It Seems
J. J. Michael
ISBN-13: 978-1-58571-305-9
ISBN-10: 1-58571-305-8
$6.99

Beyond the Rapture
Beverly Clark
ISBN-13: 978-1-58571-306-6
ISBN-10: 1-58571-306-6
$6.99

April

A Heart's Awakening
Veronica Parker
ISBN-13: 978-1-58571-307-3
ISBN-10: 1-58571-307-4
$6.99

Breeze
Robin Lynette Hampton
ISBN-13: 978-1-58571-308-0
ISBN-10: 1-58571-308-2
$6.99

May

I'll Be Your Shelter
Giselle Carmichael
ISBN-13: 978-1-58571-309-7
ISBN-10: 1-58571-309-0
$6.99

Careless Whispers
Rochelle Alers
ISBN-13: 978-1-58571-310-3
ISBN-10: 1-58571-310-4
$6.99

June

Sin
Crystal Rhodes
ISBN-13: 978-1-58571-311-0
ISBN-10: 1-58571-311-2
$6.99

Dark Storm Rising
Chinelu Moore
ISBN-13: 978-1-58571-312-7
ISBN-10: 1-58571-312-0
$6.99

2008 Reprint Mass Market Titles (continued)

July

Object of His Desire
A.C. Arthur
ISBN-13: 978-1-58571-313-4
ISBN-10: 1-58571-313-9
$6.99

Angel's Paradise
Janice Angelique
ISBN-13: 978-1-58571-314-1
ISBN-10: 1-58571-314-7
$6.99

August

Unbreak My Heart
Dar Tomlinson
ISBN-13: 978-1-58571-315-8
ISBN-10: 1-58571-315-5
$6.99

All I Ask
Barbara Keaton
ISBN-13: 978-1-58571-316-5
ISBN-10: 1-58571-316-3
$6.99

September

Icie
Pamela Leigh Starr
ISBN-13: 978-1-58571-275-5
ISBN-10: 1-58571-275-2
$6.99

At Last
Lisa Riley
ISBN-13: 978-1-58571-276-2
ISBN-10: 1-58571-276-0
$6.99

October

Everlastin' Love
Gay G. Gunn
ISBN-13: 978-1-58571-277-9
ISBN-10: 1-58571-277-9
$6.99

Three Wishes
Seressia Glass
ISBN-13: 978-1-58571-278-6
ISBN-10: 1-58571-278-7
$6.99

November

Yesterday Is Gone
Beverly Clark
ISBN-13: 978-1-58571-279-3
ISBN-10: 1-58571-279-5
$6.99

Again My Love
Kayla Perrin
ISBN-13: 978-1-58571-280-9
ISBN-10: 1-58571-280-9
$6.99

December

Office Policy
A.C. Arthur
ISBN-13: 978-1-58571-281-6
ISBN-10: 1-58571-281-7
$6.99

Rendezvous With Fate
Jeanne Sumerix
ISBN-13: 978-1-58571-283-3
ISBN-10: 1-58571-283-3
$6.99

2008 New Mass Market Titles

January

Where I Want To Be
Maryam Diaab
ISBN-13: 978-1-58571-268-7
ISBN-10: 1-58571-268-X
$6.99

Never Say Never
Michele Cameron
ISBN-13: 978-1-58571-269-4
ISBN-10: 1-58571-269-8
$6.99

February

Stolen Memories
Michele Sudler
ISBN-13: 978-1-58571-270-0
ISBN-10: 1-58571-270-1
$6.99

Dawn's Harbor
Kymberly Hunt
ISBN-13: 978-1-58571-271-7
ISBN-10: 1-58571-271-X
$6.99

March

Undying Love
Renee Alexis
ISBN-13: 978-1-58571-272-4
ISBN-10: 1-58571-272-8
$6.99

Blame It On Paradise
Crystal Hubbard
ISBN-13: 978-1-58571-273-1
ISBN-10: 1-58571-273-6
$6.99

April

When A Man Loves A Woman
La Connie Taylor-Jones
ISBN-13: 978-1-58571-274-8
ISBN-10: 1-58571-274-4
$6.99

Choices
Tammy Williams
ISBN-13: 978-1-58571-300-4
ISBN-10: 1-58571-300-7
$6.99

May

Dream Runner
Gail McFarland
ISBN-13: 978-1-58571-317-2
ISBN-10: 1-58571-317-1
$6.99

Southern Fried Standards
S.R. Maddox
ISBN-13: 978-1-58571-318-9
ISBN-10: 1-58571-318-X
$6.99

June

Looking for Lily
Africa Fine
ISBN-13: 978-1-58571-319-6
ISBN-10: 1-58571-319-8
$6.99

Bliss, Inc.
Chamein Canton
ISBN-13: 978-1-58571-325-7
ISBN-10: 1-58571-325-2
$6.99

2008 New Mass Market Titles (continued)

July

Love's Secrets
Yolanda McVey
ISBN-13: 978-1-58571-321-9
ISBN-10: 1-58571-321-X
$6.99

Things Forbidden
Maryam Diaab
ISBN-13: 978-1-58571-327-1
ISBN-10: 1-58571-327-9
$6.99

August

Storm
Pamela Leigh Starr
ISBN-13: 978-1-58571-323-3
ISBN-10: 1-58571-323-6
$6.99

Passion's Furies
AlTonya Washington
ISBN-13: 978-1-58571-324-0
ISBN-10: 1-58571-324-4
$6.99

September

Three Doors Down
Michele Sudler
ISBN-13: 978-1-58571-332-5
ISBN-10: 1-58571-332-5
$6.99

Mr Fix-It
Crystal Hubbard
ISBN-13: 978-1-58571-326-4
ISBN-10: 1-58571-326-0
$6.99

October

Moments of Clarity
Michele Cameron
ISBN-13: 978-1-58571-330-1
ISBN-10: 1-58571-330-9
$6.99

Lady Preacher
K.T. Richey
ISBN-13: 978-1-58571-333-2
ISBN-10: 1-58571-333-3
$6.99

November

This Life Isn't Perfect Holla
Sandra Foy
ISBN: 978-1-58571-331-8
ISBN-10: 1-58571-331-7
$6.99

Promises Made
Bernice Layton
ISBN-13: 978-1-58571-334-9
ISBN-10: 1-58571-334-1
$6.99

December

A Voice Behind Thunder
Carrie Elizabeth Greene
ISBN-13: 978-1-58571-329-5
ISBN-10: 1-58571-329-5
$6.99

The More Things Change
Chamein Canton
ISBN-13: 978-1-58571-328-8
ISBN-10: 1-58571-328-7
$6.99

Other Genesis Press, Inc. Titles

A Dangerous Deception	J.M. Jeffries	$8.95
A Dangerous Love	J.M. Jeffries	$8.95
A Dangerous Obsession	J.M. Jeffries	$8.95
A Drummer's Beat to Mend	Kei Swanson	$9.95
A Happy Life	Charlotte Harris	$9.95
A Heart's Awakening	Veronica Parker	$9.95
A Lark on the Wing	Phyliss Hamilton	$9.95
A Love of Her Own	Cheris F. Hodges	$9.95
A Love to Cherish	Beverly Clark	$8.95
A Risk of Rain	Dar Tomlinson	$8.95
A Taste of Temptation	Reneé Alexis	$9.95
A Twist of Fate	Beverly Clark	$8.95
A Will to Love	Angie Daniels	$9.95
Acquisitions	Kimberley White	$8.95
Across	Carol Payne	$12.95
After the Vows	Leslie Esdaile	$10.95
(Summer Anthology)	T.T. Henderson	
	Jacqueline Thomas	
Again My Love	Kayla Perrin	$10.95
Against the Wind	Gwynne Forster	$8.95
All I Ask	Barbara Keaton	$8.95
Always You	Crystal Hubbard	$6.99
Ambrosia	T.T. Henderson	$8.95
An Unfinished Love Affair	Barbara Keaton	$8.95
And Then Came You	Dorothy Elizabeth Love	$8.95
Angel's Paradise	Janice Angelique	$9.95
At Last	Lisa G. Riley	$8.95
Best of Friends	Natalie Dunbar	$8.95
Beyond the Rapture	Beverly Clark	$9.95
Blaze	Barbara Keaton	$9.95
Blood Lust	J. M. Jeffries	$9.95
Blood Seduction	J.M. Jeffries	$9.95

Other Genesis Press, Inc. Titles (continued)

Other Genesis Press, Inc. Titles (continued)

Other Genesis Press, Inc. Titles (continued)

Other Genesis Press, Inc. Titles (continued)

Magnolia Sunset	Giselle Carmichael	$8.95
Many Shades of Gray	Dyanne Davis	$6.99
Matters of Life and Death	Lesego Malepe, Ph.D.	$15.95
Meant to Be	Jeanne Sumerix	$8.95
Midnight Clear	Leslie Esdaile	$10.95
(Anthology)	Gwynne Forster	
	Carmen Green	
	Monica Jackson	
Midnight Magic	Gwynne Forster	$8.95
Midnight Peril	Vicki Andrews	$10.95
Misconceptions	Pamela Leigh Starr	$9.95
Montgomery's Children	Richard Perry	$14.95
My Buffalo Soldier	Barbara B. K. Reeves	$8.95
Naked Soul	Gwynne Forster	$8.95
Next to Last Chance	Louisa Dixon	$24.95
No Apologies	Seressia Glass	$8.95
No Commitment Required	Seressia Glass	$8.95
No Regrets	Mildred E. Riley	$8.95
Not His Type	Chamein Canton	$6.99
Nowhere to Run	Gay G. Gunn	$10.95
O Bed! O Breakfast!	Rob Kuehnle	$14.95
Object of His Desire	A. C. Arthur	$8.95
Office Policy	A. C. Arthur	$9.95
Once in a Blue Moon	Dorianne Cole	$9.95
One Day at a Time	Bella McFarland	$8.95
One in A Million	Barbara Keaton	$6.99
One of These Days	Michele Sudler	$9.95
Outside Chance	Louisa Dixon	$24.95
Passion	T.T. Henderson	$10.95
Passion's Blood	Cherif Fortin	$22.95
Passion's Journey	Wanda Y. Thomas	$8.95
Past Promises	Jahmel West	$8.95

Other Genesis Press, Inc. Titles (continued)

Other Genesis Press, Inc. Titles (continued)

Soul to Soul	Donna Hill	$8.95
Southern Comfort	J.M. Jeffries	$8.95
Still the Storm	Sharon Robinson	$8.95
Still Waters Run Deep	Leslie Esdaile	$8.95
Stolen Kisses	Dominiqua Douglas	$9.95
Stories to Excite You	Anna Forrest/Divine	$14.95
Subtle Secrets	Wanda Y. Thomas	$8.95
Suddenly You	Crystal Hubbard	$9.95
Sweet Repercussions	Kimberley White	$9.95
Sweet Sensations	Gwendolyn Bolton	$9.95
Sweet Tomorrows	Kimberly White	$8.95
Taken by You	Dorothy Elizabeth Love	$9.95
Tattooed Tears	T. T. Henderson	$8.95
The Color Line	Lizzette Grayson Carter	$9.95
The Color of Trouble	Dyanne Davis	$8.95
The Disappearance of Allison Jones	Kayla Perrin	$5.95
The Fires Within	Beverly Clark	$9.95
The Foursome	Celya Bowers	$6.99
The Honey Dipper's Legacy	Pannell-Allen	$14.95
The Joker's Love Tune	Sidney Rickman	$15.95
The Little Pretender	Barbara Cartland	$10.95
The Love We Had	Natalie Dunbar	$8.95
The Man Who Could Fly	Bob & Milana Beamon	$18.95
The Missing Link	Charlyne Dickerson	$8.95
The Mission	Pamela Leigh Starr	$6.99
The Perfect Frame	Beverly Clark	$9.95
The Price of Love	Sinclair LeBeau	$8.95
The Smoking Life	Ilene Barth	$29.95
The Words of the Pitcher	Kei Swanson	$8.95
Three Wishes	Seressia Glass	$8.95
Ties That Bind	Kathleen Suzanne	$8.95

Other Genesis Press, Inc. Titles (continued)

Tiger Woods	Libby Hughes	$5.95
Time is of the Essence	Angie Daniels	$9.95
Timeless Devotion	Bella McFarland	$9.95
Tomorrow's Promise	Leslie Esdaile	$8.95
Truly Inseparable	Wanda Y. Thomas	$8.95
Two Sides to Every Story	Dyanne Davis	$9.95
Unbreak My Heart	Dar Tomlinson	$8.95
Uncommon Prayer	Kenneth Swanson	$9.95
Unconditional Love	Alicia Wiggins	$8.95
Unconditional	A.C. Arthur	$9.95
Until Death Do Us Part	Susan Paul	$8.95
Vows of Passion	Bella McFarland	$9.95
Wedding Gown	Dyanne Davis	$8.95
What's Under Benjamin's Bed	Sandra Schaffer	$8.95
When Dreams Float	Dorothy Elizabeth Love	$8.95
When I'm With You	LaConnie Taylor-Jones	$6.99
Whispers in the Night	Dorothy Elizabeth Love	$8.95
Whispers in the Sand	LaFlorya Gauthier	$10.95
Who's That Lady?	Andrea Jackson	$9.95
Wild Ravens	Altonya Washington	$9.95
Yesterday Is Gone	Beverly Clark	$10.95
Yesterday's Dreams, Tomorrow's Promises	Reon Laudat	$8.95
Your Precious Love	Sinclair LeBeau	$8.95

Dull, Drab, Love Life?

Passion Going Nowhere?

Tired Of Being Alone?

Does Every Direction You Look For Love

Lead You Astray?

Genesis Press presents
The launching of our new website!

RecaptureTheRomance.Com

Ignite
The Flame!

Order Form

Mail to: Genesis Press, Inc.
P.O. Box 101
Columbus, MS 39703

Name _____
Address _____
City/State _____ Zip _____
Telephone _____

Ship to (if different from above)
Name _____
Address _____
City/State _____ Zip _____
Telephone _____

Credit Card Information
Credit Card # _____ ☐ Visa. ☐ Mastercard
Expiration Date (mm/yy) _____ ☐ AmEx ☐ Discover

Qty.	Author	Title	Price	Total

Use this order form, or call 1-888-INDIGO-1

Total for books	_____
Shipping and handling: $5 first two books, $1 each additional book	_____
Total S & H	_____
Total amount enclosed	_____

Mississippi residents add 7% sales tax